Scamp

Roland Camberton

Also available from
New London Editions

Rain on the Pavements
Roland Camberton

Scamp

Roland Camberton

Introduction
by Iain Sinclair

New London Editions

Scamp
by Roland Camberton (Henry Cohen)

Published by New London Editions in 2010
New London Editions is an imprint
of Five Leaves Publications
PO Box 8786, Nottingham NG1 9AW
www.fiveleaves.co.uk

Scamp was first published in 1950
by John Lehmann

Cover illustration: John Minton,
courtesy of the Royal College of Art

Painting of Henry Cohen (Roland Camberton)
by Julia Rushbury

Photo courtesy of Dom Ramos

ISBN: 978-1905512942

Typeset by Four Sheets Design and Print
Printed in Great Britain

Five Leaves is represented by Turnaround
and distributed to the book trade by Central Books

Five Leaves is a member
of the Inpress group
of independent publishers
(www.inpressbooks.co.uk)

Man In A Macintosh:
Roland Camberton, the Great Invisible of English Fiction

Iain Sinclair

You can't tell a book by its cover, but it's not a bad place to start. The design of the fiction put out by John Lehmann in the late Forties and early Fifties had the louche swagger to complement an edgily cosmopolitan list: Jean-Paul Sartre, Saul Bellow, Gore Vidal, John Dos Passos, Paul Bowles. You could smell fierce French tobacco lingering on tanned pages and sample exotic locations filtered through fugues of premature sex tourism. The books looked good enough to frame, we took the contents on trust. And being by 1975 a trader in forlorn and forgotten literature, I slid copies of two London novels published by Lehmann under my stall; in the fond belief that the John Minton dust-wrappers would give them a market value at some unspecified future date.

The novels were credited to someone called Roland Camberton. I set them aside: until the time was right to make the discovery that the most exotic location of all, the true heart of darkness, was on my doorstep in Hackney; a slack-waisted borough of which Camberton was the unrecognized laureate. Despite the gentile surname, he wrote within a recognized Jewish tradition: the unsentimental education, the investigation of a wider city and the breaking away from the clinging embrace of an orthodox family. Rites of passage involved expeditions to the real East End, before sticky experiments with Soho cafés and clubs. Versions of this story with greater or lesser degrees of cynicism and panache would include Simon Blumenfeld's *Jew Boy* (1935), Alexander Baron's *The Lowlife* (1963), *The World is a Wedding* (1963) by

Bernard Kops, Emanuel Litvinoff's *A Journey Through a Small Planet* (1972) and even Harold Pinter's *The Dwarfs* (1990). Naturally, the authors denied any familial connection and dismissed the lesser titles in the series as incompetent, fraudulent and not worth ten minutes of any serious reader's time. Baron, more generous than the rest, was interviewed by Ken Worpole as background for Worpole's first book, *Dockers and Detectives* (1983). The Hackney author moved the discussion straight back to Lehmann. 'The people you speak of were all discoveries of John Lehmann, a part of his attempt to find a proletarian literature. This had its condescending side. There is, from Lehmann and his ilk, a homosexual attitude to the working class.'

Litvinoff confirmed this accusation when I talked to him for a film on submerged London writers in 1992. He recalled, when still in uniform and heavy boots, being invited to Lehmann's elegant flat, where the publisher was waiting, draped in a Nöel Coward dressing-gown, drink in hand. There was a vampiric thirst for fresh blood, hard male prose, the subterranea of the city. Lehmann had other sources of income, shadowy business interests, publishing was a superior hobby, a way of meeting interesting young men. Much of the zest in English fiction comes from rogue individualists looking for new ways to lose money by leaving orphaned books for future scavengers to discover and promote.

One of Lehmann's tricks was to pair off a modest working-class writer with a posh but troubled artist such as Minton. The zones where the tribes collided, in apocalyptic blind dates, were Soho and Fitzrovia. Moneyed dilettantes, professional scroungers and the thirsty dead: shoulder to shoulder, they fought for space at favoured bars. They worked much harder than nine-to-five civilians to promote their own legends to the point where some other mug would write the book for them. The point, as Dylan Thomas and Julian Maclaren-Ross soon learnt, where you become an actor in the anecdote of a rival is the point where your words are no longer required. It's time to disappear. To play the final card: suicide by other means. The last train to the suburbs. Stiff nights on the bench in the Russell Square Turkish baths. Trembling hands failing to get cold coffee, unspilled, to scabby lips. Late-bohemianism is a career better recollected than experienced.

Scamp, published by Lehmann in 1950, is Roland Camberton's first novel. It is set in Soho, Bloomsbury and Fitzrovia; in the rented rooms, pubs, all-night cafés where the author could well have come across Minton and certainly did lurch against Maclaren-Ross. Ivan Ginsberg occupies a rat-infested bathroom-kitchen, while trying to scam the funds for a stillborn literary magazine. The cancelled cheque stubs of Camberton's own life are an audition for the real business: the manufacturing of fiction.

'Ginsberg found himself confronted with the type-writer... A story a day, that was his minimum task; two thousand words, preferably with a plot, development, a climax, and a twist. After six months of this routine, he was beginning to feel an intense hatred of the short story, in fact, of all writing. What an abominable occupation it was!'

Camberton's prose is feisty, but there is something fugitive about the Hackney writer: if he has broken away from his roots, he knows they will reach out to choke him. The novel is heady with the delusion of freedom, but it's on parole. Delivered like an over-researched thesis, *Scamp* is quietly triumphant about coming into existence, but crushed by the horrible labour of composition. Nobody wants a new recipe for oblivion.

Maclaren-Ross reviewed *Scamp* with withering condescension: 'Mr. Camberton, who appears to be devoid of any narrative gift, makes this an excuse for dragging in disconnectedly and to little apparent purpose a series of thinly disguised local or literary celebrities.' One of whom, although he doesn't mention it, is Maclaren-Ross himself, lightly disguised as the 'former commercial traveller' Angus Sternforth Simms. 'That he found time to write at all puzzled the little crowd of habitués which watched him and heard him every evening, with respectful animosity, at his corner of the bar.'

Other notices were more encouraging. *Scamp* won the Somerset Maugham Award for 1951. Maugham took against the other principal contender, *Lucky Jim*, finding Kingsley Amis boorish and provincial. Camberton was invited around to the Ritz to be inspected by his lizardly benefactor. A friend wondered how they had got along. 'Oh, marvellous,' Camberton reported. 'He asked if I wanted tea or whisky. And I said whisky. Maugham said, "That's right, good show! I'm going to have both." And then we put English fiction to the sword.' Maugham left the judging of his prize to a committee. The winner in 1955 was already the dominant voice of his generation: Kingsley Amis. By that time, the author of *Scamp* was drifting out of print and into Grub Street anonymity.

The second book is always hard. Camberton, in choosing to set *Rain on the Pavements* (1951) in Hackney, was composing his own obituary. Blackshirt demagogues, the spectre of Oswald Mosley's legions, stalk Ridley Road Market while the exiled author ransacks his memory for an affectionate and exasperated account of an orthodox community in its pre-war lull. Competing voices shout across a crowded kitchen where loyalty to family battles against hairball claustrophobia. The novel unfolds through a sequence of discrete but connected short stories, which fade away into sudden darkness; an untimely return to Poland, erasure, silence.

I suspect that the character of Uncle Jake is a refracted self-portrait by the author. A midnight cyclist and compulsive autodidact, Jake wobbles between ideologies, short- lived enthusiasms. He taps on his nephew's window, asking to share the narrow put-u-up bed. Like Camberton, Jake decides to join the Royal Air Force. He has to get away from everything that makes him what he is.

'The family realized that the mystical cord which, for all his eccentricities, bound Jake to them and to all that was reasonable and normal, had snapped, cruelly, inexplicably, and unnecessarily. Jake was, voluntarily and alone, descending to the lowest section of society; he was going to become a homeless casual labourer, a tramp, a criminal even. A young man who had no money, no job, no home, no wife, no friends, was, in essence, a criminal.'

Jake's guilty secret is that, without letting friends or family know, he has published a novel. And it's title is: *Failure*. There is a schizophrenic moment when David Hirsch, the narrator, opens the book written by Camberton's alter ego: 'With what strange feelings David opened the thin, ill-printed, yellow-wrappered volume. It was as though the past itself had been drawn, temporarily but without noticeable change, from the vaults of the museum.'

Then Camberton vanishes, nothing is heard from him again; he publishes no third book. John Minton's dust-wrapper for *Scamp* takes on the jaundiced colouring of the uncut pages of *Failure*. A balding man, left hand in pocket, right hand gripping a furtive typescript, slouches down the cobbles; past the pub, out of the frame, into the wilderness.

I asked Patrick Wright, who had befriended Emanuel Litvinoff and written very effectively about his work, what the acerbic old man felt about Camberton. 'He was totally dismissive,' Patrick said. 'Those two books, Litvinoff reckoned, had nothing to do with the East London he had known as a young man. They were opportunistic, banal. He preferred to remember Wolf Mankowitz. Now there was a man who knew how to make money.' As to Camberton's later career, Litvinoff thought he had spotted him once, going into the offices of the *Reader's Digest*, but he couldn't be sure.

Alexander Baron, put by Ken Worpole to recalling the 'Jewish East End writers' of his acquaintance, finished with the Litvinoff brothers. And then, after a long pause, he mentioned one more. 'Oh yes, I'd almost forgotten him:

Roland Camberton. I saw him once at a party. I think, like Pinter and myself, he went to Hackney Downs School. I can't remember whose party it was, except that it was somewhere in St John's Wood. I didn't venture very often into these exotic territories. I had this little uneasy chat with Camberton, a strange man. That's it. That's all I know.'

And there it would have finished, with no more information than you could retrieve from the flap of one of Camberton's novels. Born in Manchester in 1921. Brought up in London. Served in the RAF as a wireless mechanic. Worked as teacher, copywriter, translator, tutor, canvasser, publisher's traveller. A future project, an autobiographical book called *Down Hackney*, is floated. But nobody I have spoken to has ever seen a typescript.

The nagging mystery was one of many I worried at, up to the point when I started work on my own memoir, a documentary-fiction called *Hackney, That Rose-Red Empire.* I projected a connection with the author of the book-within-a-book, *Failure.* Camberton's topography, his questing excursions, haunted me; becoming, in their fashion, a kind of model. 'It was necessary to know every alley, every cul-de-sac, every arch, every passageway; every school, every hospital, every church, every synagogue; every police station, every post office, every labour exchange, every lavatory; every curious shop name, every kids' gang, every hiding place, every muttering old man. . . In fact everything; and having got to know everything, they had to hold this information firmly, to keep abreast of change, to locate the new position of beggars, newsboys, hawkers, street shows, gypsies, political meetings.'

Amen! Huzzah! My mad creed in a single paragraph.

Having absorbed Hackney, its lost rivers, demolished theatres and built-over market gardens, Camberton's continued existence was tautologous: he had become the spirit of place. And through place, miles walked, he was to be recovered. Or so I excused my failure as literary snoop, uncommissioned private eye. Until, in the most unexpected way, the name of the vanished writer jumped out at me. A slender booklet, *Walking the London Scene (Five Walks in the Footsteps of the Beat Generation)* by Sydney R. Davies, dropped on my doormat. Here was permission for a jug of coffee and a rest from my researches. I followed with interest the story of how a person called Douglas Lyne, described as an 'archivist and Chelsea habitué', met William Burroughs. They drink together. Lyne lends Burroughs a pound. Returning from Tangier, the notorious junkie repays the loan. A line of double brandies is fired back in celebration. When the two men meet again, in a pub called The Surprise, they are joined by a third: Henry Cohen. Lyne decides that they will go back to his flat and make a recording on a creaking reel-to-reel machine.

They are now, all three, quite drunk. The man from the pub, Cohen, the one who will operate the recording machine was himself, years ago, a published writer. That might have been the source of his irritation. His books were classically constructed, widely reviewed and completely forgotten. To hide the shame of his alternative career from his strictly religious family, Cohen took another name: Roland Camberton. This Chelsea night must have been one of the most fantastic conjunctions in literary mythology: like a posthumous nightmare for Somerset Maugham. William Burroughs, the hierophant of fractured modernism, interrogated by a champion of the local, the specific, Hackney picaresque.

Naturally, I had to track down the tape. It became a grail, all of my interests converging on a single elusive object. The full story of that adventure belongs elsewhere. I made contact with Sydney Davies and he arranged a meeting, south of the river, a long way from Chelsea, at the house where Douglas Lyne now lived. Mr. Lyne was a person adrift in memory, calling up anecdotes of military life, intertwined with genealogies of the Welsh Marches and musings on the rogue priest, Father Ignatius, who raised a girl from the dead in Wellclose Square. He was a charming and discursive anecdotalist, the years in pubs and clubs had not been wasted. He wouldn't be deflected, by my Camberton probings, from the unravelling of an invisible thread. There were mugs of slow tea and many chocolate biscuits. Mr. Lyne, with his swept-back silver hair, trim moustache, milky eye, was like a benevolent General Pinochet.

Roland Camberton — or Henry Cohen, as he had known him — was one of his closest friends. Lyne moved in the post-war Soho world of documentary films, drinking clubs where he mingled with writers, painters, adventurers on the lookout for new islands. 'Johnny Minton was one of us. He did the covers for Henry's books.'

The first meeting between Lyne and Cohen was in Chelsea at the Pier Hotel. 'All the local mandarins were lolling about,' Lyne told me. 'Dregs and real dregs. With the great Henry. Who was an extremely distinguished-looking Jewish man. Like a great composer. Huge brow. We drank and we chatted away. We bought – it must have been me — a bottle of wine. And we went back to Henry's room. He said, "I've just won a prize. Somerset Maugham has given me £500." Maugham thought Henry was a good storyteller. And he was right. Henry could do colourful characters. He had great warmth. He loved listening to what you had to say, but he didn't like wasting his time doing practical things.'

And so, inch by inch, a narrative of the lost years was teased out. Cohen learnt to write in the Air Force. 'When I had a spare moment in the office,' he told Lyne, 'I would scribble bits and pieces and read them out at lunch-time and see who laughed at which passage. I was quite surprised, they liked my stuff. But the bits I liked they found high-fallutin' and boring.' Coming across an article by John Lehmann in which he said that he was searching for English authors with the urban fizz of Saul Bellow, Cohen decided to make an approach. He took his RAF gratuity and moved west. 'I was spending all my time in

Soho. Living it up as far as I could. Drinking. Courting the girls. I'd come from a stuffy orthodox Jewish background. I found Soho life fascinating and I thought other people would want to hear about it. I wrote *Scamp*. And I remembered John Lehmann.'

After *Scamp*, there was talk of a film. But nothing happened. Cohen produced some journalism for trade magazines. He kept his head resolutely down. 'You couldn't say that's what Henry was doing, free-lance journalism,' Lyne reported. 'You couldn't ask. Henry wasn't a man who did things. He just ran out of ideas. I should have learnt more from him. I didn't take him seriously. I think he had an interior purpose. He hated to be known. He was a very secretive person.'

The pseudonym Cohen adopted was resolutely non-Jewish. He cast himself as a matinée idol rescued from some forgotten Hollywood programmer witnessed at the Clarence in Lower Clapton. Ronald Colman, Madeleine Carroll and Roland Camberton in *The Prisoner of Zenda*: such was the fantasy. The reality of this grubbing, scratching post-war era was membership of a literary underclass described by Maclaren-Ross (in a letter to Lehmann) as being made up of those who 'live like rats among the ruins which they themselves have helped to honeycomb.'

The family didn't give up on the decamped eldest son. Lyne remembers an afternoon in his studio flat. 'This very Hatton Garden sort of chap came around. He had a set of sacrificial knives which he used for cutting animals' throats. Henry jumped up. "This is my brother." The brother said, "I've come to bring you home to Hackney." Henry told me that the same scene happened every week. His father was ill.'

Lyne got married, changed pub, lost touch with his friend. Years later, in Soho, he bumped into Henry again. 'He was with a very attractive woman. I think he must have been knocking about with her for quite a long time. She was very gentile, very county. Enormously devoted to him in a distant kind of way. She didn't like being associated with Soho or drink.'

Cohen said that things were going rather well. 'She's got lots of money. She wants to get married. She's got a house, with hunting and that kind of thing. I go down there. My family have cut me off, they don't want to see me. I can't go on. I don't really have anything to do.' Roland Camberton had grown into the situation that befell Uncle Jake in the novel written so many years before. 'He lost touch completely with the family. . . their relationship was quietly wrapped up, as it were, placed in the cupboard of limbo, and locked away.'

Ducking and diving, Henry Cohen had the painful task of reading other people's novels for MGM: could they be turned into films? He brought Douglas Lyne on-board – and Douglas, in return, set Cohen up with a trial, writing copy for EBIS (Engineering in Britain Information Services). 'What's this fellow done?' said the boss. 'A picaresque Soho novel and a book about Hackney.' 'Good god! I can find twenty people to write picaresque novels about Hackney. I want someone who writes dull-as-ditchwater technical material.'

At the end of Cohen's first month, Adrian Seligman who ran the operation told Lyne they were going to have a big party. 'What are we celebrating?' 'Henry's departure. He's a marvellous writer, but it takes him weeks to polish a paragraph.'

After this set-back, news of Henry came by way of an accountant, Leslie Periton. Periton was a partner in the firm of A.T. Chenhalls who represented Terence Rattigan, Benjamin Britten and Leslie Howard. Lehmann persuaded them to take on the promising young winner of the Somerset Maugham Award. Periton and Lyne had lunch together, once a year. 'Henry was exactly the type Periton wanted,' Lyne said, 'a man who didn't have any interest in making money. Periton probably got him the job at MGM to keep him afloat. Nobody knows if Henry ever wrote anything else under another name. My view is, at the times I ran into him, he was a declining person. He had problems with his inamorata.'

At one of these epic lunches, somewhere in the mid-Sixties, Periton said to Lyne, 'It's all up.' 'What's happened?' 'Henry's not so good. In fact, he's dead.' Nobody knew the details, aorta, aneurism. Showing me his inscribed copy of *Scamp*, without the Minton dustwrapper, Lyne was visibly moved. 'Accumulated memories do work their way to the surface. I have a notion Henry married his lady. They had a child. It could be a whole new chapter in Henry's story.'

From time to time, in a half-hearted way, I tried to interest publishers in bringing Camberton back into print. I was an admirer of the series of London Books Classics being put out by John King and his partners. In considering *Rain on the Pavements* they made the usual attempts to find the person who held the copyright and they came up with a name: Claire Camberton. Could this be the child mentioned by Douglas Lyne? I was given Claire's details and a meeting was arranged.

A woman with bright eyes, animate but tentative, arrived on my doorstep, dragging a large red case on wheels. She was, as she told me, no stranger to Hackney. She brought reams of documentation, photocopies of letters, snapshots, books: the fruits of twenty years research. She was astonished to meet another Camberton enthusiast and we were instantly exchanging snippets of information, trying to fit the jigsaw together. Claire was indeed the daughter of Henry Cohen, but not the child of the late marriage. Her story was unexpected and poignant.

'I was born in December 1954. My mother's name was Lilian Joyce Brown. She was from Andover in Hampshire. She lived in London during the war, working as a silver-service waitress at the Savoy. She was three years younger than my father. She died twenty years ago at the age of sixty-four. She was a bit reclusive towards the end of her life and fairly secretive too.'

Lilian Brown was in her late twenties when she met Henry Cohen. She attended one of the evening classes he gave, in short-story writing, at the City Literary Institute in Covent Garden. She was by then working in an office as a qualified bookkeeper/clerk. Lilian, her daughter recalls, was a pretty woman who was frustrated by her lack of formal education. She had a sharp eye for antiques and secondhand books and she haunted street markets. Very soon an affair was underway: 'Mum liked Jewish men, it was a bit rebellious at the time. My father pursued her and chatted her up. Mum told me, in her rather prim way, that he was very *virile*.'

They came to an arrangement: Lilian Brown would carry Henry Cohen's child and, after giving birth, hand her over. Cohen's mistress of the moment, a Jewish woman, couldn't have children and they wanted to adopt a child. Claire's mother was living in Thornton Street on the Stockwell-Brixton border, and she received an allowance of £26 a month from Cohen's solicitors. She changed her name by deed poll to Camberton. The Camberton pseudonym had a simple explanation. 'My father made the name up by combining Camberwell and Brixton. He hated coming south of the river.' The artist Theo Ramos, who knew Henry very well at the time, has a different story. He suggests Roland Camberton was an amalgam of Leslie Periton (Henry's accountant and mentor), Ronald Colman (a film star greatly admired by Henry) and Camberwell.

Lilian decided to keep the baby. A terrible scene ensued, the last time the infant Claire saw her father. 'It was all Hollywood then. Everything was a story, a romance.' The estranged couple met on Clapham Common in 1955. 'My father produced a huge stack of legal papers and presented them to my mother. Isn't that dramatic? I was in the pram. That was their final parting, the end of the relationship.' It was like a replay of an image from Graham Greene's Clapham Common novel of secrets and betrayal, *The End of the Affair*.

Claire said, 'That's probably why he didn't want my mother to read it.'

Scamp presents an anti-hero, Ivan Ginsberg, who courts failure, relishes obscurity, and has an eye for a waitress. 'Ginsberg was very much aware of her desirable presence by his side; so delightful were her little moues and winks that he... felt like... whispering into her ear an invitation.' There was another woman in reserve. 'Until Lolita became his mistress, Ginsberg was delighted with the novelty of this courtship. But afterwards there was nothing to sustain their relations except recrudescent desire... Ginsberg was also still ashamed of Lolita's background, which, though it might supply colour for an adventure, an anecdote, made a long-term affair impossible. At the same time he was ashamed of being ashamed...'

Among Claire's papers was a photocopy of 'Truant Muse', an article by June Rose published in *The Jewish Chronicle* in 1965, just before Camberton died. Rose wanted to discover why certain writers 'whose names were once well known... sped into obscurity'. Henry Cohen, she decided, was 'the kind of individual who finds it pleasant to vegetate.' He retreated to a bungalow beside the sea. 'London history is his special subject and he writes with erudition and clarity in small reviews'. The article is accompanied by a photograph: a balding, melancholy man. Like a cinema organist after the coming of sound. Here, without question, is the stalking figure drawn by John Minton for the cover of *Scamp*. That image is taken from life.

And there is one more surprise: a 'major work', never published, *Tango*. The journal of a hitch-hiking odyssey around Britain, an English *On the Road*. 'The writing is at times Orwellian,' Rose enthuses. Camberton laid out his plans in a letter to *The Jewish Chronicle*. 'My intention is to make two journeys: one, partly on foot, through Europe... and the second to North America.' *Tango* was rejected by his publisher and has not resurfaced.

'Roland Camberton is essentially an isolated figure,' Rose concluded. 'A man in a mackintosh, dignified, anonymous, alone. He is isolated from other writers, from the Jewish community. . . and his essential anonymity implies almost an element of choice.'

A firm of Wimbledon solicitors informed Claire's mother that Henry Cohen had changed his name a second time, shortly before his marriage. The new name was never to be revealed. The allowance would stop. The site of the grave would remain a secret.

I had been chasing the wrong story. Dying at the age of forty-four, Roland Camberton left behind books that are worth searching out, as well as the lost manuscript of a journey on foot across Europe. At that point in my own life, I had scarcely begun; a bookseller in Uppingham was considering taking a punt on my first eccentric novel. I had lived in Hackney for twenty years without becoming part of its dream.

Previous versions of this article have appeared in the *Guardian* and *Hackney, That Rose-Red Empire*

CHAPTER I

THE BELL RANG with shattering stridency. It carried to a remote top-floor in Guilford Street an early morning briskness which set Bellenger and Ginsberg cursing in their respective rooms. What right, they thought, what right had he to make that infernal row? Had he not been told often enough that the bill would be paid at the shop? Merely by putting his thumb on the bell-push he was able to thrust his *own* way of life, his *own* hours, his *own* convenience upon *them*. And he did it, no doubt, with a sense of virtue, as though it were a crime to be still sleeping at nine o'clock in the morning.

But the tyrant, unaware of the horrors that were being wished upon him, set their nerves on edge again with a few short, sharp rings; and not on their bell alone, but all the way down the house, while with the same dæmonic energy he rang half a dozen bells next door, and two doors along, and banged door-knockers on the other side of the road, all to the accompaniment of the clashing of milk bottles.

On the fourth floor it was now a battle of patience, endurance, and calculation between Bellenger and Ginsberg.

"Bellie!" shouted Ginsberg. "It's your turn! Go down and give him hell!" There was no reply.

"Pretending to be asleep, I suppose!" Ginsberg shouted in mock anger. Still there was no reply. The bell rang again, this time a long, continuous discord. Bellenger had his fingers in his ears. Ginsberg squirmed in ineffectual protest, finally jumped out of bed, put his slippers on, and rushed downstairs.

His long, black hair in disorder about his face, the sleeves and legs of his pyjama jacket and trousers ludicrously short, one big toe poking through a hole in his slippers, he was in no state to argue at the street door in full view of passers-by. So, without exposing himself, he thrust his arm round the door and meekly handed the milkman his money, leaving his hand outside for the change. The transaction completed and the door mercifully shut, he climbed slowly up the silent gloom of the staircase to their eyrie on the top-floor.

He examined the four letters he had picked up: three for Bellenger, normal letters, the sort that anybody might care to receive, and one for himself, a large, fat envelope, creased in three places where it had been previously folded, and addressed to Ivan Ginsberg in his own handwriting. He had no need to open it; it was clearly a rejected manuscript. Out of breath, he reached the top-floor, drew the blinds in his own room and in the joint kitchen, and sat down to recover from the first assaults of the day. The sun streamed through the window, the birds twittered among the chimney-pots, the hen in the backyard squawked continuously, and very soon a fresh, morning buoyancy asserted itself over the blank despondency which he had felt at the sight of his rejected manuscript.

Ginsberg now began the elaborate routine which was as much an end in itself as a preparation for the day. For one thing, no day, however full, however varied, could be worthy of so much preliminary shining, brushing, gargling, shaving, and washing; for another, the shine did not last beyond lunch, when already his beard began once again to assert itself. But first he had to rehabilitate himself with a cup of tea. While the kettle was boiling, he considered the daily problem of whether to clean his teeth, have breakfast, shave and wash, brush his clothes, and polish his shoes — in that order; or to clean his teeth, drink tea, shave and wash, have breakfast, brush his clothes, and polish his shoes. The former was the easy-going, pleasurable way, the latter was on the right road towards a day of disciplined hard work and timetable orderliness.

There was a movement in Bellenger's room. A door was flung open and the hard heels of Bellenger's slippers clattered across the bare floorboards of the landing. The broad, firm features of a red-faced countryman were thrust round the kitchen door, grinning derisively.

"You're up, I see," said Bellenger.

Ginsberg said nothing. It was a convention between them that he was ill-tempered in the morning. In fact, he preferred to have the kitchen to himself until he had breakfasted, smoked, and put the last touches to his morning preparations. The appearance of Bellenger just as he had decided to shave, an act which above all others required absolute tranquillity, produced a momentary irritation; followed by resignation; which was followed irresistibly by some cause for laughter. For this reason they were unable to sustain their quarrels. Their recurrent antagonism ended always in a snigger and deep gasps of laughter. They had an identical sense of the ridiculous.

Bellenger turned on the tap and rapidly wetted his face. His eyes half closed, he snatched at a pile of dirty towels and dish-cloths and dried himself. Then he filled the kettle and put it on to boil; took the frying pan, in which there were mouse tracks on the congealed fat, and set that above another strong light on the gas stove. Soon the fat began to splutter madly. The water was still running from the tap on to a piece of soap left in the sink, and Bellenger was scrabbling among a pile of crockery for a clean plate on which to set his breakfast. Ginsberg looked on with a mixture of amusement and annoyance.

"I've got to see the professor at eleven," said Bellenger.

In five minutes Bellenger was gone. Two gas-jets were left burning, the tap was now dripping copiously on to the frying pan, which he had left in the sink — a lamentable result of remonstrances about allowing dried egg to cake on its sides; and beneath the frying-pan a soggy piece of soap was melting into squelchy liquidity. Ginsberg sighed, cursed, and shaken by a spasm of laughter, righted some of the havoc. Living in an environment where bookish types prided themselves on their outrageous behaviour, he yet marvelled at Bellenger's uncanny ability to destroy any sort of order or coherence in the domestic arrangements of the flat. Still, it was Bellenger's flat.

Breakfast, washing, and brushing were prolonged; but inevitably and reluctantly Ginsberg found himself confronted with the typewriter — Bellenger's once again. A story a day, that was his minimum task; two thousand words, preferably with a plot, development, a climax, and a twist. After six months of this routine, he was beginning to feel an intense hatred of the short story, in fact, of all writing. What an abominable occupation it was! What a struggle! For what meagre prizes! Only the middlemen, he felt, were to be envied; the publishers, editors, anthologists and functionaries who stood between the raw material of the writer and the public purse. Especially the editors; they had the best of all worlds. For some time his mind had been turning upon the idea of editing his own magazine. The three necessary elements were money, a printer with paper, and contributors. All three had to be kept separate one from the other. Each might be secured by pretending that the other two existed; a confidence trick which was the very essence of business. Of his ability to merge the three elements into a successful enterprise he did not doubt.

On this fine April morning, the thought of writing another short story disgusted him. He had had enough of battering his head against a brick wall. In six months, three acceptances, by obscure magazines published from addresses deep in the countryside. Three stories at three or four guineas each; a little over ten pounds for six months' hard labour, exclusive of expenses or paper, postage, and so on.

He put the cover on the dusty typewriter and went downstairs. Though the top attic flat was bright enough, the staircases of the tall, decaying house were dank and gloomy. The other tenants had long left for work and all doors were shut. The utmost depth of gloom was reached by the massive street door. But when the handle was turned and the door unwillingly swung back, there, bright, fresh, and full of movement was the street. Bloomsbury, for Ginsberg, was home. He never tired of its façades, morning, afternoon, or evening, lit by sun, glistening with rain, or overcast by cloud.

At the Librairie Continentale he ran into Peter Stranshaw Firth, a tall, erect young poet whose Grecian features were marred by a complexion reddened with drink.

"Aha," said Firth, "good morning."

"Wotcher," said Ginsberg cheerfully.

"Just looking at the magazines," said Firth. "There's a poem of mine in *The Southlander.*"

Firth threw his head back and appeared to laugh, though he did not make a sound.

"Let's go and have a cup of tea," he said.

They went into a café occupied by bedraggled young prostitutes and louts, talking in every variety of Irish, Welsh, Scots, and provincial accent. Firth pulled out a file from his portfolio and said, "Tell me what you think of these. They're some translations I've just done from the Spanish." Firth was creating for himself in the magazines what was almost a monopoly in Spanish translations.

Ginsberg scanned them quickly; he wanted to talk about something else.

"The translations are very fine," he said, "though I don't think some of the poems were worth translating. Still. . . "

"I don't suppose," said Firth, with a short and now audible laugh, "I don't suppose you've got five bob to get rid of."

"As a matter of fact," said Ginsberg, in rapid and automatic defence, "I've only got five bob on me." It was true. "I'm pretty hard up myself."

"You're teaching, aren't you?"

"Yes, private lessons. For the moment, anyway."

"Lucky man. At any rate you've got some sort of regular

income. I often don't know where my next meal's coming from. I was going to try and sell you," he said, with a great, soundless laugh, "a copy of my book of poems. It's published at seven and six. This copy is brand new and I would let you have it for five bob. Still, if you've got no money it's no use talking." He sighed. "It's impossible to make one's living as a writer."

Ginsberg thought: it depends on the writer. Besides, what right had Firth to complain? He did about two hours' work a day, work of his own choice, agreeable work, highly individual work; he refused to do anything so dull and unbecoming as teaching, tutoring, or working with his hands; and then he complained about living from hand to mouth.

"Yet in a way you're lucky," said Ginsberg. "You're at any rate struggling from the inside. I'm right outside and I can't even feel righteous about it. I'm nothing and nobody if I'm not a writer, and the sad fact is that I'm not."

"You have time," said Firth, "plenty of time. How old are you?"

"I'm thirty."

"I'm thirty-three."

They stared into their cracked teacups and brooded.

"The only consolation is," said Ginsberg, "that the longer I remain in the wilderness, the more I shall have to say. Because the wilderness is life."

"Mmmyes," intoned Firth, and put an end to the conversation.

Ginsberg had wanted to tap Firth on the subject of his uncle, who was a partner in the publishing firm of Scrowicz and Scrowicz. But Firth was inaccessible, his motives obscure, his poverty wilful, his unhelpfulness extraordinary. He was really a man to avoid, or to know only remotely as part of the Bloomsbury landscape. Firth swung off abruptly on some gloomy mission.

Ginsberg crossed Russell Square. The first spring flowers were blooming, here and there, where they had escaped six years of wartime nocturnal trampling. The symmetrical white mass of Senate House reached out into a blue gap in the sky. The morning was fresh and brisk and brought to Ginsberg a sense of renewal. He decided, without further ado, to attack the enemy personally, in his office.

The house of Scrowicz and Scrowicz was two squares away, in a terrace whose discreet and graceful line had miraculously remained unbroken. The publishing house had a back entrance in a mews, where the vans of the trade department were massed. Ginsberg threaded his way among them and went down a flight of steps to a cellar labelled "Enquiries". In reply to his ring, a little panel slid open in the door.

"'Ullo," said a thin, pale little girl of sixteen.

"I'd like to speak to Mr. Firth, please."

"'Oo shell I say?"

"Ginsberg's the name, Ivan Ginsberg."

The panel closed. Ginsberg lit a cigarette and paced up and down. A quarter of an hour passed, twenty minutes; then the panel slid open again.

"What is it about?" said the thin little girl.

"About a magazine."

The girl went away and a woman who might have been her elder sister came to the panel and said, "Will you go two doors along the mews and take a seat in the waiting room. Mr. Firth won't keep you a moment."

Ginsberg waited a further ten minutes. Then the door of the waiting room opened and a tall, bald-headed man with furtive eyes came in and held out his hand. Without looking at Ginsberg, his eyes darting from corner to corner of the room, he said, "You wanted to speak to me about a magazine?"

Ginsberg had risen to meet him. They both remained standing awkwardly, not looking at each other, for Firth's mumbling embarrassment had infected Ginsberg, too. He realized that he could not talk to this man. All he now wanted was to get the interview over as quickly as possible.

"Yes," he mumbled, "I wanted to suggest a sort of literary and political magazine, a review... highly controversial..."

The door opened; an office boy darted in, gasped, and quickly withdrew.

"Of course, we are book publishers... we don't really go in..."

"Yes, of course," said Ginsberg, as though the idea had just occurred to him.

They went on muttering and grunting together, still standing up, for another twenty minutes, until at last Ginsberg escaped. He cursed himself for having behaved like a fool. Why on earth had he gone to Scrowicz and Scrowicz? And, having gone, why had he not spoken forcefully, decisively, clearly? Or alternatively, given that fumbling idiot a slap on the back and marched out firmly at the first "No"? That was what always happened in success stories; and that was what he had presumably begun, a success story, as initiator, organizing spirit, and future editor of *Scamp,* the liveliest and most provocative magazine ever to be published in weary London.

He jerked his shoulders back and strode on towards the British Museum.

CHAPTER II

MRS. CHABBERS felt like running into the back-room and locking the door. A man was standing in the front porch. She could see his shadow on the glass pane. He just stood there. What was she to do? There was no one in the house; the maid had just gone out shopping. Mrs. Chabbers crept over to the phone, ready to call for the police. Suddenly there was a sharp "Rat-tat!" on the door-knocker which made her jump and then sigh with relief. It was the postman; she saw now the outline of his cap and profile as he waited for a reply.

"Parcel," said the postman.

"You shouldn't knock like that," said Mrs. Chabbers, with a little giggle. "I mean, you shouldn't. . . you shouldn't stand. . . and then knock like that I mean. You know, knock! Knock-knock! Rat-tat! Enough to frighten the life out of me. . . Makes me jump."

She giggled again, coyly, and bared her large white false teeth. She kept her teeth bared in an unhappy smile of false cheerfulness until the postman had closed the garden gate and walked away up Hampstead Lane. Then she abruptly closed her lips and began tearing clumsily at the paper of the parcel. Getting the string and paper wrapping mixed up in an unnecessary mess, she gasped and grunted with annoyance.

She was stupid this morning, jumpy. She was always jumpy, it is true, but particularly so this morning. And now it was half-past-twelve; if lunch was not ready in ten minutes she would be late for her Russian lesson. That wretched maid, never there when you wanted her. She would be late for the Russian lesson, anyway. She was always late. Still, Mr. Ginsberg might be even later, that was one consolation. What a strange man he was! What an interesting man! Was he married or was he not married? And what did he do with his time? Apparently he had no job and no family; he gave one lecture a week at the Literary Institute and a few Russian lessons. He never went to shows, he had said that, and scarcely ever to the cinema. He sat up there in that room all day, typing. What did he write about? She wondered if he had ever written about her. If only he would show the least sign of interest in her. . . But that was silly! Of course he wouldn't!

She hurried through her lunch, left the house, dashed back for her Russian Grammar, rushed to the tube, and arrived twenty minutes late in Guilford Street. She rang the bell and waited; he was not in. Good; that would give her time to recover her composure. She turned round to see if anyone was looking and dabbed at her nose with a powder-puff. Unfolding the *Evening Standard,* she glanced at the headlines, nervously turning from page to page. Five minutes passed. Perhaps he had got tired of waiting. Oh dear! That was a nuisance! She would have to write and fix up another appointment. And what was there to do now through a long, dull afternoon? The cinema again. . .

Ginsberg turned the corner from Lamb's Conduit Street and his stomach gave a dull shudder at the distasteful sight of Mrs. Chabbers. She strolled along the pavement to meet him, teeth already bared in a smile. They began as usual.

"Sorry to be late," he said, though he had deliberately come as late as he dared.

"I was late too," she said, casually enough to begin with; but very soon the torrent of words which had been dammed up within her began to pour forth in an incessant jabber.

"Oh, what a morning it's been! Dreadful! That woman I've got — I told you the old one's gone — well this one, she's no good at all. Awful! But you can't get anyone nowadays, it's not like before the war — and then there was the postman, what a fright he gave me! He stood there. He just stood there! I saw him —"

"Shall we have the lesson upstairs or shall we go to the Empire?" Ginsberg knew what her answer would be. Thank God he did not have to be shut up alone in his room with her. Though sometimes he felt so wretched at the idea of having anything to do with her at all that he thought it almost better to suffer in private. In either case, the hour's lesson, however whittled down by late arrival and early departure, was utterly revolting.

"Yes," said Mrs. Chabbers, "the Empire. Well," she went on excitedly, "he just stood there. I thought goodness knows who it was. I got ready to telephone the police. I did, you know, I was just going to telephone, when he knocked at the door. Rat-tat! Oh, he *did* make me jump! Rat-tat, he went. Rat-tat! Knock-knock!. . . "

Ginsberg looked the other way, deliberately ignoring her, absolutely disassociating himself from anything she said. It was the least he owed his self-respect. That the human race could include so abject, so ignoble a member!

They mounted the steps of the Empire Hotel in Southampton Row and chose the most obscure corner table in the lounge. A waiter looked at them curiously; a queer couple, he thought. Three times a week they came after lunch to this corner table. The woman copied something from a book into an exercise book; the man sat with the newspaper held in front of him and scarcely glanced at his companion. From time to time he picked up her exercise book and wrote something in it, then buried himself once again in his newspaper. The woman was big, red-faced, and dressed in tweeds, the man, tall, thin, and rather shabby. When the waiter came round, the woman pressed the man to have a drink; yes, he must have a drink, he *must*. This afternoon Ginsberg consented to have a whisky; Mrs. Chabbers decided to have a glass of sherry. Ginsberg knew that the sherry would be fatal. Nothing would stop her now, nothing. She would jabber without a stop until he could stand it no longer; when he would demand his fee, hurriedly fix another appointment, and leave her there to cool off on her own.

Sure enough, when she had drunk her sherry, her face became redder, her dentures gleamed nakedly, and she swung round on Ginsberg.

"I'm always talking about myself," she said. "I know it, I'm a terrible chatterbox. But my sisters are worse. Oh dear, when they get together it's terrible, you've never heard anything like it. Still, it's good to get things off your mind, don't you think? Now *you* don't say much. You think a lot, I can see that. You know, I don't feel like any work this afternoon." She pushed the Russian Grammar away impatiently, as she did one lesson in three. "Here, have a cigarette. No, *do.* Really. Keep the packet. No really, I don't want it. I've got another packet in my bag. Look." She waved the second packet in front of his nose.

"All right, thank you. It's very nice of you," muttered Ginsberg, and pocketed the cigarettes which she had thrust in his hand.

"What do you do with yourself? Are you still writing? What are you writing about? I wish I could see some." Under the influence of the single glass of sherry, she lost all restraint and babbled like a child.

"Oh, I'm still plugging away," murmured Ginsberg.

"Will you have another whisky? Yes, have another whisky. Yes," she giggled, "why not? *I* mustn't have another. I mustn't, I *daren't.* I'm feeling whizzy already, it makes me all whizzy. But *you* have another. Yes, *do.* Waiter! Waiter! Where *is* that waiter?"

Ginsberg had another whisky and looked at Mrs. Chabbers a little more tolerantly. She was a good sort, really. Quite helpless, though; she ought not to be let out on her own. Although he knew that it was unwise to give her the smallest conversational opening, he could not resist telling her about his plan for a magazine.

"Oh," she said, "oh. How interesting! What a good idea! I should think you'd be the very person to edit a magazine, with your literary interests and your languages. Yes, a very good idea, I'm very interested. I should like to help. . . "

The idea hit Ginsberg like a flash. Of course! Why had he not thought of it before? Of course! The best way of all! He would publish his own magazine. And the backer was sitting with him here, tête-à-tête, ready to help, anxious to help. . . Or was she? When it came to money, she was far from being a fool. When she got to thinking things over, she knew what she was doing. Look at the way she had sold her car, holding out for an outrageous price and getting every penny of it. Yes, he had heard about that enough times. Still, the magazine was a sound proposition. He was sure of that himself, if no one else was. Five hundred pounds would be enough to begin with, until it paid its own way. Four hundred pounds, even. Three hundred pounds. . .

"Have a cigarette," he said, offering Mrs. Chabbers one of her own cigarettes.

"Oh, thank you, thank you."

"Why don't *you* found a magazine?" said Ginsberg.

"I? What, me? Oh, I couldn't, I wouldn't know. I mean, I'm too silly." She rolled round in her chair in a contorted giggle.

"Why don't you found *this* magazine, the one I'm going to edit? You see, it needs, of course, a little capital to begin with. If you supplied the capital, once it got going you'd be the owner of a magazine."

Mrs. Chabbers kept her eyes on the ground. She ceased squirming and became suddenly evasive, cautious. Money. One had to be careful about money.

"Oh," she said, "oh."

"It would be a sound proposition, I'm convinced of that." Ginsberg waved his cigarette airily. He sniffed, picked up the paper, and let the idea sink into her brain.

She blew her nose, wriggled, fingered the Russian Grammar, pushed it further away.

"I should like to help. . . I should like to help you start this magazine. I should have to think about it. You know, my husband and I once ran a magazine, a little country magazine for nature lovers. Of course, it was only a tiny affair. I mean, you know... We wrote it all ourselves. Then, of course, the divorce... Well... " She shrugged her shoulders. Ginsberg took no notice and continued to read the paper.

She leaned across confidentially; Ginsberg could almost feel the heat of her fevered nervous excitement. "You know, I'd like to help. It's awfully interesting. I've always wanted to do something like that. Really, I'm not half as dull as you think. I read a lot... I want to see things done. That's why I'm studying Russian. It's terribly difficult and I know I'm an awful dunce. You must think me a dunce. You do, don't you?" She waited hopefully for a reply.

"No... not at all," muttered Ginsberg unwillingly, and remembered how amazing was her inability to absorb the simplest and most elementary grammatical rule.

"I'm not a communist, you know," she gasped. "I think there's good and bad in all. But I think it's very interesting, it's very interesting, that's why I'm learning, because after all if you waste your time only on stupid things, I can't stand people who just won't look any further than their own doorstep. Oh, and there are such people, I can tell you —"

She babbled on until she was exhausted. Having paused to recover breath and direction, she leaned back and said demurely and quietly, "What do you... what do you think it would... er... cost? I suppose it would be frightfully expensive. Of course. Why, even the —"

"Three hundred pounds," said Ginsberg grimly, "three hundred pounds would set it going and keep it going for some time. At the worst, if each number of the magazine made a loss, it could not possibly make a total loss. Let's say each number loses fifty pounds. The magazine will at any rate last six months. That's looking at the thing from the worst aspect. But why shouldn't the magazine *make* money? Why shouldn't it, after the first number, make a *profit* of fifty pounds per issue? Why shouldn't you have, not only an *interesting* investment, but a highly *profitable* investment? I see no reason at all why not," he concluded.

"I am absolutely confident that I can make a success of this business. The only difficulty is getting it started."

"I must think about it," she said. "Yes. I should like to help. It'll be awfully interesting, I've always wanted to do something like — but I must think about it. I'll let you know. There. Will that be all right? I'll let you know next time."

"Now is the chance for a magazine like this," he continued relentlessly. "Firstly, everything is selling well; it's practically impossible to lose in the publishing world to-day. Secondly, there hasn't been a really lively intellectual magazine for years. I can get the contributors all right. Now is the chance."

"Wouldn't you write in it yourself? I mean, er, wouldn't you write in it yourself?"

"Very little," he said modestly, "just the editorials."

He looked at his watch; they had been together an hour. It was more than enough. He began the manoeuvre whereby he could collect his fee, arrange a future lesson, and leave the lounge without her; thus avoiding the embarrassment of passing for a second time beneath the severely mocking gaze of the commissionaire. On his own, he could get out through the side entrance, by the Gentlemen's Lavatories.

"I'm afraid I've got to go now," he said, in a formula suggesting that only some prior and important engagement compelled him to leave. "Are you staying to tea?"

"Yes," she agreed submissively, "yes. I think I shall stay to tea. Then I'm going to the pictures," she giggled. "Well. . . why not?"

He folded the paper slowly, buttoned his coat, straightened his tie, and waited. Would he have to remind her? He hated doing so, since somehow it seemed to draw attention to the fact that they had done no work together. But she remembered her cue at the last moment and gasped, "Oh! I've got to pay you. Of course. What *am I* thinking about? I don't know what's the matter with me to-day. I'm silly, that's what it is. I've got one of my silly moods on. I'm keeping you waiting. Am I? Am I?"

He said nothing, but stared intently at the nervous movement of her hands as they fumbled with the clasp of her handbag. It did not matter what she said, so long as she did the right things. The ten-shilling note was the only reason for their being together; if that was handed over, all was well.

At last she found her notecase, drew out a note, and laid it triumphantly on the table, at the same time turning round to see if anyone was looking. The vast, faded lounge was empty.

"There!" she whispered. "Is that right? Is that right? Do you owe me anything? Do I owe you anything? I mean, do I owe you anything?"

"That's quite right," said Ginsberg, pocketing the note. "Now I must hurry along. You are coming again on Thursday?"

"Yes," she said demurely, "Thursday. Same time. And I'll try to be more sensible. I've been awfully silly, I'm going to stay and have some tea now. There's nobody here, it's quiet, I'm going to learn those two lessons, I really am. I'm really going to learn those two lessons. I'm determined to, I'm determined to master — but you must go now, I'm keeping you."

"Goodbye," said Ginsberg. "Thursday."

He went out of the side entrance into the street. The street: he breathed deeply. Ah, how sane the street was, how reasonable, how civilized, how normal. The interview with Mrs. Chabbers made him feel grateful for the vastness of the metropolis, where everything could be avoided, where the paltriness of a single personality could be lost in an immense, cool anonymity.

He made, once again, for the British Museum. For Ginsberg, going to the British Museum was a sort of religious rite. Where others might pray in a church, he went to the Reading Room to reflect, purge his spirit, and reacquire a sense of philosophical detachment. No sooner had he passed by the massive pillars of the portico, than his step became more ponderous and self-assured, his bearing grave and sober. Beneath the great dome of the Reading Room, his preoccupations and ambitions seemed fantastic, tiresome, unnecessary, and worthless. He lived for a couple of hours in the atmosphere of scholarly calm to which he felt himself rightly to belong.

Mrs. Chabbers, for her part, experienced a somewhat similar feeling in the huge lounge of the Empire Hotel. She liked hotels, and frequently went away for weekends to towns like Cardiff and Manchester in order to have an excuse for spending a few days in a large hotel. She liked also this mid-afternoon quiet in the lounge. Presently people would come in for tea; meanwhile she could sit and think and feel pleasantly sad. Her melancholy would not yet turn to bile, as it did in the evening. Now she felt like just crying softly and gently, not too miserably, about nothing in particular, about everything.

CHAPTER III

THE CORNEY ARMS was situated in an alleyway behind Charlotte Street. Its outstanding patron at this time was Angus Sternforth Simms, former commercial traveller, whose books of short stories, *Gotcher Mate, Shooting the Line,* and *Autobiography of a Pickpocket,* marked him out as one of the coming younger writers, a master of dialogue and a sophisticated commentator on the life of Inner London. That he found time to write at all puzzled the little crowd of habitués which watched him and heard him every evening, with respectful animosity, at his corner of the bar.

"I get up at the civilized hour of half-past ten," he would say. Well and good; few among them got up very much earlier. But before mid-day he was at his station in the Corney Arms. He did not leave the pub till it closed for the afternoon at three o'clock. Towards seven in the evening he was back again, and stood tirelessly at the bar until closing-time at half-past ten, when he moved to the Milano Restaurant on the other side of Charlotte Street for supper. At midnight, passing bums admiringly watched him, usually accompanied by his girl-friend, hail a taxi and give the address of his rooms off Piccadilly, while they, the bums, drifted into some workshop basement to spend the night on improvised beds on the floor.

When did he write? Perhaps in the late afternoon? But on his return to the Corney Arms at seven, he always claimed to have spent the afternoon in the cinema or some such place. After midnight? That was possible; though it was staggering to think of anyone writing that slick, economical prose with half a bottle of gin inside him. And in any case, the radio scripts? The film scenarios? The weekly story in *Mary Ann?* The brilliant sketches in *Bank Holiday Pudding?* The new novel which he said would be ready in three months? His work, his pose, his daily feat of physical endurance, were an amazing tour de force.

Tuesday night was a good night at the Corney Arms, a gay, sociable, crowded night. Tuesday, Friday, and Saturday nights were good nights. Monday, Wednesday, and Thursday were bad nights. Sunday was a pallid nightmare of enforced retreat. On this Tuesday evening, Simms was at his post early, firmly planted in his recognized corner of the bar, head erect, jaws clamped, eyes staring straight ahead into the distance. He was looking grim, as he always did when alone. no one had yet joined him, no selected acquaintances, no visitors from the outside world or favoured members of the Corney Arms aristocracy. If anyone wanted to speak to Simms, they had to come and find him. They had to find their way to the alley at the back of Charlotte Street, they had to come over to his corner, they had to say, "Hullo, Angus." Then they were received in audience; his welcome filled them with a warm glow. The anecdotes began, of which Angus's, told in his own inimitable style, were inevitably the longest and the loudest. It was obviously, from start to finish, Angus's party, except in the matter of buying the drinks, where complete equality reigned, Angus buying his share and no more than his share. No matter how distinguished the visitor — a fellow-writer, a publisher, a film-director, perhaps — if he met Angus at the Corney Arms — and it was flatly impossible to coax Angus anywhere else — he was entering on to Angus's chosen ground. He had to laugh with Angus, listen to Angus, drink with Angus, and play Angus's game, "Scrag".

He was looking grim because his face, when not talking or laughing, was shaped on those lines. The Corney Arms had not yet filled up and he saw no one with whom to play "Scrag". Only the failures, the Soho bums, were sitting gloomily at the back of the pub, and on them he resolutely turned his back. In order to make life tolerable in the West End, it was essential either to ignore people decisively or to acknowledge them decisively. With the bums he did not hesitate; they were most decisively ignored. There was no one here whom he could drink with; no one, even, who had the nerve to try and drink with him. He had stopped that sort of nonsense too ruthlessly in the past. Yet having already drunk two gins, he was feeling sociable; and above all he wanted to play "Scrag".

The pub door squeaked open. Without turning his head, Angus shot a quick glance at the new arrival: a tall, rather haggard fellow. Shabby enough, but not a bum. Not quite a bum; on the fringes, touch and go. Angus remembered having met him once in the Milano Restaurant. They had had an argument about Dostoevski. That was it: Ivan, his name was, and some Jewish name afterwards. He was all right, he was tolerable, he would do.

The newcomer glanced rather nervously at Angus before making his way to the back of the pub. He was not sure whether to hazard a nod. He admired Angus Sternforth Simms immensely, and felt slightly abashed in his presence. But once, after their meeting in the Milano Restaurant, he had passed Simms in Rathbone Place and prepared to smile pleasantly and say, "Good morning". And Simms had looked straight ahead, firmly and grimly. Of course, it might have been a mistake. Perhaps Simms had not seen him. But ever since then, on entering the Corney Arms, though his eyes could not avoid resting for a moment on the great man, Ginsberg had turned quickly away towards the obscurity of the back tables. On this occasion Simms stared at him as he bought his drink. Ginsberg was undecided. But as he walked past the yellow-overcoated figure of the successful writer, Simms called out, loudly and cheerfully, "Hullo, Ivan!"

"Let's have a game of 'Scrag'," said Angus, without further ado. "Ah, look, there's Panjit!" he exclaimed, as an unusually thin, young Indian, with a vast, untidy mop of hair, slunk in, grinning sheepishly. It was Panjitawarelam, the poet and leader of the "mystical" school of young writers.

"Got any money, Panjit?" called Angus. "We're going to play 'Scrag'."

"Oh no," grinned Panjit, flashing his white, uneven teeth, "I'm broke. Who's playing?"

"Just the two of us to begin with," said Angus. "This is Ivan — do you know Ivan? He's an authority on Russian literature. This is Panjit — do you know Panjit?"

"Hullo," said Ivan, shaking hands with the poet. "Yes." Everybody knew Panjit. He remembered how, years before, he had walked home from a party in Chelsea holding the arm of a girl. Holding the other arm was Panjit. It was a long walk with one end in view. The only snag was Panjit. As they approached nearer to the girl's flat in Fitzroy Square, each squeezed the girl's arm, trying to communicate, by this pressure, the special nature of his relationship and the urgency of his desire. The girl made secret signs to both, gratified by her power and smiling serenely. At the entrance to the house in which she lived, she drew out her key, ran to the door, blew them both a kiss, and slowly and mockingly shut the door behind her.

But Panjit had forgotten that episode. He had forgotten all episodes. There had been so many, night after night, year in and year out, since his arrival twelve years before from India. He had drunk so much, slept in so many different rooms, been involved in so many situations. It had been too much, in fact; now he was subdued, defeated. He trailed along behind his sheepish grin from pub to pub, borrowing a few pounds here, publishing a poem there, an amiable, vague inhabitant of bed-sitting-rooms from Chiswick to Swiss Cottage. Everything was forgotten except the simplest needs of survival, fundamental vanity, and money. Above all, money.

Panjit pondered for a moment.

"I'll come in," he said. "I've got just enough money for one round if I lose."

But they knew, of course, that he wouldn't lose. He had never been known to lose at "Scrag". And he probably did not have enough money to pay even for a single round; or, if he had, it would not be forthcoming.

Ginsberg had two pounds, which were to last him till the end of the week. But he was exalted by the idea of his projected magazine. The magazine would make or lose comparatively large sums of money. However shadowy its future existence, it rendered paltry the thought of worrying about a mere pound or two. And in any case, he was too overwhelmed by Angus's invitation to refuse. So "Scrag" it was.

"Now," said Angus, in high good humour, "I will remind you of the very simple rules of 'Scrag'." At the sound of his booming voice, the habitués of the back tables, accustomed though they were to its nightly insistence, looked up in dull, horrified wonderment. There was no getting away from that voice. On the noisiest evenings, above the rising conversation, above the shuffling of feet and the rattling of glasses, above the protestations of inveterate boasters, above the shrill, disturbing cackle of Taffy, the anarchist, above the muttered threats of violence, above the lies, the declarations, the discreet enquiries, above the shouts and jokes and uproar, above it all the voice of Angus Sternforth Simms went its own implacable way. Presumptuous strangers, casual, uninitiated visitors had at times tried to drown that voice, to interrupt it and disconcert its owner. But in vain: Angus was an old hand, too tough, too knowing, too experienced, to allow anyone or anything to ruffle his composure. In due course, therefore, the regulars lowered their heads in melancholy resignation. Another session had begun at the Corney Arms; Angus was playing "Scrag".

"Each player," continued Angus, "has four buttons. Here you are." He took from his pocket a handful of buttons and invited Panjit and Ginsberg to select four each.

"Now," he intoned, "you place in your right fist, without letting the other players see, nought, one, two, three, or four buttons. We hold up our fists and guess in turn the total number of buttons in our three hands. As soon as someone guesses right, he drops out. The last man left buys the round of drinks. As you know, I drink gin, so if you only drink beer that's your own Look-out. O.K.?"

The other two nodded acquiescence; they decided to drink gin too. Angus lost the first round with good grace.

"Popsy!" he shouted to the manageress behind the bar. For Popsy the siege had already begun. From Hampstead and Harrow and Mornington Crescent, bearded and corduroyed, the customers had arrived. They pushed and squirmed to the bar, waving glasses and calling Popsy in special, pleading voices. But on hearing Angus's boom, Angus, the best, most distinguished, and also most profitable customer, she turned her back on them and hurried over to the "Scrag" corner, her severe features cracked into a cringing smile.

"Yes, Angus," she said.

"Three," he replied briefly.

"Take your glasses," said Angus, when Popsy had poured out the drinks. "Now —" He held his glass high; the others followed suit, and Angus uttered the ritual cry, "To the loser!"

"To the loser!" they responded.

Bellenger had arrived with Joan, an art-student whom he was attempting, with simple cunning, to inveigle into the flat in Guilford Street. This was her first, routine visit to the Corney Arms. She looked around her with wide-eyed and somewhat gratified alarm. Bellenger agonised uncomfortably and ecstatically in his chair, as he sought to convey, with the subtlety of a Yorkshire mandarin, how much he was at home among the West End types and at the same time how guileless, how apart, how deeply wounded was his sensibility by the grotesque crudity of the scene. Catching Ginsberg's eye, he winked, and by that tiny muscular movement was able to experience a blessed, momentary relaxation from the strain of the part which he was compelled to play. Ginsberg winked back conspiratorially, expressing likewise his separateness from the Corney Arms carnival.

But he was quickly called to order by Angus.

"Drink up," said Angus, "drink up. We'll have another round, shall we?"

Ginsberg assented with inward apprehension; because in spite of his recently acquired contempt for a paltry pound or two, he could not yet view with complete happiness the prospect of half his week's money falling into Popsy's hands in order to pay for a few rounds of "Scrag".

Panjit guessed with uncanny insight. Ivan and Angus were left. They went on guessing against each other for ten minutes, without either achieving the necessary lead of two correct guesses. Finally Ivan lost and laid his first pound note on the counter. Two beefy novelists came in. Angus invited them to join in the "Scrag"; but no, they were firm, they had principles about this sort of thing. They were willing to buy a round of drinks, but not to "Scrag". Ivan lost the next round, too; but no matter. His face was red, he was feeling optimistic, confident, aggressive. Now was the moment to fetch out the typed prospectus of *Scamp*.

"I've got something to show you," he said to Angus. "Perhaps it may interest you. Here."

Angus took the prospectus, held it high in front of him, and read aloud:

"Contributions invited to new occasional publication. Lively, controversial, informative. SCAMP, magazine for the younger generation. Payment at the rate of a guinea per thousand words. All communications to SCAMP Publications, Guilford Street, W.C.1."

"I've never heard of these people," said Angus. "SCAMP Publications, who are they?"

"SCAMP Publications, *c'est moi*," said Ivan proudly. The beefy novelists looked on disinterestedly. Panjit restlessly turned his head this way and that, seeking in the pub, in life itself, something to hold his attention for a moment. But there was nothing. He returned to looking intensely, penetratingly, into the bottom of his glass.

"Ah well," said Angus, "it wouldn't interest me. Got no time for anything like that now. Besides, I've given up writing short stories; run out of ideas."

"But how about one of your stories from *Gotcher Mate?"* Ginsberg insisted. "What about that one on the fellow who lived in five different hotels at the same time? Couldn't I have that one?"

"You can speak to my agent if you like," said Angus grudgingly. "As it's a reprint, he'd probably let you have it for ten or twelve guineas. Now let's get on with 'Scrag'. 'Scrag'," he roared, "'Scrag'."

A minor shudder ran through the packed crowd. Really, it was almost too much. Almost, but not quite. Because in the last resort nothing could be done about it; just as nothing could be done about thunder, lightning, war, pestilence, famine. The game went on. By the end of the evening Ginsberg had lost all except a few shillings of his two pounds. But he was anaesthetized with gin. What did it matter? What did it all matter?

"Do you really think you'll get this magazine going?" asked Panjit, waking up suddenly from his mystical trance.

"Yes," replied Ginsberg, "because I don't give a damn. Therefore, in one way or another it's bound to succeed." He smiled triumphantly. In his present state of alcoholic exaltation, his words seemed not merely true, but highly significant.

"It's very difficult," said Panjit, faintly and abstractedly. "Paper, you know, and so on." Panjit had lived for twelve years among embryonic magazines. He found the whole subject totally uninteresting, scarcely even depressing. But with his bored and shattered finesse, he kept on talking, since Angus had quite suddenly turned his back on them both to give his exclusive attention to the beefy novelists.

As closing-time approached inexorably, the Corney Arms lashed itself into a final frenzy. The voice of Taffy, the anarchist, rose high above the din, shouting excited and universal denunciation and breaking into long yells of shrill laughter:

"Hahahahaha hohohohooo!" he screamed, "Hahaha — they'll blow up all Europe just by pressing a button! Hoohoohoo! Oh dear! Hoohoo!"

Leaning against the wall and pressed into odd corners by the crowd, philosophical, isolated bums watched the scene with bitter understanding. They held in their glasses the dregs of mild beer; they were alone, out of it, sober. In the revelation of closing time, they saw an immense, terrifying vista of the future, with themselves caged for ever in this environment of dismal and helpless neurosis. For the thousandth time they determined never to come again, to pull themselves together, to extricate themselves from their shoddy Bohemia.

If the depressive current crept round the walls and into the corners, great manic gusts swept the main body of the saloon bar. Angus was declaiming an uproarious anecdote from his commercial traveller repertoire; Bellenger had an arm round his intended conquest, and was resting his lips with an expression of sublime languor on her slightly averted cheek; Ginsberg thumped the bar and repeated to a couple of thickly scarved students against whom he was wedged:

"Just wait and see! Just wait and see!"

The manager, Sid, called plaintively, "Time! Time! *Do* hurry along! *Do* hurry along, *please!* Ladies and gentlemen, *do hurry along please!"*

After a few minutes of pandemonium, the show was over. The customers were driven out into the cool, half-lit night. Ginsberg found himself alone in the alleyway, between the high walls of warehouses. Where now? Should he pay a visit on Lolita? He hesitated; it was five days since he had last seen her. But he wanted to talk, and it was impossible to talk to Lolita except in monosyllables. Besides, he wanted to gather support for his magazine; now, without delay, while he was full of enthusiasm and slightly drunk.

Kagaranias; he would go and see Kagaranias, make one last attempt to get the old miser to part with some money for a worthwhile business venture. With Mrs. Chabbers nothing was certain. It was as well to have more than one iron in the fire.

Ginsberg stepped out smartly and unsteadily towards Oxford Street, crossed, turned into Dean Street, and made for the Restaurant Souci, where Kagaranias had sat, from eleven o'clock onwards, every night for the last thirty years.

CHAPTER IV

THE RESTAURANT SOUCI had recently changed hands. The sign: "Under Entirely New Management" was, however, an old one. It was almost a fixture, because the Restaurant Souci had been bought, rebought, part-transferred, and renamed a dozen times during the previous ten years. For twenty years before that it had been owned by Fraternelli and run successfully as an Italian café-restaurant with a varied Soho clientele. When Fraternelli died, the new owners, with an eye solely to money, tried to convert the site into an expensive little dinner and supper restaurant. They turned out the idlers, who used to spend two or three hours lolling about over a single cup of coffee, and waited for new customers to arrive on their way to and from the theatre. But they waited in vain. The theatregoers were prepared to eat expensively two doors along, three doors back, over the road, and round the corner; but for no understandable reason they avoided the Restaurant Souci.

As new owners, part-owners, and managers came and went, and as the restaurant steadily lost money, policy was modified a little. The management from time to time ungraciously allowed the idlers to return; except a few whose sandals were really too worn, beards too frayed, habits too aggressively individualistic for the occasional well-to-do suburban customer who might accidentally stray into the Restaurant Souci from Shaftesbury Avenue.

The latest change in management had brought a hardening in policy towards the Soho bums. They had been sifted once again. Prices on the menu had been raised slightly, a vase of flowers installed on the counter, and the latest of a series of desperate attempts to attract the moderately wealthy diner-out had been initiated. On this Tuesday evening, three pretty waitresses stood expectantly by the counter, the manager, in soiled evening-dress, waited by the entrance and looked up and down Dean Street; and at ten to eleven, there was only one customer in the place.

The manager surveyed Ginsberg, saw no definite reason for barring his way, and held open the door for him to enter. The white-jacketed server behind the counter and the three waitresses glanced up hopefully and immediately returned to their melancholy contemplation of the rows of empty tables. Ginsberg was clearly no jocular and dynamic theatregoer to be followed by a little crowd of gay suburbanites supping in Soho before motoring back to Pinner and Golders Green. They saw in him a quasi-respectable idler who might at the most order the cheapest item on the menu and leave a threepenny tip.

Their estimate was justified; Ginsberg headed for the solitary customer, sat down opposite him, and ordered a coffee. The waitress disdainfully shrugged her shoulders.

Ginsberg's companion was an acquaintance from the Café Royal named Storringham. He was a young man with thick, horn-rimmed spectacles and protruding teeth, from between the upper and lower rows of which hung a fat glittering fountain-pen. His back was against the wall, his legs were up on a chair, and his eyes almost closed. Beside him, on the table, lay a pile of manuscript which he had been correcting.

"Hullo, hullo, hullo," said Ginsberg, with alcoholic heartiness.

Storringham made no gesture except that of slightly opening his eyes. Ginsberg gently detached the fountain pen from Storringham's teeth.

"Thanks," Storringham sniggered. "I've been trying to summon up the energy to do that for the last half-hour."

"Kagaranias not here yet, I see," said Ginsberg.

"No," said Storringham, with a sigh of comfortable boredom, "it's not eleven yet. Kaggy comes on the dot. Don't blame him myself. Can't see the point in coming to this place a moment before you have to. I only come here to write when the Café Royal closes."

"Do you write in public, then?"

"Always. Can't bear to be alone." Storringham sniggered lengthily at this.

Ginsberg tried to make out the top few lines of the manuscript, reading upside down.

"Is that... er... your usual?" he said. Storringham wrote pornography for private circulation.

"No," said Storringham, "and I don't know what you mean by my usual. That" — he flicked through the fat pile of manuscript — "is a great work of art, a tremendous psychological study of homosexuality and all kinds of sexual perversion. An American publisher has already offered me ten thousand dollars for it. I shall probably water it down a bit and accept. What one has to do for money!" Storringham sniggered again.

At that moment an old, bent tramp with a stick went tap-tapping through the restaurant to the furthest corner table. His hat was broad-brimmed and dusty, his coat of moth-eaten, patchy fur. A ragged, roll-necked pullover, frayed trousers, and a muddy pair of heavy boots, one of whose soles was adrift from its upper, completed his ensemble. His head was bent and he looked neither to right nor left. It was Kagaranias, owner of extensive property in the West End, book connoisseur, and demi-millionaire.

Storringham looked at his gold wristlet watch. "What did I tell you? On the dot of eleven. My watch must be a minute slow."

Ginsberg made ready to go and join Kagaranias. "I hope your book succeeds..." he said. He never knew whether to take Storringham seriously or not. The man was obviously a lunatic. Most of what he said was demonstrably false. Yet he remained at large, spent a good deal of money, was not without talent.

Storringham leaned against the wall, stretched himself out more luxuriously on his two chairs, and shut his eyes.

"Don't worry about me," he said. "I'm not all that interested in writing. I've got my theatrical business, my film agency, my cosmetic factory, my extensive black-market distributing system —" He broke off and chuckled softly and helplessly.

What fraction of what he says is true? Wondered Ginsberg. One tenth? One fifth? One quarter?

"Run along, dear boy," gasped Storringham, between quiet sobs of laughter.

Ginsberg felt a little more sober and therefore more disquieted. These late night encounters with people like Storringham upset him in a disturbing, unaccountable way. They seemed to take place on the furthest borders of reality. But he returned to his homely preoccupation with money and walked over to Kagaranias.

"Good evening, Monsieur Kagaranias," he said, and bowed in respectful greeting. Kaggy liked these little touches, which presumably reminded him of the commercial politenesses of his youth in the Balkans and among the dependencies of the Ottoman Empire.

Kagaranias lifted his head wearily and fixed Ginsberg with a gloomy stare. Then, as though he had been fumbling for some dilapidated switch in his ruined circuit, he arranged the folds, bags, hollows, and lines of his face into a sudden smile. The effect was disastrous. So unaccustomed were his features to an expression of cordiality that they now hung shapelessly in uncoordinated groups. Ginsberg, as an old acquaintance, understood the significance of their collapse and was encouraged to sit down.

For thirty years Kagaranias had been coming to the Restaurant Souci; first in the days of Fraternelli, then through all the changes of ownership and policy of the past ten years. The Restaurant Souci was the first call in his nightly round of restaurants, cafés and coffee stalls. During the day he dealt with the business relating to his property from a basement office in Old Compton Street. Agents, chosen apparently for their shabbiness in appearance and spirit, collected rents in the slums of the West End and south of the river, arranged with solicitors to fight recurrent, niggardly legal actions, and returned to bargain about their wages and commission with Kagaranias. In the evening he found solace among his books, which were stored in a warehouse off Covent Garden. He bought them by the barrowload; they were mostly junk, but included one or two rare volumes. He did not read them, but liked handling them. At night he roamed the streets, searching for coffee-stalls, all-night restaurants, and tea shops which opened in the small hours for early-morning workers.

Everyone in the West End knew him by sight. He had a reputation as a miser and elderly, hole-in-the-corner libertine. Passing prostitutes in the back-streets sometimes pecked at his cheek; or alternatively shouted abuse:

"Dirty old Kagaranias! Dirty old rat!"

The imagination boggled at the sordid haggling and betrayal which must have taken place to arouse this vituperation. But since many of them lived on his property, and he was tolerant of their means of livelihood, he never came to any violent harm. As the years passed and he grew older, more solitary, and more wretched, he aroused a sort of affection and pity among the riff-raff which slouched about Leicester Square in the hours before dawn.

Ginsberg knew him as well as anybody. Indeed, Kagaranias had shown meagre signs of a desire for friendship. But Ginsberg was on his guard against intimacy with the funereal eccentric. This evening, however, in the interests of his projected magazine, he was prepared to discuss things à fond and listen to Kaggy's melancholy confidences.

Kagaranias took time to adjust himself to the proximity of another human being with whom he was supposed to be on friendly terms.

"So dere you are. . . " he muttered. "Pipple come and pipple go. . . and pipple come again."

Coming from anyone else, such a greeting would have been hardly encouraging. But Ginsberg knew his Kagaranias. The old metropolitan hermit, riven with suspicion and anxiety, was thawing. Soon his bonhomie would be overwhelming. There would be no restraining his offerings of cigarettes and coffee, his horrific and sentimental anecdotes, and his flirtatious comments on the three pretty waitresses.

Kagaranias kept his eyes fixed on a single sheet of Greek newspaper, some two years old.

"Det's de way it is. . . " Kagaranias mused. "No one cares about de ole man. Who wants ole Kagaranias?. . . And you? You're all right, you got plenty time yet. You're a young men."

Ginsberg waved his hands deprecatingly. A few stray customers came into the Restaurant Souci; before midnight it did a certain amount of business. The little blonde waitress tripped up to their table, daintily balanced on her excessively high heels. She smiled at Ginsberg and winked; then, catching Kaggy's eye, she smiled and winked at him too. She was a girl who knew how to handle her West End customers. And though she turned her back coldly on the sprawling, non-tipping idlers at the tables by the door, Kagaranias and any protégé of Kagaranias' could be sure of her highly effective coquetry. Her cheeks dimpled and Kagaranias cheered up decisively.

"She's very cuddlesome," he said, with his terrifying, atomised smile.

The dimples receded further into the smooth round cheeks.

"Isn't he awful!" exclaimed the blonde delightedly. She was a London-Irish girl, a war-immigrant, who had come to terms with her adopted city by means of a marriage to an American soldier, a divorce, a subsequent baby, and a bed-sitting-room in Maida Vale.

"You don't see many gels like det nowadays," continued Kagaranias, "so clin, so nice, so swit. . . "

The waitress looked on with unfeigned amusement. She knew also something of the reality which lay behind Kaggy's ancient and ungainly compliments — There had been a grotesque and frightening episode in the gloom of his deserted warehouse. She, like many others, had been tempted by curiosity and stories of wealth to come and look at the old man's "rare books". She had been driven to defend herself against his extraordinary advances by throwing books at him, desperately and with all her strength. Only when he had been bruised and cut by a succession of massive, dusty volumes had he given up the idea of adding her photograph to his gallery of five hundred nudes. Later his hopes were re-aroused, and Mary, the waitress, had by no means dismissed the idea without serious consideration. But really, he was too disgusting. And there were more elegant fish floating about the sea of Dean Street; though none offered the hard-cash terms which Kagaranias whispered into her ear nightly as she laid the table for supper.

"Isn't det right, my lovely?"

She lowered her eyelashes with demure charm. "I really don't know, sir," she said.

"Seh! Seh! Who calls Kagaranias "Seh'?"

"Now, now, be a good boy —" She became motherly. She was indeed a first-rate waitress and wasted on the Restaurant Souci. "— There now, you're hungry. Look through the menu and make up your mind what you're going to have."

Kagaranias made his usual choice in the lower price levels of the menu, while Ginsberg and the waitress looked on. Ginsberg was very much aware of her desirable presence by his side; so delightful were her little moues and winks that he almost felt like following Kaggy's example and whispering into her ear an invitation or a request for a phone number. It was scarcely conceivable that she should refuse. She had the same effect on everybody. Only when she had gone did her customers catch sight of themselves in the mirror and realise how worn, battered, and washed out they were. But Ginsberg knew only too well that there was always a snag with these pretty girls in the West End; especially when they found themselves there late at night and surrounded by twenty or thirty hungry, lonely males.

The twenty or thirty hungry, lonely males had now arrived. They sat with their backs to the wall, staring at each other across the centre row of empty tables. They were mostly of some indeterminate age between thirty and forty-five, wearing American-type shirts and suede shoes. They read the last edition of the evening newspaper and rolled their magnified eyeballs around, behind their rimless glasses, with discreet suspicion. Many had come from the Afro-Cubano club round the corner, where they had danced once or twice during the evening, squashed up on the confined, unlit dance floor against a negress. They were not absolutely the sort of customers the management had hoped for, particularly with the bowl of flowers on the counter and the latest increase in prices on the menu. But at any rate they were customers, could pay for what they ate, and only rarely broke into fierce, psychotic arguments about trifles.

The pretty waitresses made their devastating way among the tables, though the customers did not easily allow their disturbing femininity to pierce the defensive surliness which hung between the evening paper and the averted, magnified eyes behind rimless spectacles. Kagaranias ate his food noisily and filthily. The management, blue-chinned and heavy jowled, stood unhappily by the counter, and Ginsberg wondered what had landed him on this remote reach of time.

Kagaranias spoke from behind the mass of food which filled his mouth almost to choking.

"What brinks you here after all dese munss?"

"Ah, now there you're asking something," laughed Ginsberg, adopting the tone of easy flippancy which he used with Kagaranias once the first spiky barriers had been penetrated.

"What you doink nowadays?" continued Kagaranias, his face almost purple with the pressure of food.

"The usual," replied Ginsberg. "At least, until this morning I was doing the usual. But to-day I started on a new course. I'm going to try and start a little business venture. As a matter of fact," Ginsberg added, as though through an afterthought, "the scheme might interest you."

At the mention of business, Kagaranias shovelled even more food into his mouth, crouched more sorrowfully over his plate. Business: he knew how to handle that — have nothing to do with it. Have nothing to do with anything unless you could see that the other person was done for and had to accept your terms. And even then, pitch your terms so low that the other person was tempted to face up to disaster rather than accept them. Only when, after much cogitation, and taking into account the feelings of his family, of his innocent children and his aged parents, the other person decided that your terms were possibly a shade better than total disaster — only then should you do business; even at this stage, think twice, think three times, don't sign anything in a hurry, and pay out in dribs and drabs — you never know. In such a way had Kagaranias, poor orphan boy from Smyrna or Istanbul or Teheran — no one knew exactly where, perhaps he himself had forgotten — amassed half a million pounds in forthright, honest-to-goodness sterling.

"Have a coffee," said Kagaranias magnanimously; "have a cigarette." He pushed over a packet of bent, limp Woodbines. In spite of his mournful expression, Kaggy was in high good humour. Here he was in his familiar Decor, in a corner of the Restaurant Souci, beneath a spider's web and leaning against a fat, jagged crack in the carious wall. To the right was a door labelled Gentlemen-Messieurs-Señores. The time was half-past eleven — his favourite hour — and he was stuffing himself with a mass of food; while opposite sat a young man bowed down before the power of Kagaranias.

"Huh is Mr. Bellengeh?" said Kagaranias.

"Oh, he's all right," said Ginsberg. "The idea is a sort of magazine, very controversial and progressive, full of life —"

"Uh megezine," said Kagaranias, nodding sagely. "Very good. I wish you luck." He took a lump of bread and wiped it round his plate till every drop of sauce had been cleaned off.

"I'm getting old," sighed Kagaranias, and death was visibly at work in him as he spoke. His voice expressed no regret, only a blank statement of annihilation. "I wek too hud. Wek, wek, wek, de whole time, sitting in de office dere de whole day. And den I go bek to my books, to de cetuloguing."

The demi-millionaire's complaints about overwork were among his most infuriating habits, in Ginsberg's eyes. They began an argument which they had been over several times before.

"Really, Monsieur Kagaranias!" said Ginsberg. "I can hardly sympathize. What is to stop you from selling up everything and living in luxury on your capital? Or putting your property into the hands of an agent or a manager?"

"Uh menegeh," said Kagaranias hopelessly, "— de ting is to find someone you can trust."

"So what if they rob you of a few pounds? What if you make a loss? What if you lose half your money? You'll still have more than enough. You could travel again — how long is it since you've been out of London, thirty years? You could go to some sunny land, to the Riviera, to California, and idle the time away between your books and a deckchair." Even as he said it, Ginsberg realized how stupid and unnecessary was his argument. He was speaking as though Kagaranias were a "normal" man, and one susceptible to argument; whereas Kaggy was as perverse and obstinate in his life-long, self-imposed penance as a human being, inwardly mutilated and deformed, could ever be.

Kagaranias attempted to smile; the disposition of his features altered uneasily.

"Dis is my life," he said. There was a rushing and flushing of water from the lavatory, and a lean man, with a scar down his cheek, held the door half open and finished buttoning his fly. Kaggy waited till he had gone and the torrent in the lavatory subsided, and then brought his face close to Ginsberg's, looked him for once straight in the eyes, and repeated with feeling: "Dis is my life, dis is ole Kagaranias' life. He weks end he weks, end he walks de strits et night because he can't slip, end he's got no femily, no frents, no nutting."

Ginsberg wriggled in his chair impatiently. He was being side-tracked, as usual, to a discussion of Kaggy's unhappy fate.

"Why don't you interest yourself," he said earnestly, "in some great project, political perhaps, or social? The only thing worth doing is creating the world state of free and equal and noble —"

"Excuse me," interrupted the little blonde waitress, smiling with a charm that, professionally laid on or no, was exquisite, revealing a state of inner grace and harmony. "We're closing now," she said. "I wonder if you would mind paying the bill."

"For you, my lovely," said Kagaranias, "anyting." He pulled from his pocket what appeared to be a small parcel; it was actually an immense heap of notes fastened together with elastic. He extracted a tattered note from the centre of this colossal pile of paper, merely one of similar bundles carried in other pockets, and handed it to the blonde.

"Shall I include. . . ?" She indicated Ginsberg.

"Yes," said Kagaranias, waving at Ginsberg's coffee as though it were something unclean. In an excess of generosity, he pushed over to Ginsberg the entire packet of lifeless and smashed Woodbines and said: "Peheps you'll hev uhnudder coffee, while dere's time."

"No thanks," said Ginsberg, "I really couldn't."

“Den let’s go,” said Kagaranias. He handed the waitress a shilling out of his change, once again with an expression of disgust on his face, as though he were bundling out of the way some object too foul to be mentioned.

A few of the hungry, lonely males were still there, newspapers in front of them, coffee unfinished, cigarette fuming in ashtray. They would not go until driven out. Besides, most were waiting in the slight, desperate hope that they might see one of the waitresses home. Otherwise, the Restaurant Souci, its brief hour of moderate animation over, was more forlorn than ever. The manager’s ultramarine chin had changed a shade on the course from blue to black; the server behind the counter stood in his braces folding up his white jacket; the bowl of flowers had been sent down on the lift to be put in the refrigerator. The waitresses were so many shadows on the door marked Ladies-Dames-Señoras.

Ginsberg knew that he ought now at any rate to go home — to stride home in long, energetic steps and shake off the cobwebs of an exhausted midnight. Instead, he found himself shuffling out of the restaurant in time with Kagaranias. Partly he did so out of inertia, partly out of a desire to put his project once for all before Kagaranias, and having been turned down, never to see the old man again.

CHAPTER V

They drifted along Dean Street in a light drizzle, Ginsberg towering, thin, fastidious, and pale, above the ragged, bulging, ancient figure of Kagaranias.

"You gut no femily also," said Kagaranias, tap-tapping steadily with his stick and leading the way round the corner into Shaftesbury Avenue.

"That's right," said Ginsberg, "I've got no family. My mother died eight years ago, and she was the last of my near relatives."

"Det's huh I was," said Kagaranias. "We gut ah lot in common — Oh, good evening, good evening." He raised his stick as though to fire it at a passing policeman.

"Evenin', Mr. Kagaranias," the policeman nodded curtly.

Kagaranias linked his arm with Ginsberg's. "Yes, we gutuh lot in common." Ginsberg shuddered. The moment seemed at any rate auspicious for nailing Kagaranias down about *Scamp*.

"You know," he said, "I really came to see you this evening about a project of mine, a magazine."

"Uhuh," nodded Kagaranias, "uh megezine."

They crossed the road and turned down Wardour Street. A tough, stocky, muscular prostitute stood barring their way in the centre of the pavement. Ginsberg and Kagaranias gently and discreetly made a detour into the roadway.

"Yeh, yer dirty old rat!" cursed the prostitute. "Where's that pahnd, ay?"

"Uh megezine," repeated Kagaranias. Abuse poured over his head like ordure wherever he went. From Blackfriars to Victoria, from Camden Town to King's Cross, people harboured against him old grudges, shared with him aged, moth-eaten sordidities. But the curses he received lacked true venom and were uttered as a matter of routine; otherwise he would many times have been beaten up, "carved up", or had a "shiv" stuck in him. In the last resort, everything was forgiven him because he was a character; and the metropolitans, hard-boiled though they might appear to be, were as sentimental as schoolgirls towards a genuine character, one who had battled on through mockery and humiliation to arrive safely at a grinning nirvana.

"Yes," said Ginsberg, "a magazine. I think the capital will be forthcoming from another source. At the same time, additional capital would always be useful. And of course, if this first source should fail, then alternative capital will be essential. That is why I should like to interest you in the scheme, both from the purely financial point of view — though that, presumably, will be no great attraction to you — and also from the point of view of enabling you to associate yourself with something worthwhile."

Kagaranias wriggled his shoulders as though to shake off the proposition which Ginsberg had so directly laid there. He hated these rough, naïve assaults. Business was not something to be spoken about openly in a loud voice. Business was something to be muttered and whispered and inferred, a matter of hints, significant glances, averted eyes, and nudgings under the table. But then, Ginsberg was no business man and was not to be taken seriously.

"I gut no education," said Kagaranias in a low voice. "I don't understend dese tings. I buy books, but I don't read dem. Fuh you it's different. You bin to univessity, you bin to Cembritch, you understend."

Kagaranias led the way into an all-night café. They threaded their way among the tables and stood awkwardly looking for a couple of spare seats. Soldiers and their girls stared at them. "Who's he?" they asked, pointing to the outlandish figure of Kagaranias.

Crooks and ponces, prostitutes during an off-hour, one or two bookies, furtive sexual seekers, a bunch of toughs of a primitive simplicity rarely encountered during the daytime, a few of the homeless bohemians from Charlotte Street — all these, the hard core of the habitual clientele, just smiled knowingly and said, "Kagaranias". He was a familiar landmark in the wastes of the night.

At last they found a table for two. More coffee; a welsh rabbit to appease the waiter. Ginsberg lit one of Mrs. Chabbers' cigarettes.

"What is mere living?" he said. "Mere living — being born, working, growing old, dying — doing all this patiently and passively without aspiring towards something noble — bah!" Ginsberg brooded sombrely over his incoherent cosmic vision. "That's not what we were born for," he muttered. "What are you saving up for? Have a go, Monsieur Kagaranias! Have a go! Do something worth-while with the power which chance has put into your hands. Or even throw the money away! Yes, throw some of it away just to set things humming a bit. What have you to lose? Start a magazine — bah!"

Ginsberg knew he had shot his bolt, as far as Kagaranias was concerned; so he broke off suddenly. He was not sure himself what he was talking about, and certainly nothing had ever stirred and nothing would ever stir Kagaranias from his perverse sloth and his determination to use his money only for the purpose of making more money and buying a lorryload or two of books. The possibility of Kagaranias bearing some part in financing *Scamp* — a lunatic notion, anyway, coming from a person who knew Kaggy — was silently buried. Ginsberg had a mind to go back now to bed. He idly forked a piece of welsh rabbit, while Kaggy looked at the advertisements on his single sheet of Greek newspaper two years old.

It was half-past twelve; but beneath the electric lights time was excluded. Toughs and prostitutes, over-tailored, brilliantined men, and women in their cosmetic masks, lolled about quizzing the pale, nervous waiters, the soldiers and sailors with their girls now drifting in after the last cinema show. At this moment, a fight, like a pustule issuing from an impure blood stream, broke out in the centre of the café. The cause of it was a bookie named Joey. Joey was drunk and unable to pay all his debts on the day's racing. He had about four hundred pounds in notes lying in front of him on the table. But he was due to pay out nearly a thousand pounds. The Boys of various factions were occupying tables round him in a circle. They kept a watchful eye on the four-hundred-pound pile.

"There's the dough," said Joey with drunken insouciance. "Help yourselves. That's all I've got." He turned his back on the pile and leaned over to talk to a neighbour.

The Boys did not move, but watched in turn their leaders and the heap of notes. Finally Big Mike got up and walked over to Joey. Big Mike's Boys half rose from their chairs so as to be quick off the mark. The Seven Dials mob turned questioningly to Sammie Keogan, their chief. Every man's hand was in his pocket, fingering a knuckleduster, a spiked ring, a length of iron bar, a razor, a "shiv", or even a loaded revolver.

The other customers were unaware that there was anything tense, dramatic, almost deadly in Big Mike's slow, deliberate walk over to Joey's table.

"You owe me three hundred," said Big Mike in a loud voice, so that all the Boys could hear and understand that he was merely collecting a legitimate debt. But Joey also owed the Seven Dials mob four hundred and fifty. It was a question of grab.

"O.K. boys," said Sammie Keogan, and the Seven Dials mob rushed for Joey's table. There was the crash of crockery, the scream of a girl, and the unexpected sight of men with neat sashes of blood running down their faces and clothes stabbing at each other with knives and razors before closing in for a rough-house.

Ginsberg and Kagaranias had a ringside view of the fight. They experienced no sense of danger, although a cut-throat razor, thrown loose in the struggle, came flying over and landed on Kaggy's lap. The fight was no general scrimmage, but an intimate, exclusive affair between specialists. Although some customers drew back and stood by the wall, and a few left the café, Kaggy merely looked on with disapproval and Ginsberg almost without interest. He had seen so many of these fights in the West End. They were like specimens from a sociological case-book. In a flash, as the toughs grappled and slashed, he pictured the simple patterns which formed this violent mosaic — the slums of Inner London, the somewhat mentally deficient youngsters, the High Street, the pin-table saloon, the fish and chip shop, the cinema, the *News of the World,* the pub, the dog-track, the racecourse, crime and Borstal, crime and prison, a ménage with a prostitute or a half witted adolescent, and then the ganging together for company's sake with Big Mike or the Seven Dials mob.

The management had swiftly telephoned the police. There was no point in attempting themselves to cope with the situation. The toughs knew they had only a few minutes in which to damage each other. One man already lay unconscious beneath a table, his head surrounded by smashed tea-pots, plates, and cups. It was Joey who had indeed taken his life into his hands by going bust in the all-night café. But then, he had been drunk and had always been known as Crazy Joe. Others had their clothes torn and spattered with blood and terrible gashes and wounds on their faces and necks.

The money had all disappeared — no doubt there would afterwards be a few internal arguments about that among Big Mike's Boys and the Seven Dials mob. One man used the butt end of a revolver to smash over the head of a cross-eyed Greek named Kiki, who joined Joey under the table. A pimply youth with a dead white face drew a revolver and prepared to fire, wildly and without aim, into the mêlée. Ginsberg saw him and covered his eyes with his hands.

When he opened his eyes, the white-faced youth was screaming with pain, clutching a dangling, broken wrist, and the gun had disappeared. A cheerful-looking fellow with a long brown moustache, who stood somewhat apart from the main scrimmage, swished a bicycle chain with which he had disposed of the revolver.

"Let's go," said Kagaranias. They rose and left, forgetting to pay the bill, just as the police arrived with truncheons drawn. At the shout — "Bogies!" — the gangsters dispersed and desperately tried to break open emergency exit doors; all except Joey and Kiki, who lay close together and seriously injured by one of the central tables.

"I'm going home," said Ginsberg, as he and Kagaranias emerged into the street.

"I tink I'll walk wid you," said Kagaranias. "Dere's uh milk buh in King's Cross open all night."

The homosexuals stood in twos and threes in shop-doorways and barred cinema entrances. They held excited, intense conversations, from which they glanced up, at first nervously, then with amusement, as Kagaranias shuffled by, tap-tapping with his stick, and Ginsberg stalked along beside him.

They carried on down Long Acre, past Odhams Press, from which came the confident hum of immensely powerful machinery. Once, thought Ginsberg, that press too was no more than an idea in the head of an ambitious outsider. Ginsberg was now feeling wide awake, and aware of every change of scene brought by crossing a road, turning a corner, peering down an alleyway; aware, also, of poor Kagaranias, muttering self-pityingly by his side, voicing his eternal regrets and lamentations. The drizzle had stopped, but the pavements glistened; cats stole across to dustbins; a mongrel stood sentinel outside the Masonic headquarters in Great Queen Street.

Kingsway was deserted — not a stray car, not a van, not a policeman. Only the traffic lights at the crossroads carried on their bright, mechanical, sleepless life. But as they passed Kingsway Hall a man and a woman materialized from the shadows. They carried bundles in sacking and had evidently been sleeping in the doorway. Finding their previous position perhaps too exposed, they dragged along towards Southampton Row. Ginsberg and Kagaranias overtook them, and, in passing, Ginsberg recognized the man — another London character, by name Carruthers Anstruther. He was a man in late middle age, with a long, straggly, black beard streaked with grey, and wild, prophetic eyes. A thick stick swung against his legs from among the bundles of sacking and old newspaper with which he was encumbered. Formerly a doctor, his name struck off the register for performing an abortion, he had for many years been a tramp. The woman, an ex-heroine of Paris in the twenties, now lived by singing in the streets. Ginsberg recognized her, too, from the angle of her neck, which she held as though permanently dislocated. This odd mannerism, entirely voluntary, was but one manifestation of her nervous disorder. Her ancient peaked cap was another, as was her refusal to speak anything other than French. She suffered from persecution mania, and often sat in one of the Soho cafés, glaring round, making fierce gestures, and cursing in French.

Ginsberg called out cheerfully, as though it were the most normal thing in the world to hurry past at one o'clock in the morning, "Hullo, Anstruther!" At the same time he set a swifter pace for Kagaranias and sped on. But it was not so easy to get away from Anstruther. The former doctor hurried after them, puffing and blowing.

"I say, old man —" he said. "So pleased to see you. How are you getting on? Let me see, what *is* your name now? I always forget it — Good evening, Mr. Kagaranias," he said in an aside. He knew there was nothing doing with Kagaranias.

"Ivan," replied Ginsberg with a laugh.

"Ah yes, Ive. Ive. . . Ive. . . Ive. . . I remember. You're the scene-shifter bloke. Or are you the fellow who was with me in Bow Street?"

"No," said Ginsberg, "I'm just Ivan."

There was a sort of bark from behind. The ex-heroine of Paris, her neck craned forward in its attitude of permanent dislocation, was complaining furiously to the section of pavement which immediately presented itself beneath her face. She was evidently annoyed with Anstruther. Anstruther urgently caught Ginsberg's arm.

"I say," he said, "you couldn't put us up for the night, could you? We were just making for the waiting room in St. Pancras."

"I'm afraid I couldn't," said Ginsberg. "I would like to. I'd like to very much." He thought to himself how hellish it would be to have Anstruther and that woman in his room. "But I'm afraid," he concluded, "it's quite out of the question."

"Ah well," said Anstruther resignedly, "we'll have to spend the night in the waiting room at St. Pancras. Last night it was Liverpool Street, the night before that Victoria."

"Huh is it dey let you stay?" interjected Kagaranias.

"Oh they usually don't mind," said Anstruther. "If they kick up a fuss, I buy the cheapest ticket available — it's twopence ha'penny at Liverpool Street and fivepence at St. Pancras. Then they can't turn us out till our train comes in in the morning — By the way" — he broke off and became very grave — "I must read you my appendix on "The victimization of Carruthers Anstruther, M.B., B.S." in my book on abortion."

"What, *now?*" said Ginsberg.

"Yes, it won't take a minute." Anstruther began to unsaddle a number of his parcels. The ex-heroine of Paris, who had now caught up with the others, made a noise between a groan and a laugh.

"Et alors?" she demanded. "Alors?"

"I'm sorry," said Ginsberg, "I've got to go." And with that he set off on his own. Kagaranias hastily shuffled after him.

"I say," called Anstruther plaintively. "I say. . . "

"Et alors?" asked the former darling of Montparnasse.

"*Et après?. . .*" The sound of their voices carried faintly as far as Southampton Row, while they stood beneath a young tree and gathered together their innumerable and fantastic bundles.

Anstruther's battle with the law of abortion had indeed been unfortunate. Not only had he sacrificed his profession and livelihood, but, as he sank fairly happily into beggary, he had lost even the respect of those who knew his story and shared his views. He was now something between a joke and a nuisance, and in appearance he was simply a tramp.

Kagaranias trailed doggedly along right up to the house in Guilford Street. Having, perhaps for the first time in months, tasted company in his wanderings through the night, he could not bear the thought of their separating. He urged Ginsberg to make a night of it; to go with him to the milk bar at King's Cross and afterwards to an all-night café in Fleet Street. Ginsberg hesitated. It was a long time since he had stayed up all night in London, and the idea was not unattractive. The sky had cleared and the light rain had left the air mild and fresh. He was feeling not in the least sleepy and Kaggy had been mercifully silent since their encounter with Anstruther.

"I know uh men in Flit Strit," said Kagaranias. "He comes in de café uhbuht two uh'clock. You'd like to mit him, especially nuh you're gone to become uhn editeh. He's uhn editeh also. He's de editeh on de *Daily Post*."

"Really?" said Ginsberg. "You know the editor of the *Daily Post*."

"He's nut de editeh himself. He's one of de editehs, de essistent night-editeh."

"Hm." Ginsberg reflected, leaning against the railings which surrounded the basement. Kagaranias waited humbly and expectantly, his eyes almost shut. The crescent moon slid out from a light bank of cloud and illuminated the scene with silvery pallor, "It's quite an idea," said Ginsberg. "Make a night of it for once. Do I understand that you're inviting me to supper, or shall I say breakfast, at this café in Fleet Street?"

"Yes. Yes," said Kagaranias. "Hev uh sendwich, uh cup of tea. . . "

"A sandwich is hardly enough to keep one going all night," said Ginsberg. He made a significant movement towards the door, as though preparing to go in.

"All right, uh suppeh, then," said Kagaranias hurriedly and grudgingly.

They set off again and made for King's Cross. In Euston Road there was a certain amount of activity. Around three or four coffee stalls there were sizable crowds of toughs, negroes, and merchant seamen, with a sprinkling of soldiers, sailors and slatternly girls. In the absence of any legitimate explanation for their standing about in the empty street at one o'clock in the morning, Kagaranias suggested that they were having a cup of tea before going to work — housebreaking, robbery with violence, assault and so on. Certainly there was no reason to believe that they had just left late trains at one of the railway termini in Euston Road. To prove that they were no recent arrivals from the provinces, but hard-boiled inhabitants of the Caledonian Road having a quiet cup of tea in the open air at one o'clock in the morning, they greeted Kagaranias with catcalls and jovial abuse.

"There 'e is, the old geezer! Don't 'e look smart! Got a pal with 'im to-night! Cor! Ain't 'e lucky!"

In Euston Road, Kagaranias was not quite so well known as in the West End proper. Here he was just "the old geezer". Had it been known that he was also a very rich "old geezer", and that he carried several hundred pounds with him in his bulging pockets, the toughs would have been decidedly more interested.

At King's Cross there were a few more of these sinister crowds spread out round coffee stalls. The milk bar which Kaggy frequented had the same tough clientele. They knew him well enough not to jeer openly, but made way for him and exchanged jokes quietly behind his back.

Ginsberg was intimidated by the faces which

confronted him beneath the fluorescent lighting of the milk bar. They were not like the faces in Soho; they were poorer, weaker, more degraded. They had the air of known criminals whose only worry was not, *whether* they would be caught, but *when* they would be caught. Ginsberg was too cautious even to stare hard at one of these faces and register its full horror. He wanted to cause no offence, arouse no attention, but simply to persuade Kagaranias to leave as quickly and unobtrusively as possible. Ginsberg edged into a corner to await Kaggy's return from the counter. As he squeezed past a little group wearing caps and dirty white scarves knotted round their necks, a hand fell heavily on his shoulder. Ginsberg swung his head round slowly, prepared for some unpleasant episode. He found himself staring into a young face, a familiar face, and at the same time a face more frightening than any yet revealed by the ghastly fluorescent lighting. All the life, all the tension had gone out of the skin, which was covered with a multitude of fine wrinkles; and were it not for the depth of these thin criss-crossing lines, one might have supposed that the skin was about to peel and disclose a new face, smooth, youthful, and in keeping with the bright eyes, the firm red lips, and the slight, stooping body. The skin of this face belonged to an old man, a very, very old man. Nature was playing one of her dirty tricks; Ginsberg recognized Tom Sirpson, two or three years his junior, whose stay at Cambridge had overlapped with his own.

"Ivan Ginsberg," wheezed the young old man.

"Well if it isn't Tom Sirpson!" said Ginsberg heartily. For a moment he was back in another environment, one in which he had once wished to spend his entire life; an environment of delicate grey shades and fine feeling. He pictured Tom Sirpson in a score of harmonious scenes, cycling along the Newmarket Road, browsing in a bookshop, strolling meditatively out of the gates of Pembroke College. Above all he remembered innumerable lazy afternoons with Tom in the billiard-room at the Union. There were few more agreeable ways of spending an afternoon than diving straight down into the obscurity of the billiard-room after lunch, knocking the balls around beneath the restricted square of light, and emerging when it was time for tea in the Copper Kettle with Joan and Phyllis and Lambert and Talukdah and a crowd of others. Surely the most pleasantly idle, the most unchangeably undergraduate of his Cambridge acquaintances had been Tom Sirpson?

"What the devil are you doing here?" asked Ginsberg. "I might ask the same," laughed Tom Sirpson, wheezing and choking asthmatically.

"As a matter of fact, I'm doing a tour of London by night with old Kagaranias over there." He indicated the dilapidated figure which was now creeping towards them, fearfully holding two shivering and half-spilt cups of tea.

"Still as dilettante as ever," said Tom offhandedly. "By the way, meet Krishna." He introduced a tiny, handsome little Indian, beautifully proportioned on a midget scale. Kagaranias, likewise, was introduced by Ginsberg, and the four stood facing each other, holding cups of tea and curiously examined by the surrounding roughs.

Still as dilettante as ever, wondered Ginsberg? What does he mean by that? Tom Sirpson would never have used such a phrase in Cambridge. He surreptitiously glanced at Tom's face again. That surface decay, like the wheezing and painful creaking of his chest, was clearly the result of some radical disease, of some constitutional rotting. Truly, a dirty trick on the part of nature, one of her damnable experiments undertaken out of sheer idle curiosity.

The result of the experiment with Tom Sirpson's withered young body was remarkable, and yet readily understandable. Tom, it appeared, now lived with religious intensity and disregard for mundane pleasure and vanity. He had become a revolutionary and was a paid agent of the New Communist Party. Earning a bare subsistence, he lived in the poorest of lodgings behind King's Cross. When he was not travelling in the provinces, selling literature, and addressing meetings, he worked well on into the night at his articles and political notes. In the early hours, he dropped round to the milk bar for a cup of coffee, sometimes with Krishna, a medical student and fellow-lodger who had formed himself into a sort of disciple of Tom's.

Tom was not priggish about his new religion.

"I've just had harder knocks than most people, that's all," he said. "You ought to read some of our stuff. Most people think we're a lot of cranks, that's what the middleclass press wants them to think. But for the most part we're people who've simply been driven into New Communism — or as we prefer to call it, Communism, as distinct from Stalinism — through lack of any suitable alternative."

"I'm afraid," murmured Ivan, "I'm just a left-winger. Very much to the left, but nothing definite. I'm an optimistic pessimist, a pessimistic optimist, full of doubt and foreboding, yet very hopeful."

Tom threw back his head and laughed hastily and perfunctorily. "Classic!" he choked through a fit of coughing. "Classic! A model answer. Classic and inevitable." He slapped Ivan on the back. "Good old Ivan. How's your billiards these days?"

Tom knew all the answers, waited without listening while the others spoke, and then came in automatically at the end with a formal and penetrating reply.

"Well, there's one thing," said Ivan finally, "whose value no one can deny, and that is discussion. Discussion, argument, controversy provide the mixture from which we can extract truth. Now you despise my activities and interests, on the whole rightly. Well" — he smiled ironically — "I hope shortly to be doing something more closely connected with politics. I hope, in fact, to become the editor of a magazine, a highly controversial and at the same time a responsible magazine, in which the views of your party will be given the serious consideration they deserve."

"Sounds all right," said Tom. "But I can hardly believe it'll bc anything more than a variation on the old arty-crafty business. Ah well — to each one his destiny." He sighed and for an instant was so still that he might have been dead.

"Shall I put you on my list of possible contributors?" asked Ivan.

"By all means, if the thing gets going. Though I must say, yours is hardly the kind of public to which we pay most attention. Our best propaganda is events themselves, and we produce literature of immediate interest to, say, unofficial strikers, soldiers with a grievance, the poorest victims of red tape, those millions who are still right at the bottom, with their noses in the mud. For the moment we're not very interested in intellectuals. We can't afford to be, not until we're a mass party — we don't want to be swamped with them, like the Stalinists."

"Aren't you an intellectual?" asked Ginsberg, nettled. "Wasn't Lenin an intellectual?"

"Just look at me!" cried Tom Sirpson. They were all shocked and embarrassed, as though he had drawn their attention to something utterly indecent, unmentionable, and taboo. Tom Sirpson pointed to his face. "Yes, look at my face. There you have the answer. Am I an intellectual, or am I one of the dispossessed, more completely dispossessed than the poorest sneakthief in this bar?" They followed his glance round the bar, from the ragged toughs to the white-faced men in cheap and flashy padded suits; and then back to Tom Sirpson's finger pointing defiantly at his withered, deathly face.

Neither Ginsberg nor Kagaranias had the courage to ask what mysterious affliction was responsible for Tom's physical disintegration. They saw, too, that his hands were as withered as his face, that every portion of his body which was visible seemed to have had the moisture, the fat, the life sucked from it. Even Kagaranias was moved, and no longer stared in his usual baleful, mummified way.

Krishna's shining black eyes remained fixed vacantly in the middle distance. Tom was seized with a coughing fit, choking and writhing in a private agonized struggle. When he had finished, they all stood uncomfortably, no one wishing to resume the conversation.

Krishna consulted his watch. It was two o'clock. Kagaranias pointed out to Ginsberg that they barely had time to get to Fleet Street by half-past two — Kaggy had never set foot in a taxi in his life. They prepared to leave; Ginsberg held out his hand.

"Glad to have run into you again, Tom," he said. He felt the lifeless touch of Tom's hand. "I hope you'll look me up some time. I'll give you the address —"

"No," interrupted Tom with sudden decision. He grasped Ivan's hand again. "Don't. I've finished with all that."

"With all what?"

"With old friends, with anything to do with the past. . . before *this*." He pointed to himself bitterly. "Without entering into details, I don't suppose I have long to live. Perhaps a couple of years, perhaps five, who knows? And during that time, here is where I belong." He indicated the milk bar, and beyond, King's Cross and the Caledonian Road. "Goodbye."

Tom — one foot dragging lifelessly behind the other — and Krishna set off past the railway arches and the long, unbroken walls of goods yards into the desolation north of the Cross. Ginsberg and Kagaranias headed up Gray's Inn Road towards Holborn.

CHAPTER VI

THE READING OF NEWSPAPERS is a habit as nearly universal and as seemingly indispensable as the puffing and blowing and inhaling of tobacco smoke; and the men of Fleet Street take second place only to those of Westminster in the national mythology. no one, therefore, travelling for the first time on a bus from St. Paul's to the Strand, fails to look eagerly out of the window at the couple of hundred yards of street which issues and receives so much publicity. And no one, nowadays, fails to be disappointed. There, it is true, are the offices of the *Daily Express,* the *Daily Telegraph,* and the *Daily Post;* there, on the other side, is Reuters' building. That little side turning is Bouverie Street, home of the *News-Chronicle* and the *News of the World.* And here are a number of small shop-windows labelled *Wolverhampton Monthly, Huddersfield Courier,* and *South Hampshire Amalgamated Provincial Press.* And that is all.

But what else could be expected? The young provincial, like all of us an assiduous newspaper reader, who has just looked along the dusty, rather empty pavements of Fleet Street in the mid-afternoon, might on reflection admit that nothing else could reasonably be expected. A street is a street, and it is somewhat juvenile and romantic to expect Fleet Street to look and feel any different from, say, Market Street, Manchester. But at any rate, he might ask, where are the journalists? There ought to be at least one little group outside a pub, wearing yellow ties and green shirts and broad-brimmed hats, among whom might be recognized James Agate or Timothy Shy or Lord Beaverbrook or the editor of *The Times.* But no; there are only two men with umbrellas shaking hands outside a milk bar, and a group of schoolboys crowding round a window displaying postage-stamps. And where are the cafés and restaurants, those crowded, smoky old eating-houses where hard-boiled newspapermen exchange gossip too confidential ever to be printed? The young provincial had time to notice only the milk bars, a branch of the Central London Chain Restaurants Ltd., and the D.E.F. Help Yourself Service. So having travelled back up north, he contemptuously dismisses Fleet Street from the story of his itinerary. "'Twere noothing to write 'awm about."

One place he missed, however, was Tim's Caff, whose entrance was squeezed back about two yards from Fleet Street proper into a passageway no wider than a child's armspan. Tim's Caff gave a twenty-four hour service, night and day all the year round. For eight hours out of twenty-four, Jim was in charge; for another eight, Tom; and from midnight till the hearty, breathless voices of early morning charwomen echoed through the street and burst into the Caff, Tim himself was in charge.

Jim, Tom, or Tim stood by the cash-register at a slight angle to the counter. Everything was under his control — door, counter, and tables. Service was prompt, too prompt even for the startled customer. The door opened, the customer entered, and Jim, Tom, or Tim, head lowered, body crouched on a high stool by the cash-register, interrupted a stream of staccato instructions down the lift hatch, to fire a polite but peremptory question:

"What will you have suh?"

Two men behind the counter were furiously buttering slices of bread, cutting off thin flakes of cheese, frying sausages, feeding the tea-urn, and keeping half an ear open for the ceaseless, rapid instructions. A waitress hurried swiftly from counter to tables, transferring cups of tea and plates of food in arc-like, unerring sweeps.

The customer considered for a moment, feeling guiltily that he was wasting Jim, Tom, or Tim's precious, relentless time.

"Er. . . I'll have a cheese sandwich and a cup of tea."

"A cheese sandwich and a cup of tea!" was the automatic lightning command.

"No, wait a minute!" cried the flustered customer. "These sausages smell good —"

"Hold that!" barked Tim to the men behind the counter, furiously buttering, cutting, frying, pouring. "Yessuh! They are good. Everything in Tim's Caff is good, and they're the best you'll get in London to-day." He waited tensely, head lowered as though to butt the customer in the stomach.

"Very well. . . er. . . sausages and chips."

"You'll want a slice of bread and a cup of tea? Right. Sausagesandchipsslicebutteredbreadanacupotea! That'll be one and ten, suh!"

The money was handed over, the cash-register clanged, zinged, and crashed to. Jim, Tom, or Tim grinned cheerfully and waved the customer to a seat. The food came flying over in two or three huge arcs, guided by the waitress's hand, and the staff transferred their attention to "the next on the list — this way, pluhease!"

Tim's Caff was always busy and cosy. You could sit in Tim's twenty-four hours out of twenty-four, eating, smoking, reading the papers as they came off the press, and listening to talk about everything from dogs to horses, from cricket to football, from "our new bloke" to "the old one what left". Tim's Caff provided an atmosphere which brought to mind the Fleet Street of the imagination, the lively, cosy, sleepless Fleet Street which possibly once was — but with one proviso. No journalist — with the exception of Bert Flogcrobber — no reporter, no sub-editor, no contributor ever set foot in the place. It was frequented entirely by men in overalls, their hands covered with grease, by lorry-drivers, machine operators, mechanics, compositors' mates, office boys and charwomen.

The exception was Bert Flogcrobber on the *Daily Post*. During his twenty-five years with the *Daily Post* group of papers, Bert had held almost every position on the reporting and editorial staff, from seventeen-year-old junior reporter at twelve and six a week on the group's

Northamptonshire local to his present post of assistant night-editor on the *Daily Post.* He knew "the game" like the back of his hand, and had done fairly well. For all that, he was a disappointed man.

Money, for instance, was a constant, nagging source of worry. He had a large family — wife, three sons, two daughters. As a responsible journalist on a conservative paper, he felt that he was entitled to bring up his children in a manner befitting a gentleman. All readers of the *Daily Post* were gentlemen (or ladies) and a member of its staff was certainly a gentleman. Yet his salary, adequate though it was from some points of view, was frankly insufficient to enable him to send his sons to a minor public school and university, his daughters to study painting and music, his wife to Torquay for the summer, and to maintain a house in Wimbledon. He could not even afford to run a car. Yet on top of these standard expenses, less obvious but no less essential, was his whisky bill. Bert Flogcrobber was one of those journalists — and the strain of the profession produces many — who could not work without a small flask of whisky in his hip pocket. He drank heavily, held his drink well, and did sound, reliable work while in a state of moderate intoxication.

To help meet his large expenses, Bert did free-lance work. When his duties on the *Daily Post* were over for the night, and his colleagues went home to their beds, Bert sat on in his office for a further hour or two tapping out free-lance articles. The articles were popular, worthless, and easily salable. But in order to keep up his powers of concentration and produce these Sunday newspaper titbits en masse and in a way that was truly profitable, Bert drank more whisky than ever; which in turn sent up his expenses — for a steady supply of whisky could be secured only at exorbitant prices. More work, more whisky; more whisky, more work. It was in the middle of these lonely, laborious, half-drunken vigils before dawn that Bert dropped into Tim's Caff for a snack and a cup of tea.

On this Wednesday morning, when he went down to Tim's at about three o'clock, he found Kagaranias and Ginsberg waiting for him. They had almost given up hope of his coming, since it was after his usual hour for a plate of sausage and chips. But the fact was, that his two younger sons' school bills were due to be paid by the end of the month, and he had to get the *Sunday Herald-Guardian* spy story in before the first morning post was collected. So important was it for him to make sure of the eighty-pound cheque for the spy story — a long one, cunningly adapted from an American weekly, and to be published in three instalments — that he had been in an awful state of nerves, old hand though he was. He had soaked in almost half a bottle of whisky, which for once had merely given him a thick head instead of livening his brain up. With the wretched possibility before him of having to withdraw his sons from Smarmingham School, he had bitten his nails and scratched his thin, dandruff-speckled hair like any desperate novice. Not until three o'clock had he satisfied himself that the article, product of four early-morning bouts, was ready to go before the editor of the *Sunday Herald-Guardian.* He wrote boldly across the first page Yvonne Bretonne, and dropped it in the post-box for his agent. Yvonne Bretonne, a familiar name on the feature pages of Sunday newspapers and popular weeklies, but whose identity was known only to himself and his agent, had completed another undoubtedly salable piece of work.

Bert was ready for a chat with Kagaranias and his companion. He felt like airing a few of his grievances to people who didn't matter, with whom it was not necessary to keep a curb on his tongue. In one way he was feeling satisfied, and pleasantly tired, after the successful completion of his spy story. Yet in a deeper way, he had never felt more bitter. This hack work, done largely in secret and sold discreetly by his agent — for it would not do to let his chiefs on the *Sunday Herald-Guardian* know of more than a part of its scope — was wearing him down physically and destroying his self-esteem.

At three o'clock in the morning the service at Tim's was as rapid and staccato as ever. Bert Flogcrobber faced the usual intensive barrage, fired by Tim himself, the swiftest and most forceful of the three masters of ceremonies, and then lowered himself carefully into a chair. He was a large, heavy man, bespectacled, and with a receding forehead from which thin, darkish hair made a further recession. His face, his clothes, his whole appearance lacked distinctive features. He was the man-in-the-street, the middle-aged, worried, tax-paying, rate-paying father of a family, a professional man who had risen in the world, but whose speech had not lost an ugly flavouring of diluted Cockney. The snarling phobias, grievances, and vanities hidden beneath this drab exterior were no more visible than with any other season-ticket holder coming out of Cannon Street station at ten o'clock in the morning. There was not even, at this moment, a bulge in his hip pocket — he had finished his half-bottle over the article and thrown the empty bottle away. His breath smelt of whisky, but not excessively. His eyes — no one ever troubled to search them out. They were somewhere behind his spectacles, since he could evidently see; but they gave no glimpse of his inner life, unless that inner life were itself, like the eyes, dirty, colourless, and befogged with a muddy resentment.

"Well, Mr. Kagaranias," said Bert, "doing your usual round, I see." He knew Kagaranias quite well, having seen him at night in Tim's Caff off and on for the last couple of years, ever since he himself had begun to combine assistant night-editorship with free-lance work. Once he had given Kaggy a splash on the feature page of the *Daily Post* — "The Wanderer in the Night. . . Kagaranias, Popular London Eccentric".

"Yes," said Kagaranias, "I hevn't bin here for uhbuht two wiks now. Uh nice night, I thought I'd drop in. I'd like you to mit uh friend uh mine, Misteh Ivun Ginsbeg." He introduced them: "Misteh Bet Flogcrobbeh, Misteh Ivun Ginsbeg." They nodded to each other without shaking hands.

"Misteh Ginsbeg," continued Kagaranias, "is uh scholeh end uh writeh. End now he is becoming en editeh."

"Oh?" queried Bert. "You a Fleet Street man?"

"No," said Ginsberg with a laugh, "I can hardly call myself that."

"Misteh Ginsbeg —" said Kagaranias.

"What was that?" interrupted Bert. "Ginsberg?" Ivan nodded. "Ah." Bert smirked significantly. "One of the *Chosen* People, ay?" The phrase and emphasis on the word "chosen" conveyed humour, cynicism, envy, and ill-will. "Smart lads, the yids," Bert went on. "Wish I had their brains. You wouldn't see me here now if I had."

Ginsberg smiled, forcing all the muscles round his mouth to exert themselves to the full; the widest, the most tolerant, the most accommodating of smiles was essential. He was used to this gambit and to the malicious flattery which was certain to follow. Arguments about the Jews, in which he was expected to answer accusations or respond to provocative sallies, wearied him beyond measure. He was not interested in the Jewish question; or, more strictly, he abominated the Jewish question, and the passions and sentiment, dressed up in spurious, windy logic, which the dreary subject aroused.

The expected follow-up to Bert's first playful thrust now arrived. "I like working with the yids; you know where you stand. You can trust a yid. He drives a hard bargain, but you can rely on him to stick to it. Besides —" Bert pointed his fork, with a piece of sausage stuck on the end, first at Ginsberg, then at Kagaranias. "Besides, if you work with the yids, you get your cut. They get on, and you get on with them. D'y'ever see a yid stand still, in one place, year in and year out? Eh?"

Ginsberg murmured noncommittally and deprecatingly, maintaining all the while a Buddha-like smile of unhappy serenity.

"Not them!" said Bert, with an energetic shake of his head. "They've got too much sense! — Another cup of tea, Tim!" he called out. "Will you two have —? Right. Make it three teas, Tim!"

Three teas, manipulated by a waiter in rolled-up shirt sleeves, arrived immediately in a sweeping double arc. Half a dozen men in overalls went out, a couple of lorry drivers came in. The cash-register clanged, the tea-urn spluttered merrily, the men behind the counter fried, cut, buttered, and poured as furiously as ever. Tim's was always busy.

"And I don't blame 'em," continued Bert, "I admire 'em. I've got no time for anti-semitism — and let me tell you there's plenty of it about, to-day more than ever." His eyebrows were raised in warning, his lips fell away in sad amusement. The muscles of Ginsberg's face had now set, as it were, permanently in their expression of disdainful joviality; while Kagaranias was lost in the antique, submerged reverie into which he always sank when not talking.

"The yids go into business," said Bert, "and they make money. That's the only way to make money — business. I wish I'd have gone into business; but it's too late now. I'm in a rut. I've got about as far as I shall ever get in my line, and I shall just have to go on being a hack for the rest of my life."

Bert was not normally so talkative, but the extra whisky had loosened his tongue as well as giving him a thick head. Besides the bottle just thrown away, he had been drinking in the Quill Club most of the afternoon, and in the Irish bar after that.

"You don't like journalism, then?" asked Ginsberg, glad to get off the subject of the Jews.

"Well, that's a thing it's almost impossible to say," said Bert. He had now finished his sausages and chips and stretched himself with loud grunts, feeling decidedly more contented; both for having got some solid food inside him to relieve the twinges in his stale, whisky-sodden stomach, and for having arrived at a subject for conversation most appropriate to his mood. Tim's sausages were quite the hottest and crispest in London; his tea was brought to a nice strength and just a little over-sugared.

"Three more teas, Tim!" called Bert. Three teas leapt to their table. Kagaranias pulled three crushed Weights from his pocket; they lit up, and Bert, his chair tipped back, continued reflectively.

"It's almost impossible for me to say whether I like journalism or not. It's in my blood. I've been twenty-five years in the game, ever since I was a boy just left school. I like working in Fleet Street — I know everybody and every corner. It's like a little village, you know. Wonderful place, it's got everything — pubs, clubs, restaurants, little cafés like this, and some of the finest chaps in the world. And some of the worst bastards. . . No, it's the work that gets me down. When you start in the game, you want work, you like work. You lam into it, you give it everything you've got, you think it's going to get you somewhere. You turn your hand to anything — reporting, sub-editing, features; the more you're given to write, the happier you are. Your money goes up, you're no longer earning the same wage as a shop-assistant, and you think you're doing all right. But when you get to middle age, you realize that journalism is just a racket like any other. Just a business, nothing more. You thought it was different, but it isn't. And the poor mug of a journalist is just a hack like any other. He has to give the boss what he wants, and the public what it wants, and himself dam'all."

"But surely," Ginsberg protested, "the journalist is no different from any other professional man —"

"Professional man!" sneered Bert. "Professional man indeed! The journalist is no more of a professional man than the blinking office-boy! Ever seen reporters mooching down the Street looking for a job? Ever seen five hundred replies to a single ad. in the Situations Vacant column of *World's Press News?* Bah! Don't talk to me about professional men!"

Bert tipped his chair forward and passed his fingertips over his tired eyes.

"And the money?" he added. "You may say union rates and all the rest of it are not too bad; and journalists on Fleet Street seem to have a bit of pocket money to splash around. I won't deny it. Take myself, for instance. I've had a salary of a thousand a year every year for the last eight years: and since I've been assistant night-editor I get more than that. But I'm getting on towards the top of the profession — I'm just as bad as you, *profession!* — assistant night-editor on a national daily. And even then I wouldn't get very far on my salary. I earn another thousand a year on top of that. Yes," he added proudly, about-turning on his argument.

"A thousand a year alone doesn't seem too bad to me," murmured Ginsberg, who lived on four pounds a week.

"Not when you've got a family to keep!" exclaimed Bert triumphantly. "I'm no socialist, I can tell you. I believe in the policy of the *Daily Post* — I'm about the only member of the staff who does. Three quarters of 'em are damn communists, and I'm not joking. No, I believe in ambition and drive and getting on and putting up a good show. I've sent my boys to a public school, and they're going on to Oxford, and I'm giving my girls a good education, too. All that costs money, not to mention the wife and the house and the grub and the booze —"

He paused, his brow furrowed and his eyes narrowed at the word booze, to show them that it was a matter of some significance.

"So I have to earn that extra thousand. And I have to work for it, yes, work — that's what I'm doing rolling into a place like this at three o'clock in the morning. And I can tell you, half the blokes in Fleet Street who've got any gumption are putting in a spot of private overtime. — It's the Machine," said Bert. The Machine had some special, private meaning for Bert; he repeated it several times. "It's the Machine driving away; you can't get away from it. The Machine. . . "

Bert brooded intensely on the Machine, forgetting Ginsberg and Kagaranias and his half-finished cup of tea and the cigarette smouldering between fingers stained deep brown with nicotine.

"Everything's a racket," he concluded.

Then, as though the fevered crisis of his melancholy fit had passed and he had reached a state of sleepy convalescence, he yawned, leaned his chin on his hand, and closed his eyes.

"What's all this about you becoming an editor?" he asked Ginsberg, his eyes still shut. "What are you going to be editor of?"

"Well, I'm hoping to start my own magazine," replied Ginsberg. "I want it to be a lively, independent little monthly for the expression of new and stimulating ideas, preferably by young people."

"What, stories, articles, poems. . . "

"Anything," said Ginsberg; "though I'm not too keen on the poems."

"But aren't there several magazines of this type in existence already?"

"Ah, but this will be one with a difference! *Scamp,* magazine for the younger generation!. . . I hope," Ginsberg sniggered.

"Hm. Sounds all right," said Bert. "Printer, paper, money, I suppose you've got that all well in hand. At any rate, you know what you're up against there — one hell of a struggle. What's the time?" he asked sleepily.

"It's uhbuht four uh'clock," said Kagaranias, who never took part in a conversation unless he was on fairly sure ground. Kaggy could be relied upon to look after the practical side of one of his night's outings. He knew the places, the way, what was obtainable, the times of first and last buses and trains. He was no more tired than usual, maintaining his usual mid-way trance-like state between sleeping and waking, between hostility and indifference, between gloom and an exhausted, tolerant contentment.

"You gut to get to Wimbledon," he said to Bert. "Dere's uh train from Wutterloo et five-twelve."

"You ought to open a blooming information service, Mr. Kagaranias," said Bert, his eyes still closed, smiling with one half of his face, while the other remained firmly twisted in the palm of the hand on which it was resting. Then with effort he shook himself awake, straightened his back, and flung out his arms in an immense yawn. "Here," he said, "let's get out of here and get some fresh air. Otherwise I shall fall asleep on the table."

Apart from anything else, Tim did not allow customers to sleep in his Caff. Not only was it unprofitable from the business point of view, but it also destroyed the artistry of the place. Jim, Tom, and Tim, all of them liked to keep things running at a brisk pace. And at no time was it more essential to keep an eye on possible recalcitrant slackers, cluttering up the Caff with their sprawling and snoring, than during Tim's shift from midnight till eight in the morning. So Tim fired a goodbye at them with hearty approval, and Bert, Kagaranias, and Ginsberg stepped out into the chilly darkness of the hour before dawn.

With an hour to kill before catching his train, Bert led the way to St. Paul's. Ginsberg was by now too numb with fatigue to do more than follow indifferently anywhere; while Kagaranias, too, was game for anything. St. Paul's, Waterloo, or going home to bed in his Covent Garden warehouse, it made no difference to him.

St. Paul's, neither too fat and solid, nor too light and flimsy, but constructed with that earthy, yet exquisite harmony proper to the land of Shakespeare, pointed the way to a nobler and fuller life. They circled it, tried to embrace in some way the perfection of its mass dimly shaped against the dark sky. Then, shivering a little with cold, they recrossed Ludgate Circus and made for the Embankment at Blackfriars, Bert once again taking the initiative.

Bert, washed out but made wide awake by the cold, looked curiously at Ginsberg. After his night out, Ivan's pale face was entirely drained of colour. The collar of his jacket turned up, his teeth chattering occasionally, Ivan strode on like a man with a stern duty to fulfil. But this impressive picture in profile was spoiled when Bert spoke to him. Ivan smiled, and his smile was shallow, foolish, and defensive.

"What sort of a writer are you, if you don't mind my asking?" said Bert.

"I'm mainly an unpublished writer," said Ivan.

"Come, come!" exclaimed Bert, somewhat testily. "You describe yourself as a writer, you must have some justification for doing so. You're not shooting a line, are you?"

Ginsberg was irritated by Bert's impolite bluntness; but he was not the man to squander himself on an exhibition of annoyance. Besides, Bert might possibly be very useful to him. He contented himself with not replying; he tried to avoid trouble rather than cope with it, to rely on flight and footwork rather than cut and thrust.

"No, look here, old man," said Bert, "sorry if I offended you, but I'm interested. Seriously, what sort of stuff do you write? What sort of experience have you had in journalism?"

"Well," said Ginsberg, smiling his shallow, defensive smile, "my published work has been mainly in the *North African Army and RAF News,* which was published for the troops during the war and to which I was a frequent contributor —"

"You've been in the army, then?"

"Yes."

"Officer?" said Bert automatically and offhandedly.

"No, private. Since then I've contributed reviews on Russian subjects to *Senate* and a couple of other left-wing publications. I took a degree in Russian at Cambridge, you see. Oh, and in the last six months I've written about a hundred and fifty, two-thousand-word short stories, of which a hundred and forty-seven remain unpublished."

"A hundred and fifty-two-thousand-word short stories! But that's incredible! It's almost impossible! Three hundred thousand words in six months — it's enough to have driven anyone mad! What on earth made you do it?"

Ginsberg shrugged his shoulders. "I wanted to make my living as a short-story writer. As a beginner, I had to break through by sheer mass. I sold three stories in six months; even that wasn't too bad, I suppose. I put in at least six hours a day seven days a week, apart from other odds and ends of work. Still, I've given it up now, it was lunacy. I shan't try anything of the sort again until I settle down to write a novel which will be really worth while. As Connolly says, the only thing worth writing is a masterpiece."

The first hint of dawn crept up behind them. Downstream a tug hooted. The day was stirring, and two or three people were already about on the streets. From Westminster a tram clanged and clattered towards the Kingsway tunnel.

"Meanwhile," said Ginsberg, infusing heartiness into his voice, "I'm going to edit my own magazine — *Scamp*. Yes, I'll have that in the shops within four months."

They climbed the steps on to Waterloo Bridge. The air was fresh, and the sky behind St. Paul's was a luminous grey; they could just see down-river now. There was a gentleness, a patriarchal simplicity about the great, flat bulk of the city, over which the spidery fingers of the dawn crept.

"You know," said Bert cautiously, "I'm always on the look-out for a "ghost" in my free-lance work; a collaborator, that is, to work out suggestions I haven't time to follow up myself. Also to polish up the stuff I write. In general, I could do with someone to make himself useful — but someone really competent and keen. I've tried people, of course, but there's always something goes wrong. I haven't time to go into it all now, but you might be interested to discuss the matter with me one day at my office; or we could have a drink somewhere, or a meal. After all, though I wish you luck, it may take you some time to get your magazine going. And the collaboration I have in mind would give you some practical experience in journalism — of a very popular kind, I admit. But it can be profitable, make no mistake about that. Last year I made well over a thousand pounds by my free-lance work, and I put into it maybe an hour or two a day. My secretary sees to the press cuttings — incidentally, I have one of the largest private libraries of press cuttings in the country — and my agent has excellent contacts and markets the stuff without difficulty. Your job, if you decided to come in with me, would be to extend the scope of the work, undertake more serious articles, for instance, and improve the style and the quality generally."

If Ginsberg had been asked what practical, professional offer might be hoped for from a man with the status of Bert Flogcrobber, he could not have improved on the one which had just been made. And it had been put forward quite unsolicited, and within a couple of hours of their meeting. Evidently Bert was one of those shrewd, battered men of the world who recognized merit and potential the moment they saw it.

"I must say," said Ginsberg, "your suggestion sounds most interesting, and I should be glad to drop in at your office some time —"

"Any time, any time... Er, no, let me see; perhaps between five and seven would be best, if I'm there that early. Phone up and make sure — unless you'd prefer to come about two o'clock in the morning," he added with a laugh.

"As a matter of fact I would," said Ginsberg. "I shall enjoy calling on someone in Fleet Street at two o'clock in the morning. But really, you know, I may not be any good. I'm far from confident of my ability to write to order."

Ginsberg wanted to be reassured, to receive an explicit compliment. Bert obliged.

"I think we'll be able to do some good work together," he

said. "It strikes me — of course, I don't know you, and I may be wrong, but I don't think so — it strikes me that you're a young man who's got what it takes, but lacks experience and an opportunity. I may be able to give you a little of both. And on the financial side, I offer my "ghosts" twenty-five per cent. Twenty-five per cent of a thousand is two-fifty, and two-fifty a year's not bad for a couple of hours' work a day. Besides" — Bert gave Ivan a light slap on the back, summoning up a feeble heartiness outside Waterloo Station — "give a yid a chance and no one can tell where he'll get! I bet if you come in with me, you'll be turning my thousand into two thousand, taking seventy-five per cent yourself, and leaving me with a few hundred just to keep me quiet, ay?"

Bleary-eyed, the uneven bristles on his chin showing in the dawn light, Bert chuckled hollowly.

"But I like working with the yids —"

Ivan's drooping expression sagged a little lower. Really, it was a dirty trick to start going back to the "yids" now... after being so helpful, so complimentary.

"What's the matter?" said Bert. "Don't you like my saying yids? Well, it's only a word, I'm always like that. With me, a Scotsman's a scottie, an Irishman's a mick, a Frenchman's a frog, what the hell? All right, the Jews then — that better? The Hebrews, the Israelites, as they call themselves in France. Well, I like working with 'em anyway, and you'll probably send my bank balance up so's I won't recognize it. Think it over, old chap."

After exchanging addresses and phone numbers and asking each other in vain who had any cigarettes left, they shook hands and parted, with that exhaustion in the bones which comes from spending a night in the open without sleep.

Bert trudged off to catch his train. He fancied he was on to a good thing in Ivan. The chap was reasonably young, his brain was fresh, he had ideas, he could probably write a decent sentence. In any case, he could hardly be worse than the other "ghosts", those hungry, savage, deceitful, secretive, and usually incompetent wolves from the backwoods of Fleet Street. The demands they had made! Wanted cash before the stuff was sold — one fellow had actually asked to be paid in advance! And they stole ideas, botched the work, weren't satisfied with twenty-five per cent, and finally marched out with their first cheques and tried to work the same markets by imitating his methods. With luck, he might be able to saddle Ivan with most of the free-lance donkey work and give himself a little time to breathe.

Ivan and Kagaranias separated at Aldwych.

"You going to see det chep?" asked Kagaranias, before shuffling off up Drury Lane to his warehouse, where he would sleep for a few hours on a broken divan in one of the cellars.

"Yes, I think so," said Ivan.

"Well," said Kagaranias, "gled if I've bin uh little help. I tought you end dis chep might be able to do some wek togedder. End es for de udder, de megezine, I wish you all de luck. If I was uh men who undehstood dese tings, den peheps — but I'm not, so what's de use of talking? Chirrio."

Kagaranias withdrew from his features the last trace of the occasional animation and interest which they had displayed during the night, and shuffled off wearily and bravely to his grim destiny. Of what use was his half a million when he could not spend it, when some inner hand stayed him with its grip of iron? The notes in his pocket, unspent, were so much paper. Only the books in his warehouse, bought by the sack and lorryload, distinguished this building from the rotting, rat-infested slums of which it formed part. Kagaranias lived among the very poor, but without their companionship. no one in the world spoke his language.

Ginsberg went home through Lincoln's Inn Fields and Red Lion Street. Above the empty, bombed spaces, rose a huge, imaginative curve of grey sky. The broadening of the view by this small area of flat desolation and the expanse of ribbed clouds stretching like waves into the early-morning sky brought to mind the sea. And of all the views of the sea he had known — from behind the barbed wire of English seaside resorts during the war, from the Libyan desert coast, from the decks of troopships, from the quayside at Naples, and from the rocks of little peninsulas in Britanny and Scotland and the west coast of Ireland — Ginsberg was reminded of only one. It was the dear, familiar, poignant view from Porth Bay, remote, unattainable, grey, and overcast for ever by the clouded Celtic twilight. Fifty miles away was the Somerset coast; to the west, the desolation and freedom of the Atlantic. The gulls swooped over the cliffs to the rocks below, the air was damp and gusty and full of spray, and he and Margaret stared out over just such an expanse of ocean as appeared to be swept up from the bare, bombed cavities into the Holborn sky.

And now Margaret was dead. Always it came back to that. No matter what he did, what he desired, what happened, Margaret was dead, and the very heart gone from the beauty of life. Once every twenty-four hours Ginsberg came to this moment. He visualized Margaret's features, he filled in the lines of her dress, he went over the details of their first meeting, recalling every word and turn of phrase. He remembered a few composite scenes, such as the one on the cliffs at Porth Bay; these scenes, with all possible jarring details omitted, represented their year together as lovers, he as an intellectual army private, horrified and amused by the life of an infantry unit, she as the Welsh farmer's daughter with aspirations towards the great world. Finally, the posting overseas and the letter; the letter, to all intents and purposes, had robbed him of Margaret. The letter had killed Margaret. He had it still in the tattered personal file at the bottom of his suitcase, along with his birth certificate, passport, army discharge certificate, post office savings' book, and a dozen photographs. The suitcase, the file, his clothes, and a few shelves of books were his only possessions; and hidden away beneath them, like a guilty secret, was the letter.

"Darling, by the time you receive this letter I shall be dead. You remember Cemr.yg cliff, the high one beyond Porth Bay? I shall throw myself over to-night and end this little life for ever.

"If I were to live, Ivan, in six months' time I should give birth to your child. I can't face the scandal of it, in my father's house, and alone I don't know what to do and where to turn. I am after all, as you see, just a silly country girl. . ."

The letter went on, six pages of it.

"No woman has ever loved a man as I have loved you. Goodbye, darling, see you in the next world. . ."

It was a strange, terrible letter, its unreality all the more weird for being read on the edge of the desert, in the harsh sunshine of an Egyptian afternoon, which understood no fine shades, no Celtic mysteries.

Had she committed suicide? That, Ginsberg had never discovered. He had written, but had received no further news from Porth Bay. Since his return to England, he had learned nothing more. How was he to find out? He dared not visit her parents, they would merely set the dog on him. He could go down to Porth Bay and make enquiries among some of the girls who had been Margaret's contemporaries. But he had neither the money nor the incentive to hang around the narrow little Welsh town. Perhaps one day, if he could afford it, he would employ a private investigator to obtain the information, just to satisfy his curiosity. Otherwise, the new Margaret, if she were alive, was of no interest to him. A pretty Welsh housewife, married to a Dai Evans or a Taffy Jones, would have no more than the most tenuous connection with the Margaret who had insisted on running about naked among the moonlit Forth cliffs and woods and had written that strange six-page letter.

So coming along Lamb's Conduit Street in the fresh dawn of this April day, Ginsberg was lost in his private, recurrent dream, half fairy-tale, half nightmare. He had forgotten his stories, Mrs. Chabbers, Kagaranias, Bert Flogcrobber, and *Scamp*. He remembered other dawns, in the Welsh countryside, and looking out first thing from the camp towards the farm. He remembered the belated dawn of his own love, its brief day, and the long night of wandering, loneliness, and indifference which had followed. Brothels in Italy, affairs in Bloomsbury, bed-sitting-room adventures, these had only robbed him, they had given him nothing. Fatigue increased his customary feeling of an appalling emptiness and isolation, as though he had been in the thick of a large crowd which had suddenly vanished, leaving him standing alone, quite alone, in an unfamiliar, deserted world. Scarcely able to lift one foot above the other, he climbed slowly, wearily up the stairs of the house in Guilford Street, reached his attic on the top-floor, and within a minute of getting into bed had fallen into a deep sleep of complete physical exhaustion.

CHAPTER VII

JULIUS KRIPKIN was probably the youngest ticket-holder in the Reading Room of the British Museum. He had secured his ticket by a fraud of daring simplicity. Museum regulations required from intending readers a minimum age of twenty-one. In his letter of application Julius stated his age to be twenty-seven.

"Not just twenty-one," he told a tableful of art-students, film extras, and unemployed catering workers in the little café behind Foyle's bookshop. "Anyone could have thought that one up, giving his age as twenty-one, or even twenty-two. But only Julius Kripkin would have dared say he was twenty-seven. Just look at me!"

Rather unwillingly, they did. There was no denying his youth; he was, in fact, eighteen. That was during the previous summer, in the golden days of the shooting of *Caesar and Cleopatra,* when not only the film extras were working full-time, but even the art-students, the unemployed catering workers, and Julius Kripkin were needed several days a week for the vast crowd scenes.

The film *Caesar and Cleopatra* had in a way persuaded Julius to send in his successful application for a ticket to the Reading Room of the British Museum. It was in other respects, too, an important influence in his life.

He was eighteen, he had just left school, he found life, London, the future stupendously interesting. There they were, all waiting at his doorstep, unaware of, yet ready for the impact of Julius Kripkin. As far as opportunity was concerned, there was an embarrassment of riches. Should he study law, or medicine, as his parents wanted, and become the greatest lawyer or doctor of all time? Should he take up painting and become the greatest painter, or acting and become the greatest actor, or business and become the richest man in the world? Should he accomplish any or all of these aims first and then become one of London's most fascinating, irresistible, and experienced lovers? Or should he take love in his stride?

In any case, his parents were wealthy, had a large house in Golders Green, did not press him, and gave him a couple of shillings pocket money each day for his jaunts into the West End, where he had discovered that cosy, steamy little café behind Foyle's, frequented by art-students, film extras, bums, and several very pretty girls. A couple of shillings was not a lot, but it was enough to buy a packet of cigarettes and a cup of tea. And what more did one want, when one was eighteen, not entirely repulsive (though far from brilliantly handsome), and potentially the greatest lawyer, doctor, painter, actor, and lover in the world?

For the first month of what would have been the summer holidays, had he not left school, Julius entertained himself in the Belgian Café, as it is called, and let everyone know quite unmistakably that life held for him boundless possibilities. Then he heard about *Caesar and Cleopatra.* In the Belgian Café and one or two similar places in Greek Street and Old Compton Street, there was prosperity such as had not been known for years. Every day, dozens of film extras set out for the sunny compound at Denham, played pontoon behind hedges, and returned to Soho thirty shillings richer. It was, Julius learned, money for jam. He joined the merry crowds at Denham and returned with them to the Belgian Café in the evening for a plate of spaghetti and reckless quantities of tea. Six weeks on *Caesar and Cleopatra* set him up in pocket-money for six months to come.

As a result, also, of philosophical conversations held behind hedges in the compound at Denham — while producers shouted vainly for the extras to show themselves — Julius's intellectual energy, ready to rush down any channel, hurled itself at philosophy. He called it "flosophy" — his eager, enthusiastic speech had no time to delay over unnecessary syllables — and he told his parents that he had decided to become a "flosopher". They did not mind, so long as he was happy. Later, perhaps, he would settle down.

"For a few months," said Mrs. Kripkin to her husband, "let him be a flosopher."

Caesar and Cleopatra not only set him up in pocket money for six months, taught him the life of a film extra, and made him a philosopher; it also made him a disciple of Bernard Shaw. Disciple is an understatement; fanatic, monomaniac, even these are understatements. Anything to describe Julius Kripkin's devotion to and preoccupation with Bernard Shaw would be an understatement. Almost every other word used by him at this time was either Bernard or Shaw. Bernard Shaw was, apart from everything else, a philosopher; Julius Kripkin was a philosopher. Bernard Shaw was the greatest living philosopher, perhaps the greatest philosopher of all time. Julius Kripkin, seventy years his junior, was perhaps even greater.

Up to a certain point Julius Kripkin's life was to follow closely the precedent set by Shaw. Beyond that point, no mortal could imagine the knowledge, the profundity, the fame, the recognition, the wealth, the honours which were to be Julius Kripkin's. But first the point had to be reached and the precedent followed. Shaw had spent five years — or was it ten, or twenty? — in the Reading Room of the British Museum. Julius, likewise, had to spend a period studying and meditating beneath the vast dome; though in his case the period might possibly be cut to three years, or even two.

A ticket had to be secured. So Julius lied about his age. He applied for a ticket on the grounds that he had to consult books in the Reading Room in connection with his philosophical studies. His first application was refused; he was advised to make fullest use of libraries other than the British Museum, where accommodation was limited to those engaged on research or other work which could not be undertaken elsewhere. Julius, naïve in some ways, had his wits about him in others. He inherited a little, at any rate, of the negotiating skill which had stood his father in good stead in the corset trade. He made a list of philosophical books long out of print which were unlikely to be stocked by other libraries; he announced that he was engaged on a work of research — *The Origins of Shavian Philosophy and Ethics;* and sent in an urgent second application backed by two letters of recommendation, forged by a waiter in the Belgian Café and purporting to be written by Professor Huk, of Belsize Park, and Dr. Le Massage (formerly of the Sorbonne), of West Hampstead.

The second application was successful, and Julius became the youngest ticket-holder in the Reading Room. A ticket, once granted, is rarely withdrawn; and Julius might have been thus established for life, what with his occasional film-extra work on the one hand, and his philosophical studies on the other. But this is to forget Julius's dynamism. He could not remain seated for long and was temperamentally quite unsuited to the study of philosophy.

He arrived on the dot of nine, rushed to the seat which he unaccountably supposed to have formerly been Bernard Shaw's, and within a few minutes was surrounded by a massive pile of reserved books. But by half-past nine — the hour at which the Belgian Café opened — he was seized with the restless malaise of youth. It was no use merely going down to the Gentlemen's Lavatory (with its two adjacent staircases and their curious frantic signs — "The ONLY Way Up!" and "The ONLY Way Down!") and hoping that this little walk would be sufficient diversion. He had to go out into the bustling, exciting world of human ambition, human vanity and human conflict, the world beyond Great Russell Street. Preparation, study, philosophical detachment were all very well. "Look where they got Bernard Shaw!" one part of him argued. But on the whole, he, Julius Kripkin, found them a strain.

At the Belgian Café these things could be discussed. He could always be sure of an audience.

"Here comes Julius, the wonder man," they said; or, "Here comes Bernard Shaw" — "Make way for Bernard Shaw!" His favourite audience consisted of three pretty, sceptical girls from the neighbouring St. Martin's School of Art, who sat in a row on one side of the marble-topped table, while he prattled away on the other.

Julius was a good-humoured lad, a giver as well as a receiver of the insulting witticism which passed as conversation in the Belgian Café; and he did not take offence at the uproarious fun which was made of his "flosophy". At the same time, after six months' restless wandering between Bernard Shaw's seat in the Reading Room and the Belgian Café, he could wait no longer. He was going to show them; he was going to show them all. His head swam with ideas. Where should he begin? The world, the world of philosophy in the first instance, and then the world of ideas, literature, art, and fashion generally, must know of the existence of Julius Kripkin. There must be no further delay. Young though he was, he must race ahead to his incredible destiny. The world must know! Bernard Shaw himself must know!

One morning in early spring, instead of going straight from Golders Green to the British Museum, and from there to the Belgian Café, he caught the train to Welwyn Garden City and rushed off in the direction of Ayot St. Lawrence. He knew exactly where to find Bernard Shaw, and after getting a lift from a lorry carrying bricks, arrived, covered with brick-dust, at Shaw's house.

A secretary opened the door and prepared, politely but firmly, to turn him away.

"No, it's no use!" cried Julius, before the secretary had time to utter a word. "I must see Bernard Shaw! No, it's no use! I must see Bernard Shaw!"

At that moment, a tall old man, with a white beard, crossed the hall and disappeared from sight.

"Bernard Shaw!" called Julius.

The old man came slowly to the door.

"What is it?" he said quietly.

"My name is Julius Kripkin and I've come to ask the favour of an interview," said Julius, in a voice choking with awed delight.

"I'm sorry," said Shaw, "I'm afraid I am unable to grant any interviews."

"If you had written before calling —" said the secretary.

"My name is Julius Kripkin," said Julius once again, "and I've called —"

Shaw smiled. "I'm unable to grant any interviews," he said. "Goodbye." He held out his hand. Julius shook it fervently, and was sufficiently overcome to accept the situation and hitch-hike resignedly back to Welwyn Garden City. He had shaken hands with Shaw, he had seen Shaw, he had spoken to Shaw. True; but he had not been able to explain to Shaw — ah! if only he had had the opportunity! — that theirs was an historic meeting: Julius Kripkin and Bernard Shaw.

This episode and this little crisis in Julius's development marked the end of his Shaw phase.

"After all, he's not so marvellous," Julius remarked to Mimi, a baby-faced, disillusioned, eighteen-year-old art-student who sat for days on end in the Belgian Café. "He's great, I admit," Julius continued, "very great. But there's others just as good."

"Uh-huh," said Mimi.

"No, he's not so hot," ruminated Julius.

"I couldn't care less," said Mimi, not because she meant it, but because this phrase tickled her, and she had been using it for the last three months at every conceivable opportunity.

Julius continued to use the British Museum. It was somewhere to head for first thing in the morning. Besides, it gave him a certain status. He liked to keep the staff of the Reading Room busy by ordering a pile of books and pretending that they were frightfully necessary for some obscure, but important work on which he was engaged. The staff, fortunately for themselves, were hardened to every oddity and piece of perverse ingenuity on the part of their clients. Julius was an angel of considerateness and sanity compared to some. But Julius scarcely made any effort to read his books now; nor was it an increased longing for the Belgian Café which distracted his attention, though he spent as many hours there as before. His mind was occupied with plans for success. The Shaw plan, he was ready to admit, had been a flop; and he had wasted valuable time on it. He was almost nineteen, he was getting old... and nothing accomplished.

Instead of reading the books which the patient and hard-working museum staff unearthed for him from the most distant vaults, he read magazines. He found it was possible to spend almost the entire day reading magazines, and still not get through even the better-known ones. He read them, however, not as a casual idler filling in a spare hour, but from a professional point of view. His mind was turning towards journalism as a first step towards conquering the universe. He looked through all the magazines before deciding which sort of article he was prepared to write, which sort of journalistic post he was prepared to fill.

Though he did not like the idea of hack work, he very soon realized that he was prepared to compromize his principles to the extent of accepting a job as film critic with *Time and Tide,* feature-writer with *Lilliput,* or book-critic on the *Daily Express.* Having come to this conclusion, he spent a morning on the telephone offering his services to these and other periodicals. He tried the *Daily Express* first. His heart beating fast with excitement, he pressed button A in the call-box opposite the Gentlemen's Lavatory in the British Museum, and asked for the editor.

"Just one moment," said a voice at the other end. "You're through."

For an instant Julius could not speak; his voice simply

disappeared. He was about to take the initial step in a process which would eventually make him book-reviewer on the *Daily Express,* either in place of or in association with James Agate.

The editor of the *Daily Express* said hullo for the third time.

"Oh hullo," Julius was finally able to reply. "This is —" Here his voice deserted him once again. He gulped desperately for the powers of speech and continued, almost tearfully: "This is Julius Kripkin speaking —"

"Who?"

"Julius Kripkin. I'm ringing up because I should like to discuss with you the possibility of my doing some book reviews for the *Daily Express.* I —"

"Just one moment," said the editor. "You want the literary editor." The editor clicked for the operator. "Put Mr. Kripkin through to the literary editor," he said good-humouredly.

Julius ran his hand wildly through his hair; he had to begin all over again.

"Hullo," he said, "is that the literary editor? This is Julius Kripkin speaking." He found no difficulty any longer with his speech. He ran on glibly to the end. He wanted to review books for the *Daily Express.* He was willing to start with a small paragraph or two on a couple of relatively unimportant volumes. He did not demand payment to begin with, since the literary editor could not yet be aware of his talents. Nevertheless, he did not doubt that the literary editor would later thank him for having got in touch with the *Daily Express.*

"Will you please send your application in in writing?" said the literary editor, when Julius had concluded. "Though I must say that in view of the shortage of newsprint, there is no scope for any increase in staff or contributions on the literary side."

Consoling himself a little with the shortage of newsprint, Julius tried *Time and Tide, Lilliput,* the *Daily Herald, The Times, The Times Literary Supplement,* and the *Daily Worker*. They were all short of newsprint. Having exhausted the considerable stock of pennies with which he had entered the call-box, Julius made a break in order to get some more coppers. There was already a queue of four people in the museum passageway, waiting to use the kiosk which he had occupied for so long. The first two were angry and Poles.

"Three minutes," they said, "three minutes is the time limit. And you have been eighteen and one half minutes." They muttered angrily in Polish.

"Wassermarrer? Wassermarrer?" said Julius, whose speech, always hurried, slurred, and abbreviated, was under the stress of his recent excitement more elliptical than ever.

"Ach!" snorted the Poles in simultaneous disgust, and squeezed into the phone-box together.

Julius, a harassed and ill-used young man, hurried out through the revolving doors and got into further trouble by colliding with a dignified old gentleman with long white whiskers who threatened to summon him for assault.

"I'll have you in a court of law if it happens again!" exclaimed the old gentleman. "Look where you're going, sir!"

"Wassat? Wassat?" said Julius, though he had heard only too well. He cursed his bad luck for having got on bad terms with the white-whiskered old gentleman, because the latter was a powerful figure among the ticket holders in the Reading Room. His walk was so slow and so dignified, with pauses to enable him to turn round full circle and inspect everything very thoroughly, that it took him fully a quarter of an hour to make the journey from the front gate, along the path, up the steps, through the revolving doors, and along the passage-way into the Reading Room. As he made the journey a dozen times a day, the chances of meeting him in and around the museum were very great. Everyone had got to know him, and he had become a sort of unofficial spokesman for the readers. Julius felt the eyes of the old gentleman upon him, and saw his whole position at the Reading Room undermined. He hurried away to the Belgian Café to get some more coppers and have a much-needed cup of tea.

Afterwards he went down into Tottenham Court Road tube station to do some more telephoning. Here the situation was maddening. Half the telephone-boxes were occupied, the other half out of order. A handful of phone-crazy people roamed about outside the boxes waiting for one of those still in order to become vacant. Time and again Julius was shouldered out of the way by hard-faced business women, coarse, dazzling young girls determined to make or break dates, and men who soon shouted down the receiver:

"What? Are you sending them round then? Well why not? Of course he is! Yes! That's right, Joe! What? Yes, of course! Well why not? Yes, that's right!"

At last Julius managed to get into a working box with all its windows smashed. With a background of escalator and distant tube, he resumed his campaign — *Picture Post,* the *News Chronicle, John O'London's,* the *Spectator.* Everywhere he received the same reply: Send in a written application, and in any case, on account of the shortage of newsprint. . .

The outermost, thinnest, most juvenile layer of Julius's skin hardened a little. He began to understand that the whole world was not desperately anxious to enable him to become its leading figure. It was not even enthusiastic about helping him to earn his living in a congenial manner. It was not even willing to give him a chance to prove his undoubted worth.

He went back to the Belgian Café and sat down opposite Mimi.

"They don't give you a chance," he complained bitterly.

"Yeah," said Mimi, who, though her father owned a public-house in Streatham, often spoke with an American accent. "Yeah," she said, "you're damn right." She was experiencing similar difficulties herself in her attempts to become a dance-band vocalist.

"You know," she said, inexplicably, and in the manner of her favourite cross-grained, temperamental screen actress, "you make me sick." She offered no reason, nor was she in any way annoyed with Julius. It was just table-talk in the Belgian Café.

A young man named Louis, who earned his living by drawing rapid pencil portraits in night-clubs and selling them at half a crown each, leaned across from a neighbouring table and said throatily:

"And shall I tell you something, Mimi? You see too many films — and they're not good films!"

Delighted at this opposite insult, Mimi shrieked with pleasure, and Gaston joined in with his deep bass. Julius stalked off moodily to meditate on some new campaign — but the last, the infallible one this time! He drifted through the back-streets brooding intensely on possibilities worthy of his powers. He had a cup of tea in Charlotte Street, then another in Greek Street, and yet another at the Belgian Café. He could not afford to have more than a sandwich at lunch-time, and was almost prepared to go home to Golders Green for a solid meal, when the idea hit him. He would print his own paper!

The idea was so simple that he was astonished at not having thought of it before. Why crawl to editors and the like when it was possible to run one's own newspaper? And here he had already wasted two or three weeks studying the requirements of existing publications, and a whole morning trying to explain himself over crackling telephone lines in kiosks with smashed windows, while angry phone-crazy people muttered and frowned and stamped their feet outside.

Julius's forehead was fevered with excitement. He ordered yet another tea in the Belgian Café. He'd show them! He'd show them all! Bernard Shaw and all the magazine and newspaper editors and Mimi and Louis and the two Poles and the old man with the white whiskers and those hard, jostling people stampeding about the telephone kiosks in Tottenham Court Road tube station!

He knew exactly what he would do; he would put an advertisement in the Personal Column of the *New Statesman and Nation,* a brief two-line invitation of the type that so often appeared. He could see it already, below the offers to share flats, to look after baby in the evening in exchange for use of piano, to get moths out of fur, to teach Russian, French, German, Italian at minimal fees, to explain the principles of yoga:

"Conts. invtd. for new lft.-wg. prog. internat. newsppr. Poems, articles, stories. Box 078965."

There was no point in marking time. He would insert the advertisement this very afternoon. Julius rushed out of the Belgian Café into Charing Cross Road. Mimi, with Louis' arm carelessly encircling her shoulder — not that she liked Louis, but the gesture had some small prestige value — called out with contemplative sweetness, "Cheerio, Julius!" During dead periods of the afternoon, particularly just after lunch, there was nothing much for her to do except sit entranced over a cup of tea and call out "hullo" and "cheerio" to people as they entered and left the café. She would do it to anyone, provided she knew their first name. As for Julius, she thought him "rather sweet" sometimes, and had once held hands with him under the table; though she had refused his first three invitations to the cinema and broken a date for a dance. Blonde Mimi, prettiest of the Belgian Café demi-vierges. . .

Julius headed purposively for Great Turnstile, down the alley by the Phoenix Theatre, past the workshop which was formerly the Coffee An' restaurant — home of a fabulous bohemia, of which Julius had heard from gaunt survivors of the 'thirties — past St. Giles' Church and into High Holborn. With difficulty he found the passageway in which were situated the offices of the "New States of Damnation", as it was facetiously called in the Belgian Café. He raced up to the advertisement office and scribbled out his cipher message to contributors. At the last moment he changed "newspaper" (newsppr.) to "magazine" (mgzne.). Perhaps, in the first instance, it might be wiser to limit himself to a magazine. He had an idea it might not cost so much money.

He was told that there was a long waiting list for insertions in the Personal Column, and it might take a few weeks before his advertisement appeared. But Julius did not mind; the main part of the job was over. He could now take it easy for a little, until the contributions rolled in, he sent them to the printer, the magazine arrived on the bookstalls — "Edited by Julius Kripkin" — and the initial step on the road to fame and power had been taken.

Julius returned to the Belgian Café, and there something happened which drove the magazine completely out of his mind. He fell in love. The right hand and most of the left hand sides of the Belgian Café were occupied by the usual types — each table containing, say, a couple of pretty girls from the St. Martin's School of Art and a dozen film extras, dish-washers, lampshade-makers, illegal divan manufacturers, and buyers and sellers of cigarette-lighters, fountain-pens, paste ear-rings, ties, and books by Henry Miller. But in the top left-hand corner, just by the counter, was a girl sitting on her own; and what was more she was the girl who sat regularly in Row E in the British Museum Reading Room.

Julius sat beside her and spoke to her — there were no introductions in the Belgian Café. She was, he found, "intelligent". What he had been looking for ever since he was thirteen, was an "intelligent" girl. And this one was decidedly attractive. He could not restrain his enthusiasm. He told the girl straight away and with heartfelt sincerity that this was no ordinary meeting; that they were meant for each other; that they were soulmates; that they were both "intelligent". Was it not extraordinary that they both went to see French films?

That they both studied in the British Museum? That they were both socialists and atheists and internationalists? And all these years they had been reading the same books, listening to the same symphony concerts, going to the same art galleries, without either being aware of the other's existence. Now at last they had met.

The girl for her part was amused and not a little touched. The decree absolute of her divorce had just come into effect, and she felt a great sense of freedom and release. She saw the world full of an immense number of charming men, delightful adventures, and touching revelations of love and sentiment. Julius was an hors d'oeuvre, young, impossible, lunatic, tender.

She was a sub-editor for a publishing house, and worked at the British Museum checking references for the firm's popular one-volume encyclopaedia. After a two-year marriage — "an experience which has to be gone through", she said — she lived alone in a tiny furnished flat in Hampstead. Pretty, harmoniously solid, flashing-eyed, and metallic, she might have been eighteen, though in fact she was ten years older than Julius. Having discreetly cross-examined Julius as to his origins, and satisfied herself that he was harmless and clean, she invited him to supper at her flat.

At two o'clock the following morning, Julius crept quietly from the house in which Rita lived, while she carefully and gently shut the door behind him. Whom she asked to her flat and when he left was nobody's business. Nevertheless, Mr. Chyerenscz, the Czech landlord, might complain, and it would be difficult, impossible even, to find a flat anything like as good for three guineas a week. Mr. Chyerenscz did, actually, mention the matter the next morning, though he was scarcely nasty about it at all. Nevertheless, on reflection, what with one thing and the other, she decided that one night with Julius was enough. It had been an adventure to celebrate her decree absolute. Henceforth, she must cultivate relationships which, while not oppressively permanent, offered at any rate a reasonable, reliable, semi-permanence; and relationships to which Mr. Chyerenscz could be discreetly habituated without undue embarrassment on either side.

Julius walked home to Golders Green in rather melancholy ecstasy. He was ecstatic because he was no longer technically a virgin and rather melancholy for no accountable reason. It was in any case a not unpleasant melancholy, while the ecstasy was terrific and intense. He, Julius Kripkin, now had a mistress; he had seduced a girl, or rather a woman, a married woman, a divorced married woman! And she was an intelligent girl, the girl he had been waiting for, and what a smasher with her clothes off! Took 'em off as casually as you please, no fuss, no bother, no nothing. And saw to everything herself, and had her own flat. . . what a girl! "Hooray!" he shouted in a deserted road by the Heath, and broke into a run out of sheer happiness.

His mother was waiting up for him. But it was easy to invent a party at a friend's house at Chalk Farm. He slept late and did not go to the British Museum the next morning. A man like himself could afford to do as he pleased, a man with a mistress, a secret voluptuary, a man who developed all sides of his personality, physical, mental, emotional, intellectual, artistic. At lunch he remembered that he had something to ask his father.

"Oh, by the way, Dad," he said, "I've decided on the career I want to take up. I want to run a magazine."

"Aha," said the elder Kripkin absently. He was absorbed in the *Daily Telegraph* correspondence, boiling with indignation at each new humiliation inflicted on the elderly middle classes; while at the rear of his brain there was a mechanical ticking and buzzing of figures and calculations about the corset trade in Cricklewood. He in no way registered what Julius had said.

"Well, I shall need some money to start it up," said Julius. "Do you think you'd be able to put a couple of hundred pounds into it? You'd get it back, of course."

"Tcha!" snorted his father, having just read that a

retired lieutenant-colonel in Twickenham had written four times to the local Labour Exchange for an under-gardener, and had not had a single reply. "God knows where it'll all end." And if purchase tax wasn't reduced on that new suspender line, they weren't likely to be in much demand; better speak to New Brassieres Ltd. about it.

"Ay?" said Julius. "Ay, Dad? Will you?"

"Will I what? Can't you see I'm reading the paper?"

"Will you let me have some money for the magazine?"

"No, of course not. I've told you before; until you start studying again seriously, or settle down to something steady, you're not getting any more pocket-money. I know Mum gives you a couple of bob every day, and I don't even approve of that. But you're certainly not getting any more."

"But it's for my magazine!" protested Julius.

"I don't care what it's for. And I don't see why you can't get magazines out of what Mum gives you every day. They're not as expensive as all that —" He stopped short. Perhaps he had hit upon some new scandal; perhaps the price of this magazine his son was talking about had gone up beyond all reason. He would write to the *Daily Telegraph* about it.

"Well, how much is it then? Has it gone up much lately?"

"Oh, leave me alone!" exclaimed Julius, when he realized that his father was showing, as usual, not an ounce, not a grain of imagination.

"How much, I said? How much?" shouted his father angrily. "Where's your respect? Remember, I'm your father!"

"Eat, both of you," said Mrs. Kripkin placidly. "Eat." She herself had only two pleasures in life, eating and watching her family eat. All her plans for Julius's future had kept this end in view, that she should be able to watch him eat, fully and contentedly, for ever and ever.

The little flare of temper between Julius and his father was short-lived. They both returned to eating and reading:

Mr. Kripkin, the City Notes, which he did not understand, but which made him feel dignified, and Julius, *Poetry Kent — Journal of the Young Kent Poets of the Forties,* to which he had recently submitted a poem, rejected with a kind note from the editor — "Shall be interested to see more of your work in a couple of years' time." Julius quickly abandoned the idea of getting any money out of his father. He had in any case almost forgotten about the magazine overnight; and if there was one thing he hated, it was sordid haggling about money. He focused on *Poetry Kent;* but instead of seeing the words of Idris Dai Morgan Evans's *Spherical Sonata for Pwlhelli,* the image of Rita undressing swam before his eyes.

For the next few weeks Julius was absorbed in phoning, writing, and pleading with an increasingly indifferent Rita. He reminded her of their meeting, of their common tastes, of the ride up to Hampstead, of the unparalleled hours they had spent in Rita's flat. At first Rita made excuses for not meeting him. Later she pretended that she was not available, being perpetually out, ill, or sent on the firm's business to Nottingham. The more far-fetched were her lies, the more desperately Julius believed them. He wrote immense letters explaining every shade of his feeling; he sent poems, prose poems, and a short story he had written about her. In vain did he wait for her outside her office; she had to dash off immediately to catch a bus, or was just leaving for Nottingham. If he phoned, she had not yet come in, or just this minute gone out. Not once did he receive a reply to his letters; not once in almost four weeks.

Then, one morning, on coming downstairs, his heart jumped madly, even before his brain had time to register the fact that there was a letter for him bearing a Hampstead postmark. It was from Rita, and told him briefly and unmistakably that though she did not regret their evening together, she did not want ever again to see him, hear from him, or in any way be reminded of his existence, past, present, or future. Julius had breakfast and left for his daily jaunt into town. A wise habit compelled him to store up all expression of emotion until he had got well away from the house. Come what might, he had eaten a solid breakfast and enabled his mother to settle down, with an easy mind, to another day's cooking and baking. He himself decided to commit suicide, after having bitterly and sobbingly protested, all the way to the station, not to Rita or anyone else, but to God. If God had not wanted him to fall in love with Rita, why had he sent her to the Belgian Café. And if God *had* wanted him to fall in love with Rita, then was it right, was it fair to make her write him such a letter?

As Julius could not swim, he had always intended, if ever the necessity should arise, to commit suicide by jumping from Westminster Bridge. It was as convenient a way as any. But instead of letting the train carry him on to Charing Cross, and changing there for Westminster, he left the train, out of habit, at Tottenham Court Road. He remembered his mistake only when he was already on the up escalator and could not go down again without making himself look conspicuous in front of the ticket collector, who would surely realize that the reason why Julius was behaving so oddly was that he was making for Westminster Bridge in order to commit suicide. So Julius gave up his ticket and allowed his legs to carry him to the Belgian Café. There was no harm in a cup of tea; after all, he had all day in which to commit suicide.

As a man about to die, he saw everything in a new light. Never before had he realized how pleasant life was. What a jolly, friendly lot they were in the Belgian Café! How pretty Mimi was! And was this her knee pressed against his underneath the table? Yes, it was. Mimi's knee infused him with optimism, subtly changed his enlivened perception from the revelation of a dying man to the springtime vision of a youthful poet, a poet who had experienced much, suffered much, smelt death, and then rushed back joyously to life and love. Mimi, ever bountiful with her knee underneath the tables of the

Belgian Café, was never to know that its firm, agreeable pressure had persuaded Julius not to commit suicide.

After the heartrending and terrifying experiences of the previous few weeks, culminating in the morning on which he almost committed suicide, Julius entered upon a period of retreat. Apart from occasional twinges of jealousy and desire, when he pictured Rita undressing so lightheartedly, with such abandon, for other, more experienced men, he was happy merely to be alive, to walk around Soho in the spring sunshine, to stroll in and out of the British Museum, to read *Poetry Kent.* If he remembered the magazine which he had once contemplated, it was only to dismiss the idea from his mind. A foolish notion, belonging to his callow adolescence, when he was still an innocent, empty-headed boy. As if a person like himself, without capital, without connections, could found a magazine!

Instead, he set about writing a play, a play about love, realistic without being harsh, delicate and unerring as a surgeon's knife. He came to the belated conclusion that, though no two human beings ever followed identical courses, there were after all many points of similarity between his own development and that of Bernard Shaw. His excursions into the cruel world had given him experience; now he would give that experience artistic shape. He was really, after all, a playwright. Fancy having doubted it!

Meanwhile, in the advertisement department of the *New Statesman and Nation,* they had at last arrived at Julius's cipher message, discarded and forgotten by its author:

"Conts. invtd. for new lft.-wg. prog. internat. mgzne. Poems, articles, stories. Box 078965."

It happened to be placed at the head of the Personal Column, and its appeal, assured in any case, was all the more successful. For the first few days after the week-end there were a mere dozen or so replies a day. But by the following Thursday they were arriving by the score. From country parsonages and forlorn private schools deep in the shires; from Oxford and Cambridge and Cornwall; from Welsh mining villages and industrial towns around Manchester and Newcastle and Glasgow; and, within London itself, from Bloomsbury and Chelsea and Hampstead — the contributions crowded in, sometimes a tiny poem handwritten on a flimsy sheet of paper, sometimes an immense manuscript contained in a bulky parcel.

The *New Statesman,* accustomed to the phenomenal success of some advertisements and to the utter barrenness of others, merely waited till the pile of replies had reached a certain size, say a sackful, and then sent them off to Julius, so that the first reminder Julius had of the announcement he had inserted four long weeks ago, was the arrival of a solid mass of contributions, measuring some four feet by three feet by two. Two mornings later, he received a somewhat larger parcel. Then the parcels began to diminish in size, until three weeks later no more than an occasional envelope had to be forwarded from the *New Statesman* office.

Julius's original intention was to burn these parcels. But he was restrained by fear of the consequences; possibly some contributors might complain to the *New Statesman.* He had to reconcile himself to the idea of returning all the manuscripts which had been sent with a stamped and addressed envelope, and keeping the others for some little while at least.

It was after having come to this conclusion that he ran into Ivan Ginsberg. They met beneath the portico of the British Museum. Ivan had been caught by a sudden shower and passed a torn, but neatly folded and laundered handkerchief over the rain-drops on his forehead. Julius leaned against one of the pillars and, struck momentarily by the beauty of the rain pouring on grey, melancholy stone, failed for once to bustle over and gabble out a half a dozen questions.

"You're quieter lately, Julius," said Ivan. He had known Julius ever since the latter had secured his reader's ticket. On several occasions they had had to wait for each other to finish with the single mirror in the Gentlemen's Lavatory, and had thus opened an acquaintance of a certain intimacy.

"I'n'it lovely? The rain, I mean," said Julius.

"It is rather," said Ivan. He had found, to his consternation, that he and Julius shared an extraordinary number of tastes and ambitions. One common taste was for the Bloomsbury scene, and in particular this calm, sad view from the steps of the British Museum.

In speaking to Julius, Ivan felt himself returning to the years of his own eager, enthusiastic adolescence; the same loud, hasty speech, the same crack-brained ideas, above all the same mistakes, the same fantastic mistakes and poses bordering on the lunatic. With these basic features in common, Julius and Ivan shared an intimacy which did not depend upon the frequency of their meetings. The very first time they had met, they had recognized in each other kindred spirits. This was before even they had spoken; the mere casual confrontation of long blue chin with long blue chin — for Julius's beard, too, was pushing through with azure luxuriance — of bright, thoughtful, disillusioned eye, with bright, thoughtful eye only a few shades less disillusioned — these alone had been sufficient to tell one another that explanations were unnecessary. Everything was understood.

So although Ivan had not seen Julius for over two months, he was in no hurry to question him about his recent activities. And when Julius finally described, hastily and deprecatingly, his expedition to Ayot St. Lawrence and his affair with Rita, Ivan simply threw his head back and laughed.

"Really, you know, you're a scream!"

Julius looked a trifle hurt, and Ivan, rarely guilty of such lapses, switched his face back to sympathetic gravity.

"No, of course, it's all very disheartening."

At the same time, Julius did not really care a great deal. The two of them formed a resilient, indiarubbery race; humour and erratic zest eventually sent them bouncing forward quite undismayed.

Almost as an afterthought, Julius mentioned his momentary attempt to found a magazine. Ivan, hardened though he was to the dreadful similarity between them, lifted his head in amazement. This was really too much! He felt like abandoning his own plans on the spot; in the light of such an apposition, they appeared really too ridiculous. Finally, Julius arrived at the bundles and crates of manuscripts which were cluttering up the spare room at his house, to the mystified annoyance of his father.

"Now I think I can solve that problem for you," said Ivan. "I too am founding a magazine —"

"What, you also?"

"Yes, I also," said Ivan, with biting, but quite ineffectual irony. "You'll hear all about it at the Corney Arms —"

"Never go to the Corney Arms," said Julius, proud to claim discrimination between one vein of Soho and another.

"All right, at the Belgian Café then. The point is that I can take over all your manuscripts and look through them for the purposes of my magazine, which is to be called *Scamp,* by the way."

"Tell me more about it," said Julius. Suddenly his pale face was drained of its last vestige of colour. He drew Ivan behind the pillar distractedly. The doyen of the Reading Room, the dignified old man with the long white whiskers, was sailing slowly, the wind behind him, up the path from the gate towards the portico. His umbrella swayed, the old man held on to it firmly, he stopped and turned full circle every now and again in order to sweep the horizon with supervisory gaze. Nevertheless, in five minutes at the most, he would arrive at the pillar behind which Julius was hiding. And Julius most decidedly did not wish to be included in one of the old man's 360 degree horizon sweeps. Since their collision outside the revolving doors, the old man had snorted more disparagingly and loudly every time he saw Julius. The snorts were becoming brayings and trumpetings, and there was no telling what might result when they had reached their peak in volume, disgust, and disparagement.

"I'll have to go now," said Julius hurriedly. "Er. . . let me see. . . what were we saying? Oh yes, about those manuscripts. Yes, that'll be fine, a damn good idea. . . Er. . . I'll fetch 'em along in my case, so much every day. No, that won't be enough. I'll have to make up a few parcels as well. Well, cheerio."

"You'll drop them round to my place in Guilford Street, will you?" Ivan called after him. "You know the number —"

Julius disappeared through the revolving door, which at the same moment ejected, as though from a conveyor belt, a brand-new Swedish doctor of philosophy, with shining brief-case, shining gloves, shining pink face, glistening spectacles, and bright grey herring-bone coat, all heading, with immense speed and energy towards unimaginable appointments.

CHAPTER VIII

HERE AND THERE, among the ten million devious, solitary campaigns being waged in London's thousand square miles of haphazard brick, a few warriors began to mention the name of *Scamp*. In the battlefields of Soho and Charlotte Street and Bloomsbury, combatants still on active service, and others scarcely more than stretcher cases, said now and again, with a yawn:

"Have you heard of this new thing — what's it called? Old what's-'is-name was telling me about it. He saw a postcard advertising it in a shop-window somewhere."

"What, those unfurnished flats going if you pay £500 for a few chairs of something?"

"No, I saw that too, that's a racket. No, this thing which that feller, what's-'is-name? Tall, thin feller, comes round here? You know him, spoken to him often — I got it, Goldberg. No, Ginsberg, that's it. Yeh, that's the feller."

"Well, what about him?"

"Well, he wants to start a magazine or something. Seems quite serious about it. *Scamp,* that's it. Of course, it's bound to flop. Still, you never know."

Such remarks were heard in the Corney Arms and the Duchess of Margaret, the twin alcoholic fortresses of western Charlotte Street; in the Belgian Café, Tony's, Fama's, the Barba-Yanny, Pedro's. Once, Angus Sternforth Simms referred to *Scamp* during a dinner at the White Tower restaurant, when the nephew of an earl and a novelist who had married an American heiress were present, as well as a couple of sly, obsequious editors, who intended to get in digs at Angus in the forewords to their forthcoming anthologies; and Angus, who was interpreter and liaison between these delicate souls and the crudities of Fitzrovia, made it the basis of a fantastic anecdote which later appeared in *Bank Holiday*

Pudding. Scamp was likewise the subject of a lively discussion at breakfast in Hinton's Dairy one morning, among a band of bohemians with bloodshot eyes who had just spent the night either camping on the floor of a basement workshop manufacturing unlicensed furniture or wandering from one all-night café to another.

Scamp was also heard of in more genteel surroundings, far away, on the other side of Tottenham Court Road, along the corridors of Senate House and behind the chintz curtains of the Ex-Students' Club in Gordon Square, where Ginsberg was a member. Many of the newsagents' shops round the British Museum carried in their windows little typed notices announcing the appearance, at some future date, of this informative, controversial magazine of the younger generation. In addition, all except one of the manuscripts sent in answer to Julius's advertisement in the New *Statesman and Nation* had been returned to their owners, whether or no they had enclosed stamped and addressed envelopes; and each returned package contained a typewritten slip giving details of *Scamp,* the most provocative magazine ever to be published in weary London.

Ginsberg had not been idle. Indeed, he was working almost as hard on correspondence setting in motion his new project, and on the "ghosting" which he had already begun for Bert Flogcrobber, as he had previously done turning out each day a two thousand word short story with plot, climax, and twist. Letters were sent off to prominent intellectuals in France and America, including Einstein and Leon Blum; to cabinet ministers, journalists, novelists, and poets at home. Had one half replied, and one tenth of that number contributed, they would have been the most outstanding set of contributors on the market: Idris Berwin, in the Cabinet; G.D. Creasley and I.N. Horster, the novelists; Hughie McPrice, the poet; John Horweil, the fast-punching left wing journalist; and Alfred Boemser, the political theorist; to mention only the beginning of Ginsberg's list. Ginsberg left it to their idealism to encourage them to contribute, because the rate of pay he offered was the same in each case; one guinea per thousand words.

Actually, one guinea per thousand was a generous offer, since Ginsberg's income was still four pounds a week (admittedly, unaudited, and therefore free of income tax) and his capital nil. Mrs. Chabbers had not yet parted with any hard cash, and more than a pound had been spent on paper and postage. Nevertheless, Ginsberg did not doubt that Mrs. Chabbers would eventually part with enough for at least one number.

She was an evasive person and hard to pin down. It was her habit to run away from anything which offered the merest hint of difficulty — to run away, literally. She had once hurried out of the lounge of the Empire Hotel after Ginsberg had reproved her for a repeated grammatical mistake; she had hurried faster and faster through the tables, knocking over a chair, dropping a glove, until finally she had broken into a run. On another occasion, when a Dutchman had stopped her in Southampton Row to ask the way to Oxford Street, she had run for fifty yards in order to get away from the awkward situation. In the same way, she ran towards things. Often, if she was late for her Russian lesson, she arrived panting on the doorstep, having run all the way from Russell Square tube station. And if ever Ginsberg happened to be watching her approach, she increased her pace, laughing and waving uneasily, broke into a trot, then a run, then a mad race for her embarrassed Russian teacher, arriving level with him as though she were breasting the winning tape in a hundred yard sprint.

So Ginsberg did not press her too strongly, in case she should take flight for a week or two and go to stay at the Grand Hotel, Birmingham, or the Royal Provincial, Manchester. She would come back eventually, of course. She would write a note apologizing, explaining, lying, protesting, pleading. But in the meantime, several lessons had been missed, which crippled him financially, since she paid only for the one appointment which had been broken. And there was always the slight worry as to whether this was, after all, the final showdown. Though she had always come crawling back in the past, she might one day — though it was highly improbable — summon up the courage and the perversity to give up studying Russian altogether. Ginsberg therefore bided his time. A decision was forming in her frantic brain; but she must always feel that the decision was not forced, that there was a means of escape, should she wish to choose it. Otherwise she would force an escape, out of sheer panic, and catch the next train for Newcastle or Edinburgh.

Capital, contributors, and a printer with paper — those were the three elements which Ginsburg had thought necessary in order to create his magazine; those, and the power and energy with which to fuse them. Power and energy were unspent, capital was maturing, contributors were even now reading their correspondence from Guilford Street; there remained the question of finding a printer with paper.

At lunch-time on Wednesday, Ginsberg co-opted Bellenger into this task. Bellenger protested a little, though the prospect really pleased him. However, a protest now was useful ammunition to have in hand in case of any future bargaining. He remembered the occasion, for instance, when Ginsberg had made such a fuss about trudging through South London and calling on pawnbrokers and second-hand shops, on the look-out for bric-à-brac which could be resold at a profit to West End antique shops. What a moan the man had made, nagging and complaining all the way through Camberwell and Peckham, standing sulkily at the back of pawnbrokers' shops and putting him off business. Or there was the time when he had persuaded Ginsberg to come with him to the Albert Hall to listen to a symphony concert. What cheap facetiousness! What East End humour! Bellenger determined to have a little of his own back; not much, since he did not want to help discourage

Ginsberg in his latest notion, but a little, to assert his independence.

Bellenger had been Ginsberg's closest friend at Cambridge, though they had first become aware of each other with feelings of intense hostility. Ginsberg, the scholarship boy from the East End, had been the most devoted of Zena Yadcott's entourage. This was in their second year at the university. In spite of his air of cynicism — due, in the main, to a piece of cartilege blocking his left nostril, which compelled him to curl his upper lip sardonically in order to breathe through his nose — Ivan's relations with Zena had been sentimental and innocent. The time came when he was head man of the entourage, when, in fact, Zena's following dropped away and he was the only one left. Ivan was happy. Zena now leant on his arm alone when strolling to morning coffee or afternoon tea or along the Backs. Then Bellenger had come along and begun an objectionable affair of jealousy, smouldering hatred, and passionate reconciliation, in which he, Ivan, was cast for the role of Zena's confidant. What was more, Ivan discovered that Zena was far from being the pure, schoolgirl-complexioned, incontestably virginal English rose he had imagined her to be; and that Bellenger was but the latest of her many clandestine lovers.

Ivan had then succeeded in entering himself into this secret band, during one of Zena's quarrels with Bellenger. When reconciliation arrived and Bellenger learned of this latest development, he swore vengeance on Ginsberg, in whom he saw a machiavellian schemer, a dastardly Jewish seducer. Ginsberg might have been involved in a fight with Bellenger, who was in those days a boxer, a rugger player, and on the fringe of the "hearties", had Zena not left them both, run away to London in the middle of term, and been sent down in her absence for passing four large, overdrawn cheques to Cambridge tradesmen. Neither had seen or heard of Zena again; but they met to talk about her. Their hostility changed to friendship.

There were two real people; Ginsberg, the scholarship boy, and Bellenger, the Harrovian — whose father was contentedly drinking himself to death in Tanganyika, having disposed of his youngest son, to the satisfaction of both sides, by giving him the correct education and afterwards an allowance of three hundred a year. But these two real people were lost beneath romantic misconceptions. For Bellenger, Ginsberg became the eternal metropolitan, born old, incredibly experienced and wise, and destined to intellectual greatness. As a corollary, he himself was the eternal undergraduate, perpetually slumming in this life, but belonging really to a more casual, light-hearted, airy plane. Ginsberg was very well read in sexual literature, could supply endless information on sexual matters, from the psychoanalytic study to the bawdy joke, from brothel anecdotes to medical pathology; while Bellenger had no other worldly ambition than to seduce as many girls as he could possibly lay hands on, and to acquire as many kinds of sexual experience as were obtainable without danger of disease or imprisonment. He required a mentor, imaginary or real; hence his admiration for Ivan; hence also, the need to assert his independence which he experienced from time to time.

At lunch-time, Ivan was sitting in front of the gas fire in his room, half attic, half studio, in Guilford Street. Bellenger had furnished and decorated this flat with simple, admirable taste. The walls were painted light blue, an ornate mirror provided a rococo touch on the chaste, bare wash of colour; and the room, so remote from the faded, graceful street below, was illuminated from without by the grey luminosity which is the daylight of the average London day, and from within by the bubbling red glow of the gas fire. The southern wall was almost entirely taken up by two large windows, suitably clouded with a film of dust and dirt. Through these windows was visible a panorama of roof-tops, towering and falling to St. Paul's, whose dome could just be seen above the jagged, uneven mass of buildings.

Ivan lay back in the easy chair and stared out at the scene spread below. He inhaled deeply the smoke of his cigarette and was invaded by a sensation of comfortable lethargy. Yes, he could dream his life away in this immortal, ruined, inner city, stupendous and inevitable casualty in the chaos of human development. The blackened countryside of south-east England had been blasted in the first industrial and commercial battles. Now it was twentieth century London, a city crippled by its own weight and mass, croaking and groaning like some gigantic monster, whose litheness had gone, but which could still shake itself hoarily and roar in a way to recall its old energy and power. And this first of industrial and commercial cities had created a "new beauty", the beauty of despair in an urban setting of gasworks, high factory walls, railway wildernesses, tiny backyards sprinkled with rubbish, and the brave, shoddy mockery of a gim-crack luxury cinema.

There was a far-away thud, as the heavy street door slammed to, four floors below. Then a scarcely audible tapping; the tapping drew nearer and grew louder, until it eventually resolved itself into the sound of Bellenger's second-hand suede shoes slowly climbing the eight flights of stairs.

Bellenger reached the top landing, pushed open the door of Ginsberg's room, and flopped onto the divan bed to recover his breath after this wearisome ascent. Ivan was ready to explode with laughter. He did not yet know at what. But in all Bellenger's activities there was something so monstrously absurd, so unreasonably logical, that he waited expectantly for Bellie to utter his first words. Not that other people were likely to find Bellenger funny. On the contrary, their reactions, after a little puzzlement, were impatience and irritation. Frequently, when Ginsberg and Bellenger were together in the company of a crowd of acquaintances, there would be an awkward moment when Ginsberg alone let out a roar of laughter at some unimportant and quite seriously intended remark of Bellenger's. Bellenger often did the same to Ginsberg; they had a thousand private jokes in common. A social-minded observer might have felt appalled at the cynicism, and indeed vicious antagonism to almost everybody, displayed in their backchat and asides. But this part of their conversation was no more than an unthinking patter for each other's amusement; a safety valve for indifference and cruelty.

Bellenger, in theory, had the highest possible ethical code. In practice, Ginsberg was the only beneficiary; for Bellenger, beneath his mildly tortured exterior, was engaged in a subtle, never-ceasing war with womankind. As a result, his relations with men, too, were uneasy, because there could be no neutrals in his perpetual war, and he wanted no allies. Even Ginsberg was no real ally, but a necessary intermediary power, a sort of Switzerland or Sweden who assisted in dealings with the outside world, with the milkman, the landlord, and anyone else who rang the bell.

In addition, Bellenger admired Ginsberg. Ivan, in his eyes, was the outlandish genius whom writers of racy biographies love to recreate: sufficiently outlandish not to impinge on his tender amour-propre. His belief in Ivan's genius was an essential part of his personal faith. He saw himself as Boswell to Ivan's Johnson, as Proust to Ivan's Bloch, as Daedalus to Ivan's Bloom, or as the more sensitive half of a host of other two-fold literary analogies. Had he been persuaded that Ivan was neither a genius nor a monstrous source of anecdote, the colour would have been drained from his romantic vision of life. He would even have lacked confidence for his war on women. Somehow, his association with Ivan was linked in his mind with sexual emancipation and the legitimization of all that was normally held to be sordid, adolescent, and undignified, not to mention immoral and indiscreet.

He had held on to his significant concept of Ivan throughout the war, when they had been separated and out of touch. Then, one night, they had met by accident in a dimly lit Bloomsbury street. But for Bellenger, their meeting was no accident. How else could fate have arranged things? He had just acquired and furnished his flat in Guilford Street, *the* flat, corresponding to some familiar reality carried over from a previous existence. He had settled in, as it were, for life. From these headquarters he would make sorties into Soho or Chelsea; he would plan and execute week-ends; he would send expeditions to Paris and Switzerland, possibly even to New York and California. Then Ginsberg cropped up, one foggy night in Marchmont Street, stalking momentarily through the hazy, smoke-filled area of light cast by a street lamp. All this must surely have already happened once before. It was so appropriate and so inevitable. Bellenger immediately flung an arm round Ivan's shoulder and installed him in the second room of his flat, specially set aside for a semi-permanent guest — a guest proper, of course, as distinct from a hostage or prisoner-of-war from womankind, for whom had been reserved the pillow nearest the wall in the huge, deep, springy, luxurious double bed which occupied his own bedroom.

So the life of the flat had got under way. In Bellenger's room, touching, sentimental encounters took place, were prolonged over three days, and then mysteriously ended. The requiem was sung by Bellenger in the early hours of the morning over a cup of tea to a sleepy, incredulous Ginsberg. In Ginsberg's room, great schemes, great enterprises, great labours were undertaken. Otherwise, nothing happened. Neither had any urgent routine. There was no fixed time for going to bed or for getting up; sometimes they got up in the morning, sometimes in the evening. Sometimes they did not meet for days. Once Bellenger went away for a fortnight, and Ginsberg knew nothing about it. They dusted and cleaned their own rooms when there was any special reason for doing so. The rent was paid by post once a month out of

Bellenger's allowance; likewise the gas and the electricity. They were certain of a roof over their heads whether they had money or not; and Bellenger magnanimously refused to allow Ivan to pay a penny of these basic expenses. As for income, Ivan had his lessons with Mrs. Chabbers, his weekly lecture at the Literary Institute, and a few odd guineas earned by his short stories and an occasional review in *Senate;* while Bellenger had the remains of his allowance, earnings from time to time as a film extra, and the proceeds of his deals in bric-à-brac, his profits as a middleman between pawnshops, antique dealers, auction rooms, and second-hand shops. At the same time, he was engaged on a vague, protracted four-year course for a thesis in psychology, which necessitated his attendance once a week, if he felt like it, at a lecture or discussion or tutorial with an aged professor of London University.

Scamp was quite in the order of things at the Guilford Street flat; obviously Ivan must now and again hatch up something of the sort in his half-attic room looking out over the roof-tops towards St. Paul's — something new and out of the ordinary, and yet quite to be expected. In the same way, if Bellenger brought back an Indian half-caste, or a blonde Scots girl who acted as prostitute among the lesbians of Chelsea and Baker Street, or an eighteen year old dipsomaniac whom he had picked up in The Fitzroy, there was something interesting and startling, and yet very ordinary, and almost dull in the latest situation on Bellenger's extended, thinly-held, amatory front.

So whatever were his feelings when alone, Ginsberg took, in the company of Bellenger, an urbane, defeatist view of his projected magazine. Bellenger had seen too many of his literary-commercial schemes flop to be able to take the latest seriously; just as he had seen too many of Bellenger's affairs fizz out to be able to imagine his friend bringing off that decisive victory in prestige and passion to which all his energies were devoted.

On this Wednesday afternoon, the gas fire in Ginsberg's room spluttered cheerfully, the smoke of cigarettes balanced horizontally in ashtrays rose in a straight line to the ceiling, and neither felt very much like moving.

"Do we *have* to go hunting around for a beastly printer!" said Bellenger with a grimace. There was more than a trace of Yorkshire in his accent; he had been brought up in a private school near Chesterfield and frequently opened his mouth wide to a broad Northern vowel.

"I'm afraid so," said Ginsberg with a grin, implying that all the farces, however tiresome, had to be worked through.

They got ready to go out, Ginsberg in a threadbare sports jacket, Bellenger in a yellow, belted jacket which he had bought in Charing Cross Road and which had been nicknamed the "zoot-suit". On the first-floor landing, they were surveyed by the glistening eyes, rolled at identical moments in the simultaneously swivelling heads of two kittens owned by the woman in the basement. Absolutely alike in appearance, the kittens were yet very different in personality. One, Betsy, had the domestic grace and placidity proper to a household cat. The other, which Ginsberg called the Supercat, was a neurotic, gay and melancholy by turns, lively, intelligent, wilfully individualistic, almost human — in fact, a bundle of nerves. The Supercat bounded forward, landed on Bellenger's shoulder in one leap, miaowed wittily, playfully leapt from Bellenger's shoulder on to Ginsberg's, and swiftly rejoined Betsy in a placid twin pose.

"The Supercat!" said Ginsberg with arch profundity, as it were Dr. Johnson making a remark, so it might now seem, for the benefit of Boswell and posterity; or Leopold Bloom, to be recorded by his James Joyce; or Bloch, to be remembered, thirty years later, by Marcel Proust. Bellenger made a mental note of the incident; while Ginsberg, for his part, played up to his future biographer by pontificating, irrelevantly:

"Life without love is an operation without an anaesthetic."

"How right you are," said Bellenger. "How right you are. I was thinking that only yesterday when seducing Lucille —"

"How many times have I told you," interrupted Ginsberg, "that that phrase is not to be taken as having any meaning. It is in the nature of a ritual phrase of prayer which means nothing except the simple anxiety behind it, like some incomprehensible verse babbled by an orthodox Jew in Hebrew, by a Catholic priest in Latin, or by a Russian priest in Church Slavonic or ancient Bulgarian. I read the thing somewhere, in a book by Cocteau I believe; it's a jingle. It's as trite in the twentieth century as saying "Your cheeks are like the rose' was in the sixteenth." The real reason for launching into this speech was to prevent Bellenger from talking about Lucille. The man was a liar, of course. Nevertheless, Lucille was a lovely girl, and it was too disgusting if she had actually been seduced by Bellenger.

They walked along jauntily, Ginsberg ostentatiously drawing deep lungfuls of air.

"The purest air in the world," he said, "is the air in Russell Square." This was another of his classic sayings. Ivan was a humorist who gained his effect by repetition. That was why so many of his jokes were esoteric and understood by Bellenger alone. Only the fact that some extraordinary statement had been made a thousand times rendered it funny. Yet there were moments, like the present, when Bellenger walked along and sat in the bus in a kind of daze, while Ivan showered jokes upon him, so funny from one point of view, so feeble from another, that Bellie smiled in wan exhaustion; occasionally he went "Hoo-hoo-hoo!" and made a gesture of holding his stomach, as though the latest joke were really too funny to be borne.

They arrived south of the river, in Battersea, and trudged along interminable High Streets to Wandsworth. Ivan called in on one printer, who was most unwilling even to discuss doing business; not so much because he was busy or lacked paper, but because of his religious, political, moral, and linguistic scruples. It was clear that he had not taken to Ivan.

"How do I know who you are?" he repeated cogently.

He went on to explain that he did no work which was against his principles. In politics, he was a Labour Party man, "but didn't hold with all this socialism". So it was no use expecting him to print "any of this communist stuff about socialism and all that".

He peered at Ivan through the gloom of the bare anteroom in which they were talking, while Bellenger's face was every now and again pressed against the window from the street, vainly trying to make out how much longer he had to wait.

"You're no working man," said the printer, and cackled at his own shrewdness. "No, it's no use telling me. I bin in the game fer thirty-eight years now. When I started —"

"Yes, yes," interrupted Ivan hastily.

"And during the war, I can tell you, in the blitzes —"

"Quite," said Ivan, "but can you give me any idea at all of your charges?"

The printer touched on religion. He was a Baptist. Formerly he had been a Unitarian, but there had apparently been a crisis. He had been through fire and the sword. He had been singed by the very flames of hell, he had felt the deathly lure of the devil, Antichrist had stalked the streets of south London, yea, he had verily been in the valley of the shadow, he had repented for the end was nigh. Now he was a Baptist, and refused to print anything atheistical, heathenish, or immoral. Which brought him on to morality. "All this love business, all this kissing that goes on, and worse. Ah, it's no use telling me. They call it love, but it's nothing more than harlotry and fornication!"

Bellenger, the fornicator, had at first managed to make out Ginsberg's face in the black shadows of the ante-room. He tried to spell out that he was going to hunt around for a gents' lavatory, but Ginsberg could make nothing of his exaggerated pointings and the fantastic gapings of his mouth and closing of his teeth. Bellenger's distraught face disappeared.

"Look at Piccadilly. Harlots and strumpets and loose women, all of them. Ah, it's no use telling me. And disease, even unto the fourth generation. Serves 'em right. The anger of the Lord; His wrath is slow to kindle and hard to extinguish. So nothing immoral — immorality's the worst of the lot."

Finally, the printer explained that there were a large number of words which he would not set up in type. These included not only the usual four letter Anglo-Saxon words, but also "damn", "blast", "kiss", and "naked".

"Thou shalt not take the name of the Lord thy God in vain," he concluded, and marched triumphantly from the blackness of the ante-room into the Pit of Darkness, the region at the back of the premises where presumably he worked.

"But give me a rough idea, at any rate, of your prices," pleaded Ginsberg, who had sat through the printer's hallelujah talk in order to get his first professional estimate.

"Two hundred pounds," called the printer from the Pit.

Ginsberg left, found Bellenger very much refreshed after having discovered a public lavatory quite close at hand, and pushed on deeper into Wandsworth. When it was almost teatime, and he had given up hope of discovering anything of interest in the district, he saw a flamboyant sign on a newly painted shop just off the main road.

"Printing", it said. "ALL CLASSES OF WORK UNDERTAKEN. LET *US* HAVE YOUR ORDER, LARGE OR SMALL. The lowest terms in the trade, and the best quality work. All the staff ex-Servicemen. Service with a smile is our motto. THE YOUNGER GENERATION."

"The Younger Generation" in particular caught Ginsberg's eye; it was the very phrase he had used in the prospectus for *Scamp,* and it was stuck rather meaninglessly on to the boldly coloured poster.

"Come on, Bellie," he said. Bellenger dragged apathetically behind.

"I'll wait outside," said Bellenger, partly because he preferred smoking a cigarette in the open air, partly in order to demonstrate his martyrdom.

The little printing firm was owned and run by two partners, an optimist and a pessimist. The optimist looked like one of those cheerful, Cockney, convict types portrayed by the actor Gordon Harker. The pessimist was one of the melancholy, apocalyptic Baptist printers of whom Ginsberg had already had one experience, and in whom South London seemed to abound. They were leaning against the mantelpiece in the converted lower floor which was their workshop, and staring at the isolated packets of paper placed here and there on the floor and at the single press surrounded by vast areas of space. The two partners were like an illustration on how to draw faces quickly. Thus, for the mouth, an arc turned downwards produces an appearance of misery — vide the thin, drooping line of the pessimist's lips — an arc turned upwards produces unlimited cheerfulness — vide the optimist. They faced each other on opposite corners of the mantelpiece in order to make the illustration absolutely clear and unmistakable.

"Ah!" said the optimist, on seeing Ginsberg, as though he had been waiting for him all his life, and as though the additional blessing of Ginsberg's arrival filled the cup of his happiness to overflowing.

"Aha!" replied Ginsberg, quick to adapt himself to other people's moods and mannerisms. Without deliberately setting out to do so, he found himself talking like a Cockney to Cockneys, like a schoolteacher to schoolteachers, like a drunkard to drunkards, and so on. He could not bear appearing to lack goodwill. He tried to adopt not only the superficial mannerisms, but something of the underlying attitude of mind of those with whom 'he was associating'.

While talking to the optimist, therefore, he was expansive — was not life full of possibility? And while talking to the pessimist, he was grave, reticent, cautious — fully aware of serious industrial crises; human frailty; the slow defeat which must await the exuberance of youthful endeavour.

Spiffhorn and Trunt had just started up on their own as a firm of printers. They had, it was evident, not much capital and not much stock. A couple of overalled boys strolled in and out discussing the greyhound forecasts in the evening paper. There was not much doing, as Spiffhorn put it. But quite enough for their meagre resources, added Trunt. They had done catalogues for some of the local tradesmen, a brochure for a cinema, visiting cards, and so on.

Could they undertake the printing of a magazine? Yes, said Spiffhorn. No, said Trunt. They were lucky in having a good stock of paper, and of excellent quality, too, with art and semi-art finish. So thought Spiffhorn. They needed the paper for their existing clients, said Trunt; it was all they were likely to get for a long time to come.

What about the cost — say, for estimate purposes, forty-eight pages measuring eight inches by six? Here Trunt was temporarily put out of action, because, on his own confession, he was no good at figures; he could scarcely add up a few shillings, let alone make calculations for a printer's estimate. Ivan, too, had no idea what all the sets of figures and odd items of multiplication and division were about. So Spiffhorn, licking a stub of pencil and putting out the tip of his tongue in an effort of concentration, got down alone to an optimistic estimate of costs.

"Sixty-eight pounds," he said finally.

Ivan thought that there must be some mistake. Almost everybody he had spoken to had placed the cost of printing five thousand copies of *Scamp* at not less than one hundred and fifty pounds. Spiffhorn reconsidered the matter.

"Ah yes," he said, "I left out — let me see, it's

seventy-one pounds. Yes, that's it, seventy-one pounds." His youngish, Gordon Harker-like face, with its broken nose, beamed with honest mathematical effort.

Trunt could say nothing. Sums of money beyond ten pounds were outside his comprehension; he left the arithmetical side of the business to his partner. He could understand a weekly wage packet, totting up so many hours at two and fourpence halfpenny an hour, deducting unemployment insurance, and so forth, although he was not capable of doing even these simple calculations himself. But as for the rest, well, all his life he had been a printer, a workman, a man who sets up type, an expert in his own field — he did not understand business. All he knew was that he had never printed anything larger than an eight-page catalogue before; and no good ever came of trying something new.

"Nah," he said, "I shouldn't think it could be done."

"I'd pay a substantial sum in advance," said Ginsberg.

"Good, good," beamed Spiffhorn, "just what we need." He turned to his partner: "We could buy that wojercallit old whatsisname's got, see. Just what we need. Just what we need."

Trunt remained unconvinced, but withdrew for the moment his active opposition.

"And of course," said Ginsberg, "if the thing should be a success and expand, well, you'd expand with it."

"Of course," said Spiffhorn, "of course!"

"This might be the beginning of something, profitable to both of us."

"It might," agreed Spiffhorn enthusiastically.

"On the other hand, it might be a flop."

"Yes, it might be a flop!" said Spiffhorn heartily. Nothing, it seemed, could be better from his point of view.

"But even that wouldn't affect your bill. You'd get paid whatever happened."

"Aha, yes, yes!" Spiffhorn nodded vigorously. He found the whole scheme admirable in every respect.

They left it at that. Spiffhorn and Trunt were to send

on a detailed estimate in writing, which Ginsberg wanted to show to Mrs. Chabbers, so that the sight of it might ginger her along a little in producing the capital. And once the estimate had been sent, Spiffhorn and Trunt were to hold themselves ready, at a month's notice, to produce *Scamp*.

"We could work overtime, if necessary," said Trunt — not that he agreed with the scheme, but the discussion of actual working details, such as a time limit, immediately interested him. He made the remark as a disinterested comment, delivered sagaciously from behind his pipe by the man on the job. Ginsberg, for his part, said that he would pay the whole bill in advance. Why not? If he had to pay, he might as well pay and have done with it.

In spite of the momentous arrangement just concluded, Spiffhorn and Trunt took up their old positions at opposite ends of the mantelpiece, as though waiting in the empty workshop for someone to arrive and take possession. Even Spiffhorn, for all his bonhomie and cheerful agreement, did not seem to feel that an important business deal had just been initiated. That was what rather disquieted Ginsberg. Nevertheless, he had decided to put his trust in Spiffhorn and Trunt and thus conclude his search for a printer. He left them leaning there, facing each other, Spiffhorn a simple illustration of how an upturned arc for a mouth creates an optimist, Trunt the converse.

Bellenger had disappeared. He could hardly be blamed for having pushed off. Ginsberg knew where he had gone — to the Belgian Café. From teatime onwards, Bellenger adhered to a timetable, none the less regular for being voluntary. Belgian Café, five-thirty to seven. Half a pint at the Pillars of Hercules from seven till quarter to eight. Eight o'clock, the Corney Arms. From eight till eleven he circulated between the Corney Arms, the Duchess of Margaret, and the Fitzroy. Eleven till twelve, supper at Pedro's International Café Restaurant. If he were with a girl, the timetable was much the same, except that it began, if possible, after lunch. He preferred to meet her at Oxford Circus tube station at two o'clock, walk to the Academy or Studio One or the Curzon to see a French film, and then continue through the Belgian Café, Pillars of Hercules, Corney Arms, Duchess of Margaret, Fitzroy, to Pedro's International Café Restaurant — after which the real struggle began. Would she or would she not come back to the flat in Guilford Street? There were a score of reasons why she would not or could not; there was one paramount reason why Bellenger wanted her to. It was not desire, though that played its part; it was the insatiable need to chalk up more and more and yet more strokes on his amatory scoreboard. If only he had been able to accomplish a final, decisive conquest, one which would make him the cynosure of Soho, it would have been possible for him to give up, or at any rate ease off the struggle. But in the end something always went wrong. The amusing oddities which rendered him interesting for an evening or two, made him intolerable on the third evening. So his affairs, transitory individually, permanent en masse, traced the pattern of his routine.

He was sitting even now in the Belgian Café, which held its usual, largely adolescent teatime crowd. Bellenger was some ten years older than most of the others, being only a year younger than Ginsberg. He was sandwiched in between Julius Kripkin and Mimi, opposite Sybil and Jojo and Sid. Julius Kripkin was telling of how his call-up papers had arrived and of how he was opting for the mines, so that he might revolutionize Britain's mining industry. Bellenger's left leg was making acquaintance with Mimi's right (the very leg which had already saved Julius Kripkin's life). Sybil and Jojo and Sid were talking jazz. Sid ran a band, and Sybil and Jojo both wanted to sing for his band; and all three felt, not so much contempt, as pity for anyone who was not in a band. Bellenger wondered once again whether it was worth while inviting Mimi round to Guilford Street, He had seen her home one night to Streatham; he himself, of course, missing the last train and having to walk back for over two hours; she would go so far and no further. It was disappointing. And she had the mind of an orang-outang. Or rather she had no mind at all. People were often described facetiously as having no minds; but Mimi, Bellenger reflected bitterly, was really lacking in a mind. Nor had she any strong feelings or passions; she had nothing, she was nothing, absolutely nothing, except a very pretty little blonde. She did not even want very strongly to become a dance-band vocalist, not like Sybil and Jojo, who were looking up into Sid's eyes with bitch-like devotion. They were urging him to advertize, to expand, to become a second Oscar Rabin, Ambrose, Lou Preager. Absently, Jojo laid a cigarette beside each person sitting at the table, though she had never seen Julius Kripkin before and knew Bellenger only vaguely as "that funny chap — gives me the shivers. Is he queer?'

This was in accordance with Belgian Café camaraderie. And when Ginsberg said jocularly, "Hey! What about me?" she handed him a cigarette too, though she had not the slightest notion who he was either. Ginsberg had just arrived unnoticed and squeezed his lanky body into a chair by the mirror which ran the length of the wall.

"Well, Bellie!" he shouted across the table. "It's all fixed up. They're going to print it for me, and very cheaply, too."

"Wassermarrer? Wassermarrer?" said Julius Kripkin. "Hullo, Ivan, 'member me?"

"How could anyone fail to remember you?" said Jojo. In the Belgian Café, just as one could give a cigarette to a stranger, so could one insult him. Julius took it in good part.

"Good old Julius Kripkin!" he said, knocking an elbow into Mimi's blonde head as he patted himself on the back. "I say, Ivan! Ivan! Is that the magazine? What you were telling me about? You know, you know? Ay?"

"Yes, that's it. *Scamp*. It ought to be out in a couple of months."

"There y'are!" said Julius. "Wha' did I tell you? Ay? Wha' did I tell you? And warrabout the cont'butions? Ay? D'you sen' 'em all back?"

"Yes," said Ginsberg, "all except one, from Ireland. I'm keeping that. A short story. It's jolly good."

"Jolly good, ay? Jolly good —"

Ginsberg could not stand the pace of Julius's conversation and glanced round the café, keeping au courant with the latest situations. Bellenger leaned across Mimi and tugged his sleeve.

"Sid wants to speak to you. I've just been telling him about *Scamp*."

Sid, pestered by Sybil and Jojo to do some advertising, had conceived of the idea of having an announcement in *Scamp*. For his own part, he didn't give a damn. He was one of the intellectuals of jazz, stooping-shouldered and goggle-eyed, and cared only for his art. His position, therefore, in the dance music world, was assured if modest; for among the intelligentsia he was known as a subtle rhythmician. However, Sybil and Jojo were a formidable combination, and the advertisement wouldn't cost much. Ginsberg promised to let him have the entire back cover for eight guineas.

That was that. With a pint of tea and three cheese sandwiches inside him, Ginsberg was ready to face his weekly lecture at the Literary Institute. He felt in his pocket to make sure his notes on Dostoevski were safe. Such as they were, they lay folded safely in his wallet. Each week his lectures were more carelessly prepared. Fortunately no one in his audience of a dozen or so, which included Mrs. Chabbers, cared very much, except possibly that pretty little Viennese Jewess, Greta Blauzimmer. She was really charming. It was to her alone that he addressed his most thoughtful, impromptu remarks. Why on earth she came to the lectures was a mystery. Surely she must realize that the lectures were just copied out of Mirsky's *History of Russian Literature?* But possibly she was interested in the lecturer? Ah! Possibly indeed... Life was full of possibilities; fortunately, or it would be intolerable. And fortunately, too, not one tenth of these possibilities could be investigated; the rest were the successful ones, untouched, unshattered.

But Greta Blauzimmer apart, thought Ginsberg, as he emerged into Charing Cross Road and made for the Literary Institute in the Strand, these Russian lectures in a gas-lit, underground room — to a bunch of disapproving spinsters and a couple of deaf, aged clerks were becoming a first rate bore. In any case, he was shortly going to get the push. He had seen the look in the Principal's eye; polite enough, for he was one professional man dealing with another, but quite decided.

There was *Scamp,* of course. He might be able to pay himself a little salary out of the magazine funds. But that was still, when all was said and done, in the air. His earnings with Bert Flogcrobber were going to be indispensable. And they were good earnings, too — about twelve pounds already. He must go and see about collecting his first fortnight's money. He kept on forgetting about it. Ginsberg stopped there and then, in St. Martin's Lane, made a note on a slip of paper — REMEMBER BERT FLOGCROBBER — and wrapped it round his last pound note, so that there was no question of his failing to see it some time.

He arrived five minutes late at the Literary Institute and, as luck would have it, ran slap into the Principal, who said good evening sadly, because he was obviously getting ready to give Ginsberg the push. Greta Blauzimmer and Mrs. Chabbers and the spinsters and the deaf clerks were waiting in the lecture room, all chewing toffees which Mrs. Chabbers had distributed.

Ginsberg apologized for being late. His throat felt dry before even he had begun; it must be the cheese sandwiches.

"The Tragedy of Dostoevski," he began.

He saw in the gloom Greta Blauzimmer's blue jumper and yellow blouse. She really did look ravishing, like some gay, cheeky little flower.

"The Tragedy of Dostoevski," he began again.

No, it was too dark in here, quite impossible. Most of the lecture rooms in the Literary Institute were underground, and this one was nothing more than an unventilated cellar.

"I'd better light the gas," he said. He lit up, blew out his chest in the mariner of lecturers who are weary of their audience, and began again. Greta's brilliant eyes were fixed upon him.

"The novels of the early period. . . "

The spinsters furiously scribbled down every word. One of the deaf old clerks was pulling cotton wool out of his ear. Greta tapped her teeth with a silver propelling pencil. And Ginsberg delivered his hastily prepared summary of the chapter on Dostoevski in Mirsky's *History of Russian Literature.*

CHAPTER IX

THE YELLOW RAYS of the sun probed the London dust. They bathed the city in unaccustomed, gentle warmth, stroked it with a decadent caress. Everybody was different, clothed in the rare personality reserved for sunny afternoons. Older people, settled in routine, were driven to fetch out from the lumber room of the past, queer, discarded summer clothes; they looked with wonderment at their poor, exposed limbs. Bald, ill-tempered, long-married men phoned up over-ripe pub acquaintances with dyed, blonde hair. Spinsters somewhat past thirty wondered whether it was worth while remaining virtuous any longer. Pretty girls now looked ravishing. Quite ordinary young men appeared handsome.

To others the May sunshine brought a not unpleasant sadness. For the first time for many months they saw all the lines on their faces, and a terrible band of new ones added during yet another winter. And in a way they welcomed the full revelation brought by the sun's rays. "So that's how it is," they said. Yet still, they decided, there was much for them to do. If they were not young, neither were they old. It was the first afternoon in summer, the tremulous, evanescent English summer.

Mrs. Chabbers was one of those to whom the sun brought a melancholy revelation. Illumined by the wisdom of its rays, she too was filled with resignation, on whose borders lingered a pervasive and by no means intolerable yearning. She spent the lunch hour strolling through Bloomsbury in a state of warm and comfortable sadness. The shops and hotels round Russell Square revived a host of memories, but they no longer seemed to matter. They were softened by time, dispersed by events. Here she had quarrelled with her husband the night they drove up to town from Lincoln. Oh, the stupid, fidgeting, fussy man he was! Ten years she had wasted on that nincompoop, ruining her nerves and wasting her youth. And there, at the Empire Hotel, she had stayed so often with her father, on his regular three-monthly visits to his brokers and his solicitor. His stuffy, dignified world was very distant now, and perhaps that was not a bad thing, though the shortages of chocolates and sweets, the difficulty in getting a maid, the clothes rationing, the general shabbiness and austerity and all the rest of it were at times really too much. . . nothing but the fault of the incompetent Labour government. Socialism was all very well — she was more or less a socialist herself, or at any rate a Liberal — but there was no need for all these restrictions. The socialists had made this country an object of scorn and pity and derision for the whole world. She would leave the country to-morrow if it weren't for —

Her train of thought was interrupted as she caught sight of herself in a long, all-revealing mirror outside a tailor's. What a dowd she looked! And quite middle-aged! And so red and horsy! If she could emigrate to a country where the sun always shone, she might acquire a sort of placidity, a brown, plump, sleepy contentment which would smooth over the wrinkles and frownings of middle age and render her not unattractive. She had been a good-looking girl, with long, brown hair, white teeth — Heavens! Teeth! She had forgotten she had no teeth of her own. But even that difficulty might be overcome. After all, what were a few teeth? If she could put the idea into his head, so that he himself might suggest that they should go together to South Africa, or Australia, or the Bahamas. . . . Perpetual sunshine, lazy days on the beach, cool drinks, servants, bungalows; he would write his stories or his articles, and she would see he lacked nothing, that no one disturbed him. And he, too, would be happier. He was obviously poor, and he must be lonely. Even she was better than no one. She felt humble and loving. The desire to pour out her affection and unfulfilled passion ran through her blood like alcohol, suffusing it with warmth and heightened feeling. Life in the bright sunshine was full of significance and infinitely different from the dull, dragging, undifferentiated days which belonged to London,

She could think now quite clearly and calmly, formulate subtle thoughts in an orderly fashion. But she knew that in a half-hour, if she arrived on time for her lesson, she would be writhing and squirming in an agony of embarrassment and ridiculously unbecoming shyness. And he might bring up the subject of his magazine. At the memory of the dreaded magazine and the demand for three hundred pounds associated with it, she almost decided to run away, to cancel her lesson and dash off to the country and spend a few days with her sister in Lincoln. He hadn't said a thing for nearly a fortnight; but it was on his mind still, there was no doubt about that. And he talked of having contributions and getting the first number out in a couple of months. Oh dear! What was going to happen? Still, he might just possibly have forgotten about it and given the whole idea up. He was always thinking up schemes and then dropping them a few weeks later. He had had about a half-dozen during the year she had known him. There was the time he was going to Brazil. He was quite serious about it, applying for a visa and so on. After a fortnight he never mentioned Brazil again. He was a funny man. . . . Mrs. Chabbers pushed aside her nervous apprehension in recalling the vicissitudes of the year's tuition in Russian which she had received from Ginsberg.

In Tavistock Square she scattered a few cake crumbs for the birds, only to hurry off because a man was staring at her too intently. Perhaps he had been following her all the way down Southampton Row, perhaps he had been just about to speak to her. Mrs. Chabbers was momentarily in the grip of her fixation; she was once again the terrified little schoolgirl desperately trying to run away from some nameless and inconceivable horror. In a flurry, therefore, she turned into Guilford Street, and panting with heat and excitement rang the bell marked BELLENGER. Before she had finished ringing the door opened.

"Ah," said Ginsberg, "I was just coming down to meet you. I saw you rushing along from Russell Square. What's all the hurry about? You're quite early."

"Yes, I know," said Mrs. Chabbers demurely. "But you see, there was a man staring at me, and he must have been following me, I'm sure he was — oh, dear! These men! They always follow me. They do, you know. Why *me,* that's what I can't understand? But there!" she concluded, only to begin again. "You can't get away from them. Only yesterday —"

"As it's such a fine day," interrupted Ginsberg with great deliberation, "I thought we might have our lesson out-of-doors." He spoke very slowly, so as to compensate in some measure for her surges of formless speech. "Would you like to do that?"

"Yes, I'd love to. I love the open air. When I was a girl. . . "

As a result of long practice, Ginsberg was able to shut her out completely. What a magnificent day it was. Suddenly, in the pouring sunshine, he felt free, released from the oppression of an obscure routine. True, he was walking along the street with Mrs. Chabbers; but he was doing it voluntarily. Even she was part of the fullness of life, an aspect of a two thousand millionfold human diversity.

They went round to a little public garden tucked away behind Brunswick Square, where old age pensioners dozed and muttered on fine afternoons. This garden had once been part of a cemetery, and a few venerable tombs remained. Ginsberg and Mrs. Chabbers found their habitual seat, somewhat hidden from the view of passers-by, behind the tomb of "Sir Caleb Jarmfon, 1723-1796, former alderman of the City of London, greatly refpected and loved for hif good workf and generofity, efpecially by needy fonf and daughterf of the clergy, for whom he made bounteouf provifion".

Ginsberg had chosen this seat the previous summer, not only for its privacy, but also because there was a curved iron bar in the middle dividing it into two. By waiting till Mrs. Chabbers had seated herself in one half, and then seating himself in the other, he prevented her from edging closer and closer and almost snuggling up to him in conversational intimacy, an appalling tendency which she had shown in other seats which lacked the dividing bar in the centre. The iron bar maintained decorum and reminded her, however slightly, that their relationship was and would remain basically that between language teacher and private pupil.

Mrs. Chabbers giggled and sighed contentedly, as though they were playing truant and engaged on some conspiratorial and delightful outing. She felt more at ease here than in the lounge of the Empire Hotel, where there was always the possibility that some waiter might creep up or an old acquaintance of her father's stare at her curiously from the depths of a straw armchair. Here she could say what she liked for a whole hour — absolutely what she liked, because she had said the most outrageous things, why she could not tolerate her husband, for instance, and Ginsberg had not lifted an eyebrow. "Dear me," he had murmured, or "Hm", or "Very understandable". So long as he did not start questioning her or persuading her to do something she didn't want, everything was lovely. But if he laughed or nagged or grew angry and impatient, then she went to pieces.

She brought out a packet of twenty cigarettes.

"Have a cigarette," she said. And then, as usual — "You have them all. No, really, I've got plenty more."

And as usual he murmured something like: "Are you sure?. . . " all the while pocketing the cigarettes. To-day she added a box of matches. "No, really, I've plenty more at home." He offered her one of her own cigarettes, and she accepted. For the sake of form he asked her whether she had learned Lesson xii in Semyonov's Russian Grammar.

To-day less than ever were they likely to do even five minutes Russian, not with the sun shining down from a cloudless sky for the first time since the previous autumn. She launched out into a terrific babbling apologia. Blowing cigarette smoke in a thin cloud into the air, Ginsberg let her words shower on him like a mass of scarcely troublesome gnats, only shaking his head every now and again to blow them away.

"By the way," he said, and Mrs. Chabbers's heart sank a little at the studied casualness of his tone, "have you thought any more about what we were discussing the other day? You remember, the magazine?"

"Well, as a matter of fact —"

"I've been very busy on the scheme, you know. Everything's going excellently. I've written to some very prominent people, and some of them have replied. I've got a couple of first rate short stories, including one by Angus Sternforth Simms and another by a talented new writer, a girl of twenty-four, whom I've discovered in Ireland. I've got a couple of poems by Douglas Vanner, satirical ones of course, and a drawing for the cover by Sophie Maslan. And I've got a printer who's only waiting for the word go to have the whole thing ready within four weeks of receiving his copy. He's very cheap, too. Probably the first number won't cost more than about a hundred and thirty pounds. What do you think of that?"

"Oh, jolly good," said the uneasy Mrs. Chabbers. "I wish you luck. I wish I —"

"I could probably get it started with a couple of hundred pounds." Ginsberg wondered whether he was not insisting too much; but he could not let the matter go dragging on like this for weeks on end. The showdown had to come, and to-day was as good a time as any. If he lost her as a pupil as well as a prospective backer, well, so much the better. He was in no mood for dilly-dallying. If the magazine idea flopped, he would push off to Brazil or some such place. He was not going to piddle around any longer on the underside of Bloomsbury. The sun had come as a dazzling revelation of the vastness and brightness and intensity of life, and of the sacrilege of despair. Perhaps it had gone to his head a little.

"Have you come to a decision?"

"Well, I should like to help," she said, in a quiet voice, with downcast eyes.

"It's very nice of you to say so." He pursed his lips and blew smoke in a thin stream into the air. The nursemaid who always walked through the gardens at half-past two came into view, pushing a glittering pram. Who could still afford to employ a nursemaid, or, rather, where were nursemaids still to be found? They were almost an extinct race. "I'm very grateful for your encouragement. And of course you're under no obligation to have anything to do with the magazine at all. At the same time, I would like you, I would ask you, to let me know definitely whether you are going to advance any capital, and if so, how much? Firstly, then, are you willing to advance any capital at all? Needless to say, the whole thing would be done in a businesslike way; we could get a solicitor to draw up an agreement —"

"Oh no!" interrupted Mrs. Chabbers. "That's just what I don't want!"

"Why?" Ginsberg was drawn aside from his main theme to consider this point with curiosity.

She spoke in a low voice as though making a confession.

"You see, my solicitor must know nothing about it. He sees to all my affairs. Ever since my father died, he's kept an eye on me; and though I know you, he might not. . . Well, he might think. . . I mean. . . "

She looked up in embarrassment, blushed, and hung her head away from him, like a shy young girl, or an imbecile.

"Quite," said Ginsberg.

"You know what I could do," she said excitedly. "I could draw it out from the bank fifty pounds at a time and say it was for current expenses. I could say I had a particularly heavy run of expenses for a month and had to pay off several bills." She was so pleased with this simple ruse that she forgot her unwillingness to provide the money at all.

"Then can we fix a date?" said Ginsberg. "Only once you give me your word you must stick to it. I mean, I shall be incurring expenses on the understanding that this money is going to pay for them. When do you think you will be able to let me have the money?"

"I'll let you have two hundred pounds six weeks from to-day." Ginsberg wondered what she had up her sleeve. There must be an odd snag somewhere. Otherwise, he could not imagine her being so definite. However, there was nothing to do but wait and see. He would get everything ready, but he would certainly wait until he had the money safely in the bank under his own name before incurring any financial obligation.

"So that's that," he said. "Six weeks to-day. In cash?"

"Oh yes, in cash. You see, I wouldn't want my solicitor. . ."

"Quite."

"Very well then, six weeks to-day in cash," he repeated, in order to hammer the point home as decisively as possible.

A shabby, stern-looking old man, wearing a mackintosh in spite of the heat, came round the path by their seat, although it was nothing but a loop from the main path, and cast suspicious, penetrating glances at them. It was easy to picture him as a witness in a case of blackmail, or demanding money with menaces, or securing money on false pretences. This was quite possibly his vocation. Having perhaps caught the word "cash", and seeing in Ginsberg and Mrs. Chabbers an oddly assorted couple, he stopped dead in front of them and stared over their heads at the epitaph on the "illuftriouf and greatly refpected Sir Caleb Jarmfon". They sat in silence; he stood there for quite a long time. At last, greatly disappointed at hearing no more and at failing to catch a glimpse of a threatening knife blade, or revolver barrel, or bottle of sulphuric acid, he shuffled back to the main path, casting several fierce, shrewd, and extraordinarily nosy glances over his shoulder.

"There you are!" Mrs. Chabbers breathed excitedly. "Things like that are always happening to me. Men follow me, men come up and speak to me. I was sitting on a park chair yesterday, right away from everybody, and a man. . . "

Ginsberg allowed his thoughts to flit away gently on their own. In a way, the magazine idea was not radical enough. Even if it succeeded, it would only be a new combination of old elements. This weather made him restless with everything that his familiar environment, England, London, Bloomsbury, could offer. The very comfort with which he slipped into his surroundings was dangerous. He could spend years in situations like the present one, extracting quite largish tips from people like Mrs. Chabbers to enable him to get along without a regular job; he could start up something like *Scamp,* possibly make it work. But it was not the worthwhile activity he was seeking. The pace of the quest must be speeded up. He must push on with the affair *Scamp,* see what it added up to, and meanwhile prepare for the next coup. Brazil? An immense, untapped continent, abundant, luxuriant, terrible, deadly, soaked with sun. . . On the other hand, Bloomsbury was home. He caught sight of Mrs. Chabbers' wristlet-watch. Three o'clock. Time to collect his ten shillings and go.

". . . and so I said, What do you mean? But you can't do that! I mean, you can't! Can you? So that's how it is, you see, they're all like that. They are, you know —"

"I'm afraid I shall have to go now," said Ginsberg, rising slightly from the seat to indicate, visually, that her time was up, and then sinking back again while she reached for her bag and dithered among its contents.

"Oh, is it time? So it is, and here am I talking. But I mustn't keep you. You have to hurry away. Where am I — I mean, where is that silly money?" She suddenly began to fling her bag around the seat, knocking it on the iron bar, dropping it to the ground, and making this inanimate object appear to possess the living mischief of a thousand red-hot devils.

"Here we are." At last she had won her usual wrestling match and game of skill with the leaping, cavorting bag, and held up in triumph the ten shilling note.

"Here we are." Ginsberg waited until it had descended, then unobtrusively took it and pocketed it. He looked round to see if the suspicious old man in the mackintosh were observing; fortunately, though still prowling around the gardens, he was now peering at a notice board of by-laws and regulations.

"I think I'll go too," said Mrs. Chabbers. They set off together, Mrs. Chabbers grinning to herself in a private train of ideas, Ginsberg stalking ahead, his eyes set on some invisible objective, looking neither to right nor left at the dozing or staring pensioners on either side of the main path. Mrs. Chabbers remembered that she had wanted something special to happen on this day. But she had been so busy on the one hand, coping with the nervous strain of being in Ginsberg's presence, and on the other, spilling over a few drops of the ocean of words which welled up inside her, that she had forgotten to invite Ginsberg to supper.

"What are you going to do now?" she suddenly brought out, grinning so much in her embarrassment that she seemed to be in the throes of an excruciatingly funny joke. "I mean, what are you? Ay? What? Oh, I'm so silly," she tailed off, hanging her head shyly. "You must forgive me, I'm terribly rude. I really am! Really!"

"I shall probably type out one or two letters connected with *Scamp."* As a matter of fact, Ginsberg had nothing to do, an unusual state of affairs. He had just completed a batch of articles for Bert Flogcrobber and was waiting for the next set to arrive. Though he wasted a great deal of time, he did so normally with a sense of guilt. But for the last couple of days he had been unable to find any justification for guilt. The absence of his customary shadow left him feeling, not so much relieved, as light-headed. He needed his sense of guilt as a stabiliser.

"Don't you get lonely?" asked Mrs. Chabbers coyly, her shoulders heaving with nervous laughter. "I mean, don't you? But of course not, you're like me, you have your interests, your ideas, your books." Her phrases were sufficiently like those he might himself use, to make Ginsberg hate her with momentary intensity. Like *her,* indeed! But he said nothing. He knew how to keep silent. If he had learned nothing else in his thirty years, he had learned to keep quiet.

"I could never be lonely," continued Mrs. Chabbers, now one of the spiritual elite talking to a fellow rarefied spirit. She waved her hand airily. "These people won't believe it —"

"Which people?"

"Why, people, *people!* The *others!* You know what I mean, ordinary, stupid people." They passed the Alsatian dog which sat on its haunches behind the gate of a basement in Coram Street. Mrs. Chabbers, who was convinced that she had a way with animals, bent her head down to the huge, dignified, and disdainful brute, and began to make the most absurd clucking noises. The dog could not be bothered even to watch such debasement, and slowly and contemptuously turned his head the other way. "They love me," said Mrs. Chabbers. "All animals love me." This was too much for Ginsberg. He let out a great halloo of laughter. The dog barked fiercely; it disliked people creating a disturbance in front of the gate.

"What I mean is," burst out Mrs. Chabbers, "would you, I mean, wouldn't you like to come and have dinner with me?"

"By all means," murmured Ginsberg. A free dinner was in no ways to be despised, even at the price of Mrs. Chabbers.

"Well shall we go and have tea first, and then go and

have dinner? Ay? Shall we? Shall we?"

"No," said Ginsberg, "we'd better meet for dinner later. I have one or two things to do." Tea was not, financially, a very profitable meal to accept, since it could be made almost for nothing in his own room. Besides, an unbroken afternoon and evening in the company of Mrs. Chabbers produced an immense pressure round his head, as though it were being knocked in by innumerable insistent little hammers.

They met again at half-past six. Ginsberg had spent the late afternoon reading, washing, brushing, and meditating in Guilford Street. Mrs. Chabbers had contrived, in a few hours, to be involved in a number of odd, embarrassing incidents which were the subject of uneasy puzzlement behind several newspapers in the tube that evening. They strolled through Russell Square and Bedford Square to Soho, where Ginsberg chose the most expensive and tasty little restaurant he knew, the Siguenza. He was feeling rather pleased with himself, what with the sunshine, the idleness, the delightful meal which the Siguenza was sure to provide. Mrs. Chabbers, it was true, made a minor exhibition of herself in the restaurant, and he had to prevent her having any wine, which would have been a disaster. But when he stepped out into Dean Street once again, into the low, broad, golden beam of the setting sun, he glowed with well-being. The weather from without, and an excellent half bottle of claret from within, turned his face a reddish bronze. In his trouser pocket he fingered the change out of two pounds which Mrs. Chabbers had slipped under the table for him to pay the bill with.

"Where now?" said Mrs. Chabbers.

"Now," said Ginsberg brutally, "home." Innumerable justifications for his behaviour lurked at the back of his mind. Behind all her agitated generosity, she wanted to buy him, body and soul; and he was simply acting in self-defence. As for accepting her hospitality, well, why not? It gave her, presumably, some pleasure to have dinner with him. He had certainly enjoyed the dinner. In any case, the money was not hers, was not his; it belonged to those who had created it with the painful effort of their bodies and the wasted hours of their time. . . agricultural labourers in Lincolnshire, tenants in Chalk Farm, tubercular, enslaved blackmen in South Africa, diseased oilworkers in Persia. For his part, he intended to spend the evening in the Corney Arms, drinking a few light ales and prolonging his state of stomachic wellbeing. Afterwards he would call on Lolita. All being well, he would stay there till about one o'clock and then amble down to Fleet Street to see Bert Flogcrobber. A delightful programme.

"Well, goodbye, Mrs. Chabbers." He held out his hand. "Thanks awfully for the dinner, I've enjoyed it immensely. I'll be seeing you next Tuesday, I trust. And in any case, I shall be relying on you now about the magazine. Six weeks from to-day."

"Yes, I think I shall be going home, too," said Mrs. Chabbers, with a grimace of disappointment. She was furious, as well as disappointed. It was not so much that she had hoped for anything definite; but it was such a lovely evening, and it was awful to be dropped flat like this.

"Six weeks from to-day," repeated Ginsberg with a cheerful wave of his hand.

CHAPTER X

JULIUS KRIPKIN'S ADVERTISEMENT in the *New Statesman and Nation* had brought an astonishing number of replies. From parsonages and private schools had come poems and sad, weary short stories. A brother and sister in Norfolk sent, inexplicably, two novels apiece. A man in Middlesbrough submitted a tattered, yellowing sheaf of handwritten manuscript — boy scout stories — accompanied by a postcard saying: "You can have the enclosed for a hundred pounds. Those are my terms, take them or leave them." A man in Bow, named, of all things, Ivan Ginsberg, sent a clever political story, but far too long for inclusion in *Scamp*. Several girls posted neatly written poems in prose, about a spring morning or an autumn afternoon, which were indeed charming and naïve, but uncontroversial. In looking through the parcels of manuscript which Julius Kripkin turned over to him, Ginsberg found it much easier to decide what he did not want than to imagine what he did want.

All the contributions except one went back. He had no need to hesitate. Many of them were good, quite as good as those which appeared in the "young writers'" miscellanies; but they were totally unnecessary. They reached a certain standard of mediocrity, conformed to certain rules of "taste"; but the world would have been not one whit the poorer without them. Above all they were dull; readable but dull.

The one exception was a contribution from Ballykelly, near Cork, in Southern Ireland. It was a story, apparently autobiographical, about the isolation of a young girl who is an anarchist, an atheist, and a would-be bohemian in a primitive Irish town. In secret she reads scientific text books, English novels, and left-wing magazines passed on to her by a friend who is a schoolmistress in Cork. But she can stand her isolation no longer. She is shortly going to run away to London, to the great world, to do great things, to die in great causes... The story was naïve, and at the same time exciting and moving. The credulity, ignorance, and simple charm of a peasant girl appeared amongst the formal, rhetorical phrases acquired from slightly out-of-date political textbooks.

Ginsberg typed her a note of acceptance, and added in handwriting — "Good luck!" Kathleen, the young authoress, reading those simple words of encouragement by the light of an oil-lamp in her damp bedroom in Ballykelly, wondered from what enchanted corner of the great city they had been penned! She wondered what the editor of *Scamp* was like and what he really thought of her and her story. She wondered whether it were really possible that in a few weeks' time she would be speaking to this inconceivable editor — for she intended to call on him in London, since she knew absolutely no one else. Meanwhile, her story was scheduled for the first number of *Scamp*.

From acquaintances in the Corney Arms and Pedro's International Café Restaurant, Ginsberg had already secured other contributions which were, in the words of *Scamp's* terse prospectus, lively, controversial, and informative. Five guineas was all that Angus Sternforth Simms' agent asked for permission to reprint "Mr. Bolonius", the story about the man who lived in five different hotel rooms at the same time. A delightful satirical poem had been written by Douglas Vanner, on a theme commissioned by Ginsberg. In the "Notes on our Contributors" which Ginsberg was tentatively drawing up, Douglas Vanner added his own paragraph:

"The finest, the purest, the most beautiful flower of unnatural truth is Douglas Vanner. He may be a man, he may be a woman, who knows? He has a blue chin and long, waved ginger hair. His clothes are neither this nor that. His eyes shine and his smile is delicate, poised, and more than civilized. His wit glitters perfectly and artificially, from the first greeting — "Tell me the story of your life!" — to the last farewell — "But I expect to suffer!'"

"What would you make of mine?" asked Sophie Maslan, who had agreed with an impatient wave of her hand — "Ah, fiddlesticks!" — to do the cover.

"I would write something terribly sweet," said Douglas Vanner, and wrote on the back of the soiled menu in Pedro's:

"Should you be walking along Charlotte Street at half-past ten at night and see a thin, middle-aged woman walking perilously on spidery legs backstage to Fitzroy Square, then, if all is well, as I trust it is, you will be seeing Sophie Maslan, the painter. Dear Sophie, thrusting bird-like glances from side to side, looking for Mary or Joan or Bill or Jack. Sophie, always half squiffy, and yet never losing her character, her independence, her genuine superiority and pride. For she is an artist. Her race is petering out, as all races must, but she has run it well. . . ."

"There," said Douglas, his head aslant, almost resting on the right shoulder, and his smile switched on like that of an experienced actor. "Six dots at the end, that's my signature. And now I must leave all you *dear* people." His emphasis on "dear" was not ironic, nor was it sincere. It was abstractly artificial. The meaningless, flippant phrases which bestrewed his conversation were a formal chinoiserie. His most devoted admirer, as it happened, was Bellenger, who followed each intricate turn of these Chelseaisms with diligence; and tried uttering them on his own, with shattering effect. Douglas Vanner drew on his yellow gloves, smoothed the elegant tails of his strange jacket, switched up his smile, and said:

"Be terribly gay! Be terribly, terribly gay!" Making his exit from Pedro's with a half bow, he vanished in the direction of Charlotte Street.

Another contribution to *Scamp* came from a journalist whom Ginsberg had met at the Ex-Students' Club in Gordon Square. Or, rather, Ginsberg had introduced himself to the man, who was known in the Ex-Students' Club as "The Journalist". The magazine project had been explained and The Journalist's advice sought.

"Meet me in the Viennese Café, Tottenham Court Road, at four," said The Journalist, and rushed out of the club. Up till that moment he had been sprawling lazily in the lounge with his legs over a chair. In the Viennese Café, The Journalist gulped down a coffee and, hat in hand and stick over arm, said:

"Put in a bit of smut." He lowered his voice. "Have an article on V.D. It always goes down well. But I must rush now. Meet me in the club to-morrow evening at six."

On the following evening, The Journalist lay as usual in the lounge, his legs over a chair and his neck and shoulders squashed into the corner of another. He immediately jumped up.

"So glad you've got here, I'm just hurrying away to the House — "

"Which house?"

"The House of Commons. Look here, can you meet me on Friday lunch-time at Mooney's Bar?"

So it went on. One day, to his surprise, Ginsberg was given an excellent article of inside gossip on political and public personalities, concluding with a paragraph prophesying universal ruin.

"You can have it for nothing," said The Journalist. "It's just on the right side of the law, so you needn't worry. And it's red-hot news."

Yet another journalist, Buchsfindlemann of the *London Daily Echo,* came up to Ginsberg in the Corney Arms one night and said gloomily:

"I hear you're founding a magazine."

"That's right, *Scamp,* magazine of the —"

"It all depends on your point of view."

"How do you mean?"

"Well," said Buchsfindlemann with an unhappy sigh, "it all depends on whether you're a dirty stinking reactionary or not."

"No," said Ginsberg, "my own views are extreme left wing, though if anybody had anything interesting to say — "

"As long as you're not a filthy bloody conservative, or a lousy sod of a liberal, or one of these hypocritical labour swine, or anything like that."

"No, I don't think so," said Ginsberg.

"In that case, I'm willing to be your art editor — if you want me, of course," he added out of politeness, smiling at the absurdity of the idea that he might not be wanted.

"Oh, that's very nice of you."

"I'm art editor on the *London Daily Echo*."

"That's very nice of you indeed."

"I'd give my services free, for the good of the cause. Anything to get a slam at those bastards."

"Quite."

There was a moment or two of silence, then Buchsfindlemann glared at Ginsberg truculently. "Well?" he demanded.

"Well. . . " said Ginsberg hesitantly. "You see, I don't know much about these things, and I'm not even sure that there'll be an art editor."

"What, no half-tones, no line drawings, no photographs, no coloured block for the cover?"

"I'm not sure whether the money will run to it."

"Tchah!" Buchsfindlemann scowled into his glass. "Well, if you need me, you can always get in touch with me at the *Echo* office. As long as it's not for those swine, those bastards, those lousy rats, those filthy stinking. . . "

Buchsfindlemann was speaking of his employers, the *London Daily Echo,* and the policy they represented. His job was Buchsfindlemann's first major grudge against society. Angus Sternforth Simms' success, in fact Angus Sternforth Simms' very existence, was his second major grudge. And the third was the fact that everyone took him for a Jew, on account of his name, whereas he was of Dutch origin. He was not an anti-semite; quite the contrary. All the same, it was galling to have people continually coming up, winking knowingly, and murmuring in Yiddish. . . . Ach! But people were a lot of swine, rats, dirty, filthy, stinking scum. . . .

Buchsfindlemann was of so violent a disposition, at any rate verbally, that Ginsberg decided to sheer off to the Duchess of Margaret. The man might be art editor of the *London Daily Echo,* but he would be nothing but a nuisance to *Scamp.* Buchsfindlemann glared after Ginsberg's retreating back. He glared at the door, he glared round the pub, he glared at objects and people with the same undiscriminating hatred, so intense that smoke and flames would not have been surprising in its wake.

Buchsfindlemann was not the only person in Soho and Bloomsbury whose interest in *Scamp* was somewhat embarrassing. From among a little crowd of lost souls, two eventually detached themselves. They were Kroganin and Philip.

Kroganin was supposed to have been a close friend of Lenin's and a member of the Politburo of the Communist Party in Moscow. He was due to have been shot in a purge of Trotskyists, but at the last moment escaped, or was allowed to escape. Even the humourless Soviet secret police, so the story went, could not shoot Kroganin, who would have gone talking and expostulating to the very firing wall. He got away to Paris, to Montparnasse, where he talked in the Dome, the Coupole, and the Rotonde for about fifteen years. Chance brought him to London. Ever since, he had been straining — so he said — to get back to Paris, but had been unable to muster the fare.

His single preoccupation was keeping alive. It was no easy task. He could not have done it anywhere outside the West End of London. He had no money and had presumably not worked, in the ordinary sense, for thirty or more years. And at present, what work could he do?

Who would employ a man with a long white beard and a flowing white mane? A man who spoke innumerable languages atrociously and who felt at home only in his native Helsinki dialect of Finnish? A man who had been out of work for twenty years and whose occupation before that had been "professional politician"? Obviously, hardly anyone. And if there was anyone who thought of employing him, Kroganin soon disillusioned him. Kroganin was unemployable, and at the same time had to be kept alive; and not merely alive, but decently alive, in a manner befitting a distinguished cosmopolitan. He was very fond of Guinness. He needed an occasional cigar, as well as cigarettes, to keep him in good humour. And his paradoxes were most brilliant after a tasty supper in Pedro's, followed by cup after cup of Pedro's excellent and very sweet Turkish coffee — "quite as good as anything in Montparnasse," Kroganin insisted.

Kroganin's demands were in a way modest enough; but satisfying them took up all his time. Since earning money was out of the question, he had to live on his friends. Everyone who met him became Kroganin's friend, no one could help liking him. So the old man spent his days and nights walking between the Ex-Students' Club and Charlotte Street on the look-out for friends. The moment he spotted one whom he had not tapped for some time he waved his stick at him across the street and took him off to lunch. Another he took to the Corney Arms for a Guinness; another to the Duchess of Margaret for a Guinness and a cigar. He preferred two or three friends to share the cost of his supper at Pedro's, since the bill, including the Turkish coffees, was rather large; while he permitted exceptionally close friends no alternative but to put him up until they could stand him no longer, when he was passed on to the next friend. Not that any of them ever grew to dislike the man himself; but they grew to detest his voice, which was booming and continuous. Speaking English it would have been bad enough, but murdering half a dozen languages simultaneously it was funny up to a point, and beyond that catastrophic.

Ginsberg was one of Kroganin's friends. Knowing Ivan's circumstances, Kroganin made only token demands — a cup of tea and a sandwich, a few cigarettes, very rarely a glass of Guinness. He also spoke to Ivan of his search for work, how he had been to the B.B.C., the British Council, the Inter-University Federation, the Workers' Educational Association, the Foreign Office, the Home Office, the War Office, the Central Office of Information, offering to write articles, to lecture in South America, to do anything — anything reasonable.

"But always turrrning me down they urrr!" he boomed. "*Orrr* you urrr too old, *orrr* no Brrritish subject, *orrr* we will wrrrite in six months time, orrr this, orrr that! — Ach!" Kroganin snorted like a hippopotamus. He would have been none the worse off for not looking for work, since he invariably received smiling refusals. But he enjoyed pestering cultural organizations for work. It brought him more friends, who had the culture to appreciate the breadth of his intellect and experience, and who were also wealthier and more influential than his Soho acquaintances. Often he was invited afterwards to dinner, where his booming voice soon assured for him the position of honour. Besides, his search for work completely justified his living on friends. They could see for themselves that he had no choice. And they knew that once he did secure a job — it was only a question of time — he would repay every penny.

To prove the earnestness of his quest, he asked for practical advice. Did anyone know of anything on the films, in television, radio? In book publishing, journalism, lecturing? Any translations, research? Would it be better for him to write or phone or present himself in person? Would it be better for him to shave off his beard and have his hair cut, or not?

On this last point Ivan had come near to offending Kroganin irreparably. The old man, having hit a stony patch, had thought urgently of taking a job as a dish-washer. "I must," he had said, "I must". For a moment the emptiness behind Kroganin's irrepressible bohemianism was visible. He belonged nowhere, he was outlandish in any environment, and he was weary. But he could not remain still like an old man and perform some mechanical job till death relieved him. He had to make a noise, to strike an attitude. Temporarily, however, he was seriously considering his chances of getting a job as a dish-washer. "I must," he had said, "or I shall starrrve." Where another person would have said, "I shall be broke," or "I shan't have a penny left," Kroganin always said, "I shall starrrve."

"Then shave your beard off and have a haircut," Ivan had said, on being asked for practical advice. "If you don't let them see you're a cut above dish-washing, and just take orders quietly, they'll as soon have you as anybody else. I should imagine there's a shortage of dish-washers now, anyway."

But Kroganin's crisis had blown over, and he had not taken a job as a dish-washer, or any other sort of job; and Ivan had quite forgotten the incident. Several months later he found himself sitting opposite Kroganin in the Thermopylae Café. He mentioned *Scamp*. Kroganin nodded abstractedly, sucking one cheek into his mouth. He seemed to be lost in memories of the remote past, of Tsarist Helsinki, Lenin in Moscow, Bela Kun in Hungary, Montparnasse. Just before Ivan left, however, Kroganin caught his sleeve and roared in what was meant to be an aside:

"Do you think I could get such a job?"

"What sort of a job?" asked Ivan puzzled.

"Editor magazine," bellowed Kroganin. Ivan did not feel like explaining that his editorship of *Scamp* was not a job, in the ordinary sense. Besides, it was impossible to explain anything to Kroganin, particularly in a public place. Every nuance and confidential hint was taken up by Kroganin, amplified a dozen times by his deafening boom, and broadcast to the entire company.

"You probably could, if you felt like it. Though," he added flippantly, "you'd probably have to get your beard and hair back to normal. They'd be a distinct asset to an editor."

After the dish-washing episode, Kroganin had, in fact, shaved off his beard and had his hair cut en brosse. Ever since then he had been somewhat undecided; a long white stubble covered his chin and his hair stood up in a massive white bush. Now he turned angrily on Ginsberg:

"But it was you," he shouted furiously, "it was you yourrrself who told me shave off bearrrd and cut hairrr!"

Suddenly Ivan remembered his previous piece of advice. The whole thing was ludicrous, but he dared not laugh, or Kroganin might explode, run amok, have a fit, or, worst of all, burst into tears.

"Ah, but that was different," Ivan explained reasonably. "I think you will agree that was quite different. There it was a question of a job as a manual labourer, that is to say a dish-washer. Here we are discussing an intellectual and prestige post. Aren't we?"

"Ach," said Kroganin with unqualified disgust, "pfeh!" But he brightened up a minute later. Once again he laid his hand on Ivan's sleeve: "Perrrhaps you will do me small favourrr?"

"I hope so," said Ivan cautiously.

"Assistant editor you will have me as, yes? Don't misunderrrstand me, I ask forrr no wages. Later perrrhaps, if you urrr grrreat success, I might ask forrr wages — and even back wages," laughed Kroganin, in a gust of cheerfulness as sudden and complete as his previous outburst of anger. "And I don't want to do worrrk. If you want me to do worrrk, I will do it, and you will have to pay me for it. But I don't *positively* want to do it. And I don't suppose you want me to, either."

"Then what exactly do you want?" asked Ginsberg.

"Let us say assistant editor I am — on paper! Assistant editor in advisorrry capacity for example. Verrry well, I go to Brrritish Council, I say I am assistant editor on magazine. I go to B.B.C., I say I am assistant editor on magazine. I go to publishers, I say I am assistant editor on magazine. I get job! Now you underrrstand?"

"Yes, but —"

In spite of Ginsberg's diplomatically worded discouragement, Kroganin advertized himself around Charlotte Street and in the Ex-Students' Club as the assistant editor of *Scamp*. There was nothing that could be done about it. And in announcing his new position, he described the magazine in such terms that people began to look at Ivan with new respect. Really! Who would have thought it! The editor of *Scamp*!

But Kroganin was harmless; if anything, he tried to be helpful. And if it came to that, why should he not be an unpaid and unworked assistant editor of an as yet non-existent magazine? The position and the anecdotes which would grow around it would simply increase his stock in trade. After a short time, they would be hauled out only rarely, and eventually would be forgotten altogether. But Philip — Philip Lank — Philip was a more dangerous proposition. Philip brooded and worried and schemed in a most determined and frightening way. Night after night he leaned up against the public bar in the Duchess of Margaret and drew pensively at his cigarette-holder. Behind spectacle lenses of impenetrable thickness, his eyes vanished into nothingness. His immensely long, immensely thin body tied itself into shapes of increasing discomfort as he concentrated on some inner problem — *the* problem, the problem of problems, the square root of the cube of the integral of the logarithm of the differential. For Philip was a metaphysician who worked in mathematical terms. These mathematical speculations were punctuated by a recurrent and urgent sexual query.

"Do you think," he once confided to Ivan, "that someone somewhere may be found to love me?"

It was very unlikely; indeed, it was flatly impossible, if by love was meant anything connected with affection, tenderness, happiness, desire, beauty. Philip was really too far gone, although he was not yet thirty. He was clever, but with a sort of cleverness that belonged to some dusty corner of a public library. One could imagine the librarians pointing out the gawky, shabby youth, crazed with scientific knowledge, and saying: "But he's awfully clever. Wins prizes and all that. You wouldn't think it to look at him. *Closing time,* please!" So Philip had won his prizes and accumulated his degrees and might have become an eccentric, unwashed don, had his mind not grown sick of textbooks and formulae and academic work and revolted with a number of nervous breakdowns. He had to give up studying; instead, he got a job in a laboratory off Great Portland Street. And to keep himself just on the right side of sanity he drank steadily every night in the public bar of the Duchess of Margaret. Afterwards, when, as the last customer, he had been driven out, he staggered back to his bed-sitting-room in Cleveland Street, muttering and whimpering to himself, and in spite of the dangers to his sick brain, devoured a quarter of a volume of mathematical philosophy. When the first light of dawn was perceptible through the blackened windows of his room, and he fell asleep with the book propped open in front of him, he sometimes felt that he was on the verge of finding the secret, the secret of secrets, of solving the mystery, of working out the problem, the problem of problems, the square root of the cube of the integral of the logarithm of the differential. . . .

What disconcerted people about Philip, what prevented them from realizing the pitiable martydom of the skinny, graceless, flopping prodigy, was the expression of his face. The face itself was as it were streamlined, the forehead above and the chin below receding from a central forward-thrusting and upward-tilted nose. And its expression was always smiling, even when he was quite alone in a corner of the pub opposite the darts board, or sitting by the door in the Thermopylae Café with his back to everyone else.

At first sight he appeared to be smiling at some private joke. At second sight he was still smiling at this private joke. And at third sight, to the uneasy surprise of the observer, he was still smiling, steadily and unremittingly. Always and everywhere, on Philip's face, there was an expression of private amusement. Perhaps he was smiling at adversity, a brave and human gesture? No, in reality, he was not smiling at all. Only Philip and the few people who ever spoke to him knew that the smile was the result of a nervous facial contortion, was an expression of inner agony. The eyebrows were lifted, the forehead was creased and wrinkled with amused surprise; but the eyebrows could not be lowered, the forehead could not be relaxed in public. The mouth was grinning, the large, uneven teeth displayed, stained brown by forty cigarettes a day; as long as there were people around, strangers, the mouth had to go on grinning. At the age of almost thirty, Philip was still too shy to face strangers without his grinning mask.

Probably Philip's closest friend was Bellenger. That is not to say that they were very close friends. They met perhaps once a week, when Bellenger had nothing better to do. But as no one else ever spoke more than a few words to Philip, his meetings with Bellenger were for him the height of intimacy. He carried on where they had left off the week before.

"So you think he was wrong?" he would begin, the moment Bellenger entered the Duchess of Margaret.

"Who?" asked Bellenger.

"Why, Pascal, of course!" said Philip irritably, annoyed with Bellenger for having forgotten that the very last thing they had been talking about ten days before was the philosophy of Pascal.

Then Bellenger, if he could, would slip away, and Philip would save up what he had to say on Pascal for another few days. But if Bellenger was in the right mood, disappointed, exhausted, frustrated, he welcomed Philip's company. Walking home from Pedro's or the

Thermopylae Café at midnight, after a fruitless round of the pubs and cafés, he could at any rate unburden himself to Philip without maintaining the slightest reserve. Suspicious though he was of everybody, male and female, in his lone sexual war, he excepted Philip. He took him back for a cup of tea to Guilford Street, and Philip was prodigiously, slobberingly grateful, drooling thanks and saliva down his burnt-out cigarette holder in a prolonged farewell at two o'clock in the morning. Often he rang the bell ten minutes later and brought Bellenger down eight flights of stairs to add in the long gasps, almost sobs, with which he spoke:

"Oh, sorry to bring you down again. But I didn't want you to go away with the impression that I'm a completely uncompromizing determinist. I do grant" — he seemed to be on the point of tears as he made this concession — "that the irrational and erratic probabilities in the case of some electronic streams do seem to offer some mathematical basis for a belief in limited free will."

Bellenger's jaw hung down with fatigue, but he had to humour Philip. Once he was persuaded to go back to Philip's room, which was the rottenest, most infested attic even in that abandoned quarter of the West End behind Middlesex Hospital. At other times they carried on desultory, speculative argument through deserted, midnight streets. All his encounters with Philip had an eerie quality, as though they were the last men left alive. Partly this was because they met only when Bellenger was too exhausted and ill at ease to do anything else; and partly it was because Philip's personality was truly macabre, gruesome, deathly. He would grin horribly in the moonlight as they passed a bombed site, and waving a long, skinny arm towards the waste ground, would gasp and sob:

"Don't you wish you'd been there when it all went up? How nice it must be to die and finish with everything!"

"Come, come," Bellenger remonstrated mildly.

"Oh, I'm sorry if I'm depressing you. I was only

speaking for myself. I'm a monstrosity — you can see that, anybody can see it. I'd be far better dead."

There was such a note of despair in his voice that Bellenger was touched. His stomach ached with pity, which overcame his disgust, and he put a friendly arm round Philip's greasy mackintosh.

"You're not a monstrosity at all," he said comfortingly if insincerely, "you're a person of brilliant qualities, which will one day be recognized."

But Philip, in these moments of annihilating lucidity, knew the truth: he *was* a monstrosity, repellent and disquieting in appearance, agitated and morose in behaviour, dirty, unhealthy, and unwanted. Yet he resented any attempt to change his habits, desperately though he yearned to be normal, to look normal, and to be received within the tolerant community which frequented the Duchess of Margaret and the Thermopylae Café. It was with a casual suggestion about buying himself a new mackintosh that Ginsberg almost fell foul of him. Bellenger had mentioned the forthcoming appearance of *Scamp,* and Philip had arrived at Guilford Street late one night with the manuscript of an article on Science and Society. The article was put aside for later reading, and Ginsberg found himself for the first time getting the full impact of Philip Lank, of whom hitherto he had received only a hasty impression. Philip hung about shyly in the doorway of Ginsberg's room. He did only what he was given explicit permission to do, and sat in the armchair as though faced with a grim ordeal. After a time, speaking haltingly in muted sobs, he came round to his question: Was it possible that someone somewhere could be found to love him? His long, thin hands twitched, his smile was fixed, graven in uncomfortable wrinkles on his cheeks and forehead.

"Do you really want my advice?" asked Ginsberg.

"Yes, I do!" gasped Philip.

"I believe I am right in assuming that you earn a fair weekly wage. You may even have a little money saved up —"

"I haven't," said Philip, with so lifelike a grin that Ginsberg wondered whether he might not after all be finding something amusing in their discussion.

"No matter. On your salary you could very soon manage to buy some clothes. To judge by appearances, you have not used up many of your clothing coupons. Very well. Buy yourself a new suit, new shirts, a new tie, new socks, new shoes, and above all a new mackintosh! Even if they are cheap, they will at least be new, fresh, and clean. Burn all your present clothes, throw away your cigarette holder, cut your nails, have a thoroughly good bath, shave carefully every morning, go to the Duchess of Margaret only twice a week, take an occasional walk in the country —"

"Yes!" cried Philip, in a harsh voice totally different from his usual whines and gasps and sobs. "That's you and your kind all over! What's wrong with my mackintosh? It keeps out the rain! Isn't that enough? Clothes, appearances, vanity — that's all you think about. You don't care about the man beneath. If someone is smart and nice to look at, you're satisfied. My clothing coupons — I give them to my mother and sister, they need them. I don't care about show and finery —"

"But you asked me —"

Philip took no notice. He was transformed and carried away by feelings drawn from an out of the way vein of childhood. Ginsberg appeared as the incarnation of mammon.

"You and your kind!" grated Philip. "Clothes, finery, scented women —"

Ginsberg found himself picking idly at his frayed sleeve end, unconsciously contrasting his actual condition with Philip's outpourings. He was shocked, not so much by what Philip said as by the fact that he said it. He had always imagined Philip to be slightly off his head, but no more so than most other people in Soho. Now he was afraid that the scientist was becoming progressively more insane, that this scene was a crisis in a progress towards certifiable lunacy. A sort of foam was appearing round Philip's mouth. He raved on with his aggressive confession; he described how he went once a fortnight to a prostitute in Shaftesbury Avenue, the humiliations he suffered, and he somehow, rather abstractly, blamed it all on Ginsberg and his kind. Sweat stood out on his forehead, he glared wildly round the room, not particularly in Ginsberg's direction. Ivan was momentarily afraid that Philip might get violent. It would be no joke to find oneself alone at midnight with a raving lunatic. But even the transformed Philip seemed hardly dangerous; and just then, the fit quite suddenly ended. Philip blinked as though he had awoken from a dream. His narrow shoulders sagged to their normal piteous stoop, his voice dropped back to a gasp. His features wrinkled unhappily into their fixed smile.

"I'm awfully sorry," he moaned. "I really don't know what came over me. . . . I think I'd better be going now." He groped his way out, as though the room were in darkness, stumbling over chairs, bumping into the wall. Ginsberg was glad to see him go, though for the sake of politeness — and as a vague precaution against drawing on himself another of Philip's crazy outbursts — he muttered a few words about it being "quite all right. . . no need to hurry away. . . always welcome."

Philip rushed blindly down the stairs, slipping once or twice. He paused two landings below. "I do hope" — his voice was so piteous and supplicatory that he seemed to be praying — "I do hope that you'll like my article."

Philip took a morbid interest in *Scamp*. In the Duchess of Margaret, when anyone spoke to him, he immediately told them about the magazine. If he caught sight of Ginsberg at the other end of the street, he hurried after him and gasped breathlessly: "When is it coming out? Have you decided about my article yet?" And if Ginsberg looked up from his beer in the private bar of the Duchess, he saw Philip's spectacles glimmering in his direction.

Philip even asked Bellenger to use all his friendly influence to persuade Ginsberg to take the article.

Ginsberg had not the courage to refuse the article outright; so he continually hedged, now saying that he had not yet made up his mind, now postponing its possible publication to the second or third issue. The article itself was largely a collection of platitudes about the power of science, with here and there a nihilistic touch, such as:

". . . though perhaps it might be better to destroy all existing humanity and leave a selected pair to breed a new race in accordance with scientific principles. . . "

Philip was a man to watch. There were violent forces at work in his brain, which was subject to dreadful pressures. He formed the habit of ringing the bell in Guilford Street almost every other midnight, after drinking beer for hours in the Duchess of Margaret. He called to see Bellenger, who had usually not yet returned from Charlotte Street; but he never failed to ask at the same time about his article. Ginsberg did not ask Philip up; eventually he did not even answer the bell. It was none the less sinister to hear that strident ringing; while Philip down below knew quite well that Ginsberg was deliberately refusing to open the door. A further step was to disconnect the electric wires which set the bell ringing. This merely diffused the uneasiness which Philip aroused. If Ginsberg were reading late or typing out a letter or an article for Bert Flogcrobber, he wondered: Is Philip down there ineffectually pressing the bell-push, or staring up from the other side of the road to see if he can spot a chink of light in the attic window and thereby confirm his suspicions? Philip's interest in *Scamp* and the Guilford Street flat was embarrassing, if not dangerous. And the worst of the matter was, nothing could be done about it.

CHAPTER XI

BERT FLOGCROBBER sat in the Irish bar holding the remnants of a glass of whisky. He felt deeply discouraged, profoundly, abysmally, bottomlessly discouraged. Outside, a gusty, heavy wind blew up the dust of the London pavements. A ray of evening sunshine, without warmth, almost without brightness, found its way through the thick, stained-glass windows of the bar and settled gloomily along the heavy leather settee. The bar was almost empty; the few people by the counter spoke in subdued voices. Bert Flogcrobber remembered the bustle of Fleet Street in the old days, remembered how the bar used to fill up at this hour with a crowd of noisy young reporters, sub-editors, and night staff. He could not account for it logically, of course, knew that he might even be wrong in fact, but in those days everyone seemed young, or if not young, alive. There was a tang, a zest about journalism, a salt about England, a solid, honest to goodness flavour about everything. Now. . . now he felt like an elderly unwanted foreigner in his own country. He, Bert Flogcrobber, as English as roast beef, he liked to say, felt like a foreigner. The children went their own way. They didn't seem to mind, they had never known the old England, when beer was beer, and whisky was Scotch, and cigarettes were sixpence for twenty, and you could tell the difference between a dustman and a duke, between an assistant editor and an office boy. Bah! Now, everything was miserable and joyless; and not merely miserable, but dishonourable. It was a disgrace; they had let their forefathers down, those forefathers who acknowledged no master save their king — the gentlemen of England, the yeomen of England, the strong armed and respectful servants and labourers of the gentlemen of England, all eating good English beef, drinking good English ale, sailing good English ships, wearing good English cloth. . .

Bert Flogcrobber's reverie went on and on, each image stamped with the word "England". "England" exalted him, made him feel jolly, forthright, clean, robust. "England" had nothing to do with the London of the 1940s; but that was the fault of the modern Londoner, who had let down the old bulldog breed.

A hand fell on his shoulder. Bert started — he was a nervous man — his knee hit the table, rocked it, sent a glass rolling off and smashing into smithereens on the floor. Ginsberg stood towering above him.

"Oh, I'm awfully sorry," said Ginsberg.

Bert forced himself to smile in welcome. They had arranged to meet for a few minutes to talk over a few articles. At the same time he thought sourly: There he is, the Jew; he doesn't care, what has he got to lose? Came from some Polish ghetto, no doubt, now gives himself airs in London. What right has he got to walk around with his head in the air like that? Looking dignified, the bloody crawler, the hack — a hack's hack! Was there anything lower in Grub Street? Calls himself a writer, Bert sneered inwardly; who wants to read his damn stories? Aren't there enough stories in existence already? It's not as if he can even sell them.

"Do sit down," said Bert. "Have a drink, cigarette. What is it you usually have, light ale?"

"Thanks," said Ginsberg, helping himself to a cigarette.

They were at the end of their first month of working together, and their collaboration was going well. Bert had an amazingly fertile mind for articles and features. He turned over the ideas in their raw state to his secretary, who sorted out for each an appropriate bunch of press cuttings. Bert then dashed off quite unthinkingly and at immense speed the rough outline of an article, and sent it off to Ginsberg. Ginsberg found himself working quite hard, not the promised two hours a day, but five or six or seven hours on most days. The fact was that Bert Flogcrobber needed more articles badly. No sooner had he paid his sons' school bills than a batch of new demands had come from his family. His wife wanted to take their two daughters to Paris. At first he had refused; but she had pointed out that practically all their neighbours and friends had been abroad. That was a point on which he was sensitive; if everyone else in Beaulieu Avenue had been abroad, then his wife and daughters must go abroad too, and spend the niggardly seventy-five pounds which the contemptible Labour government allowed tourists to take out of the country in one year. Still, three times seventy-five pounds was two hundred and twenty-five pounds, and two hundred and twenty-five pounds was decidedly two hundred and twenty-five pounds, apart from fares. It was fortunate that he had lighted upon Ginsberg, who was making a reasonably good job of writing up his articles — give the man credit where it was due — and it might be possible to pull out of this latest financial swamp. There was also a chance of securing a most important commission — the biggest he had ever achieved — from the Amalgamated South African Press Syndicate. It was this he had wanted to discuss with Ginsberg.

"Now listen," he said, "I want to tell you about a chance we've got with some big South African papers which pay very well. My agent's been talking to one of the directors, who's over here, and if he likes the synopsis he's willing to commission a series of six articles on life in this country to-day. We'll split the country up into six regions and do a piece on each. The whole thing's worth three hundred pounds, in other words seventy-five pounds to you, what do you think of that?"

"Sounds admirable," murmured Ginsberg. He wondered how much Bert already owed him. The trouble was, he had no check on which articles were sold and which not. If one quarter of the articles he had done for Bert Flogcrobber were sold even at four guineas a thousand, Bert must already owe him something like twenty-five pounds. A pleasant sum of money to a man with eight and fourpence in his pocket.

"So I want you to make a specially good job of the synopsis," continued Bert. "Put in more of your own ideas. I'm not complaining, mind you, but you've been leaving the main body of the articles as I've written them. Now I dash them off in ten minutes; and though I'm an experienced journalist, I'm not so vain as to believe that the article couldn't be entirely rewritten. You write some very nice paragraphs, but what about putting a little more ginger into my ideas? See what I mean? Rewrite the whole thing, if necessary."

"Quite," said Ginsberg. What it amounted to was that Bert wanted him to do more for his twenty-five per cent.

They discussed in detail the synopsis for the Amalgamated South African Press Syndicate, Ginsberg listening rather apathetically to Bert's ideas, issuing forth with mechanical, supremely boring efficiency. A month before he would have been interested, enthusiastic. He would have been dazzled by the seventy-five pounds and taken up with what would have appeared to be an ambitious project. Now the seventy-five pounds was just an abstract figure; he could not see it fluttering in delightful pound notes to his lap. It was not that he actually distrusted Bert, but just that the relationship between them seemed to have lost all financial significance. One pound would have made all the difference, one single crisp note, one cheque. But Bert said that he did not pay his "ghost" till the end of the quarter, when his agent prepared an account. It was all very businesslike, but very remote. Meanwhile Bert refused to pay out a penny. As for the articles themselves, nothing could be more dull, more appallingly boring than those bright, chatty, newsy, gossipy, facile outpourings. At the end of three weeks he was already sick of them. And to think that he had once wanted to be a journalist on a Sunday paper!

"I'm relying on you, then," Bert concluded, "for the benefit of both of us. Actually there's no hurry; a week's time will do."

"Right," said Ginsberg, "I'll post it on." After two or three visits, Ginsberg had lost interest in calling on Bert at the *Daily Post* office. "My secretary will send you some cuttings and my outline to-morrow. You come round and see me in a week's time."

"Right you are. Or if it's quite straightforward, I'll post it on. Look, there's just one other thing. I hate to bring it up again; but I've been doing quite a lot of work for you — far more than we arranged, in fact. And now this new thing, if they commission it, is going to need a lot of time and effort. Well, how about letting me have a few pounds out of my quarter's commission?"

"I've already told you that I'm not an employer, in the ordinary sense. You and I are collaborators, we're partners. I might just as well ask you for payment in advance as you ask me."

They stared at each other with naked dislike. Then Bert, the more experienced negotiator, laid his hand on Ivan's arm.

"Don't worry," he said, "it'll be all the more welcome when it does arrive. Have another cigarette."

Ivan took another cigarette and went. Bloody Jew, thought Bert. It did not take him long to get on bad terms with his "ghosts". In one sense he was boss, and in another sense he was partner, fellow conspirator even, because there was something hole-in-corner about this free-lance work. Bert did not like it, but there was no alternative. He kept on reminding himself that he was a professional man of standing, assistant night-editor on the *Daily Post,* a newspaper whose readers were gentlemen. Yet he had to have dealings with such riff-raff as Ginsberg. "Bloody Jew," he muttered to himself. He felt automatically in his hip pocket to reassure himself about his nightly half-bottle of whisky and left the Irish bar.

A dark, curly-headed young man with a beaky nose was walking towards the Strand, his arm round the waist of a pretty, fair-haired girl. As Bert passed, the young man nestled his beaky nose against the girl's cheek, while the girl giggled affectionately. "Bloody Jew," muttered Bert Flogcrobber, annoyed by the beaky nose, annoyed by the windy evening, annoyed by his own rumbling stomach, annoyed by the prospect of a night's work stretching ahead. His animus directed itself against the Jews. He had just been reading a leaflet, left by someone in the Irish bar, entitled: "Britons ARE Slaves!" — "Britons!" it said. "In times of old your forefathers knew how to draw the sword for liberty. It was they who carried the flag to the furthest corners of the globe... Alien influences dominate our native land. Everywhere the Cohens, the Levys, the Abrahams, the Isaacs, and the Moses are in control. Behind the Labour government, which is rapidly choking the country, is held the hidden hand of International Jewry... British blood is being shed in Palestine by Jewish terrorists, too cowardly to emerge into the open... Britons! Awake! Arise! Join the Association of Freemen and Yeomen of England!" Bert was not impressed by this crude sort of stuff; but there's something in what they say, he reflected. He looked back to see the young man still resting his beaky nose against the girl's cheek. He looked ahead again and saw a fat, prosperous looking little man getting into a taxi with an equally fat, prosperous looking little woman, who, in entering the cab, revealed a stretch of fat, silk-stockinged leg. "I bet they're Jews," said Bert to himself. Otherwise, Fleet Street was deserted.

Sometimes Bert admired the Jews, and sometimes he had for them a pathological hatred. At the present moment he saw their hand everywhere, and their very existence seemed a crime. Were they poor, then they had infected England with their Eastern European poverty. Were they rich, then they had no right to be. All these chain shops were Jewish, half the Cabinet were Jewish, all the highbrows were Jewish, damn them. The highbrows, the Jews, the Labour government, they were linked together somehow in a conspiracy. Perhaps there really was a vast secret International of Jews, Freemasons, communists, socialists, and highbrows. Of course, that was what Hitler had said, but perhaps Hitler was right? Reaching his office, Bert took a deep swig from his half-bottle of whisky. Aaaah! The whisky tore like fire through his throat, warmed his stomach, revivified his entire body. When he had sat down in his comfortable swivel chair, lit a cigarette, and relaxed, his mood changed completely. He liked the office, he was at home in this chair. Life was good, comfortable, he had done well for himself. England would pull through; even the Labour government weren't so bad; they didn't go too far, a lot of 'em were coming round already. As for the Jews, they weren't such a bad lot. Of course, they were clever, you had to keep on your toes with them. But what was wrong with that? He admired clever people. He himself wasn't such a fool. Look at the way he ran his free-lance sideline. No one in Fleet Street knew, or even suspected that Yvonne Bretonne and Man about the West End and Philip Dangelas and Frank Antonius and a crowd of others were all Bert Flogcrobber. And — he chuckled aloud at the thought — he even had a yid working for him; and on whose terms? On his, Bert Flogcrobber's terms. And how much was he going to get? He'd be lucky if he got a couple of fivers. He'd find that ninety per cent of those articles he'd written up had been rejected. The chances of his actually coming across one of the articles published in the provinces or in one of the Dominions was negligible. Who was smart now?

Bert Flogcrobber arrived early at the office as well as leaving late. He liked to have time to smoke and drink a bit before the rush started. He took another swig of whisky, felt alive to the fingertips, and, struck by a thought, went over to a set of metal drawers in the corner. He unlocked the top drawer and glanced round the room out of excess of caution, before drawing out a heavy Service revolver. He could not have said exactly why he had bought the revolver and kept it fully loaded at the office. He certainly contemplated no crime of violence; nor had he envisaged any occasion when the revolver might be necessary for defence; while even in his gloomiest moments he had not seriously thought of suicide. He was simply fascinated by its sinister beauty, and out of bravado he kept it filled with live cartridges. It made him feel powerful to look at the exquisitely turned and shaped weapon and reflect that death was contained therein — a clean, neat, mechanical, impersonal death, the death of the detective novel, without, apparently, the splashing of blood and guts and the crushing of bones such as he had seen once after an air raid.

A soldier had sold it to him in a pub off the Strand. Without thinking, Bert had slipped the lad a pound note and put the gun into his pocket. Ever since then it had been his favourite toy. He fondled it, he gloated over it, he held his finger on the trigger. All over the country, as the Sunday newspapers showed, similar transactions had taken place, and these unnecessary lethal weapons lay conveniently loaded and to hand in drawers, ready to be seized in a fit of anger or a moment of fear. "I don't know what came over me," said the accused; or, "I only meant to frighten him, but the thing went off". Nevertheless, some unconscious homicidal instinct had completely prepared him for the fatal accident.

CHAPTER XII

GINSBERG KNOTTED HIS BEST TIE. Dissatisfied with the result, he knotted it again; and again, and again, until at last it dovetailed perfectly into his shirt collar. He would have liked to be a dandy from head to foot; but his pocket permitted only a change of ties — one tie for everyday wear, one for evening wear, and one for very special occasions. The tie he had just knotted was the yellow one for evening wear. He would not have troubled to put on even that, just for Lolita's sake, but he himself felt a trifle renovated by the change.

Lolita was in a way the ideal mistress. When he was a curious, open-mouthed youngster in the East End, he had heard "wide-boys" boast of having such a mistress. He tried to overcome his deep distaste for Lolita by reminding himself of the achievement. She made no demands, had her own room, was sensible, tolerably good-looking and had an excellent figure. She more or less loved him, did not require him to love her in return, asked for nothing more than to prepare him a tasty supper, hold his arm on an evening stroll down Euston Road, and spend long hours in bed. Theirs was a casual relationship of convenience around which had grown some affection and a great deal of mutual understanding and tolerance. Nevertheless, they both wanted something better. Many times they had decided to separate, never to see each other again. But they could not hold out against their desire, and perhaps their loneliness too, for longer than a couple of weeks. And so they remained lovers and rather indifferent strangers.

The affair had begun with a late night pick-up the previous summer. Ginsberg was walking along Euston Road from Warren Street, when he saw, strolling along the deserted pavements towards him, balanced comfortably on plump haunches, the silhouette of an attractive young woman. The silhouette materialized into a blonde about whom there was something sufficiently unusual to arouse his curiosity. Normally no woman would be walking slowly on her own down Euston Road, at just before midnight, unless she were a prostitute, and a distinctly proletarian one at that. This solitary stroller, however, had a gentle and averted expression on her face, a thoughtful weariness in her step, which did not belong to the professional street-walker.

They were the only two people on the wide stretch of pavement facing Euston station; in fact there was scarcely a soul in sight, from the traffic lights at Warren Street to the coffee stalls towards King's Cross. They were alone, a man and a woman, walking slowly on stone, in the middle of a vast empty space, surrounded by stone. They were not using this street as a means of going from one place to another; they were here because they did not want to lie alone in bed on a warm summer night. The chances were not one in ten that they might interest each other, but only one in ten that they might not. So reasoned Ginsberg, as he advanced towards his pick-up with an experienced glibness acquired in the army during six years and in four countries.

The pick-up was Lolita, and it had not taken him long to place her, to dispel her fears about talking to a stranger, and momentarily to fall very much in love with her. She was a member of the Gibraltese colony which occupied a number of dilapidated houses in Hampstead Road. They had been evacuated from Gibraltar by the government during the war and more or less forgotten; with innumerable people demanding shipping space, the authorities left the humble Gibraltese at the bottom of the waiting list. No one was more pleased about this than the Gibraltese. In Gibraltar they were poor, members of a tiny, backward community. In London they could earn enough for everything; for meals three or four times a day, for clothes, shoes, cigarettes; and not only for these, but for gay luxuries, cinemas, theatres, concerts, dance halls, all-night cafés, and all sorts of wonderful things.

Lolita had been strictly married in the Spanish fashion, and therefore sheltered from affairs with American soldiers and the like. In the middle of London she had led the life of a peaceful, hard-working young Gibraltese housewife. She cooked, scrubbed, queued, and then spent ten or twelve hours a day at the sewing-machine, doing piece-work. Late at night, the dark, plump, throaty, vivacious Gibralterinas sat at open windows looking out over the unspeakable wilderness of Hampstead Road, and spoke, sang, argued, and shouted furiously in Spanish. Sometimes their voices grew still; someone "touched the guitar", as their language expressed it. Their menfolk, like good Mediterraneans, spent the evening on their own. So it happened that Lolita's husband, an impossibly handsome forty-year-old Spaniard, had several mistresses during their stay in London. With one of these, the owner of a large, prosperous sweet-shop in Birmingham, he went off, leaving Lolita a brief note, saying that he would never return, and would she please leave him alone and not ask him for money? Lolita worked the edge off her grief at the sewing machine, doing twelve, fourteen, fifteen hours a day on piece-work. Now and again, when the Gibralterinas were exchanging their last furious Spanish gossip at open windows, and some dapper working man was lightly "touching the guitar", Lolita went for a stroll on her own. Men spoke to her, taking her for a prostitute; but she still understood little English, she had the good sense that came of innocent domesticity, and they grew impatient and went off.

It was June, the nights were fine and warm, and Ginsberg used to pass late in the evening in front of the row of houses in Hampstead Road. Fat materfamilias, with the rough, placid fecundity of the earth itself, arms folded over immense bosoms resting on the window sills, nodded good evening and smiled down approvingly.

"Lolita! Tu amigo!" they called to one of the top windows, behind which Lolita was still bent over her sewing-machine.

Later, Ginsberg was invited onto landings and passageways and front steps, where groups of Gibraltese spoke passionately and tumultuously about nothing; until Lolita came down, took his arm, and they walked off beneath the gaze and comment of the entire Gibraltese colony.

Until Lolita became his mistress, Ginsberg was delighted with the novelty of this courtship. But afterwards there was nothing to sustain their relations except recrudescent desire. Like a long-married couple, they had nothing to say to each other. They walked straight round from Hampstead Road to Guilford Street, kissed perfunctorily, undressed, and made love with silent concentration and thoroughness. Then they looked at each other with an affectionate tolerance and gratitude, chatted a little, combed each other's hair, and strolled back through the squares smoking cigarettes.

Lolita would have wished to move into Guilford Street a little more effectively, to cook an occasional meal, darn socks, and add a few feminine touches to the bachelor harshness of the flat. But Ginsberg was ashamed to let Bellenger see that he might hanker for the simple domesticity supplied by Lolita. The understanding was that he and Bellenger could do without women, "except for one thing". And though he thought Bellenger's attitude a piece of adolescent bravado, he was nevertheless influenced by it. Ginsberg was also still more ashamed of Lolita's background, which, though it might supply colour for an adventure, an anecdote, made a long-term affair impossible. At the same time he was ashamed of being ashamed and not rising above such petty snob-consciousness.

After a couple of months, such feelings of remorse drove Ginsberg to tell Lolita that they must not meet again. He wanted to make it clear, to himself as well as to her, that theirs was an adventure, the prolonged result of a pick-up. Lolita was quite passive in accepting his decision. She was equally complaisant when, a fortnight later, he wrote to her pleading forgiveness and a resumption of their meetings. The same thing happened three or four times; until they began to accept it as a matter of course, a process of behaviour inevitably resulting from their psychologies, their physical needs, their social disharmony.

On this evening, when Ginsberg had finally knotted his tie to his complete satisfaction, he felt bitterly defeated. He had just come the the end of his longest period of abstention from Lolita since their first meeting. It was over four weeks since he had left Mrs. Chabbers outside the Siguenza in Greek Street, stoked up at the Corney Arms, and ambled along to Hampstead Road for his blonde Gibralterina. That had been a very pleasant evening; suddenly, at the end of it, surfeited with Lolita, he had made the irrevocable resolution never to see her again. And now, here he was once more, treading the old, unsatisfactory path. He had written to her again, apologizing and explaining; in the past she had always come back, without reproach. But would she accept him this time? Some day, surely, she must lose patience? And there were his own obscurer feelings; with Lolita he felt trapped, drawn down into the London slums from which he had come. She had the same warm-hearted vulgarity, the same small-time ambitions and fears as the basters and cutters, the seamstresses and machinists and finishers in those Jewish quarters of the East End whose memory filled him with a sort of homesick horror. In going back to Lolita, he was going back, back, right back. He was thirty; there seemed to be no escape from the endless London slum. Having no other hold on him, it compelled him to sunk back for a woman. One day something would go wrong and Lolita would have a baby, and then he would be really done for. . . .

Yes, reflected Ginsberg, as he dodged through Tolmer

Square, a gloomy, sooty little tombstone of human effort, it is not so easy to get away from oneself. It is not so easy to do what one really wants to do, even when there are no material obstacles in the way, or when they are of slight importance. What was to stop him making that trip to Brazil? Difficulties about money, visas, passage, they did not worry him, they could be overcome. What was to stop him then — *Scamp,* Lolita, Bellenger, his friends in Soho? Bah! And yet. . . it was all very well to exclaim inwardly "Bah!" — he did it automatically; it was absurd to suppose that he, Ivan Ginsberg, the future writer, traveller into the furthest corners of the globe and of the mind and of experience, was going to be held back by this stale old London. But a man must attach himself to something. Perhaps, after all, this was his destiny, to fritter his life away in these mean streets among these ignoble activities, to idle about between wars till the great catastrophe came and cleansed the earth of all its rubbish. What was to stop him from going to Brazil? Nothing but his own sense of failure; but that alone was too strong for him.

If *Scamp* were to succeed, what good would that be? Very little, he now saw. The publication of the magazine would not release him from Lolita, with her odour of dried sweat, from his dependence on Bellenger for any sense of permanency, from his pleasureless round of Soho cafés and pubs. It was necessary to go right away, as far away as possible, to strike out in new directions. His six-year absence from London during the war had deceived him. There were no threads to pick up, there was no new life to knit in with the old. Too much had happened in this city. He did not want to settle down here, to grow into it once again, to share its grim fate. But perhaps, even at thirty, it was too late to start afresh? Perhaps the outer decay which he attributed to London was nothing but a reflection of his own inner decay? Perhaps in the harsh tropic reality of Brazil he would only be plunged more deeply into an appalling failure? All this was possible.

But there was a point beyond which reason and caution were merely cowardice; to stay in London and play the obvious game of becoming a journalist, a literary journalist, a short-story writer, and novelist — to accept with a grin and a shrug Lolita, Bellenger, and the rat-ridden flat in Guilford Street — to know always that a bus-ride away lay the East End, with the memories of his orphaned childhood — all these would be a crime against himself, a denial of the aspirations which gave an individual life its direction, a monstrous piece of self-abuse. He would bring out one number of *Scamp* and then clear off.

But Ginsberg's resolutions veered and pulled at their moorings like so many hydrogen balloons. When he arrived at the Gibraltese colony in Hampstead Road, he was ready to abandon any intangible sense of freedom, any self-esteem, for the familiar, pleasurable routine with Lolita. The buxom Gibraltese housewives were there as usual, their copious bosoms resting on the window-sills of the row of blackened, dilapidated houses. They smiled down from broad, moon-like faces. "Tu amigo, Lolita!" they shouted. For a moment the opulent lines of Lolita's figure, crowned by a blonde mass of hair — the somewhat lined, coarse-skinned and reddish face not distinguishable from below — was silhouetted invitingly at a top window. But instead of waving, and asking him to wait a few minutes till she had tidied up and got ready, Lolita instantly disappeared. Ginsberg was a little disturbed, but waited for her none the less. He entered into conversation with a few young men who were lounging by one of the gates smoking cigarettes. They told him that José was "touching the guitar" on the back steps of the second house, and José was reputedly the best guitar player in the colony. Ginsberg found diminutive, black-moustached José, a midget Adonis, surrounded by a group of children and composedly plucking the strings. His eyes were shut, and the dry notes danced in the dust of the evening air. Ginsberg leaned against the doorway and tried to wait patiently; but he was unsure of himself. He went out into the street again and looked up at Lolita's window. Two fat Gibralterinas on the third floor gossiped to each other from sill to sill. Ginsberg whispered gently upwards. From several windows people watched him; behind the women he caught glimpses of men in shirtsleeves, one with braces hanging down, another in the middle of shaving. Still Lolita did not appear. The women sensed the new situation; they were now neutral, that is to say indifferent and unhelpful.

"Is Lolita up there?" called Ginsberg to the two fat Gibralterinas on the third floor, though he himself had already seen her.

"Don' know," said the fatter of the two. Her heavy jaw, resting on the palm of her hand, remained firm, while the upper part of her face moved up and down as she spoke. Ginsberg drifted uneasily back to José. The dry notes tapped the dust. José's eyes were now open. "Evenin'," he said, and Ginsberg imagined in his voice, too, a certain reserve, a sort of detachment that people have when they sever themselves from somebody who is being destroyed. Back again to the street; Lolita's window was still wide open, a bottle of milk and a jar stood as before on the sill, and Lolita herself remained completely out of sight.

Ginsberg went up to a little black-haired girl who was holding on to some basement railings and listlessly jumping up and down.

"Here," he said, "I want you to do something for me." The battery of watchers was on the alert. They might never have seen Ginsberg before; he was a suspicious stranger. So he was preparing to interfere with little schoolgirls, too, was he? The man who had been shaving stopped to watch, the safety razor motionless against the soaped half of his face.

"Go up to Lolita," said Ginsberg, "and tell her Ivan is here. Tell her that he would like to speak to her. Ask her if he may come up."

He wanted to explain, though what was there to explain? He had long expected this showdown. Yet already, during his brief ordeal, he had rapidly brought up new plans and sketched a new way of life. He would take her to the cinema, buy her little presents. Perhaps. . . no, that was too much. . . he could not, even at this moment, honestly suggest that one day they might marry.

The little girl came down. "She doesn't want to see you."

"What!" He could not picture this new Lolita. He would have liked to catch another glimpse of her, if only to see the expression on her face. The message was a blow, almost a physical blow. His shoulders drooped. He slouched away down Hampstead Road, back to his habitual quarter beyond Warren Street.

Lolita was right, of course, absolutely right. There was nothing with which he could reproach her. And yet he felt bitter. He had trusted her, expected from her certain behaviour. Now the entire year they had spent together was soured, and made worthless by deeply concealed treachery.

The streets behind Tottenham Court Road were at their worst, empty, hot, oppressive. In the little teashop which he frequented, a blowsy domineering waitress stood with one hand resting against the tea-urn; beneath her armpit was a great rent in her shabby yellow blouse, and through it a glimpse of hair. A stubble-chinned Cypriot sat in the corner, so still, so resigned, that he might have been a dummy inserted as part of the décor. Outside the clouds gathered for a storm. Soho had never seemed so rotten. Ginsberg went to the lavatory. In the neighbouring backyard, behind a restaurant, a couple of diseased chickens pecked lackadaisically at the overflow from the kitchen. An indescribable stink of waste food and stale urine filled the tiny space between high black walls. Everywhere decay; truly a wasteland; without love, even without the mixed, dullish feeling he had shared with Lolita, his familiar environment was nothing but a desert, an ugly, unhealthy desert half destroyed by war and neglect.

A would-be Satanic young man, with deep black rings under his eyes had meanwhile arrived in the café. Penshaw by name, he manufactured divans without a licence and employed half the bums in Charlotte Street. Ivan had once worked for him as a traveller, but found the experience too nerve-racking and gave up the job after the first day. Penshaw smiled at Ivan, as though they shared a conspiracy of cynicism.

"'Lo," said Penshaw, grinning sardonically. "How's the magazine?"

"Oh Christ!" said Ginsberg. The last thing in the world he wanted to speak about just then was *Scamp.*

"Business on the up and up? I hear you're taking on staff," Penshaw chuckled.

"Who's that?"

"Kroganin."

Ginsberg flapped his hand down. "Bah!" In the first instance, his gesture implied, any piece of news about *Scamp* was false, any statement a lie. Between him and Penshaw it was understood that nothing could be what it appeared to be, that Soho was phoney right through.

"Heard the news?" said Penshaw.

"What?"

"About Storringham. Got eighteen months."

"I didn't know he was pinched. What for?"

"Oh, his perfume racket. They wanted him for a lot of things. But that's all they could hang on him. No licence, non-payment of tax — it came to about ten thousand, I think — buying stolen goods and Christ alone knows what."

"Well, well. Poor old Storringham. They'll get *you* one of these days."

"Gah, nerts! There's nothing they can pin on me, nothing. I've got it all taped. There's not a President of the Board of Trade who's been able to stop the divan racket in Charlotte Street; that's one thing all the bloody totalitarian governments put together can't do. Come an' 'ave a drink?"

"No, I'm going. Thanks all the same."

Ginsberg wandered gloomily homewards. On the other side of Tottenham Court Road, the streets were clean and sad, empty of people. The clouds hung ever blacker and heavier in the sky, but no rain fell. In the square, the dark green leaves of the trees were swollen with pap.

Unwilling to go home, Ginsberg looked in at the Ex-Students' Club. The white-haired, professionally cheerful spinster at the hall desk smiled energetically as he passed, and then returned to *The Times* crossword, wondering if she had ever seen him before and whether he was a member. In the ping-pong room, an Indian was playing with a Chinese, three Africans looked on. The late summer night had almost fallen, but the lounge was unlit. Several Indians sat with girls on settees; one or two whispered and giggled, but most couples lay back in silence, close together, watching the sky through tall windows. By one of the windows, in the last fading grey light of the day, a game of chess was being played. Ginsberg strolled over quietly, almost on tiptoe — the atmosphere of the lounge was like that of the innermost sanctuary of some infinitely holy place of worship. One of the players, a middle-aged woman wearing a beret, lifted her head and peered at Ginsberg over her spectacles.

"Ah, the master!" she whispered. Ginsberg was far and away the best player in the club, and was indeed known only to the chess section, but he never troubled to play. Repetitive amateur games had no interest for him. He appraised the game in an instant, saw how futile it was, and made to turn away.

"How's the magazine?" whispered the woman.

Ginsberg shrugged his shoulders, in a gesture that indicated nothing whatsoever except his utter boredom. Curse the magazine! He sat down in an armchair and strained his eyes to read the cartoon captions in an old copy of *Punch*. Giving it up, he lay back, as the lounge sank into complete darkness. It occurred to him that the pleasanter sort of death might be something like this. Things grew quieter and quieter, dimmer and dimmer, till you floated away in darkness and silence and eternity, feeling nothing, thinking nothing, a vague aura of nothing floating in a spaceless, timeless infinity of nothing. . . .

The religious atmosphere of the lounge was broken by the sound of a violent argument in the hall. Only one voice seemed to be taking part in the argument. It grew louder and louder as it approached the door, then it shut up. The door was opened, and distinguishing a suggestion of white beard and white hair in the darkness, Ginsberg realized that the argument had only been Kroganin. Kroganin had been passing the time of day with someone in the hall.

Accustomed to thundering from the rostra — possibly against vociferous opposition — at Eastern European revolutionary meetings in the 'twenties, Kroganin could not help roaring. His most hushed murmur was a loud boom. If he wished to raise his voice and emphasize a point — and there was never a man more inclined to emphasize a point — the volume of sound increased in geometrical progression. Hence the paradox of his status at the University Club — where the silence was normally broken only by the squeaking of shoes on highly polished floors — Kroganin was greatly liked, yet entirely shunned.

He held the door open. A light in the hall faintly illuminated the lounge. "Ach," said Kroganin, for no obvious reason other than a general and long-matured disgust with life. As he said it, he sucked in one cheek and chewed. No regular member of the club would speak to him, but to Kroganin's delight Ginsberg was caught in the faint beam of light from the door.

"Therre you urrr, my good sirrr," roared Kroganin. He continued, with his charming, wry smile: "Ach, but you urr lucky man! Editorr magazine, securre position, no worries, rrrelaxes in lounge Ex-Students' Club considering editorrial policy." To show that he was joking, Kroganin clucked and shook his head from side to side several times, and smiled as broadly as he could. Still not sure whether he had made his intentions quite clear, he added: "You rrrealize I am joking, of courrse!" Then, more seriously, he added: "What is news prrrogrress magazine?"

The peaceful couples on the settees, the chess players sunk finally and irrevocably to rest, chin on hand, consciousness gone, were brought to indignant life by Kroganin. Damn the man; it was not the first time he had done it, not the first hundred times; they would raise the matter at the next meeting. It had to stop — There might have been an unpleasant scene, with someone calling out: "For heaven's sake please do shut up Mr. Kroganin!" But a voice called from the door, over Kroganin's head: "Closing time, we're closing now."

In Gordon Square, Kroganin continued, roaring and thundering like a pneumatic drill. "I was to-day Brrritish Council. I tell them I am assistant editorr magazine. Mr. Rrruperrtson — do you by any chunz gnaw him?"

"No, I'm afraid not."

"Mr. Rrruperrtson, verrry churrrming men, took me lunch Clerrridges. Verrry nize lunch, verrry nize vine, verrry nize cigurrr, verrry nize chet, but no chop!"

"Ay?"

"No jawp. Jawb, ach! Job."

"Oh, hard luck."

"Sometimes I sink it is perrhaps better put my hat in guess oven," Kroganin said good-humouredly, and almost quietly, as though all he had said hitherto was for the sake of appearances, and now he was expressing a sincere, sober opinion.

"Oh, I shouldn't do that."

"You sink nought?"

"For our sakes not. Think how we should all miss you. Life is bleak enough as it is. Without you it would be infinitely bleaker."

"But I hev only two shilling in pocket. I will sturrrve. Ach!"

Kroganin dealt — though only verbally — in the stark realistic terms of Siberia and the plains of Turkestan. There were no half measures. If you had no money, you starved. Once, for instance, Ginsberg had mentioned to Kroganin that he had considered emigrating to Brazil.

"What do you think of the idea?" he had asked.

"It iss quite simple, sirrr."

"Really?"

"Quite simple. You will sturrrve."

"But —"

"Ach! But rrreally! I tell you, it iss quite simple. In Brruzeel, *orrr* you urrr millionairre, *orrr* you sturrrve."

If Kroganin's friends were at all hesitant about buying him a meal or a drink, he used the same stark arguments.

"If I donot have drrrink and meal beforre nightfall, I die of hungerr and thirrrst."

So it was now. Kroganin reflected to himself "Ach!" once again. He sucked in one cheek in a characteristic mannerism and chewed it vigorously. His ordinary expression was a frown of theatrical ferocity. The only other expressions of which his face was capable were expostulatory impatience and the sunniest good humour. He switched rapidly from one to the other. Flashing back momentarily to theatrical ferocity, he returned to good humour.

"It iss verrry nize of you, kind sirrr," he repeated. "I do not want put hat in guess oven, though perrhaps it iss betterr. Ach. Can you by any chunz lend me fife pop. If you hev not got it, police say so. But rrrrreally! Police say so!"

Ginsberg hesitated, and was lost. He would have to lend Kroganin something; the question was, how much? He rummaged in his pocket, feeling what coins were there.

"I'll see how much I've got."

"Gnaw, but, police say so —"

"I can manage half-a-crown. Will that be all right?"

"Urrr you surre you can sparrre it? But rrreally, urrr you? But rrrreally — It iss verrry nize off you, kind sirrr. Sank you verrry much. It isss verrry nize off you. You sink it iss betterr nought put hat in guess oven then?"

"Definitely."

"Sank you. Good night."

They parted in Southampton Row. A few drops of rain had fallen. Suddenly the storm broke. Torrents and sheets of water gushed from the sky with tropical violence. In a moment Ginsberg was soaked to the skin. He did not trouble to hurry; but as wet as though he had plunged into a swimming bath, squelched up Tavistock Place, trod in a flooded gutter, and whistled despondently the tune which José had been playing on the guitar.

CHAPTER XIII

HITHERTO THE PROGRESS of *Scamp* had been desultory, meandering, and rather hopeless. But nothing decisive had occurred, one way or the other. Now, some three months after its inception, there began a steep and unmistakable fall.

Scamp was all along an idea with no reality behind it. But there is no cause for excessive derision. A man may count himself a millionaire or the dictator of an empire. Yet what is he, what has he? He is a naked mortal, who shivers when he is cold, shrieks when he is hurt, and grumbles when he does not get what he wants. And what happens if the bank refuses to accept his cheque? If the soldier at the gate refuses to salute? If the strong arm men refuse to beat up his enemies? The idea that he is a millionaire or dictator quickly disintegrates. . . . Everything human is frail, temporary, and illusory. *Scamp* was an extreme instance of this general truth.

Had it been blessed, had it received the grace of God, by which all things exist, its history would of course have been very different. The writers of articles celebrating its centenary would have insisted on the audacious vision of its founder and editor, the pertinacity of its assistant editor, the enterprise and workmanlike resource of Spiffhorn and Trunt, the munificence of Mrs. Chabbers, arising from her self-sacrificing love and generosity, and on the colourful society of Soho and Bloomsbury which was its background and inspiration.

But fate or God willed otherwise. Spiffhorn and Trunt, for instance, might well have shown enterprise and workmenlike resource, and it might well have paid them to do so, as Ginsberg suggested. But they showed nothing of the sort, they were totally unreliable, and they are now both working as simple compositors for a large firm in Walworth Road.

Spiffhorn had told Ginsberg that the printing of five thousand copies of *Scamp* would cost seventy-one pounds. It had seemed too good to be true; but Ginsberg waited for the written confirmation of Spiffhorn's optimistic estimate before bothering his head any further with this tedious subject. Absorbed in the editorial side of *Scamp,* in his Soho and Bloomsbury round, in his occasional inner debates about going to Brazil, or at any rate leaving London, in his introspections and resolutions and their effect on his amatory life — absorbed, in other words, in the same activities and unfinished projects with which he had occupied previous years, he let several weeks pass without worrying very much about Spiffhorn's estimate. Spiffhorn, Ginsberg felt, might be mistaken in detail; he might be twenty or thirty or even fifty pounds out, but basically the man was sound. If he said he would send in an estimate, he would send it in. He might be three, four, or five weeks late, but he could be relied on to write some time. And if he said he would print the magazine, then he would print it. There might be difficulties, delays, alterations, frustrations, but there was no doubt in Ginsberg's mind that Spiffhorn could ultimately be relied on to print *Scamp*. It never occurred to him that there were other people, ordinary, unpretentious, uninteresting people, who were as completely and breathtakingly unreliable as he himself and his acquaintances. Anyway, behind Spiffhorn stood Trunt. And if ever a man had his feet firmly planted on London asphalt, that man was Trunt.

But weeks had passed; no letter had arrived from Spiffhorn and Trunt. Ginsberg went down to Wandsworth one afternoon. Superficially nothing had changed. Spiffhorn was alone when Ginsberg arrived, but in a moment he was joined by Trunt. They leaned on opposite corners of the mantelpiece. They looked optimistic and pessimistic respectively. Perhaps Spiffhorn was a shade less optimistic and Trunt a shade more pessimistic? It was difficult to say. More exactly, Spiffhorn was a shade less enthusiastic, rather than less optimistic. Why? What was wrong. Did he not *want* business? Was not Ginsberg's money as good as the next man's? He was not to know that so far, in actual negotiable cash or available credit, there was no money. The threadbare sports jacket? The devitalized clothes? That was nothing — clothes rationing, no coupons; in any case, many a business man, particularly in publishing and journalism, did not trouble about his appearance. No, it was all very puzzling and rather disquieting.

"Ah," said Spiffhorn, "I was just going to write to you."

Yes, he said, he had just been on the point of writing. There, he pointed out, on the mantelpiece, lay the sheet of paper on which he was going to write. Beside it lay the pen and ink with which he was going to write; further along, the envelope in which the letter was to be enclosed and the stamps which were to supply the necessary postage. Everything was ready, insisted Spiffhorn, Ginsberg could see for himself.

That Spiffhorn should, after so many weeks delay, be just on the point of writing at the very moment when Ivan entered the workshop was an extraordinary coincidence. It did not occur to Ginsberg not to believe him. Life would be intolerable if one did not believe everything one was told unless there was good reason to think otherwise. Frequently a liar himself, Ginsberg automatically assumed others told the truth.

Oh, and there had been a mistake in the estimate, added Spiffhorn. The cost would not be seventy-one pounds, but a hundred and fifty-eight. He had got his working wrong. He seized on a piece of paper, quickly scribbled a few rows of figures, altered a figure here and there, crossed out the whole lot, did it all again, and showed the result to Ivan — exactly a hundred and fifty-eight pounds.

"But," said Spiffhorn triumphantly, "if we cut out the overtime, that'll knock nine pounds off the expenses. A hundred and forty-nine pounds, see. Nine pounds less.

That'll be a lot cheaper, see, without the overtime."

"Oh yes, bound to be," said Trunt. Even he conceded this. "Stands to reason, if you cut out the overtime. Bound to be less."

Ginsberg was at once startled and relieved; startled at the vast increase in the estimate, relieved to find the cause of Spiffhorn's slight hesitancy. Obviously the man had been worried about his mistake in calculation, Perhaps that had subconsciously made him forget to write. Now all that was past. They were on the right road, the straight road, the royal road. . . . The only major obstacle yet to be surmounted was Mrs. Chabbers.

A hundred and fifty pounds was of course a lot of money, but it would not prevent at least one number of *Scamp* appearing. And Ginsberg's ambition was now limited to one number. It was not so much that he wanted to see that number, as that he wanted to see the last of it. It was not so much that his life would be, as he had at first confidently expected, broadened, revivified, and redirected by the appearance of *Scamp,* as that it would be intolerable if he could not get the wretched business off his hands and done with once for all, and so leave his energies free to take the future boldly and force it into some worthy mould — a new mould, a really new mould!

Ginsberg assured Spiffhorn that the revised estimate was quite all right by him; he fully understood and he was grateful. Payment would still be in advance, the whole of it, if Spiffhorn wished, on the day the manuscripts were handed in. So a new arrangement was reached, confidence seemingly re-established; and for the second time Ginsberg left Spiffhorn and Trunt's workshop, with its solitary machine standing in state in the centre of an empty floor, feeling that a major business had been safely concluded. For the second time he asked Spiffhorn, with complete confidence and trust, to confirm their understanding in writing.

Trunt he was never to see again; and Spiffhorn only once, for a second, in the Lushamor Palais de Danse.

On that bright, fresh April morning when *Scamp* had been conceived — ah! how distant it was, with its spring flowers, its breezy sunshine, the light symmetrical mass of Senate House towering gracefully towards a blue gap in the sky, and its sense of renewal, its urge to leap forward nimbly and gaily into yet another summer of youth and hope — on that spring morning three elements had appeared necessary for the founding of a magazine. They were: money, a printer, and contributors. A clever man, it had seemed, might make any one of these elements conjure up the other two. For instance, contributors alone, if they were really outstanding, would undoubtedly attract money; and money, if there was enough of it, would attract a printer.

With this thought in mind, Ginsberg had put in two or three weeks quite hard work writing letters to prominent intellectuals, begging, not without a certain dignity, for contributions. "Speculative thought alone," he emphasized, "offers some hope for the future. Where no course of action has yet been discovered which will satisfy the urgent needs of our time, we must at least search, and search courageously, for that hidden path. *Scamp,* a magazine for the younger generation, invites contributions that are lively, controversial, and informative. . . Payment is at the rate of one guinea per thousand words." These letters, with variations designed to appeal to individual celebrities, had gone out to Einstein and Blum — Ginsberg had considered writing to Stalin, but eventually turned down the idea — Idris Berwyn, G.D. Criesley, I.N. Horster, Hughie McPrice, John Horweil, Alfred Boemser, the Rajah of Katakanak, and a score of others.

Most of the intellectuals and celebrities had not troubled to reply; while of those that replied, the majority simply sent ten word regrets that they were unable to contribute. G.D. Criesley, in his friendly, schoolmasterly way, advised Ginsberg to give up the idea. "Believe me," he wrote, "you require a lot of capital to do this sort of thing well, and if it is not done well, it is not worth doing at all." The letter addressed to Alfred Boemser came back unopened, after having been forwarded by air-mail to half a dozen addresses in four continents and failed to reach him.

Katakanak, it so happened, a Pacific island the size of Switzerland, and owned by the Lemills family as a private estate for two hundred years, had been quietly annexed to the British Empire one weekend. The occasion had provoked a few letters to the press, a question in Parliament, and a letter of sympathetic indignation from Ginsberg, in his capacity as editor of *Scamp,* to the Rajah of Katakanak. The Rajah of Katakanak, alias Stevie Lemills, while regretting that his more or less royal position prevented him from contributing to Ginsberg's magazine, as invited, enclosed a cheque for a guinea. So Scamp Publications received its first and — to anticipate — only cheque — "As a token of appreciation for the sympathy extended to Katakanak; and to help your publication in its fight for Katakanak independence and freedom everywhere."

The most stimulating and encouraging of the replies was from Idris Berwyn in the Cabinet. "Dear Ivan," it began, and was signed: "With very best wishes, Idris." Go right ahead, was the gist of Berwyn's message; don't be discouraged. But Ivan would understand, added Berwyn, that as a member of the Cabinet he himself could not contribute. Having received this note, Ginsberg would willingly have followed Berwyn's political flag to the end of the earth. He had always been an admirer of Berwyn, who had for years enlivened Fleet Street and the House of Commons with his outspokenness. Now, though Berwyn sat in the same Cabinet as Prudence Featherleigh and Honest Levin, Ginsberg's admiration was unlimited. He made up his mind that the first number of *Scamp* would headline Berwyn as the hope of progressive England, the man for the prime-ministership.

However, as far as contributors were concerned, Ginsberg could not claim any great success. It was true, he had a story by Angus Sternforth Simms. But the story was only a reprint, and Angus Sternforth Simms, the lion of Soho, was merely a highly successful second-rater in the world at large. The cover, again, was to be by Sophie Maslan. But could Sophie be trusted to have anything ready by a given date? And might she not suddenly deny ever having promised to do it? Besides, Sophie Maslan, a name to be bandied about in the 'twenties along with the heroes of Chelsea and Montparnasse, was now almost forgotten. People no longer point her out in the Fitzroy or the Corney Arms. And as for Douglas Vanner, his was decidedly a slight, delicate talent which would appeal to his friends alone.

This was not to disparage the quality of the contributions accepted. They all appeared to Ginsberg excellent, especially the naïve, yet startling story from Ireland by young Kathleen O'Flanagan. But commercially their value was small. Unknown contributors introduced by an unknown editor were not going to draw out capital and a printer.

"Six weeks time." Those were the words which Mrs. Chabbers, in her period cottage up in Hampstead Lane, found herself repeating apprehensively. It was not that the decision which she had promised to make was in itself so important. A risky investment of two or three hundred pounds would not greatly affect her finances; though, living on income derived from a fixed capital, she had to watch carefully over such sums of money. It was rather that she dreaded having to come to a decision about anything, particularly at a given date. She tried going away to Cardiff for a weekend, staying at the Royal Welsh Hotel, and later she spent three days at the Worcester County Hotel in Worcester. But these provided only respites from her preoccupations.

She had said, "In six weeks time", quite hastily and unthinkingly, simply in order to avoid immediate questions. But the six weeks drew inexorably to a close.

Meanwhile, a new factor, or rather a whole host of new factors, had entered the situation. The first of these new factors was the beginning of an urge to give up Ginsberg entirely. His rudeness after their dinner at the Siguenza was responsible for such an unprecedented notion. She had been so shocked by the abrupt farewell on the pavement in Greek Street — especially after her generosity in the matter of dinner and wine — that she began to reconsider in their entirety her relations with Ginsberg. She remembered a hundred other rudenesses and humiliations. He had taken so much — money, presents, meals, drinks, cigarettes — and given her literally nothing, not even at Christmas. And ten shillings an hour, when you came to think of it, was a lot to charge for a Russian lesson; the Twentieth Century School of Russian charged only seven and six, Professor Lezhnitsky only five shillings, and he was a very charming old gentleman, too.

Having once begun a revaluation of Ginsberg, she adduced all his peculiarities as faults. What had previously rendered him interesting, out of the ordinary, enigmatic, now made him appear an ill-bred boor. A man of his standing, a B.A. and a lecturer at the Literary Institute, leading such a life! That filthy flat! She had once peeped into the kitchen, and heaven help us, you never saw such a mess in your life — there was a bath in it black with dirt, there were pails of refuse overflowing and filling up an entire corner, there was dirty crockery weeks old lying about the floor, and she was sure she had seen a frightful animal, larger than a mouse and smaller than a cat, shoot out from under the gas stove and dive down a great hole with rotting edges by one of the water pipes. He himself was clean and frightfully particular, she had noticed that, but he hadn't once changed that shabby sports jacket during all the eighteen months she had known him. It was no use talking about not having money — he could get money soon enough if he worked. He wanted to have his time free for writing, did he? Well, if he was so marvellous, why wasn't he famous and rich?

She had read in the papers about people getting fifty pounds just for one short story — Ginsberg couldn't get fifty pence for his! Why couldn't he be ordinary, like other people? Not *too* ordinary, not like anybody — she didn't believe in going down to other people's level — but, well, like herself, for instance? He thought himself too good for her — well he wasn't! So there!

Such was the defiance which hid in the recesses of Mrs. Chabbers' mind. Outwardly she was just the same, she could not help herself, nervous, giggly, babbling. But within, conflicting streams of emotion frothed and bubbled. Rising defiance and steady caution met habitual deference, admiration and — this was the most incalculable and disconcerting current of all — a wilful little eddy of desire.

Her recent aversion demanded a complete break. Caution strongly advised her against parting with three hundred pounds. She had never been sure of Ginsberg's financial honesty, and she was now even less sure. She had no proof that the whole magazine idea was not an elaborate fraud to get her to part with a few hundred pounds. He had promised to show her an estimate from the printers; where was it? He *had* shown her a letter purporting to come from Idris Berwyn, but could it be genuine? Of course, she had no reason for disbelieving him, and it was absurd to think of a lecturer at the Literary Institute being a swindler. On the other hand, she had no reason for believing him, and she knew nothing of his background. Habitual deference and admiration — these were responsible for her actual behaviour during the six weeks, which was as docile and fussily attentive as ever; but there was no strength behind them. It was her frustrated but persistent desire, that nagging, dangerous, indestructible, twisting, crawling, secret, debasing, maddening, terrifying little traitor, which in the last resort prevented defiance and caution together from getting rid of Ginsberg.

Ginsberg, with his long, black hair, his disillusioned eye,

his blue chin, his sardonic expression, was associated in her mind with sex. She could not have said why. Perhaps it was because he was a teacher, and her earliest, dismal sexual experience had been acquired at the age of thirteen from her elderly music teacher. Whatever the reason, from the very first time she had set eyes on him at the Literary Institute, he had started appearing in the dreams which she had every night, when he regularly swooped on her, bore her down with savage insistence, and ravished her. It seemed absurd, on seeing him once again in waking life, to suppose that he was unaware of what had happened the previous night in her dream. That was why she so frequently and inexplicably blushed the colour of beetroot in Ginsberg's presence. There were times when, unmistakably, that bright, bland, and thoughtful eye of his held hers for a moment, and he seemed to know perfectly well every detail of her dreams. Yet he remained quite indifferent, neither reproving nor in the slightest bit interested. She could not help comparing him with her ex-husband — she shuddered at the thought of those ten years of fuss and fumbling and moralizing — and even with Jim. Jim was a dear, of course, but the hot, giggling, gasping battles she fought with him on the sofa, and which he always lost, made him appear an excited child, for all his forty-two years, beside Ginsberg.

She had to admit, however, that so far Ginsberg had given her not the slightest encouragement. If she so much as laid her hand on his, he snatched it away as though he had been stung. And sometimes she just longed to snuggle up to him on the park bench and feel his protective bulk beside her; but he edged along to the other side of the bench, or sat so that the wretched iron bar in the centre separated them. Was she so ugly, so revolting? Surely she wasn't too bad, and Ginsberg was nothing to write home about either. No doubt he thought of her as middle-aged, but did he know she was only thirty-nine? Why, she was still in her thirties, and he was just about in his thirties, too, so there was scarcely any difference between them. Plenty of men thought her attractive; why was he so standoffish?

It was a fact that Mrs. Chabbers had many suitors, though none under forty. To some of the elderly and lonely professional men, business men, and commercial travellers who made her acquaintance in first class carriages, hotel lounges, London parks, whist drives, and the like, nothing appeared more desirable than a rich, red-faced, healthy-looking, giggly, sporty, talkative, forty-year-old divorcée (a widow might have been even better). The most constant of these suitors was Jim, a solicitor from Lincoln, her home town. She had almost married Jim in the first place, instead of her husband. Jim was still a bachelor, and his feeling towards her had remained constant. After the divorce he had resumed his suit. During his frequent visits to London they wrestled and struggled on the large sofa in Mrs. Chabbers' drawing room. From these bouts they rose, with aching heads and parched throats, their dress disarranged, their cheeks flushed, their temples throbbing, and nothing accomplished.

"There!" Mrs. Chabbers would say triumphantly, as though she had achieved some magnificent end. "You shan't." She giggled hysterically. "You see! You can't get the better of me!"

"Oh, shan't I!" said Jim; and then, more seriously: "Well, why don't you marry me then?"

"You must give me time. I won't be rushed. I must have time to think."

She was now in her fourth year of thinking. Jim was as constant and ineffectually aggressive as ever. Meanwhile, as friend and solicitor, he handled more and more of her investments. In that field, at any rate, he had control over her. It would be very difficult for Mrs. Chabbers to sell two or three hundred pounds' worth of shares without Jim knowing. And she did not want Jim to know about Ginsberg. The two belonged to quite separate compartments of her life. Jim belonged to slow, solid, sober Lincoln, where her father had been known and respected, where she herself had deep roots. Ginsberg belonged to the strange pressures and lonely, arid wastes of time in London, to the nervousness and the obsessions which had gripped her increasingly since her marriage. With Ginsberg she might at times have thought of starting a new, rather distinguished and vivid life abroad, in the Bahamas, South Africa, the Riviera; but essentially he was someone to be worked out of her system. While Jim would always be there; he was something permanent, like Lincoln, like Hampstead Lane, like her investments.

The weeks passed, and Mrs. Chabbers found herself no nearer to a final resolution of her inner conflict. But she hit upon a characteristic temporary solution. Ginsberg had asked for three hundred pounds with which to bring out his magazine, two hundred pounds at the very least. She decided to let him have forty pounds. Why forty pounds? Well, for one thing forty pounds could be drawn from her banking account without Jim knowing. For another, forty pounds was not so large a sum as to be really worrying if Ginsberg turned out to be some kind of obscure confidence trickster. And thirdly, the forty pounds would help her to reach a final decision. If Ginsberg behaved a little more affectionately, in such a way as to indicate that there was some future in their relationship, then more money would be invested in the magazine. If, on the other hand, after receiving such a substantial sum as forty pounds, he continued to ignore her, to treat her as though she were a rather distasteful half-wit, then she would throw him over entirely.

Mrs. Chabbers never really seriously considered the practical connection between any money she supplied and the possible appearance of *Scamp*. Her own motives were so confused, partial, hesitant, jumpy, that she saw the whole scheme as a vague, indeterminate idea; nothing so definite as so many thousand copies of a magazine, each containing so many pages of such and such a size, the whole requiring such and such a sum of money. If two hundred pounds would finance a magazine, then forty pounds would do something or other, she wasn't quite sure what.

Meanwhile, the weather was fine, and she spent a great deal of time gardening, sometimes in the small front garden, but usually in the large one at the back, with its lawn, its pond, its creepers, and the clump of bushes and trees at the end. She was happiest gardening in the morning, when the night, with its dreams, its worries, its twistings and turnings, was quite forgotten. By lunch-time she was already restless; after tea her private torment began.

Sometimes, working in the front garden, she noticed a rather shabby saloon car parked at the end of Hampstead Lane, with its driver, she might almost have fancied, staring at her. Although normally a nervous person, she attached no importance to the saloon car and its occupant. There were plenty of people about — the milkman, the postman, errand boys, Miss Lint next door; the sun was shining, there was nothing to worry about till lunch-time. After a few days, if she had been asked to design a painting of Hampstead Lane, she would undoubtedly have suggested including a rather shabby saloon car at the lower end. It was appropriate, it fitted in. So quickly does the mind become accustomed to rearrangements of old scenes. On the afternoons when Mrs. Chabbers left the house after lunch, as she usually did, the car drove off to a telephone box by the Heath, and the driver put through a call to Shoreditch.

CHAPTER XIV

GINSBERG, like the soaked survivor of a shipwreck, was washed up in Guilford Street after having left Kroganin. He flung all his sodden clothes into a corner of the joint kitchen-cum-bathroom, jumped almost a foot in the air as a rat shot past him to the dark foul, cobwebby space under the bath and sink which was its headquarters, exploded the geyser, and set the bath going.

The inside of the bath was in two main colours. The top few inches were more or less white; the remainder was a greyish black. Bellenger maintained that this was the actual colour of the bath, and that the paint had come off. Ginsberg said that the greyish black colouring was dirt, and to prove his point once took a scrubbing brush and, by working away for ten minutes at a narrow strip, disclosed the white enamel beneath. However, Bellenger remained unconvinced. In any case, as they both agreed, it was pointless cleaning the bath up or even painting it, because Bellenger would undoubtedly filthy it again as quickly as was humanly possible. Bellenger never emptied a bath; the dirty water was left standing for hours or days. Also, if Bellenger ever took it into his head to do any washing up, into the bath went plates, saucepans, frying pans, ashtrays. The geyser was exploded, the scalding water thundered down, Bellenger cleaned two saucers and a spoon, and the remainder of the unholy mess was left to stew. This was the bath into which Ginsberg lowered himself gingerly, after having wiped away the most recent layer of dust and scum and poured in several tablespoonfuls of disinfectant.

He was thinking at one and the same time about Lolita and the heavy noises under the bath. The ponderousness, the massive effect of those noises was extraordinary. It was scarcely credible that a colony of even the largest rats could move over the floor-boards and against the wall with such beefy thuds. When all was said and done, he could not get used to the rats. Mice had been different. In the summer there had been hundreds of them. He and Bellenger had not realized how many till they opened one of the dresser drawers and found it entirely covered with tiny black oval-shaped fragments.

"What on earth can they be?"

And then it had dawned on them — those black oval-shaped fragments were the thousands of droppings left by hundreds of well-fed mice. But mice, at least, had a certain fear of human beings; some people even liked the abominable vermin. One could accommodate oneself to their presence in the flat. Ginsberg had therefore stored all his food in a suitcase in his own room, and let it go at that. Bellenger — who was really delighted with the mice — left a broken mouse-trap about, in which one day a dead mouse was actually found, though it must presumably have died a natural death.

At the beginning of the summer the mice disappeared, suddenly, mysteriously. One day they were there, the next day they were gone. It was eerie at first. Where previously the flat had been full of squeaking, scamperings, scurryings, loud gnawing and sawings, little thuds and, a general hurly-burly of activity, it was now silent. Ginsberg felt perturbed. Where had they all got to? Were they ill? Were they quietly breeding in their thousands? An old neighbour and occasional visitor, Dr. Patteoti, teacher of Italian, said they had gone off to Brunswick Square for the summer. He himself had seen them there. Food was left about again and was untouched, unnibbled; dishcloths remained unholed, newspapers were no longer discovered in tatters. Bellenger, who had never really minded having his food crawled over and nibbled by mice, and who had only locked away a token packet of margarine or hunk of cheese out of deference to Ginsberg, left his entire week's rations unashamedly on the kitchen table.

A few weeks after the mice left, there were a number of disappearances from this pile of food, noticeable disappearances of quite solid items — a loaf of bread, a pound of carrots, a half-pound of margarine. They vanished without a trace. There was no question of their having been taken by mice; no crumb, no shred of paper, no trail indicated such a possibility. Bellenger and Ginsberg each thought that the other was playing a practical joke. A towel disappeared, a couple of dishcloths, a bar of soap, a whole *Daily Telegraph,* a pound of potatoes.

The mystery was solved when the first rat was seen, and that explained also why the mice had gone. The hordes of mice had been pushed out by the rats, large, powerful rats with massive appetites and unlimited energy. A couple of these apparently found no difficulty at all in carrying a loaf of bread under the bath and down one of their broad holes. The towels and dishcloths were recovered more or less undamaged from a hiding-place under the sink; though what the rats wanted with the *Daily Telegraph,* when they had all Bellenger's rations at their disposal, was never explained. And another fact about them which puzzled Ginsberg was the noise they made. He lay in bed at night and listened. The scraping of chairs, the battering against walls, the creaking of floorboards, the occasional clashing of crockery, the steady thudding of heavy objects or beings dropping from some height to the floor — all this nerve-racking din was inexplicable. How could a mere colony of rats make it? If there were half a dozen of them in the kitchen at the same time, all busily shifting potatoes and carrots and bread down their hole, and doing it very noisily, and bumping into chairs and tablelegs in the process, that would not explain the busy marching and tramping and prowling all through the night. And if he seized a walking stick and old tennis racket, crept on to the landing, and flew into the kitchen, hoping to beat one to death, there was not a rat in sight; there was not even to be heard the last echo of one scurrying down a hole. It was as though, the moment he touched the door handle, every rat in the room instantaneously vanished, without a sound, without a trace. Yet if, forgetting all about them, he walked noisily and carelessly into the kitchen, then, sure enough, a rat would bolt from under his very legs and another would dash out from under the gas stove and shoot down the hole.

Or now, for instance, while he was lying in the bath, splashing water and singing — not because he felt cheerful, but in order to warn them that there was a human being in the room and they must keep down their hole — were they afraid? Did they lie still? They scampered about merrily underneath, having a run, exercizing themselves, working up an appetite; because soon it would be midnight, and they would be able to feed, feed to their heart's content, on Bellenger's rations, on the bucket of waste, on the congealed fat in the frying-pan, and on all the odds and ends that were lying about the kitchen.

Yes, there was much to mystify one. There was he, Ivan Ginsberg, a man of thirty, a man of some experience, a man of some education, and he understood so little, so very, very little. . . . He did not understand these rats, certainly; he did not understand why they should be hurrying about even now underneath the bath, how they could be so brazen, not showing — even for the sake of form — any respect for the noise he was making in order to frighten them into silence. He did not understand how to get rid of them; as long as he stayed in Guilford Street he had to live with them; there could be no divorce, no separation, no legal redress. That man from the town hall was coming again in a few days, but the man himself knew that his traps and poisons were quite useless. . . . No, he did not understand this rat question at all. And he did not understand other, deeper things, if not more immediately urgent, at any rate altogether more fundamental and significant.

Lolita, for instance; why had she refused to see him? What had she really been thinking this last year, during the long silences when they walked through the squares smoking cigarettes, or when they lay in bed, staring out of the window, each lost in thought? Common sense told Ginsberg that there was no mystery, that Lolita had grown tired of his unemotional routine lovemaking, in which nothing could disguise his boredom with her as anything other than a female body. She had either made up her mind quite deliberately, or a new lover had made it up for her. In any case, she, like most people — but unlike himself — having taken a decision, was capable of sticking to it; word and thought bore a direct relation to deed. The only cause for wonder was that she had not made this particular decision months before. And yet, another part of him argued, she at least owed him an explanation — no, not an explanation, but an announcement, a sentence, a phrase, a *word* of farewell.

This last argument was unanswerable. They had always been polite to each other; and while Lolita had been affectionate, Ginsberg too had shown all the kindness and consideration possible without feigning an interest he did not feel or wasting money on entertainments that neither really wanted. Not once had they spoken to each other in anger. Not once had there been any apparent conflict of will, for his had always been accepted by both. And now. . . this!

There must be some mistake. Ginsberg thumped the side of the bath with conviction six times: *there must be some mis-take!* A sharp, heavy movement of rat under the bath was followed by an extraordinary silence. Those six thumps had momentarily impressed the rats, an achievement which no amount of singing and splashing could have accomplished.

Ginsberg made up his mind to write Lolita a letter. It was difficult to imagine what mistake there could have been. But if one started off with the assumption that there had been a mistake, certain possibilities existed;

remote and scarcely conceivable, but nevertheless possibilities. Thus she might not have received his previous letter, she might not have seen him from the window — but wait, the message sent with the little girl? Ah, there was after all no room for a mistake of that sort. . . . Perhaps Lolita had been unwell. Yes, she might have been feeling terribly out of sorts, and that, on top of everything else, had made her do something which she would undoubtedly regret later. It was obvious that he must write a letter, his first sincere, heartfelt letter to Lolita — expressing, indeed, what were his first sincere, heartfelt sentiments towards her since the previous summer.

Ginsberg rose from the bath and towered nakedly upwards to the congeries of pipes, deeply coated with black dust, which sprouted from the geyser. In the unaccustomed silence of the kitchen, the only sound was that of water dripping from his limbs, as the rats continued to lie low underneath the bath.

The whole of the tall, decaying house was silent; the street was silent; outside the rain now drifted in a vague drizzle, lightly and inaudibly. The tenants downstairs, dim, quiet people, who crept out to work early and crept back in the evening, had long ago crept into bed. This melancholy silence was shattered to fragments by the terrible top bell. Ginsberg had forgotten to disconnect it, and its shrill, ear-splitting insistence indicated that Philip Lank was downstairs, had seen the light left on in Ginsberg's room, and was waiting in the rain for news of his article. The door would have to be opened this evening. Some time had passed since Philip had been given any information about *Scamp,* and it was as well to keep on the right side of him.

Ginsberg hastily dried himself, put on his ludicrously short flannel pyjamas, slipped over them his overcoat, and, the big toe poking through one of his slippers, hurried down eight flights of stairs to answer the door. Meanwhile the bell had rung again several times. It rang continuously as he rushed downstairs. There seemed to be something especially desperate in its note to-night.

Ginsberg turned one lock and pulled back the other; the massive street door swung slowly open, and, scarcely able to wait till there was sufficient space, a long, thin, ungainly figure squirmed and twisted through, arms and legs waving and gesticulating disconnectedly.

"Where's Bellenger?" gasped Philip Lank wildly and breathlessly. "Where's Bellie? I must see him. I *must see* him," he hissed.

"I don't think —"

"If I have to wait all night, I must see him. He isn't upstairs?"

"No, he —"

"This is really important."

"What's it about?"

By the thin shaft of light which found its way from the top landing, via the well of the staircase, to the dark ground floor passage, Ginsberg tried to make out the expression on Philip's face, to discover a clue to this episode. He was in any case relieved to find that Philip's first words were not about *Scamp* and his article. As a matter of fact, the article was not mentioned at all. It had been driven out of Philip's mind by an altogether bigger, more important conception, the Great Revelation, deriving from the mathematical function which Philip had so long been seeking, the square root of the cube of the integral of the logarithm of the differential. . . . But this Ginsberg was not to learn until the morning.

"I can't tell you," sobbed Philip. "I can't tell anybody, not a soul in the whole world, except Bellenger. I must see him."

"I've no idea what time he'll be back. Maybe he won't come back to-night at all."

"I must see him."

Philip Lank crouched against one wall, he shot over to the other, he paced up and down in long, uneven steps. He floated before Ginsberg's eyes in the darkness like some weird, flimsy growth blown about by the wind. Ginsberg wondered what to do. Bellenger would probably be back soon, but one could never be sure. For all he knew, Bellenger was taking a girl home to Balham or Battersea or Ealing Broadway, in which case he might totter back at four in the morning after having trudged six or seven miles through unknown streets. Or Bellenger might have decided to sit up in an all-night café with the Charlotte Street bohemians; or he might have hit on a girl with her own room in Chelsea and be spending the night with her. If Philip persisted in his present mood the poor scientist would simply hang about in Guilford Street until the morning; or even — should Bellenger still not have arrived — all the following day, and the following night, and the day after that, until he just withered away. . . . On the other hand, he, Ginsberg, was not having Philip up in the flat, not for anything. The best thing seemed to be to leave him down here in the passage.

"Look, Philip," he said, "I should like to invite you upstairs, but —"

"I must see him."

"— as I am just going to bed, and I'm very tired —"

"I must."

"— you will understand that it's impossible for me to invite you up. But you're quite at liberty to wait down here if you want to."

"I've got to see Bellenger."

"So I'll leave you now. If you decide to go, see that the street door's closed after you."

"I must see him."

Ginsberg slowly mounted the first flight of stairs, looking dubiously over his shoulder at the unfortunate scientist. A match flared and went out; a cigarette glowed in the darkness by the door, then moved erratically towards the staircase. Philip's spectacles reflected a glimmer of light; the red cigarette end floated away once again into the blackness. There was a muttering and breathing of incoherent phrases. Ginsberg climbed to the top flat, listened for any sharp, dramatic sound from below, closed and locked the flat door after him.

Poor Philip. He felt a helpless pity, not for Philip alone, but for himself and all mankind. What had Philip done to deserve this odd torture? And what could be done to help him? Who could afford to help him? Philip had done nothing, nothing could be done for him, no one could afford to help him. The only thing to do, reflected Ginsberg, was to see that in future people like Philip were never born.

Ginsberg sat down to write his letter to Lolita. Very soon, amid his own preoccupations, he forgot Philip prowling about in the passage downstairs. At first he wanted to pour his heart out, to tell Lolita of new feelings born in him since their last meeting. This was not Ivan Ginsberg writing to her, he wanted to say, but a different man, older, gentler, more chastened. He could not bear to live alone any more, he did not want to start again with someone new. . . he wanted her to forgive him, to take him back. . .

Then he pulled himself together. This sort of maundering was inexcusable, tired though he was. A new Ivan Ginsberg indeed! The lines of Blake occurred to him:

Never seek to tell thy love
Love that never told can be,
For the gentle wind doth move
Silently, invisibly.

He tore his first letter up and threw it out of the window. Shreds of paper fluttered in the drizzle to the pavements of Guilford Street below. This time he wrote a brief, business-like letter, addressed it, and sealed the envelope. It was designed, not to express his feelings, but to persuade Lolita that her refusal to see him was either a complete mistake or a strange aberration on her part, which he was ready, without any recrimination whatsoever, to excuse. After all, it was no use denying that if he could not get Lolita back physically, and more or less immediately, he had no inclination to waste his time writing her letters which she wouldn't in the least understand. He included a few formal phrases of affection and asked her to meet him at Tottenham Court Road tube station. He was quite explicit and fairly urgent. Now there could surely be no room for a mistake — as indeed there had not been previously. If Lolita failed to turn up, it was finished — another affair discarded.

Staring out of the window over the mass of buildings towards St. Paul's, he had once again his unfailing daily vision of Margaret. He saw himself sitting in the low kitchen of a Welsh farmhouse. The dogs lay outstretched in front of the fire. On the walls and from the ceiling hung pots and pans and sticks and guns and old-fashioned bed-warmers and rustic odds and ends. Margaret brewed tea. From nearby sheds came the dull grunting of animals. The wind blew round the house, a wind that came straight from the Atlantic. As a gust rattled the windows, he and Margaret looked up and then looked at each other. It was a long, firm glance that they exchanged, from which a smile of trust and intimacy curved away; it was this glance which he now remembered poignantly.

That had been his one visit to her house, on an evening when her parents were away. Margaret did not dare even mention him to her father, and he himself was intimidated by the grim, chapel-going Welshman. The fanatical old farmer would as soon have received a Zulu as prospective son-in-law.

Yet Ivan had often imagined himself settling down as a Welsh farmer. If, after a few pints at the Corney Arms, he spoke of his nostalgia for the damp, misty valleys round Porth Bay, he received a cackle of facetious comment:

"Ginsberg *bach*!"

"Ginsberg of Llanfachmachllollen!"

The backbenchers at the Corney Arms asserted that without London, without the company of people like themselves, he would grow rusty. Ginsberg snorted at the thought. Without them! Why, there wasn't in the whole world a bent nail on an abandoned piece of driftwood as rusty as those backbenchers in the Corney Arms! On the farm at Porth Bay there would have been work and love and children and writing. Writing was for him like air, and at Porth Bay it would have been fresh and salty. Ivan saw himself sitting in the low-ceilinged farmhouse kitchen. The dogs lay outstretched by the fire, the wind carried straight across from the Atlantic, cattle grunted and lowed in the sheds, Margaret brewed tea. . . .

Bah! Ginsberg braced his shoulders and blew out all the air in his lungs. There was only one thing to do if one was tired, and that was go to bed; not hang around regretting, fidgeting, hankering. In a moment, if he was not careful, he would fall into a night-long reverie about his mother and childhood and everything. . . . Fuss. Fuss was no good to anybody. Fuss only bred fuss. Bah!

He crept downstairs to see how Philip was getting on. There was no sound or sign of the scientist. Ginsberg lit a match. Three cigarette ends and a pile of ash lay on the centre of the hall stand. Philip was gone; that at any rate was a relief.

CHAPTER XV

A MILLION WORDS might be insufficient to describe the actions and thoughts of a single person during a single hour of the day. It is accepted, therefore, that only momentary, partial glimpses can be obtained of Ginsberg; while as for Mrs. Chabbers, Kagaranias, Angus Sternforth Simms, Bellenger, Julius Kripkin, Spiffhorn and Trunt, Bert Flogcrobber, Kroganin, they are no more than shadows which flash across the screen and vanish, leaving behind a confused and bewildering impression.

Once again these gesticulating, agitated shadows, our brothers and sisters, are flashed on in rapid, indeed lightning review, if only to show what kind of change has occurred in three months. Change there must have been, since there is no verb "to be", only "to become", and for the metropolitans of Inner London the tempo of becoming was fast and irregular. With a second point plotted, the direction, at any rate, of a periodic movement on one of their zooming, fluctuating curves is indicated.

Peter Stranshaw Firth had retired to the country for the summer in order to translate Spanish verse and summon up the courage to face London again in the autumn. He was staying with an aunt in a hamlet some ten miles from Oxford. On most days he spoke no more than forty or fifty words to his aunt. In the afternoon he recited poems to the hedges, he declaimed verse heroically to the wind. Twice a week he got drunk at the village pub. On these occasions, the country people looked at him with disquiet. Reading Garcilaso de la Vega or Garcia Lorca, he swallowed pint after pint of watery brew. At pint seven or eight he began to read aloud, furiously rolling the Spanish r's. On Sunday, the curate, who despised Firth for having been a conscientious objector during the war, came to tea at his aunt's, and the two men quarrelled with hissing politeness. When Firth was particularly annoyed, he threw back his head and laughed his great, long, all-absorbing, soundless laugh.

Angus Sternforth Simms' routine was unchanged. He was still stationed firmly and unyieldingly by the bar at the Corney Arms. But there had been, perhaps, a slight decline, a scarcely perceptible lowering of prestige. It was not so much that he had gone backwards as that he had failed to advance. The radio scripts, the film scenarios, the short stories and sketches continued to pour forth. But the radio scripts and film scenarios were after all merely radio scripts and film scenarios, and could affect only unfavourably those discriminating bums and coldly amorous, raised-eyebrowed, rimless-spectacled bluestockings whom Angus secretly wished to impress. While even the short stories and sketches, in which Angus had created his own, highly accomplished genre, tended to be rehashes of his earliest and most original work. Literary critics who had described the Corney Arms as a phase in the development of one of England's coming younger writers, began to wonder in print whether it was a phase; or whether Simms was not getting more and more firmly fixed in a genre which he had outlived and which was rendering his work stale and second-rate.

Stale and second-rate. Angus was tough and experienced and not easily moved by the genteel reproaches of the critics; but somewhere within him there was a living core of intolerable sensitivity, and there the words "stale and second-rate" were like salt on an open wound. It was Panjitawarelam, of all people, discreet, softly-spoken, self-effacing Panjitawarelam, who inadvertently brushed this raw and tender abrasion and brought on a most painful scene — Angus lost his temper; it was as though a bishop, an archbishop, had himself started a shrieking brawl on the very altar of his own church.

Early one evening, before Angus had finished his first

gin and orange, Panjit made a remark — no one could be quite sure what it was — which irritated Angus.

Angus did not take the remark with his usual sophisticated off-handedness — as he did almost all remarks addressed to him by anyone below the rank of managing director in a publishing firm. The words jolted him, immersed as he was in his own train of thought, into a momentary irritation and then into uncontrollable anger.

"Oh, do shut up, Panjit," he said testily.

"But really —" Panjitawarelam scarcely murmured the words, they were little more than a sigh. But they were too much for Angus.

"Shut up!" screamed Angus. "I'm sick of you!"

There were a few people in the pub at the time, and they all stared in horror at Angus. He had accustomed them to his high, insistent monotone, which nothing could alter or deflect; and here he was losing his temper over nothing at all, and screaming, positively screeching. It was obscene. And with Panjitawarelam! Everyone knew Panjit; Panjit was an institution. One didn't quarrel with Panjitawarelam, leader of the "mystical" school of young poets.

"Go away!" continued Angus in a frantic scream. "I'm tired of you. You're nothing but a guttersnipe! I want nothing to do with you! Or your beastly poems! Mystical poems!" sneered Angus. Ah, that was in truly bad taste, bringing in the poems, because everyone knew Panjit hadn't written a poem for years. It was kicking a man when he was down.

Panjit tried to reason quietly, to murmur discreetly, but to no avail. Angus, his face chalk-white, was trembling with fury. Panjit, too, was as pale as his brown skin permitted. He turned away, to sympathizers at the other end of the bar, leaving Angus alone with his girl-friend, towering over her, hypnotizing her, like a snake preparing to strike, and hissing with assumed calm:

"My dear, did you read the review in the *Observer* of that new collection of stories Hutchinson are bringing out?"

One of Panjit's sympathizers was heard to say loudly:

"Don't bother about that sort of thing, Panjit. We've got no time for bogus geniuses *here*!"

Popsy behind the bar looked down her nose disapprovingly. She didn't like it, she wouldn't stand for it, not even from Angus. Any more of this nonsense, and *out they'd go!* Yes, *Angus too*! Vigorously and angrily she wiped beer from the bar counter, slopping her wet rag from side to side.

In three months, Kagaranias had grown even older, even wearier, still more impossible. By fairly heavy bribes he had added seven more photographs, including one of the delightful blonde waitress at the Restaurant Souci, to his collection of five hundred-odd nudes; and had been able to indulge in the strange practices associated with the photographic act. Out of some dustbin he had fished a different hat and a different filthy sweater, for it was summer, and time for a change. He went rather more to the Victoria coffee-stall than to the milk bar at King's Cross, and scarcely ever to Tim's Caff in Fleet Street — one got tired of going to the same places. He had bought several lorryloads of books, which had been tipped out into his warehouse. But there was one thing he did not know; that in three weeks' time the whole lot was going up in flames, books, warehouse, photographs, and memories of scarcely credible sordidities to be consumed in one of the most rapid blazes ever seen in Central London. If he had known, it would not have made any difference. He could hardly have been more gloomy, more derelict, than he was already.

Douglas Vanner did not appear to have changed. Change there must have been, but the process had kept itself well out of sight, somewhere behind the bright, false smile, the permanently waved hair, the powdered blue chin, the arched back, the slender, dangling hands, tipped with crimson fingernails, and the high-heeled shoes. Douglas Vanner, it was to be hoped, would never change outwardly, for that would have been disastrous. His polished, absurdly artificial personality, a masterpiece of decadence, would have withered swiftly and shrivelled into pathos. His entire energies and considerable talent were devoted to keeping things the same. That was civilization, he felt; a state of affairs in which nothing ever happened, in which novelty and change were the worst of barbarisms.

"Tell me all," he said. He tried not to move very far from a dozen or so formal phrases. "Be terribly gay," was his never-failing injunction, "be terribly, terribly gay." Douglas Vanner intended to carry on to the end. From within his position might be undermined; he would never give way before a frontal assault. One day he would just collapse quietly; a heap of infinitesimally thin, brightly-coloured tinsel would lie on the ground, drift and rustle away in the wind.

Julius Kripkin was still awaiting his call-up papers to the mines. Knowing that his carefree, irresponsible mode of living was to be interrupted for a considerable time, he savoured to the full the round of Soho cafés and the simultaneous love affairs in all stages of development except the final one. He was indeed the most balanced of the philosophers in the Belgian Café.

"There's time for everything," he said, "there's time for everything."

Becoming the second Bernard Shaw, writing plays, attaining world prominence — all these were postponed till he had done something for the mining industry. It was good to be able to postpone things, to take it easy for a bit. After all, he was young. He had a right to enjoy himself.

"First things first," he said. "First things first."

The only urgency was girls. You couldn't get away from

the fact, a chap had to have a girl; even a chap like himself who'd recently had his heart wrung out in one of the most tempestuous and passionate affairs it was possible to have. Now in one sense he had girls. There were probably half a dozen girls he could take to the pictures any evening in the week, and about sixteen more he had his eye on. But in another sense he hadn't a girl. And he needed one. Oh, he didn't only mean physically, though he wanted that badly enough, too. He wanted a girl who was a friend, a real friend, a girl with whom, complementarily, he could form a common front, a self-sufficient, indivisible unity.

Kathleen O'Flanagan, in her damp bedroom in Ballykelly — the room was damp even in midsummer — was thinking the very same thing. She wanted a lover to whom she could surrender herself completely and with confidence. Not just anyone — there was no shortage of boys in Ballykelly who would have been delighted to accept her surrender — but *the* lover, the man for whom she had been waiting throughout ten or eleven long, oppressed years, the man in whose person sex, love, revolution, and gaiety were combined — a *man*! Anyone who was the opposite of her father, that slobbering, foul, tyrannical, cowardly brute, who beat her with a stick, even now when she was twenty-four, and then moaned curses, threats, and pleas when, more in disgust than pain, she rounded on him and tore at his face with anger-blind, groping fingers.

Soon she would be in London, and there, in the young, ardent circle of contributors to *Scamp,* she would meet the lover who was to mould her shy, awkwardly virginal body into that of a young woman, balanced, calm, complete. God, she prayed — though she was almost certain there was no God — God, be kind to me, let nothing interfere with my going to London. God, she said, if you stop me going to London, you will kill me. I may go on living, but I shall be dead. Every minute of the day, every activity, had meaning and interest only in so far as it brought nearer her departure from Ireland. This departure had already been delayed several weeks, since it was necessary, when she *did* leave, that not the tiniest hitch should occur. At last, in consultation and co-operation with the indispensable schoolmistress friend in Cork, everything was arranged. The shillings she had hoarded for years were counted over once again; the documents and ticket, sent to her friend's address, were examined down to the last by-law and regulation on the back. Kathleen's heart seemed scarcely to beat; it floated high, high in her body, palpitating with a light, airy rhythm of its own, as though it might leave her altogether and sail away on the wind to impossible lands. The day was coming, the day when she was to begin that for which all her years hitherto had been a preparation, a struggle, and a test. Soon she would live, soon she would be *born!*

At just about the end of this period of three months, Louis — "Do your profile, half a crown?" — abruptly disappeared from Soho. He had done it before, stayed away for seven years, and returned. Now, once again, the broadbrimmed sombrero encircling a cheerful, fat face, the deep chuckle trailing away into a continuous gurgle, the cloak, and the dramatic poses of a stage grandee in front of the long mirror in Pedro's International Café Restaurant, all these, so inimitably Louis, were missing. Where he had gone, what he was doing, who could say? Did his new acquaintances cry out, with the affection of the old: "Here's Louis; he makes me sick"? And did Louis parry, with dignity: "Madam, you too cause me to vomit"? And would he return to Soho this time? Would he still be young enough and strong enough to face it all again? No one could say. All that could be said was that Louis was away. Each man belongs to a village, though that village be in the centre of a metropolis. The mind is too human and intimate to take in the vastness of the world, the multitudinousness of its people; it needs to fasten itself on something small, familiar, and comprehensible — a few streets and places, a continuous thread of people, such as Soho. Thus Louis, no longer in Soho, was away, away from home, away from his native village, his normal point of reference in uncharted time and space. Soho might disappear materially, might be lost in memory. . . but always it would be the place from which Louis was "away".

Sid, at the instigation of Sybil and Jojo, had booked a full-page advertisement on the back cover *of Scamp.* But both he and Ginsberg, and even Sybil and Jojo, had more or less forgotten about the preposterous idea — since what type of reader *of Scamp* (lively, controversial, informative) was expected to be interested in:

"Sid's Red-Hot Rhythm Sextet — starring vocalists Sybil Panzonli and Jojo Kaminik — bookable for all functions, large and small, guaranteeing sweet music and rip-roaring swing-it boogie, with all the latest dream-hits straight from Hollywood (Telephone: MAIda Vale 01032)?"

Sid, the swing intellectual, the advocate of Higher Swing, had let himself be jogged along by Sybil and Jojo. Ginsberg, preoccupied with the very existence *of Scamp,* less interested by now in making the magazine pay than in throwing away such money as Mrs. Chabbers would provide in a single fling on one number, could not bother his head with advertisers. As for Sybil and Jojo, they had more important things to think about.

Jojo was pregnant, with only, so far, a "slight touch of pregnancy", as Louis put it, but, nevertheless, indisputably pregnant. As weeks nine and ten passed, the matter began to grow serious. She, silly urban adolescent, was being edged slowly down to those dark abysses which lay underneath Charing Cross Road; underneath Foyle's bookshop, the cafés, the American-style outfitters, the milk-bars, the rubber-goods shops, the run-quick fruit-stalls, the dance-saloon; even underneath the roadway, the electric cables, the gas-pipes, underneath the tube, underneath the sewers, underneath the last defensive outpost of those who walked above — underneath them all, far, far underneath, lay the dark abysses of birth and death. And Jojo, slight, seven stone, eighteen-year-old, pretty little Jojo, was naturally afraid, all the more so because she was completely unprepared for birth and death. She had never seen either a newly-born baby or a corpse. She had been educated — had, in fact, matriculated — she had once known and now wisely forgotten the battles in the Crimean War, the exports of British Columbia at the time her geography book was written, how to do quadratic equations, how to conjugate deponent verbs in Latin, how to prove that two straight lines which are parallel to a third straight line are parallel to each other, and so on. But what to do when an unwelcome, indeed disastrous pregnancy was beginning inside her, that she had not learnt; for that she had to go to Sybil, who was almost twenty. Sybil took her to Valerie, who was twenty-four, and Valerie, in turn, took her to a dirty old woman in one of London's dingiest slums, thirty yards behind Regent Street and not far from Great Marlborough Street police station. Jojo's regime of pills, hot baths twice a day, great doses of gin, and jumping down flights of stairs was brought to an end by an appalling episode on the old witch's sofa; after which Sybil and Valerie nursed Jojo for two weeks in a furnished room in Bayswater. Sid gladly paid up eighty pounds, thanked heaven that Jojo was still alive, and made up his mind to have no more vocalists in the band, a resolution effectively maintained for three long summer months.

Jojo was restored to apparent normalcy after a few weeks. A glimpse of the abysses of birth and death was, however, something that once experienced could never be forgotten. In spite of her eighteen years she was now curiously mature, and six months later was married to a chartered accountant many years her senior. Still later, the effects of that monstrous abortion on the sofa began to show itself in cysts and growths and all manner of ovarian complications. Her reproductive system, which had formerly functioned so smoothly and agreeably, became the curse of her existence, chronically out of order, erratic, morbid and sterile. Such — for all her chartered accountant and eighth floor flat obtained at an exorbitant rent — was the unfortunate lot of pretty little Jojo, upon whom the grinning old monsters of sex and the city, with their dusty files of antique, cruel laws and customs, with their sordidities, their slums, their underhand ways and means, upon whom sex and London revenged themselves.

It so happened that on the very evening when Jojo was agonizing on the sofa by Great Marlborough Street police station, four other girls — out of the hundreds privately swallowing mildly poisonous pills, sweltering in unbearably hot baths, drinking sickening draughts of gin, and crashing down flights of stairs — were undergoing the same ordeal in more or less similar circumstances in other parts of London. Three lost, in addition to the unwanted embryo, nothing more than their money; the fourth died, her abortionist spending as a result six crippling years in a women's prison built in the early nineteenth century. Yet within a quarter of an hour's walk of each of these five painful scenes, Carruthers Anstruther insisted in his book on abortion, there were admirable hospitals, hygienic, and humane, with every modern surgical and anaesthetic facility; hospitals which shelved moral considerations in the unequivocal treatment of diseases undoubtedly resulting from gluttony, alcoholism, lack of sexual restraint, laziness, criminal negligence. . . .

Carruthers Anstruther himself had left London, with the fine weather, and set out on his annual summer tour of casual institutions in Devonshire, known to all tramps as the most hospitable county in the British Isles. If the night was exceptionally mild, he slept by the roadside, under a hedge; but normally he joined a crowd of tramps at the casual ward and distinguished himself by his grumbling, or "binding". His complaint, delivered in those assured Kensington accents which the years had in no way marred, was always the same:

"Damn it all! I can stand for a lot, but I do draw the line at this!"

"Gah! Shut yer trap! 'Oo asks yer ter stand fer i'? Why 'n cher piddle off back where yer came from?"

"When I want your opinion, I'll ask for it," Anstruther said to his interrupter. "Damn it all, I draw the line somewhere, and this is about the limit!"

Anstruther's companion, the former darling of Montparnasse, still wandered about the West End at night. Her neck remained cricked forward at its peculiar angle. The police left her alone, although she complained increasingly that they were persecuting her; and anyone, at two or three in the morning, might see her standing in the middle of an empty roadway, staring, staring, down, down, down into the asphalt.

CHAPTER XVI

BERT FLOGCROBBER WAS NOT AT ALL WELL. He suffered from a whole host of minor ailments and irritations. His digestion was poor, his sight was bad, and overwork gave him dull, throbbing, incapacitating headaches. Occasional sciatica tugged at his right leg, slight rheumatism gripped his feet and ankles. His bowels were usually and infuriatingly either constipated or diarrhoeic. He was unable to sleep soundly more than a few hours in twenty-four. Most of the morning his face smarted uncomfortably from shaving; late at night his gums began to ache. His drooping shoulders were covered with an irritating acne. Although he did not eat enough, beer and whisky and total lack of exercise had given him a flabby little heap of stomach. If, once in six months, he broke into a trot, he felt that his heart was on the point of racing itself to death. He smoked forty cigarettes a day; his fingers, lungs, tongue, and teeth were coated and stained with tobacco. He drank half a bottle of whisky while he worked, on top of other drinks during the afternoon, and his liver was finding it increasingly difficult to handle these injurious doses of unconsumable alcohol. Two other factors, tiny yet crippling, contributed perennially to Bert's discomfort. His size in shirt collars was awkwardly midway between fifteen and a half and sixteen, and his size in shoes just as awkwardly midway between nine and a half and ten. For thirty years, therefore, he had been periodically choked and lamed by new shirts and shoes. He preferred being a martyr to looking, as he oversensitively imagined, a fool; consequently he chose the smaller sizes and suffered pains which, if forcefully imposed by one person on another, would have been called torture.

So though Bert was not ill enough to go to bed and call

in the doctor, he was decidedly unwell, physically wretched, mentally on the point of breakdown. He could not afford to be ill and take a rest; it would have meant ruin. If he gave an inch, he would lose everything. He always tried, as he boasted to one or two of his cronies in the Press Club, to live beyond his income. That was the only way to keep going. It was with his approval that his wife and two daughters, keeping up the Flogcrobber prestige in Beaulieu Avenue, had gone over to Paris for a few weeks, at a cost (to his free-lance account) of three hundred pounds. He was working as hard as ever, in spite of being able to delegate much of the hack work to Ginsberg, and he was drinking perhaps more than usual. The articles for the South African syndicate were going ahead, and he had got some excellent dope from Inspector Sly for one or two in the series. "London's Square Mile of Vice" was his own material. Ha! He'd used it a few times before, too, almost word for word! But "Britain fights the Terrorists" was red-hot stuff straight from Sly on the Jewish thugs (it had been agreed at a meeting of the Journalists' Association to refer to the terrorists only as thugs).

Bert had been finding Sly a great stimulus to his work. They had first met, years before, when Sly was in the Racegang Squad at Scotland Yard and Bert was a reporter. They had met again from time to time, and most recently at a meeting, in a room above a pub off the Strand, of the Association of Freemen and Yeomen of Britain. Bert went partly out of curiosity, after having picked up the association's leaflet in the Irish Bar, partly with the idea of shaking up a column on them in one of the Sunday newspapers. Sly was there in his official capacity, keeping an eye on the association for Department XY. The two men got on well together, and Sly was an excellent tip-off at a time when XY was expanding its activities. XY was the most curious of departments and had strange ramifications. Questions had been asked in Parliament: "Who was the minister responsible for XY?" No one knew. "What were the functions and duties of XY?" No one knew. "Out of which vote of credit did XY receive its funds?" Out of the special non-departmental secret list. Sly, of course, kept his mouth shut about many things; but about others he was helpful and communicative. As a result, Bert's articles on the Jewish bandits — these did not pass through Ginsberg's hands and meant a lot of extra work — on the international Jewish currency smuggling ring, linked up with the Palestine thugs, on drug-taking in Mayfair, blackmail at Marble Arch, and the protection racket among prostitutes in Leicester Square, all these were among the most startling, vague, apocalyptic, lurid, and unsubstantiated in the whole of the Sunday press. Sly was more of an inspiration than an informant. He dealt in hints and heavily significant nods. But even so, he helped Bert Flobcrobbber's free-lance work to expand along with the activities of XY, although there was no direct relationship between the two.

Bert went several times to the meetings of the Association of Freemen and Yeomen of Britain. The members, he felt, whatever their faults, were moving in more or less the right direction. Of course, the debates in themselves were rather silly; the debate on Honest Levin's speech, for instance. Honest Levin had spoken bluntly, as man to man, straight from the shoulder: "I honestly think that if we can get together, round a round table, honestly doing our best, I can solve this. Your Palestine Arab is a good man, one of the best, the salt of the earth, and I'll never let 'im down, even if I go down with 'im. And your Jew is a good chap, too, if you treat 'im firm, because that's the talk 'e understands. And I honestly feel that if we — that is, you and I and they — can't get together round a round table and 'ave this out, then I honestly say. . . " And so on. It was hailed in the press as one of Honest Levin's best efforts. But the Freemen and Yeomen were far from unanimous in their support. What did he mean, complained a large minority, by that bit about "your Jew is a good chap, too"? It certainly did look suspicious. There was a smaller, but vociferous and determined minority, which was completely anti-Levin. "Levin!" they sneered. "The man's name is Levene! And he's in the pay of the Yids!"

The last argument was quite laughable, reflected Bert. Most of the Freemen and Yeomen were thoroughly crude and naïf. Nevertheless, there was something in what they said. He was becoming increasingly convinced of it. There was, somewhere and somehow, a vast, secret, international conspiracy of Jews, Freemasons, communists, and highbrows, as well as most of the accursed Labour government, with the possible exception of Honest Levin. He put it to Sly; what did Sly think? Sly was not committing himself. Instead, he tipped Bert a wink, a great, meaningful, all-inclusive, solemn wink.

By an unfortunate coincidence, Bert had a new shirt and a new pair of shoes at the same time. He could scarcely hobble out of the house to hail a taxi, or cross Fleet Street from the Irish Bar to the office. He had to clench his fists in order to bring himself to take a step, and the veins stood out on his temples in agony. His two big toes went blue and their toe-nails black. This was normal; he invariably lost the greater part of his big toe-nails when breaking in a new pair of shoes; and he preferred to get the torture over and done with, rather than ease up after a day or two and change back to an old pair. But on this occasion, for a few days at any rate, while his feet were held in their terrible leather clamps, his new shirt was simultaneously cutting into his bulging red neck, pressing murderously on his Adam's apple, and strangling him. With the external pressure on his windpipe, and the fumes of alcohol and tobacco circulating internally, it was a wonder that Bert was able to draw through his lungs enough air with which to remain alive.

Bert's escape from these, as from all his other aches and pains and worries, was to go up to his office early, take off shoes, collar and tie, pour himself out a tumblerful of whisky, light a cigarette, and work at his free-lance articles; so that he might send his wife and daughters for more expensive holidays to the right places, pay another term's fees for his sons at Smarmingham School, buy himself more fifteen and a half collar shirts and nine and a half size shoes, and above all more whisky and more cigarettes to enable him to write more articles with which to buy more whisky and cigarettes to enable him to write more articles with which to buy more. . . .

Cogitating a ticklish paragraph, he would get up, pace up and down the room in stockinged feet, pull his loaded revolver from out of the set of drawers and absent-mindedly fondle it. One late afternoon, as he was caressing the blue steel, there was a deferential tap on the door and Ginsberg entered; said that he had come to ask about one or two points in the articles for South Africa, and then raised once again the question of Bert advancing him some money. Bert was furious with the *Daily Post* day-porter for having let Ginsberg come up unannounced. But he covered up his annoyance, offered Ginsberg some whisky, and very soon got rid of the man.

"The money'll be all the more welcome when it does come," were Bert's parting words. "That's half the fun in free-lance journalism, hanging on till your cheques come in, and then having a glorious blue. The end of the quarter'll soon be round, don't worry."

Ginsberg went off with a distracted air. Bert disliked his "ghost" more and more as time passed. For one thing, he was the only Jew with whom at this period Bert had any dealings; Ginsberg therefore served as a focus for Bert's dispersed hatred of the syllable "Jew" and its associations. For another, there was the frequent discussion of Ginsberg's commission, a matter which ought to have been considered as definitely over until the end of the summer. Finally, there was Ginsberg's abstracted air, his tall, shabby aloofness; and the way he implied that, though he might casually and irritatingly raise the subject as often as he liked, he didn't really care about the money — or about the articles, or Fleet Street, or the whole of journalism! He had other things to think about, he seemed to imply. Oh, did he! Who the devil did he imagine he was? He was nobody, he was nothing, he was less than nothing! He was an utter, complete, and absolute nonentity. So he'd better damn well get rid of his abstracted air. He'd learn one day that earning your living was a serious matter. You had to worry about it, at least!

But really, though it might not appear so at first, Ginsberg's attitude was a part of this Jew business. Most Jews thought and spoke and lived money. Ginsberg pretended he didn't. By doing so, he showed how important it was to him to seem not to care about money. Thus he was as much of a Jew as the others, but a bit more cunning. He was one of these clever-clever, arty-arty highbrows. Highbrows! Bert, kindling himself, as it were, by spontaneous combustion, flamed with indignation. Highbrows! Communists! Socialists! Jews, the whole damn lot of them! Bert's temples were throbbing; one of his great headaches was coming on. He felt, as he had felt several times lately, that he might at any moment run amok, screaming and yelling and cursing and beating and smashing everything within sight. Picking up the revolver, which he had pushed under a folder when Ginsberg came into the room, he rushed over to the remainder of the tumbler of whisky and drained it. He grew calmer. His animosity disciplined and concentrated itself, at the same time recognizing its own limitations. He raised the revolver — ah! what power was contained in its sleek beauty! He imagined Ginsberg was still standing there. He imagined himself pulling the trigger. It was out of the question, of course; one didn't commit murder. But he imagined it all the same, every detail of it. One's finger tightened on the trigger. One pulled — ping! Or better still, six times — Ping! ping! ping! ping! ping! ping! One Yid the less.

CHAPTER XVII

BELLENGER, TOO, WAS CHANGING. He was reaching the end of a ten-year period in his thirty-odd years of life. The last ten-years had been a decade of protracted undergraduateness, of incessant sexual search and experiment — nothing else had really held his imagination for a single day — of dull, inward pain and damped-down fever. He was even now not disappointed in his chosen environment and mode of living; but there were moments when he felt unable, as he muttered to himself, "to stand the pace".

Yet Bellenger was the last person whom anyone would have suspected of not being able "to stand the pace'; of giving under the strain of people, of the betrayals and frustrations, the let-downs, lies, malicious gossip, and sheer ill-will which sooner or later seeped through the thin tissue of Soho bonhomie. With his fresh, red, countryman's face, his beefy body, his careless assurance, he seemed good for another twenty years of drinking and indiscriminate love-making. Not even the food in his favourite restaurants was able to upset his metabolism. Terrible things issued from the kitchens of the West End restaurants; blue and purple potatoes lay in a pool of gravy alongside the nameless parts of unidentifiable little animals and birds, the whole masquerading under such titles as "Vienna steak", "Hungarian goulash", "mousaka", "stewed steak" (which those in the know always ordered, in the belief that it was reasonably fresh stewed horse), "kebab", "Cambridge steak" (as ex-residents of Cambridge, Ginsberg and Bellenger tried in vain to interpret the significance of this horror), and, most deadly and indeterminate of all, the "mixed grill" and "hot-pot" which appeared to contain the scraps and leavings of what the gamblers had been eating in the back-rooms the night before, during one of their all-night sessions at poker and pontoon. Eating twice a day in Soho, Bellenger forked his way through the entire menu; and he not only enjoyed, but thrived on this diet. Nor was he upset by the beer of the Corney Arms and the Duchess of Canterbury. He swigged gallons of it, and next day was as fresh and rosy as ever. Having got up at lunch-time, he went off in the afternoon to the second-hand bookshops, bric-à-brac dealers, and pawnshops of south and west London as though he were striding through a ploughed field. Thus supplementing his allowance, he then squandered his earnings with whole-hearted eagerness on "kebab" and "goulash" and mild and bitter for himself and any number of prospective seducees.

Bellenger was hardly sensitive to the general wearing effect of the small community of four or five hundred people which frequented his habitual pubs and cafés. He was unaffected by the sudden, inexplicable, and quite unnecessary insults and hatreds which kept busy those smaller and poorer than himself. He did not take these things seriously; he was no bum. He could not be bothered with them; he was in fact, hardly aware of their existence.

He came to Soho because it was the ideal hunting ground for girls. The rest of what went on in its back streets or in the minds of its habitués was irrelevant. And it was only a succession of pretty, twenty-year-old girls, with their special brand of betrayal, let-down, lie, malicious gossip, and sheer ill-will, which could cause him to mutter bitterly to himself, late at night or walking home in the dawn: "I can't stand the pace."

Time was beginning to tell, not yet on Bellenger's body or appearance, but on the youthful resilience of his spirit. So many blows could be received in his amorous warfare, and he could flick them lightly aside, closing in for more; until there was struck one blow too many. It might seem, as it did to Ginsberg, for instance, that Bellenger was impervious to injury in his sexual and sentimental encounters; but there came a moment when, small in itself, a blow was received which, on top of all the others experienced during ten years, beat Bellenger to his knees.

There is the Shavian story of a man learning to ride a bicycle. He continually falls off — until one day he no longer falls off and he is able to ride. There is to the spectator scarcely an intermediate stage between falling off and not falling off, between riding and not riding. Visibly, the acquired accomplishment of riding a bicycle is manifested overnight, or even while the spectator's back is turned. But invisibly, of course, the evolution of this accomplishment has been gradual and steady.

So it was, but conversely, with Bellenger. For ten years he had been experimenting with sex. For ten years he had been experiencing new exaltations and disappointments every fortnight or three weeks. Each of these affairs had come to an end, and the end of each affair, usually accompanied by some brutal gesture, had struck a blow at Bellenger's heart. Even to so intimate an observer as Ginsberg, Bellenger's latest affairs seemed no different from the affairs of five, six, and seven years before. But it was not so. For ten years Bellenger had been riding a precarious bicycle. Every fortnight a new triumph or a new piece of feminine baseness made him wobble more wildly. Somehow or other the bicycle kept moving. Essentially Bellenger was maintaining his balance, because there could be no halfway between maintaining a balance and falling to the ground. But there came a final triumph, followed by a last betrayal; Bellenger wobbled more wildly than ever, he flung up his arms, he clutched the air — to no avail. There was a crash of desires and vanities and habits, and Bellenger lay on the ground. When he picked himself up, he was no longer a man who wished to ride a bicycle. He clambered on to something slower and more permanent, less exigent and less precarious — as it were, a tricycle. Bellenger, Bellenger the immortal, with the secret, the tirelessness, the fresh buoyancy, the bright-eyed, rustic good looks, and the incorrigible idiocy of eternal youth, Bellenger had

had enough, Bellenger could not "stand the pace", Bellenger was earnestly and circumspectly anxious to get married.

The main agents of fate during this summer were Joan, the art-student, Rana, the Indian half-caste, Mac, the lesbian prostitute, and Lucille. . . the exquisite. There were, too, minor agents, whom Bellenger fruitlessly pursued to Battersea and Finchley Road and Holland Park. Lucille it was who concluded Bellenger's decade of love and indiscriminate sexual experiment. He had casually held in his arms scores, perhaps hundreds of girls. Lucille was the last of them. She was to be followed only by Prue Cummings, of the Cambridge School of Domestic Economy (Housewifery), Bellenger's future wife. Of course, five years later, after the birth of his second son, Bellenger was to break out again, first with the maid, then with the girl at the tobacconist's. . . but those affairs were of a different order, not in Bellenger's grand manner, altogether in a minor key.

The *affaire* Lucille was a classic illustration of an affair in Bellenger's grand manner; the simple opening movements, the early and masterly triumph, the lingering, jarring, and futile diminuendo, the brutal and irrevocable conclusion.

Someone brings Lucille to the Corney Arms. She is introduced to Bellenger, or Bellenger introduces himself to her, or she is wedged up against Bellenger on the back seat. Lucille is exquisite, truly a miracle of nacreous beauty, as yet only half aware of its devastating perfection. Were there not so many other legitimate claimants to a distinction which, once given, would merely appear banal, one might say she is the loveliest girl in the world. In a way it is inevitable that she should meet Bellenger. It is her own fault, the price she has to pay for being so lovely. Others, too, shoot covert glances at her, Angus Sternforth Simms, Panjitawarelam, Ginsberg. But they dare not stake their entire dignity on the slender chance of pulling off a coup, especially when there are so many — but so many! — competing punters. Besides, they are wiser than Bellenger, they learned the lesson years before; no good can come of it. And so, with the pain of regret, they turn their backs on Lucille — "Hm, not bad. . . " — and seek to efface the memory of that mother-of-pearl delicacy.

Lucille admits to Bellenger that she is a "neurotic". Bellenger obtains her telephone number, discovers that there is nothing to fear from her mother, who is also a "neurotic", and arranges to take Lucille to the Academy on Thursday afternoon — his favourite day, his favourite cinema, his favourite film, *Quai de Brumes.* Walking along Oxford Street afterwards, he will make a gesture with his hand and say in a low voice, quoting from the film, "I am interested in what lies behind things — les choses derrière les choses!"

During the film, Bellenger follows a well-defined routine. Five minutes after settling down, the first cigarette; and after that has been accepted, left arm carelessly and lightly round Lucille's shoulder, elbow resting on seat back. Fingers begin tentatively to play with Lucille's hair, then to caress her arm and shoulder. When the first cigarettes have been stubbed, Bellenger's grip tightens, his whole body moves over, his left leg makes contact with Lucille's right flank, his cheek rests against her cheek, his left hand works its way round through her armpit to come to rest on her left breast. Lucille offers only a mild, formal resistance. The next move is to bring the right hand over and begin a circular, caressing movement on the left breast, at the same time lightly brushing her right cheek with his lips and occasionally nuzzling his nose in her right ear. Overwhelming forces having thus been brought to bear on the left breast, it becomes the point of breakthrough, and Bellenger is able to advance all along the line. Lucille now co-operates delightfully, and Bellenger is once more amazed and gratified at the intimacies which ingenuity renders possible in a cinema without disturbing the decorum of the darkness.

Tea in Guilford Street. The flat has previously been transformed by Bellenger. The dust has been swept out of sight under the beds, the rooms have been tidied, some of the washing up has been done, the remainder hidden away in the kitchen cupboard. In Bellenger's room, blinds have been drawn, barring the view to the inquisitive back-windows of the tenement opposite. The gas-fire glows cosily, the reading-lamp sheds a discreet light over the portable gramophone — on permanent loan from a friend named Pam — which lies by the bookcase surrounded by poufs and cushions. On these, it is indicated to Lucille, she may lie and handle the books. Filling half the room, the vast, low bed spreads out its soft, luxurious spaces, its immensities of amorous terrain. Bellenger pads in and out with the tea-things. He speaks in a hushed voice, as though he were a butler or attendant nurse. Lucille says:

"What a lot of books you've got."

Bellenger assents in a subdued whisper. Then he makes a feeble joke. It hangs uncomfortably in the air; it is out of place. Lucille does not notice; she is turning over the pages of a book on Cezanne. She stares thoughtfully at a nude.

"He's awfully good, isn't he, Cezanne?"

Bellenger nods gravely. Tea is over, cigarettes are lit. The day is charted with cigarettes. Pin-points of lighted tobacco signal through the afternoon. The glowing twin beacons flare their calls to each other across the evening.

The gramophone is wound, the music plays. Bellenger's favourite records, Ravel. This is Bellenger's moment; not later, on the bed, but now — the flat in Bloomsbury, the drawn blinds, the glow of the fire, the cushions on the floor, the books, Lucille's pale face lost in thought, the music of Ravel. Finally, the last records are reached — *The Bolero*. Delicate sentiment is dissipated:

"*Bang*-tiddedy *bang*-tiddedy *bang*-tiddedy *bang*-tiddedy *bong*. . . Ding-dong ding-dong ding-dong *dong* diddy *dong. . .*" It is time to set to work.

Everything goes smoothly, as Bellenger has anticipated, since Lucille is a self-declared "neurotic". At twelve o'clock the bath thunders in the kitchen-cum-bathroom. Lucille is about to have a bath before going home to mother. It is a curious part of the rite, this having a bath after the bed-ceremony is over. Bellenger himself does not have a bath, but he likes the female participant to bathe before leaving; certainly not for hygienic reasons, but as part of his aesthetic. Also, he perhaps wishes to impress Ginsberg, who returns at this hour from the West End and may wish to eat his supper in the kitchen.

Lucille leaves. She comes again once, twice, three times at the most, and then she comes no more. Why? There is a question which Bellenger, invoking the help of Ginsberg, has long tried to solve. Of one thing he is certain: "Before meeting you," all the girls assure Bellenger, "I never knew what it was to make love." Then what can it be?

After midnight Bellenger makes tea — by dropping half a fistful of tea-leaves into the cold brown brew already in the pot, and then filling up with hottish water — he sits at the foot of Ivan's bed and goes once again over his entire sexual history. He outlines his original objectives, touches on individual campaigns, adduces localized actions, draws some general conclusions, and, somewhat consoled, goes to sleep till the following afternoon.

When Lucille lets him down for the first time, Bellenger's pride is aroused. Oh, she thinks she can play around, does she? Well she can go to hell! There are plenty of other fish in the sea; and Bellenger mentally enumerates a few score of them. But irrespective of Lucille's special attractions, Bellenger is quite incapable of maintaining this attitude. He cannot bear to think of any girl, let alone Lucille, disappearing for good, slipping irrevocably out of his grasp. So after a few weeks he relents.

He telephones: "Hullo, darling. Bellie speaking. Haven't

seen you lately. Was wondering what was the matter. Can you manage next Thursday afternoon at Studio One?"

Lucille is unable to manage Thursday afternoon.

"The symphony concert at the Albert Hall on Sunday?"

No good.

"The theatre on Tuesday?"

Nothing doing.

Bellenger plays his ace.

"Then how would you like me to take you to the Afro-Cubano Club on Friday evening?"

Ah; there he has something. Bellenger wins the trick. . . but his ace has now gone.

Yes, Lucille would like very much to visit the famous Afro-Cubano Club. Bellenger has a triumphant evening showing her off to the negroes, half-castes, and West Enders. He goes up yet another peg in the estimation of the Afro-Cubano proprietor, who there and then makes Lucille — as he has made all Bellenger's other partners — an honorary life member. On a few square feet of floor not occupied by the Black Rhythm Trio and the tables, several couples, comfortably squashed together, are making vaguely dance-like movements. Lucille is in great demand; first — "droit de seigneur" — by the proprietor, who whispers into her ear simple invitations indirectly connected with an honorary life membership. Then Panjitawarelam asks for the privilege. He introduces her to a painter, who immediately arranges to paint her the following afternoon; to a sculptor, who insists on doing her torso as soon as possible; to a bookshop proprietor, who offers her a job on very favourable terms. Later a dance-band leader invites her to visit the palais-de-danse as his private guest, a drunken American comes over to tell her "she's the sweetest thing"; and a funny little man, who is persuading as many people as he can to let him buy them drinks, tells her that if she will come and see him in Wardour Street to-morrow, he will build her up into a screen star.

"I mean it, too! You think I'm kiddin', don' cher?

Everybody thinks I'm kiddin''. Well I'm not, see. Jus' ars' fer Morrie, dahn Wardour Street, they'll tell ya. Or in 'Ollywood, if it comes ter tha'! 'Ave a drink. I said, *'Ave a drink!"*

Bellenger leans back in his chair with an expression of masterly confidence. He takes credit for everything, for the Afro-Cubano, the Black Rhythm Trio, the proprietor, Panjitawarelam, the painter, the sculptor, the bookshop owner, the dance-band leader, the American, the film-man — he has arranged them all. While as far as they are concerned, he takes credit for Lucille. It was he who arranged that she should be so lovely, that she should come to the Afro-Cubano; it is with his permission — "Are you sure you don't mind, Bellie?" — that she is dancing with them; it is with his connivance, even though he has not been openly informed, that they are going to paint her, sculpt her, train her, and generally put her over. Bellenger is the man who holds the strings in this little puppet show.

But he really knows, as they all know, except perhaps Lucille, that no good can come of it. . . . He knows that Lucille will not come back to Guilford Street with him, this night or any other night; that she came to the Afro-Cubano only out of curiosity. These pretty girls learn quickly; and in three weeks, if she has any sense at all, she will have had enough of the Afro-Cubano and the Corney Arms. She will go back to her mother and her nicer, well-brought-up boyfriends, perhaps to the one who originally took her to the Corney Arms; and it is he, Bellenger, who will be left high and dry, stranded in his top-floor, rat-ridden flat in Guilford Street. Watching her dance, he is able to register in yet another light the exquisite perfection of her loveliness. He knows that he can never possess her. The fact that she has slept with him means nothing. She belongs only to herself.

As he has foreseen, so it happens; but every step of the painful, familiar farce has to be gone through. She has to be dragged reluctantly away from Panjitawarelam and his crowd; detached from the bookshop proprietor, extricated from the gaily self-pitying Wardour Street group. She darts back once or twice to cancel an appointment, arrange another, exchange telephone numbers. Outside the Afro-Cubano, and again in Piccadilly tube station, there has to be a little scene, silent but deadly, in which Lucille refuses to come back to Guilford Street. In subsequent weeks she breaks three appointments. For a time she is seen around with the sculptor, later with the painter, then with another painter; then she is seen no more. Bellenger writes a couple of letters. The second brings the inevitable, conclusive, and unmistakable reply:

"I loathe you. You sicken me. I hope I make myself clear. You make me want to vomit. . ."

The affaire Lucille was a weighty blow, among the heaviest, though not *the* heaviest, Bellenger had ever received. It caught him squarely on the jaw — bash! — and knocked him flat. In the past he had got up, nimble and fresh, ready to weave in for more. But he was now a man who had been in the ring for ten rounds, ten year-long, hard-punching rounds, and lying there in the sawdust, he rubbed his jaw reflectively. Even then, so powerful was his libido, he might have raised himself before the count was over and taken another few pastings from his pretty female antagonists. But a pleasant, firm voice, stern though not combative, whispered in his ear:

"Come along, Hugh."

Not Bellie, but Hugh, the name on his birth certificate, used only by his relatives. And the voice had behind it all the authority of Cambridge and the assurance proper to a member of a family which had appropriated land in Shropshire two hundred and fifty years before and held on to it ever since. It was the voice of Prue Cummings, calling him back to his senses after eight years of slumming in the army and the West End.

When Prue Cummings came to the Corney Arms in the company of Pam, she did not accept it; least of all did she find it "interesting".

"It ought to be abolished," she said firmly.

"Oh, I don't know," said Bellenger, to whom she had been introduced by Pam; "what's wrong with it?"

"Well, this sort of thing is all right for a lot of foreigners," said Prue, "but it's not the place for a gentleman."

Bellenger looked at her reflectively; good, healthy figure; nice, fresh complexion, like a soap advertisement; no cosmetics; tweedy. Not the sort of girl with whom to impress the proprietor of the Afro-Cubano or Panjitawarelam or Angus Sternforth Simms; nevertheless, a good hockey-playing sort. And after this latest Lucille business, and one or two other affairs that had been slugging into him lately, he could think of nothing better than a good hockey-playing sort.

Prue Cummings, for her part, looked at Bellenger with a critical, but not unfriendly eye. He had obviously been in bad company lately. He would need a little cleaning up and pulling together. But he would do.

"Come along, Hugh," she said later, "let's go and have some supper."

"Good idea," said Bellenger. "Do you know Pedro's International Café Restaurant?. . . "

He trailed off. What was the point? Pedro's was a preliminary to an invitation back to Guilford Street. . . ." The full extent of the difference between Prue and the suburban adventuresses who frequented Soho was brought home to him.

"Let's go back to my place," said Pam. "I'll fix up something."

Bellenger hesitated. He hated leaving Soho in the evening, he hated deviating from his traditional round. His was a conservative temperament which liked to do the appropriate thing at the appropriate time. At no time, as far as he was concerned, was it appropriate to visit Pam's abominable flat in Victoria and listen to her dreary gossip about the Cambridge of ten years before, about the people who had "gone down" or "gone up", about the jobs they had taken, the wives and husbands they had married, the children they had begotten — "reproducing their ignoble kind", as Ginsberg put it — and the time and place at which Pam had last seen them. But he was lying, as it were, in the sawdust, after ten long, bitter rounds; he was still dazed by the terrific smack in the jaw with which Lucille had floored him; he was being counted out:

"— two, three, four —"

Was it worth getting up? Was it worth going on? Had he the strength to go on? Could he stand the pace?

"— five, six, seven —"

A stern but friendly voice, a firm, assured, hockey-playing voice whispered in his ear: "Come along, Hugh. Enough of this game. You are a gentleman, you are one of us. Come along, Hugh."

"— eight, nine, ten!" Too late! He was out! Bellenger was out for the count!

"Come along, Hugh."

"Yes, let's go," he said.

Pam, a "booksy girl", as she laughingly called herself, who at thirty was not only writing her first novel — "Shows a delicate touch" *(Spectator)*, "Careful portraiture" *(Sunday Times)*, "A promising first novel" *(Observer)* — but had become a quite relentless match-maker, happily linked arms with both Prue and Bellenger and took them off to Victoria. She had long reproached herself with leaving Bellenger — and Ginsberg, too, for that matter — on the loose. But now she had begun a thoroughly good job between Prue Cummings — the Cummings of Cambridge, used to live in Shrewsbury, one of the Shropshire Cummings — and Hugh Bellenger — only son of the Bellengers of Tanganyika. Ginsberg, of course, was rather a hopeless case; Ginsberg of — where was it, Stepney? Though something ought to be arranged even there. Some nice Jewess, perhaps. . . .

It was Pam who, over supper, first suggested Bellenger's leaving London for the remainder of the summer and going to Cambridge. It would be an ideal change and holiday, since he was not going abroad, and at the same time he would be able to do some reading at the Union library for his psychology thesis. As far as Pam was concerned, Bellenger's index card at this period read: "He's in London, working on his psychology thesis, under Professor Pfueffer, the Jungian." Bellenger himself scarcely remembered the fact from one weekly lecture to the next, and he busied himself with his studies in psychology chiefly when offering to psychoanalyse female "neurotics" at the Corney Arms. As a matter of fact, poor Professor Pfueffer had died a few weeks before, and he had not yet written to the University to ask about new tutorial arrangements during the next session.

Prue backed Pam up.

"Why don't you come and stay with us?" she said, bold and blushing. "I'm sure Peter" — that was her brother — "would be awfully pleased if you came. And I would, too," she added, a still deeper blush rising to join the apple-red of her cheeks.

Peter? Bellenger asked himself. What the devil had *he* got to do with it? Then he remembered certain quaint, hockey-playing conventions and modesties from the remote past. Floundering around for the right thing to say, he murmured:

"I suppose we should get in plenty of sport?"

"Oh, plenty.'"

"But I wonder if the section in the Union library on Jungian psychology will be extensive enough for my purposes. You see, Pfueffer was the man who stocked up our library. . . . No one can replace Pfueffer. . . . It might be a snag."

"Oh," said Prue, "yes. It might be a snag. Of course, your thesis comes first."

Yes, even Pam was forced to agree that this was a possible snag. The thesis came first.

Bellenger clung on to it. It gave him time to think; while a firm, friendly, unspoken voice whispered:

"Come along, Hugh."

In this thoughtful frame of mind, and not definitely committed, Bellenger left Pam's flat, where Prue was staying too, and headed for Bloomsbury. He strolled along Whitehall in the light drizzle which was all that remained of the earlier rain, crossed Trafalgar Square, and outside St. Martin's Church ran into Kagaranias. The old man was muttering to himself rather more distractedly than usual.

"Hullo, Misteh Bellengeh. Huh you? Huh's Misteh Ginsbeg? Busy wit megezine? I'm just going to all-night café in Strent. Well, chirrio."

Without waiting for a reply to his questions, Kaggy shuffled off to join the night queue outside a Strand all-night café. Never, surely, had he been quite so filthy and bedraggled. Perhaps he had a premonition that in a few weeks' time his warehouse was going up in flames.

Bellenger, as a result of his recent experiences, stared after Kagaranias as though seeing him for the first time. He scratched his head. Did such a person really exist? Could *anybody* become like that? Were the last ten years merely a dream filled with such dilapidated phantoms, weird and unsubstantial? Bellenger felt extraordinarily unsure of himself, unsure of everything. He scratched his head in puzzlement so hard that his hair stood up in a tousled mop. To-morrow, no doubt, he would wake up in the dormitory at Harrow. "Come on, Bellie, old chap," someone would say, "you've been snoring like a pig. Hurry, or you'll be late for breakfast. . . ."

It was with relief that Bellenger turned into Guilford Street. Though it was not long after midnight, and he did not usually go to sleep till three or four in the morning, he felt very tired. He would make a cup of tea, have a chat with Ivan — Ah! Ivan was the man to put his ideas straight! — and go to bed for about eighteen hours.

Bellenger pushed back the massive street door and stood on the threshold of the pitch-black passage. He sensed the presence of another person.

"Who's there?"

There was no reply.

"Who's there?" repeated Bellenger loudly. He struck a match. Philip Lank was cowering against a wall.

"Philip! What on earth's the matter?"

"I've found it," muttered Philip, grinning crazily to the wall and rolling his eyes upwards.

"Found what?"

"At last, I've found it."

Bellenger waited, ready to hit Philip hard on the jaw if he became violent. The poor fellow had obviously gone off his head, since he did not appear to be drunk.

"I've found the secret, the mathematical secret of the universe. . . . The square root of the cube of the integral of the logarithm of the differentia. . . ."

He straightened himself. He advanced on Bellenger with right arm outstretched and laid it on his shoulder.

"Bellie," he said, "you are the new Christ, the deliverer of mankind. Only you helped me, stood by me. . . . I am God." Philip repeated this several times very calmly. He turned round full circle and chanted it. "I am God. I am God. I am God. Everything is solved. You and I together will build the new Jerusalem on scientific principles. . . . From now on, you and I must never be separated."

Bellenger took Philip's arm to lead him to the door.

"You'd better go and sleep it off, Philip," he said, trying, by casualness, to edge Philip back towards normality.

"Don't be so silly!" cried Philip in a harsh voice. "You're coming with me."

"I'm not, you know."

"I shan't go unless you come with me," said Philip, his voice rising. "Understand, you're dealing with God now. And what's more," he added, lowering his voice again to its customary sob, "if you don't come I shall do someone in. It may be myself, it may be someone else. One thing is definite, to-night someone must die. . . . Only you can save me. . . ."

Bellenger took the scientist's arm and led him out into

the street. He could feel Philip's long, thin body trembling. The streets had been washed clean by rain; the pavements were covered with a fresh, glistening sheen. It was now a night of immense, clear spaces, a night for starry speculation between men like gods.

"God," Philip resumed, as they approached Tottenham Court Road, "I am God. You take one "o" from "good", and what do you get? God!"

A blue car came up smoothly and swiftly from behind and stopped a few paces ahead of them. A police officer beckoned them to the window.

"Identity cards, please," he said.

Bellenger drew from the large pocket of his "zoot-suit" a tattered handful of ration-book pages, tickets, envelopes, coupons, contraceptives, and notepaper, and extracted from it two torn separate half pages of identity card. Philip, after desperately searching every pocket and feeling in the lining of his jacket, found his identity card, as might have been expected, in his wallet. The police officer glanced at the identity cards, stared up at their faces, memorizing them in case of any future trouble; the radio in the car issued an instruction, and the car slid off.

"Evil," pursued Philip. "You turn round "evil", and what do you get? Live!"

Bellenger now welcomed Philip's talk and his lunacy. The resolve was crystallizing in his mind; he would go to Cambridge, he would accept Prue's invitation and all that might result from it. He wanted this night to go on for a long time, so that he might touch bottom, really rock-bottom; and then, choking for want of air and very nearly drowned, to shoot up and away to Prue, to her firm, friendly voice, to the early-to-bed reasonableness of Cambridge — and to marriage. Yes, marriage. Never had it seemed so attractive to lie in bed beside a thoroughly reliable, legally-wed wife. . . instead of tramping midnight streets with a lunatic who might at any moment become violent.

In Howland Street four Indians stood, hands in the

pockets of their flannel trousers, whistling up to a third-floor window in an attempt to attract someone's attention and to be let in for a night's sleep. The latest and humblest of London's immigrants, they were glad to bed down six or seven to a room. After the French, the Jews, the Italians, the Greeks, the Cypriots, the Maltese, had come the Indians, little chattering men with flashing smiles, and wearing a standard costume of cheap navy-blue overcoats and flannel trousers. Philip Lank shambled past, neck jerking backward and forward; he towered over them like the thin remnant of a prehistoric animal, a dinosaur or a pterodactyl.

"Philip," he said, "you turn it round, and you get Pilihp, Bellenger; you turn it round, and you get Regnelleb —"

This was too much for Bellenger. He gave several loud, uncontrollable hoots of laughter which echoed strangely through the empty streets.

"Hoo-hoo-hoo! Hoo-hoo-hoo-hoo-hoo! Hoooooo!"

The Indians stopped whistling and jabbered excitedly amongst themselves. One of them frisked a few paces in front of Bellenger and halted him.

"What uh matter wid you. What you laugh?"

Bellenger gave another few hoots, at the same time bending and pressing his stomach as though the comedy of the situation were really too much for him.

"You no laugh at us!" cried the Indian angrily. "You no laugh at India mans!"

The other Indians gathered behind their excited compatriot, more out of curiosity than in support.

"I wasn't laughing at you," said Bellenger, still holding his stomach.

"Yes you laugh!"

Bellenger straightened himself. "Look," he said to the Indian, with a note of impatience in his voice, "I wasn't laughing at you. Do you understand that? I was not laughing at you." He repeated the last sentence very slowly, carefully articulating each word: "I — was — not — laughing — at — you."

The Indian still looked at him suspiciously and uncomprehendingly; and his companions behind watched with the same bright-eyed, open-mouthed curiosity. Bellenger laid the flat of his hand against the Indian's chest and prepared to push him gently away. Suddenly the Indian bent down and bit Bellenger's finger. The action was so unexpected and painful that Bellenger gave a sharp yell, while, almost involuntarily, his left fist came round in a powerful swing and punched the Indian in the stomach. The Indian doubled up, groaned, pretended to be more hurt than he was, then craftily aimed a kick at Bellenger's groin. Fortunately the kick merely glanced along Bellenger's thigh. The other Indians closed in; curiosity gave place to action. One held a knife by its blade between thumb and forefinger, then regretfully put it away again. The occasion was not worth a knife.

There was a confused moment when Bellenger was striking out in all directions, while four little Indians, who all appeared to be on his back, were showering sharp blows on him in the most painful places and Philip Lank called impatiently:

"Do come *along,* Bellie. I wish you wouldn't stay and *argue* with these people."

An instant later, the four Indians, Bellenger, and Philip were each running as fast as they could in different directions. The Indians started it. They shouted something to each other, each repeating the monosyllable several times, and hared off. Bellenger turned round, half dazed, and saw the cause of their flight; a blue police car, almost certainly the same one which had stopped previously, was drawing up to the kerb. Quite automatically he too began to run. Even Philip, startled at last into a normal response, shot down the nearby alleyway. Bellenger bolted unthinkingly and blindly. He ran like someone in a dream who tries desperately to escape from a swifter pursuer. The menace, whatever it is, draws closer and closer; ever more menacing, it goes on drawing closer and closer and closer. . . Then, like the dreamer awakening, Bellenger realized that the pursuit was entirely imaginary; he slowed down in Whitfield Street, no one was running after him. The police must be chasing Philip and the Indians. Or more probably, since they were motorized police, they did not feel inclined to leave their comfortable car and run around after petty malefactors.

At any rate, he had shaken off Philip for the night; that was one consolation. It occurred to Bellenger, slinking back to Guilford Street in the shadows, that it might be an idea to leave for Cambridge this very morning. Then he need never see Philip again. What a delightful thought! Never to see again Philip or Kagaranias or any of the people who were always touching him for half-crowns. Never to set foot again in the Corney Arms or Pedro's International Café Restaurant. Never again to be enveloped in the miasma of Charlotte Street with its pollution of memories. Never again to be tempted by the enchantresses of the suburbs. Ah! That was not so easy. But if he ran away at once, it would be easier.

Bellenger did not bother to make any tea; he was far too tired. Instead, he flopped straight into bed. The next thing of which he was conscious was the ringing of the bell. The dreadful, strident bell penetrated right into the most exhausted profundities of his sleep and pulled him straightway into the following morning.

"Bell," it said. "Bell! *Bell! BE-E-E-E-ELL!*"

Who could be it? Eight o'clock. Too early for the milkman.

"Bellie!" came Ginsberg's voice from the room across the landing. "Bellie! — Bell. Bell — Bellie! Ha-ha! It's your turn, blast you!"

Bellenger turned over and closed his eyes again. The bell continued to ring. He put his fingers in his ears. Muffled, the din continued; it was joined by other, more ordinary noises. Bellenger dozed. The bell must have rung again; there must have been other noises and silences. Then Ginsberg was shaking him.

"Bellie, wake up. Come on, Bellie, I want you to get dressed. We've got to go round to the King's Cross hospital."

"Wha's ma'?" said Bellenger, without parting his eyes and leaving his mouth open.

But Ginsberg would not let Bellenger have his yawns and sighings and stretching whereby it took him three-quarters of an hour to sit up in bed. He pulled Bellenger into an upright position, put a cigarette in his mouth, lit it, and told him what had happened.

Philip had come round at eight o'clock and started ringing the bell. He had gone on ringing and banging at the door for about an hour, then he had begun to shout:

"I am God! I am God! God the scientist! God the mathematician!"

Then, Ginsberg had gathered from the woman downstairs, who had been watching the whole thing from the basement window. Philip had starting hammering on the door with his fists and calling through the letterbox hole:

"Bellenger! I want Bellenger! I must have Bellenger!" The woman downstairs had sent her little boy for the police, and just before they arrived Philip had drawn a razor-blade from his pocket and held it against his Adam's apple. He had stood there, with his back to the door and the razor-blade held ostentatiously against his throat, every now and again making a rapid gesture of drawing it across his windpipe. He appeared to be enjoying the scene he was creating. He grinned and rolled his eyes behind their thick spectacles and called:

"God here. I want Bellenger!"

It took three policemen and a great struggle to get him carted into the police ambulance and strapped down; and as he fought, razor-blades were scattered from one of his pockets. The woman downstairs had come up to fetch Ginsberg, who, dozing rather more lightly than Bellenger, had been wondering why the bell had stopped ringing. The police, it appeared, wanted both of them at

King's Cross hospital.

The rain was falling again, a steady, cold rain out of a dirty London sky. When Bellenger and Ginsberg arrived at the hospital, they discovered that they were not after all wanted. The police had found all the information they required in Philip's pockets; and they were already in the course of sending for Philip's father, a bank clerk in Birmingham..

"What's going to happen to him?" asked Ginsberg.

"Oh, he's having a lunacy board next Friday," said the young policeman to whom they spoke. "Poor chap, I feel sorry for him. What was it? Overwork, I suppose. That's the trouble, if you overdo it. These brainy chaps." The young policeman sighed. "Who's this Mr. Bellenger he keeps on asking for?"

"That's me."

"If you want to give evidence before the board, about his molesting you, or anything like that. . . ?"

"No, thanks," said Bellenger hastily. Eager to put an end to a conversation which might involve him in lunacy boards, police investigations, and what-have-you, he urged Ginsberg out immediately into King's Cross Road. He also remembered his flight from the police in the early hours of the morning. Perhaps, on the first occasion when the car had stopped, they had noted the name on his identity card. Since the officers in the car were almost certainly attached to the Bloomsbury division, he might very well run into them. Not that it mattered greatly. Still, what would the Cummings, a branch of the Shropshire Cummings, think of it all? The best thing to do was to clear off without delay. This very morning. The eleven-fifty from Liverpool Street. The good old eleven-fifty. His spirits rose when he thought of it. He needed a rest, by Christ! A damn long rest with a good hockey-playing sort! He would have tea on the lawn this very evening. He glanced at his watch. Half-past nine; do it easily.

The sky was the colour of an old floorcloth; the cold rain

continued to fall. Everyone was soaked and miserable. Ginsberg led the way into a Help Yourself Tea-Shop in Euston Road. Pale, slatternly waitresses and kitchen hands flopped about in broken down slippers.

"What you got?" asked Ginsberg.

"Nothing." Then, relenting a little: "Only tea."

Tea it was, the palest of pale, watery ochre in colour. With a tea-spoon chained to the counter, they were allowed to stir imaginary sugar in the frothy liquid. Unshaven, they stared at each other across a table. Bellenger brought out a squashed cigarette, whose survival into the morning would normally have been a miracle, since he smoked absolutely every cigarette he had before going to sleep (he even, in the middle of the night, crept around the flat picking up fag-ends and rolling them into bent, disintegrating cigarettes on his cigarette-rolling machine). However, the previous night had obviously been an exception. Bellenger broke the squashed cigarette in two, gave Ivan half, and realized by this act — one of innumerable joint eccentricities — how much he loved the pale, bony-faced Jew on the other side of the table. In his cogitations and calculations of the previous few days, he had left Ivan out of account. It was necessary and unavoidable to do so. Friendship was not, like marriage, or having an affair, something which followed a set course through defined channels; it could not be consummated, legalized, formulated. It was the most elusive of relationships. After the armistice which had recently been declared in his war with women, Bellenger was able to take stock of his affections. He found himself turning back towards his earliest loyalties, personified in Pruc; while of all people he had met since childhood, only Ivan meant anything. They had to part, but they would always be friends. How would they be friends if they never met and never wrote (no personal letters arrived at or left the Guilford Street flat)? Oh, somehow. . . .

Both Bellenger and Ginsberg disliked any display of sentiment. So after Bellenger had explained to Ivan his intention of leaving the flat, of going to stay in Cambridge as a suitor to Prue Cummings, and of completely changing his mode of living, neither said anything very much, except:

"You'll have to step on it to catch that eleven-fifty train."

"Yeh. Just sling a few things in a case, go round to the bank, and get the number eight bus."

"Better get a taxi."

"Yeh, that's right, better get a taxi."

"Of course, it doesn't affect the flat till the end of the month."

"No, the rent's paid till the end of the month. I'll come down before then for a day or two and see about things."

Their lives had grown together in a hundred ways. Besides, the end of anything was sad. Later, it occurred to Ivan, this moment would no doubt appear significant. But watching the rain, he was thinking of something else, something else entirely. The rain fell. Corporal Lenton said:

"Ginsberg."

"Corporal!"

"You take this list down to the village and go over it with the manager of the Welsh Groceries. It's for the officers' mess, so if there's any bollox up, gawd help you!"

It was raining; he took the short cut through the back gate and across the fields by the cliff top. As he got near the lane leading into the village, he saw a girl walking along, swinging a shopping bag. It was Margaret. He whistled. She waved and waited for him; and they stopped under a bush and kissed. Rain from the overhanging leaves dripped on to their heads, and a few drops rolled down his neck. There was the odd smell of Margaret's mackintosh and the momentary, shining happiness in her eyes. Then she walked off first, so that they should not be seen together.

CHAPTER XVIII

THE SHOREDITCH BOYS, they liked to call themselves, just the four of them. Pleasant-mannered and capable young men of the slums, they were above all determined to remain independent of any "boss," to get up in the morning what time they liked, to have suits and overcoats with thickly-padded shoulders, and to feel always in their left-hand trouser pockets a fat roll of notes held compactly together with a band of elastic. They might have gone into business. Indeed, they had gone into a business of sorts. But lacking capital, talent, assurance, and knowledgeability; lacking also the ambition to do anything other than laze around in the East End during the day, and round dog-tracks, cinemas, and dance halls during the evening, they had gone in for crime.

They owned a lorry and a shabby blue saloon car, both stolen several months before. It was this blue saloon car which had been parked in Hampstead Lane during several mornings. From its driving seat an eye was kept on Mrs. Chabbers' house and on her movements. The Shoreditch Boys were no scatterbrained young rascals; they planned things thoroughly. Not until they were entirely sure of themselves did they act, and then they acted with disconcerting whole-heartedness.

They spent a week getting the "low-down" — their slang, their accents, their entire inspiration were film-American. They spent a further week waiting for the correct moment to strike. Mrs. Chabbers' house was, of course, the target, selected as the most suitable in the whole of Hampstead Lane, on account of Mrs. Chabbers' habit of leaving after lunch and not returning till evening. Two of the Boys waited in the car, two others were ready with the lorry in Shoreditch. One afternoon, shortly after Mrs. Chabbers had rushed down the lane in her usual fluster, the maid left, too, all spruced up and clearly taking her half-day off. This was the moment. The blue saloon car drove round to the call-box by the Heath.

"O.K.," was the message.

Three-quarters of an hour later a large Removals lorry came to a halt outside Mrs. Chabbers' house. Two cheerful-looking, overalled workmen stamped up the path; one of them fumbled for a minute with the lock, and the street-door was open. They were joined by one of the men from the car, and the operation began. Miss Lint next door peeped curiously out of her window. She hadn't known Mrs. Chabbers was moving? But perhaps she was just having some things transferred to Lincoln, as she had done in the past. One or two other neighbours glanced occasionally from behind their curtains at the lorry. So Mrs. Chabbers was moving. . . .

It was hard work. For two hours the men sweated with tables and wardrobes and chests-of-drawers and armchairs and settees and carpets and beds. The drawing-room carpet was a devil, vast, thick, and heavy; one would scarcely have thought a carpet could weigh so much. Then there was the china; that had to be packed away hurriedly in the bedclothes for safety. The Shoreditch Boys were careful and thorough; they hated breaking crockery or damaging any of "their" property. By tea-time the lorry was full, economically though its space had been used. A few bits and pieces had to be left behind. The Chief, who had been sitting in the car all the while, gave a last look round. He came out with a stout metal box which had been left in a corner of Mrs. Chabbers' bedroom.

"You mugs!" he said. "There's dough in here!"

"'Ow jer know?"

"I seen one o' these before, in that job up Finchley Road. It's a portable safe."

"Stone me!"

The Chief was right. The little portable safe, which he took with him in the car, contained not only some of Mrs. Clubbers' jewellery, but also the forty pounds which had been got ready for presentation to Ginsberg on the following day.

The convoy drove off, the huge Removals lorry trailed by the shabby blue saloon car. In a quiet side-street behind Hampstead Lane, buttons were pressed in both the car and the lorry, and their number-plates transformed themselves with smooth, mechanical efficiency. The operation now over, cigarettes were lit, brows were mopped, and home to Shoreditch.

The Hampstead coup was but one of more than a dozen similar raids made by the Shoreditch Boys in the course of the summer. Just before Christmas, however, they were caught. The Chief got four years, the remainder two years apiece. Part of the loot was recovered, but most of it had long been disposed of and the money tucked safely away to provide nest-eggs for the Boys when they came out.

Mrs. Chabbers returned from St. James's Park, where she was sure three men had been trailing her at different periods of the afternoon, and found the front-door of her house wide open, the rooms denuded of furniture, and bits of fluff, glass, straw and sawdust scattered about the passages and up the garden path. For some time, she was simply mystified. What had happened? Had she come to the wrong house? Then she realized that she had been robbed, not merely of this or that, but of everything; everything, at any rate, that she had in the house. She registered, as she felt she ought to — even though no one was looking — shock, horror, consternation. And for a moment she did really feel faint. But behind these light, automatic reactions, there stirred a great feeling of joy. She could not have said why she was so happy about the robbery; nevertheless, she had the utmost difficulty in restraining herself from breaking into song.

"I have been robbed! I have been robbed!" The words ran like a gay, dancing refrain through her mind. And her joy was not really so surprizing. Firstly, there was the excitement of it all. Nothing so newsworthy had ever happened to her. The reporters would be round, and the press photographers. Her photo would be in the evening papers — "Hampstead Daylight Robbery". There would be questions to answer, interviews with the police, all sorts of comings and goings.

But more important than the immediate pleasure which the robbery would give her was the general, beneficent shaking-up of her life as a whole. Things which are functioning well, a good watch for instance, can only be harmed by a sudden jolt. On the other hand, those mechanisms which are functioning badly may click back to efficient normality by being knocked, turned upside down, and thoroughly shaken about. So the first thing which Mrs. Chabbers did was to wire to Jim from the post office in the High Street:

"Have been robbed. safe and unhurt apart from shock. Please come at once. Need you."

Now she could throw herself gratefully into his competent, rescuing arms. And she could leave London; the robbery was the excuse, the inspiration for which she had been waiting. Now she need no longer go through with the ordeal of being an independent woman, in search of intellectual and emotional emancipation. She could go back to Lincoln, grow stouter, perhaps have children. . . . It struck her as extraordinary that she had held Jim at arm's length all this time. In the past she had owned a house of her own, of which she was compelled to be proud; it was an expression of her personality. Now her personality was gone. What a relief!

Meanwhile, the department of Mrs. Chabbers' brain which dealt with money had established that the robbery was not financially disastrous. Her property was insured against burglary; and there had been no money worth talking of in the house. Suddenly she remembered the forty pounds destined for Ginsberg and locked away in her portable safe. That was gone along with the rest! What was she to do?

At the thought of Ginsberg and her vague obligations towards him and his magazine, all Mrs. Chabbers' distraught fluster returned. She just could not face telling him. Of course, she could draw another forty pounds from the bank. But never had she felt less like giving away forty pounds. The best thing to do was to take this opportunity for a complete break with London; to clear out, leaving her empty house, her loneliness, her desperate dashings to and fro, her Russian lessons, Ginsberg and his magazine, and all the hundred complications of her weekly round in London, leaving all these to solve themselves. Or alternatively, placing any of those which would not solve themselves in Jim's capable, solicitorial hands. Let Ginsberg try any funny stuff with Jim!

Having been shocked by the robbery into making a complete break with Ginsberg, Mrs. Chabbers felt no charity towards him. She was not one to sentimentalize about the past. On the contrary; now that she was engaging on a new course, it was necessary, in order to show the superiority of that course, to denigrate the past as much as possible.

"London!" she was to say for years to come in Lincoln. "I don't know how anyone can bear to live there! Great, big, dirty, ugly old place! And the people! The people!. . . Why, I was robbed by a man I took pity on and employed to give me private lessons. Of course, I've got no proof, and the police didn't take it up against him. But I'm absolutely certain he was a member of the gang which robbed my house. What? You haven't heard how my house was robbed? Oh, well, I haven't got time to tell you *all* about it, but I think I've got time before tea to give you some idea. It was like this. The man Ginsberg. . . ."

If Mrs. Chabbers had been taken quietly aside from the heat of the tea-table and asked to make a statement of sober truth, she would probably have admitted that she did not really believe Ginsberg to be behind the robbery. What earthly connection was there between his forty pounds and the carting away of all her furniture? Since he was to receive the money from her the following afternoon, why, if he were connected with the gang of burglars, should he have chosen that day of all days for the robbery? How could the fact that she had drawn forty pounds from the bank for Ginsberg on the very day she was robbed be anything other than a pure coincidence? But such confrontations with the need for sober truth are rare. So Mrs. Chabbers' great anecdote about the robbery, entirely false, grew to fabulous size, simply for lack of a cool, steel pin of truth with which to deflate its swelling balloon of hot gas.

Material for the anecdote collected in her mind as she made her way to the police station. The basis of it was the strange coincidence that on the very day when she had a moderately large sum of money in notes in the house, the place was robbed. Of course, the thieves had taken furniture and property worth hundreds, perhaps thousands of pounds. But that was all insured. The forty pounds was a dead loss. Almost certainly, ran the argument — which she realized would be helpful in maintaining her decision never to see Ginsberg again — Ginsberg had guessed the day when the money would be in the house and had informed the thieves. He might even have taken part in the operation himself.

With the police she was cautious. She did not want to go into details about the forty pounds; why she had drawn it, for what purpose it was destined. But she mentioned her acquaintance with Ginsberg and the suspicion which had crossed her mind that he might have given the thieves information about her. By the time Jim arrived, however, on the next morning, the legend was growing. Ginsberg had held her in an evil, hypnotic grip during the previous two years. She had not wanted to tell Jim about it, because while she was under Ginsberg's influence, her will to be open and clean and frank had been undermined. Ginsberg had tried to seduce her, to get money out of her under false pretences. He had cooked up a ridiculous story about wanting to found a magazine and asked for three or four hundred pounds. She had managed to put him off, but eventually had consented, more out of pity than anything else, to hand over forty pounds. Ginsberg, angered by the thwarting of his base plans, had then organized the robbery of her house.

Had a client of his come along with such a story, Jim would have put the client through a severe questioning. On this occasion, however, he was delighted to accept the story, since it gave him encouragement to ask an entirely non-legal question. After murmuring vague solicitorial threats against Ginsberg, he whispered:

"Darling, will you marry me?"

His tone of voice, his humble, doggish entreaty were the same as they had been when he first asked the question twenty years before.

"I don't know what to say," said Mrs. Chabbers, game to the last.

Jim seized her in his arms. She scarcely resisted, only placing her hands against his chest and exerting a gentle pressure to push him away.

"You must marry me!" he cried. He knew it was now or never, and rather fancied, with immense inward exultation, that it was now.

Her eyelids fluttered. She coyly averted her lips when he tried to kiss her. Then at last she brought the words out. After twenty years and an intervening marriage and divorce, she granted him the honour and favour of becoming her second husband:

"Well, darling, if you think it will make you happy, I don't mind. Let's hope it will be for the best. . . ."

Having thus opened the road for retreat into Jim's safe, welcoming arms, she hurried along it as quickly as her dignity permitted. Jim took charge; Jim took her over, as it were, lock, stock, and barrel; Jim saw to everything. And what a relief that was!

They stayed for a couple of days at the Empire Hotel in Russell Square, while Jim attended to her affairs with professional efficiency. He was anxious to leave London as soon as possible and begin to make arrangements for their wedding in Lincoln. She, for her part, once installed in the Empire, was agreeably apathetic. The huge, faded hotel immediately re-established connection with Lincoln and the past; for it was here she used to stay with her father, and later, on several occasions, with her first husband. The past crept into her mind, spreading itself into every sad, forgotten corner. She made no resistance; youth was over, the last incongruous remnants blown away during the previous few days. There were no struggles on the bed in their neighbouring single rooms at the Empire. Jim bided his time, was more than correct, and waited patiently and responsibly for the wedding-day. Once, in the morning, he came into her room while her teeth were still in a tumbler. Toothless, she was more naked than if the bedclothes had been pulled down and her nightdress torn off. Jim stood for a moment in surprise, registering her sunken mouth, her bare gums, and the queer, indistinct sounds which she uttered. Then, oddly enough, he came over and kissed her tenderly. He had seen her for the first time in all her pathetic helplessness and human weakness; and the sight had aroused with new force his old protective instincts.

They both enjoyed driving by night and staying at first-class roadside hotels. So on the fourth evening after the robbery, when the late summer dusk was already falling, they started off from the Empire with the intention of putting up outside London somewhere on the Lincoln road. As the car plunged forward past the traffic lights of Guilford Street, Mrs. Chabbers felt a momentary pang of intolerable regret. She was saying goodbye to youth. Dying was merely sad and painful; whereas the decisive moment when one crossed the line into middle age was heartbreaking.... Far away down Guilford Street she caught a glimpse of a tall man walking along with his arm round a girl. She fancied it might be

Ginsberg. How pleasant it would be to walk along with his arm round her waist; and then to sail away to a sunny land, to the Bahamas, South Africa, or the Riviera, there to lead a distinguished, gay, bronzed life of perpetual sunshine, cocktails on the beach. . . . Too late; never, now, never in all eternity would she know romantic love. At that instant of crossing the traffic lights she had entered middle age.

"Well, old girl," said Jim, "we're off! How do you feel about it?" He chucked her under the chin playfully.

For answer Mrs. Chabbers slipped her hand through his arm. She turned round from staring up Guilford Street and faced ahead. Before her stretched the traffic lights of Southampton Row and the regulated, undeviating future.

CHAPTER XIX

GINSBERG LEANED up against the ticket machine in Tottenham Court Road tube station. The escalator jogged away. Every now and again it bore up a great mass of people, held them poised momentarily for inspection, and then ejected them. No sign of Lolita. Since she was already twenty minutes overdue, it was certain that she would not be coming. But Ginsberg continued to lean up against the ticket machine. He felt curiously detached; he would just as soon be watching the escalator with its human display as doing anything else in the world. He went on leaning for another twenty minutes. It seemed, somehow, that if he went on leaning long enough, Lolita would eventually arrive; the rendezvous was surely a place to which Lolita must some day return. Not that he cared any longer; once the appointed minute had passed, the affair was over, like so much else during these last few days. He went on leaning solely out of inertia.

Finally he shook himself upright and shambled off. He ought, he reflected, to be feeling discouraged, depressed, truly ill-used. In a couple of days the whole structure of his life in Guilford Street had collapsed. Bellenger had gone, not merely in space but in time; the Bellenger he had known for ten years was now thoroughly buried in a past already remote. *Scamp* was finished. The last tenuous remnant of it, which was all he had hoped to salvage, had disappeared as a result of Mrs. Chabbers' desertion. And the suddenness of Mrs. Chabbers' flight, the cause of which he had learnt from a sympathetic detective making routine enquiries about her absurd allegations, had produced an effect more immediately catastrophic than the destruction of *Scamp*. There were to be no more Russian lessons. Half his weekly income was gone. As if that were not enough, he had received, the previous morning, a polite, affectionate, almost lyrical note from the principal of the Literary Institute, announcing that his services would not be required for the following session. How valuable those services had been, said the principal, it was scarcely possible for him to express, but. . . . Therefore no overdraft, at any rate no justifiable overdraft from the bank; the other half of his weekly income was gone, too. There was, of course, the money Bert Flogcrobber owed him; but that was a question apart. Meanwhile, thirty shillings in his pocket was all that stood between him and the pawn shop.

Then there was Lolita. He had now to undergo not only the subtler deprivations of her absence, but the straightforward corporeal ones; he had not made love for over four weeks. This alone was normally enough to make him feel as flat and stale as a jug of sour beer.

And the rats. Ha! One could not but admire them, with their pertinacity, their resourcefulness, their desperate courage! And they were, after all, fellow-occupants of the flat; *they* were not likely to leave Bloomsbury. They had found out where Ginsberg hid his rations, in a small fibre suitcase tucked away under an armchair in his room. Bold as you please, with amazing and violent energy, they had one afternoon torn away the entire back of the suitcase and made off with the week's rations. Their official opponent, the rat-catcher from the town hall, had made one of his routine visits the following morning. This rat-catcher, or "rodent operative", as he was officially described by the borough council, was a funny little man with absolutely no pretensions. He arrived once a week with a small bag, patiently laid his uninviting poisons and set dangerous traps on which Ginsberg and Bellenger were terrified of doing themselves injury. The poisons, of course, were no concern of the rats. Why should they eat poison when they had all Ginsberg's rations? As for the traps, they might carelessly have nuzzled round the bit of mediocre cheese which served as bait, had they not been so wise, resourceful, and experienced. One foolish young rat, it was true, had its tail caught in a trap; but it got away by biting the tail off.

"Have you ever caught a rat?" Ginsberg asked the rat-catcher. The rat-catcher was not offended. It was his duty to explain, patiently and modestly, and to persist.

"Oh yes," he said, "lots. Only yesterday I found one in a trap, over in Kentish Town. A whopper he was, too. Great big feller. Stone dead. Ah yes." He scrambled up to inaccessible corners of the flat, overlaid with dust, and placed his new traps and poisons.

"Well, see you next week," he said, and tripped off with his queer little bag and his gentle, shy smile.

Things were, if anything, worse than ever, on the rat front.

So, reflected Ginsberg, he had indeed every reason to be feeling discouraged, depressed, and truly ill-used. The curious thing was that he now felt for the moment quite cheerful, as optimistic as he had ever been, and full of vitality and heightened, positive sentiment. He wanted to shake hands with people, to do good, to sing, to dance. He had shaken off the lethargy of the tube station and felt that he was on the point of experiencing one of his crises of boundless optimism and energy. He walked several times round Soho Square, admiring the trees, admiring the tall buildings, admiring the evening sunshine, admiring the passers-by. In Frith Street, Ginsberg's favourite organ-grinder was turning the handle of his dilapidated instrument. The mournful, red-eyed veteran of Mons and Ypres and long-forgotten battlefronts of the 1914-18 war touched his cap expectantly. Ginsberg was known to all the organ grinders and pavement artists in the West End as a man who never passed the old cap without dropping in at least a penny. Not that Ginsberg believed in charity. "I pay them for the pleasure they give me," was his argument. Now he pressed a half-crown in the hand of the former soldier-hero. This act made him feel even better. What a decent chap he was at heart! How kind! How considerate! How well-disposed towards everybody!

He turned into the Italian café-bar for a coffee. The place was filled with the babble of Italian Cockney. Wonderful people the Italians, thought Ginsberg, wonderful; and yet there was no people in the world finer than the English, except perhaps the Welsh. None whatsoever; he frowned over his coffee-cup in case anyone should be wishing to contradict him.

Meanwhile, a tiny, impenetrable area of calmness at the very centre of his mind — "the observation-post" he called it — was viewing Ginsberg's high spirits with wonderment and caution. It distrusted these crises of optimism. The last one had produced *Scamp*. What would this one produce? A trip to Brazil? Retirement to a monastery? Or just another short story?

But there was no question, observation-post or no observation-post, as to what was immediately necessary. The thing to do this hot summer's evening was indisputably to find himself a girl. The Corney Arms was no good; too much competition. The street was no good, he did not feel brave enough to accost girls in broad daylight. Besides, he had given up that sort of thing; he was too old to do it with any initial enthusiasm, and without enthusiasm it was an uncomfortable farce. The only alternative was the Luxor Dance Hall at Marble Arch. True, the entrance fee was sheer robbery (no wonder Lushamor shares had risen so spectacularly), true, the heat, the dust, the sweat, the fug, and the jostling were intolerable. Nevertheless, the fact remained that two thousand pretty girls, frantically unconcerned with heat, dust, sweat, fug, jostling, and the spectacular rise in Lushamor shares, were even now queueing up at the back of Oxford Street so that they might exchange the wages of five hours spent at the sewing machine or behind the shop counter for the privilege of meeting two thousand boys in the Lushamor Palais de Danse.

Ginsberg bought an evening paper and caught the bus up Oxford Street. He glanced at the leader in the paper. The article was bad, debased, truly low, in the worst tradition of cheap journalism. Ginsberg felt momentarily sick. He crumbled the paper up into a ball, pushed it under the seat, and ground it with his heel. What a horror! It needed all the main force of his mood of optimism and positive energy to transmute this sheer momentary disgust into a larger understanding and tolerance even of the evening paper. The conductor came to collect his fare, and in his voice there was so much weariness and resignation that Ginsberg looked up and saw in imagination a hundred thousand other conductors and labourers and mechanical functionaries with heads bowed and spirits subdued; while above them, in the modern world, was held, not the whip nor the gun, but the hypnotic repetition of newspaper and book and magazine, the unctuous hypocrisy of the radio, the infantile wooziness of the film. Truly the people of England — and for Ginsberg, as well as Bert Flogcrobber, the word England held a patriotic magic of lost, beautiful associations — the tolerant, subdued, kindly, cheated people of England, truly they deserved something better than the leader he had just read. Admittedly, not all popular newspapers were as bad as this one; and even in this paper, not all leading articles were quite so low. Nevertheless, the vast machinery of contemporary culture, which would survive any mere change of political regime, was on the whole one for the perpetuation of falsity, meanness, narrowness, drabness, and inequality, and for the permanent emasculation of this bus- conductor and his fellows.

Ginsberg collected his change and reproached himself for slipping back into a pessimistic inner querulousness. That was not the spirit at all, not the spirit at all. Here was Marble Arch.

Men of England, heirs of glory!
Heroes of unwritten story!. . .

He murmured the lines to himself as he clattered down the steps of the bus.

"Marble Arch," said the conductor sadly and wearily, a defeated urban descendant of Kentish farmworkers driven from the soil in the late eighteenth century.

An historical phase, thought Ginsberg; you can fight against anything you like, a battleship, an airliner, an atomic bomb, but you can't fight against an historical phase. The most you can do is help, after great effort, in edging it along another half-inch. So lying, meanness, drabness and misery must have their day out yet. And it was no use grumbling, even to oneself.

"An historical phase," he said to the girl in the cash-desk at the Lushamor. It was nine o'clock, and the last queue had already gone in.

"How many?" she snapped.

The commissionaire shifted his weight slightly, ready to deal with any funny stuff.

"Ticket for one," said Ginsberg.

The Lushamor was always overwhelming; now the noise and the heat and the pressure of bodies struck at one like a great sledgehammer covered with velvet.

The band was playing a waltz, and the hall was almost in darkness. Electric starlight played on the ceiling. A thousand couples circulated, in a packed but shifting mass, on the four thousand square feet of dance floor. A thousand men and a thousand women looked on.

"Stand back off the floor, *please!*" bawled the loudspeaker above the dreamy music. "Make room for the dancers, *please!*" no one moved. Everyone was wedged as tightly as before.

At the back of the hall, a packed and plunging mob pushed and yelled and fought its way towards an unseen objective. That was the bar. Ginsberg felt thirsty, but it was useless trying to get an alcoholic drink. He made for the soft drinks' bar. Here the crowd was slightly less dense. He squirmed, he threaded, he apologized, he ducked, he shoved, he twisted, he edged, he stood on tiptoe, he moved round, he advanced bodily, and very soon found himself standing against the bar. Here it was only a question of catching the waitress's eye, a mere quarter of an hour's wait. He looked to right and to left, at the undifferentiated faces. One detached itself from the rest, a pretty, familiar face which he could not immediately identify. Greta Blauzimmer! That was a stroke of luck. He was sure, from the way Greta Blauzimmer used to stare at him during his lectures, that she was really waiting, always had been waiting for such a chance meeting. And she would more than compensate for Lolita. Indeed, in the presence of Greta Blauzimmer's vivid colouring and dainty, graceful gestures, Lolita appeared gross and coarse, a vast piece of heaving blubber, a she-elephant or a whale.

"Greta Blauzimmer," he said.

She turned round, looked at him questioningly, and then said:

"*You* here!"

"Why not?" Ginsberg smiled ingratiatingly and shrugged his shoulders.

"A lecturer at the Literary Institute!"

"Well, you're here, aren't you?"

Ginsberg knew nothing at all about her. In fact, he had never spoken to her before alone. It was strange, having stared at a person long and hard once a week for nearly a year, and remaining a total stranger.

"Well," he said, with beaming confidence, "how about a dance?"

The band was now playing a foxtrot. The mass of dancers pushed against each other to a different rhythm.

"Stand off the floor, *please!*" bawled the loudspeaker. "Make room for the dancers, *please!*" Still no one moved.

Ginsberg had just caught the waitress's eye and broke away for an instant to buy a couple of orangeades. As he did so, Greta Blauzimmer touched him on the shoulder.

"Will you excuse me one moment?" she said.

Ginsberg managed to keep her in sight as she threaded her way through the crowd and up the stairs and on to the balcony, where she stopped at the ladies' handbag depository. Having got her handbag, she moved round the balcony to the opposite side and stopped at the counter of the ladies' cloakroom. Ginsberg stood for several minutes, very puzzled, holding two orangeades, and watching her move along with the small queue till she reached the counter. She was handed her coat and disappeared into the ladies' lavatory. Someone charged Ginsberg in the back and spilt most of the two orangeades. He remained with the two almost empty glasses staring up at the door of the ladies' lavatory. When Greta Blauzimmer came out, she did not so much as glance in his direction. She wore her light swagger coat, had her handbag under her arm, and stepped smartly to the exit staircase. That was that. Had she cleared off? There seemed scarcely any doubt about it.

"Stand back off the floor, *please!*" bawled the loudspeaker. This time some force caused the crowd to surge backwards. The two orangeade glasses were crushed against Ginsberg's waist. Could they stand the pressure? The crowd leaned steadily backwards. Spiffhorn, the printer, bobbed into view phantasmagorically in a visible section of the dance-floor, and an instant later disappeared from sight and mind. A fat girl stood on Ginsberg's toes and his back was in turn pressed against some bodies behind. One of the orangeade glasses cracked. He held the other high above his head, till the crowd eased forward again and some sort of movement and respiration was possible.

Ginsberg was sweating and exhausted. He disposed of the orangeade glasses under a chair at the side of the hall, wiped the spilt drink from his jacket with a handkerchief, and asked the nearest girl to dance. Perhaps Greta Blauzimmer would be back. Maybe she had gone out for a breath of air.

The girl whom Ginsberg had asked to dance was a pretty little gum-chewing blonde with a white jumper drawn tightly over a pair of round, high breasts.

"O.K.," she said nonchalantly.

They pushed through to the dance-floor. The girl pressed herself against Ginsberg, chewing gum all the while and looking away disinterestedly over her shoulder. Ginsberg could feel the entire length of her body moulded into his.

"Some baby!" he thought.

There were hundreds like her all around. They chewed gum continuously, their jumpers were drawn tightly over round, high breasts, they looked away disinterestedly to right and to left. Suddenly they began to shriek enthusiastically. All dancing stopped and hundreds of girls, Ginsberg's blonde among them, shrieked piercingly.

"What's the matter?" asked Ginsberg.

"It's Jackie Sambo," said the blonde between two yells.

Jackie Sambo?

"Jackie!" screamed the girls. "Eeeeeeeeeeeeee!"

Jackie Sambo turned out to be the young man who had just begun to beat the drums. He banged away as hard and as loud as he could, grinning ecstatically. Every now and again he banged even harder and louder, and the girls went into a paroxysm of screaming delight. The applause was thunderous, but above it, or below it, the noisy drum rattled and banged and clattered away with rhythmless, headachey insistence.

The sweat, the noise, the pointless discomfort of the Lushamor Palais de Danse were proving too much for Ginsberg. He had to get some fresh air and a gallon of cool drink or he would collapse. He decided to try, too, the "Will you excuse me one moment?" stunt. The blonde was staring open-mouthed at the drummer and every few seconds uttered a shrill yelp. Her back was turned to Ginsberg. He nudged her on the waist; she felt for his hand and drew it round her. Ginsberg nudged her again with his free hand.

"Will you excuse me one moment?" he said.

"Gee!" she said. "Jackie Sambo! Ain't it a shame they keep him off the radio! It's a real shame, that's what it is, a real shame!"

"Yeh," murmured one or two gum-chewing neighbours, "it's a real shame. They're frightened to let him on, that's what it is."

"Will you excuse me one moment?" repeated Ginsberg.

The blonde became aware of his plaintively muttered request.

"What's that?" she said.

"Will you excuse me one moment?" said Ginsberg for the third time. It seemed that he was back at school asking if he could leave the room and go to the lavatory.

"Wha'd'y'e mean, excuse you? Ain't you well or sumpthing?"

"No, it isn't that, but —"

"Well, woss the idea then? You arst me te darnse, didn't yah? Woss the idea tryin' te run aht in the middle?"

"But we're not dancing," said Ginsberg shamefacedly. Several people were glaring at him with curiosity and hostility.

"Well, go on then, buggar off!" said the blonde. "Anybody would think *I* arst *you* te darnse! Go on then, wotcher waiting for? Buggar off! Stone me!" she said to her gum-chewing neighbours in general, "the nerve of some o' these geezers!"

Ginsberg slunk off, tripping over people's toes, brushing against serried rows of breasts, squeezing past ravishing mounds of backside. At last he found himself in the street. Ah, the street! In the last resort, there was always the street! Thank God for the street!

Opposite Marble Arch he spotted a lemonade barrow. He drank four glasses of lemonade, lukewarm water faintly, delicately discoloured with the merest drop of fruit juice, paid for it the justifiable price for a bottle of champagne, and feeling much refreshed crossed over to the park.

It was now dusk, a late summer's dusk, a moment when, on a hot night and in Hyde Park, anything could happen. Ginsberg hoped so at any rate. Legs twinkled mysteriously in the half-light and the distance. Solitary and apparently lovely women strolled thoughtfully across the grass. From some corner of the park, cut grass emitted a faint scent of hay. At Speakers' Corner the usual quiet hubbub, the peaceful tumult of singing and praying and exhorting and arguing was in progress even at this late hour.

Ginsberg drifted through the strange crowds of salvationists, revivalists, community singers, guardsmen, serving girls, exhibitionists, political preachers, tramps, policemen, lunatics, cheerful prophets, agents of the Public Morality Council, plutocrats from the Park Lane hotels, and miscellaneous wanderers like himself, till he came to a large circle of people singing lustily and tunefully in Welsh. On one side of the Welsh, a band of Irish chanted a ragged and sentimental chorus. On the other side, a group of seventeen-year-old girls led by a large, black-haired momma, thickly bedaubed with rouge and paint and mascara and lipstick and nail-varnish, and all giggling hysterically, surrounded a number of elderly men arguing about anarchism and sang

> "Lay that pistol down, bo,
> Lay that pistol down!
> Pistol-packing momma,
> Lay that pistol down!
> Yippee! Yoohoo! Yippeeeeee!"

But the orderly and forceful singing of the Welsh, like a trained and disciplined army confronting a loose rabble, overcame all other voices with "Cwm Rhonnda" and "Land of My Fathers".

Ginsberg stood entranced among the Welsh. The wide-open mouths, the lusty, harmonious voices, the stern men dressed in black, the special charm of the girls immediately transported him to Porth Bay and to Margaret. "Margaret, where are you?" he whispered, "Margaret, why have you left me in this world alone?" Then, adopting the stern expression of the men around him, he roared such Welsh words as he knew and made up the rest.

At eleven o'clock the Welsh went home, and Ginsberg, no longer wishing to investigate the restless sordidity of the park, ambled down Oxford Street, hands in pockets, tie undone, shirt collar wide open. "Margaret!" he whispered to himself every now and again, "where are you? What are you doing at this moment? Are you alive or dead?" Or, "Margaret, life without love is an operation without an anaesthetic. Perhaps you think of me as often as I think of you? Perhaps we shall meet in the next world? Perhaps we shall relive this life and be permitted to choose alternative courses? And then?. . . But of course! Somehow, in some inexplicable way, you and I are one. . . Always, always, you hear me! You and I are one. . . "

At the same time Ginsberg savoured the possibility of each pair of female legs which crossed in the darkness, mysteriously and beautifully, on the other side of the road. Those possibilities did not bear investigating — how many shapely legs were crowned by a horsy face! — but it was good that they should exist. Possibilities. . . he thought with bitterness and bewilderment of Greta Blauzimmer. She had been a possibility, too, for a whole year, a delightful, wonderful, charming possibility. And now. . .

Ginsberg reached Guilford Street. Home sweet home, home to the rats! What romantic, what voluptuous companions! But wait; what was this? An unprecedented phenomenon, a miraculous apparition, obviously a direct result of unspoken prayer — God was on his side after all — a beautiful, long-legged, fair-haired girl with a suitcase sitting on his steps.

Ginsberg walked round her and up the steps, inserted his key in the lock of the street door; then, having established his legitimate position on the doorstep, he turned and said, "Hullo."

"Hullo. Are you Ivan Ginsberg?" The girl spoke with

unhesitating although shy friendliness. Her voice was high, soft, and feminine, with an agreeable trace of Irish accent. She seemed to Ginsberg to bear a wonderful resemblance to Margaret; and he immediately sensed that she, like Margaret, would transform the entire aspect of things, would return to life its significance, its beauty, and its completeness. But what stimulated him most of all in the first instance was the sound of his name uttered in a friendly and enquiring tone by another person. So even on this night there was someone in London who wanted to see him and speak to him!

All the dismal, solitary experiences of the previous few hours were dispersed and blown away by the girl's words and her presence. She enabled him to re-establish communion with the human race. Once again, as in Soho Square, he was invaded by an intoxicating sense of optimism. "That is my name," he replied, "Ivan Ginsberg."

"Oh. . . you see. . . I am Kathleen O'Flanagan. . . You see," she continued with a rush, "I called earlier, but you weren't in, and the woman downstairs said you might be back later, so I thought I would wait. I hope you don't mind. This is the first time I've been to London, and you're the only person I know. Of course, I don't really know you properly. . . I hope you don't mind."

"I've never minded anything less in my life," said Ginsberg. "You're Kathleen O'Flanagan of Ballykelly, I take it. Your story was the only really worthwhile piece of original writing submitted for my magazine. By the way, I'm sorry to have to tell you that *Scamp,* which has been dying unnoticed for the last four weeks, finally expired two days ago. A proper abortion — or rather miscarriage."

"You mean your magazine's not coming out after all?" said Kathleen, and there was a warmth and sincerity in her voice which made Ginsberg ashamed of his disillusioned cynicism.

"I'm afraid not," said Ginsberg. "I was going to return all the contributions in the next day or two. But look here," he broke off, "this is a pleasant surprise finding you on my doorstep. I take it that you've run away from home, as you said you'd do in your story. Congratulations!" He held out his hand.

"You mean that?"

"Of course I do. Life is too short to spend eating one's heart out. I'm also glad you've come for purely selfish reasons; I'm delighted to see you."

Kathleen took his hand. At the same time he took her other hand and helped her to rise from the step to a standing position. They stood face to face, holding hands and staring earnestly into each other's eyes. They had no need to speak as they separated and Ginsberg picked up the suitcase. Eyes, hands, voices, ordinary common-sense and calculation, as well as those radiations which every human being emits, had established that they were in harmony, that they were tuned in to the same frequency.

Kathleen was delighted with the flat.

"It's lovely," she said, "just as I'd imagined it."

"It's not bad," admitted Ginsberg, rather grudgingly. Viewed abstractly, the flat was ideal — central, self-contained, tastefully decorated and furnished, "with every modern convenience". Give Bellenger his due, he had fitted himself up a pleasant flat. The initial idea was good; what had gone wrong? Ah, that. . . For one thing, there were the rats.

"Of course, we have rats here," he said, expecting her to spring back with alarm and disgust as other visitors to the flat had done.

"Of course," she said placidly. "It's the same in Ireland. Rats everywhere. We've got hundreds at home. I don't like them, do you?"

Ginsberg choked with only partly feigned indignation.

"Like them!" he growled. "Like them! I really can't express myself on the subject; my feelings lie too deep for words. Let's talk about something else."

"Have you been doing any writing lately? I suppose you do write, as well as edit?"

"I did once," said Ginsberg, "but I gave it up when this magazine idea got hold of me. Writing's a mug's game. No, I don't really mean that," he added, noting the rather exaggeratedly hurt and puzzled expression on Kathleen's face. All her expressions were charmingly and unconsciously overdrawn.

"Which reminds me," he continued, for it had, indeed, reminded him, "I must tear up all the stories I've ever written and start afresh. Or perhaps write nothing at all, I don't know. Anyway, all that I've written up till now is a lot of trash. Bad-time trash at that; you know, whatever you do, don't be happy or pleasant or useful or positive or brave or stoical or optimistic or co-operative or magnanimous. Of course, I was just following the fashion unthinkingly." Ginsberg shrugged his shoulders.

"I'm afraid I don't understand all these things as yet," said Kathleen. But she looked at Ginsberg with admiration. She had come to London to hear incomprehensible outbursts of this kind.

"Bah," said Ginsberg, "it's easy to understand. That's part of the racket, to make you think there are things you don't understand. But it's all quite simple, really; truth is simple. Anybody who tries to make truth complicated is an intellectual racketeer. I've been a dupe of those boys for years. . . "

He went over to a drawer and pulled out a pile of manuscript nine inches high.

"The collected works of Ivan Ginsberg," he laughed, and began to tear the manuscript there and then. They were so easy to tear, amazingly easy. In ten minutes they could all be in shreds; yet how long they had taken to write.

"Oh, don't tear them all!" cried Kathleen in dismay. "There may be some worth preserving."

"None," said Ginsberg. "I'm suiciding this section of my life, you see. Then I can start afresh." He looked at her significantly.

"Let me hear just one of your stories," she said, "before

they all go. Just to give me some idea of what you mean."

"Better not. Oblivion is oblivion. Once you start making concessions —"

"Just one. Please." She picked up the top half of a sheet as yet torn only into two, and began to read aloud:

BALLAD OF RUSSELL SQUARE

"The lift gates clang to savagely; the lift goes down, the lights go off. The slam of the gates says, that was the last, now sort it out among yourselves.

"The prostitutes and drunks and flotsam hanging about in doorways feel a last uneasiness. Is there no hope? They kick around in the bitter street. Midnight silence; only the call of a wayward flapper tears the night. Then they feel a terrible hatred of themselves and the horror that hems them in.

"Suddenly it happens. Ah, at last! What they have all been waiting for — a fight. Words and threats and blows, terrible blows with all a man's strength. They would like to murder each other. They would all like to murder each other. Instead, they watch the two men. no one interferes.

"One man goes down, the other is on him, hitting and hitting and hitting. Others now join in, all of them hitting the man who is down. They go on hitting so long that the onlookers wonder when they will grow tired. But harder and harder and more and more! A man calls out from far away, ready to run: "One at a time, you dirty swine! One at a time!" They take no notice.

"Then quite suddenly they stop. Without a word they stroll away, wiping their hands, brushing their coats. They are tired, they have had enough.

"The beaten man lies in the road. He lifts his bleeding head and crawls on hands and knees towards the kerb. He has no strength, collapses, crawls. . . They all watch breathlessly, because a car is coming along the road. Will it overtake him? Will its wheels roll over him? The man crawls on, falls flat on the pavement. A woman wipes the blood with a handkerchief. The crowd disperses. But while the hitting was going on, they had exulted. That was what they wanted to do, to hit and hit and hit with all the strength they had in them, strike out and kill and avenge themselves.

"The man raises his head, sees the street from an unusual angle, a worm's eye view. He reaches for —"

"Where's the other half?" said Kathleen.

"It must be somewhere at the bottom of the wastepaper basket."

"Oh, I should have liked to read the rest of it. I thought it was awfully good, you know. Are you sure you ought to tear them up?"

"I must say, I liked it better after hearing you read it. I think I'll go through them carefully and see what's worth salvaging."

Ginsberg retrieved the nine-inch thick pile of manuscript, only the top few inches of which had been already destroyed. "But there's no question about this lot," he added, and rushed over to a bundle of sheets prepared for Bert Flogcrobber. He had to do something in Kathleen's honour, and this was a step he had been wanting to take for several weeks. Finish with Bert Flogcrobber!

"What's that?" said Kathleen in alarm, wondering what Ginsberg was tearing up with such ferocious energy.

"That," said Ginsberg, hurling the screwed-up shreds into the wastepaper basket, "is the lowest form of activity known to man — dope journalism. A prostitute merely pretends a few gestures, opens her legs and spreads syphilis. Whereas the dope journalist feigns sincerity in our most profound activities, politics, social life, public affairs; and he spreads war, famine, tyranny, general misery, and what have you. Of course, he has his excuse. I'm only a minor agent, he says, I've got to earn my living; and if I didn't do this, someone else would. And he's damn right there, unfortunately. As Bernard Shaw wrote somewhere, the population of Great Britain is forty-five millions, ninety per cent of whom are free-lance journalists. However, that ninety per cent no longer includes Ivan Ginsberg."

"What do you do for a living, if I may ask?"

"At the moment, nothing. But that's a problem which will have to be faced in the morning. How about you? How are you fixed financially?"

"Well," said Kathleen, "I've got about five pounds with me, which represent my secret life-savings. Apart from that, the only job I really know how to do is milk cows."

"Well," said Ginsberg cheerfully, "the situation, though desperate, is far from being serious."

Kathleen, sitting on the side of the bath in the kitchen-cum-bath-room, fidgeted with the lock of her suitcase. Something was clearly on her mind, and her expression was excessively troubled.

"Look," she said, "of course, I didn't think. . . I was so excited at the idea of coming to London. . . but, I mean, I'm intruding, of course. . . I mean, is there anybody else here?"

"As a matter of fact there isn't."

"Aren't you married or anything?"

"No. And I'd like you to stay here."

Kathleen stopped fidgeting with the lock of her suitcase. Ginsberg exploded the geyser, set the bath thundering, lit the gas beneath the frying-pan, whose fat was miraculously untouched by the rats, and turned round to find Kathleen staring at him fixedly. He held out his hand.

"Shake," he said.

They shook hands.

"And now," said Ginsberg, "no doubt you'd like a bath. Of course, the bath isn't much to look at —"

"At home we haven't got a bath at all."

"— but there's a bottle of disinfectant on the dresser. Meanwhile, I'll try and rustle up some supper out of what the rats have left of my week's rations. Unless, that is, you'd like the room to yourself while you're having a bath?"

"No, not at all."

The hot water thundered down from the geyser, the fat in the frying pan, beneath a full light, spluttered and fretted madly, and Ginsberg struggled to open a massive tin in which he had secreted — out of rats' way — a half pound of salame sausage.

Chapter XX

It was Pam who first suggested that Ivan and Kathleen should get married. Unmarried herself, Pam had a positive passion for marrying off her friends. Once every six or nine months she checked up, as it were, on Ginsberg; and making, shortly after Kathleen's arrival, one of her rare visits to the Guilford Street flat, she lost no time in suggesting that a visit to the Registry Office in Russell Square would set the cap of legitimacy on their ménage. As for the practical arrangements, she, Pam, would provide the cakes, cut the sandwiches, pour out the beer, and so on.

"Of course," said Pam with a laugh, "I know you've got all sorts of theoretical objections to marriage, but it's about time you grew out of those. After all, you're thirty now. And maybe at the back of your mind is the idea that marriage between two faiths — though I know you're not religious — won't work because of the children. Well, there's something in that —"

"Pam," said Ginsberg. "I know you mean well. But good intentions are not enough. I warn you, if you go on any longer, I shall kill you. It's not that I want to kill you, but I can't restrain myself. Once you start talking, my hands tremble with desire to get at your throat and strangle you. Only the fact that I am so completely a civilized being has saved your life so far. But don't presume on this for too long. Somewhere within me, terribly powerful, is a yearning to shut you up once for all."

Ivan kissed her on the neck, and Pam slapped his face quite hard, so that the cheek went red. After getting her friends married, slapping them playfully and hard on the face, or the buttocks, or anywhere convenient was Pam's favourite sign of affection.

"And what do you find so annoying?" she asked Ivan.

"When you start talking about marriage and faith and

children, it makes me see red, really it does. Particularly the faith part. What right have you got to saddle me with the Jewish faith? I want nothing to do with the beastly thing. I hate the Jewish faith more than all others, not because it's any worse than the rest, but because it's the one whose abominable practices were thrust on me when I was a helpless child by a gang of nasty old rabbis and pasty-faced, mealy-mouthed ministers."

Kathleen's arrival had loosened Ivan's tongue. Normally he said little, except to Bellenger. It was not worth arguing with anybody, a waste of breath. Better to keep quiet, watch other people making fools of themselves, and save your own energy and temper. Now, for the first time for years, he had someone who was really interested in his opinions. The result was, that not only with Kathleen, but with all his acquaintances, he was laying down the law with unaccustomed violence.

"Well at any rate," said Pam, "if you do decide to settle down, you can rely on me for the practical side. There's nothing would give me more pleasure. Besides," she added, "think of Kathleen. It's always easier for the man —"

Ginsberg tore wildly at his hair and ran round the room whooping in mock frenzy.

"Pam you're too much for me. Your platitudes are too terrific. I have lost my reason."

Pam left, and Ginsberg, alone, granted that there was much in what she said. Of course, Kathleen would need some persuading — marriage was against all their principles — but when all was said and done, for a girl, no matter how advanced her views, there was no prouder moment then when the ring was slipped over the old third finger. The only snag was his name: Ginsberg. O'Flanagan, Ginsberg; Ginsberg, O'Flanagan. It was hard on the girl. Still, she probably thought it a perfectly wonderful name.

Yes, there were certain advantages in getting married. If they left London for a couple of months, and went to work on a farm in the country, as they planned to do; or if they went abroad together and tried to settle in Brazil, as they also planned to do, marriage would be essential. Otherwise they would have to sign false declarations in hotel books and face all sorts of condemnation and nasty scenes, in which their private relationship would be discussed by every species of abominable functionary.

Besides, when one was happy, what did the legal tie matter? There would be, in trotting along to the registry office one afternoon, no sense of doing anything drastic. It would simply be a rather good joke, paying over the old fee, signing the old book, making the old promise, and slipping on the old ring. Yes, marriage it should be.

Kathleen, when she came home for tea from the illegal divan factory in which she was working, was at first completely opposed to the idea. It was against every principle in which they believed. But eventually, just before it was time for Ivan to leave for the Sophisticated Revue Theatre, she came round to the point of view that the legal ceremony was something not worth arguing about, and that they might just as well go through with it for the sake of convenience and their future plans. Here, in Bloomsbury, in Bellenger's flat, the old ring and the old certificate didn't matter. But in the country, and crossing frontiers, and applying for visas and jobs, they would be all-important.

For the moment, Ginsberg was working as a dish-washer at the Sophisticated Revue Theatre. The job was only a temporary one, while the Chinese student whose sinecure it really was spent a few weeks at the seaside. Dinners were served during the show at the Sophisticated Revue Theatre; and for washing all the dishes — the kitchen fortunately contained a miraculous oil-cleanser, kept off the market by a soap cartel, otherwise the work would have been considerable — Ginsberg received a free dinner, a pint of beer, and five shillings. The job was a cushy one while it lasted, though not to be compared with teaching Mrs. Chabbers Russian.

That had been a job among jobs, with cigarettes and matches provided, and drinks, and occasional meals. However, dish-washing was not bad. One couldn't complain.

And it left him time free during the day to meditate in the British Museum Reading Room and to work on the novel which he had just begun — *the* novel. The trouble about the novel was that he had got stuck, as usual, in chapter four. The first three chapters were easy, laying down the plot, introducing the characters, getting the style going. But afterwards. . . In six previous novels he had got stuck at chapter four. He had a good mind to scrap *the* novel and begin novel number eight. Start afresh; but really *the* novel. Or maybe wait until they had arrived in the country.

They planned to leave very shortly for Carmarthenshire. Ginsberg hungered for green fields, cattle, few faces, and those new, and the possibility of totally immersing his imagination in the projected novel. Alone he could not bring himself to leave London; with Kathleen, nothing was easier. At the same time, Kathleen would be able to do milking on one of the farms, which were all short of labour, and he himself would probably be able to earn a pound or two at something or other. Such earnings would help them along. What was really necessary, however, was the eighty to a hundred pounds which Bert Flogcrobber owed him. It was disgusting to evaluate himself in this penniless way, when all the while he was worth close on a hundred pounds. Not a fortune, but nevertheless a hundred quid. It was true he had given up free-lance journalism abruptly and worsened still further his relations with Bert Flogcrobber. It was true that not for a thousand quid — no, a thousand was already a temptation — not for two hundred quid, would he "ghost" another article for Bert Flogcrobber. But this money was earned, that was the annoying part about it; it was *his money*. And he had to go begging for it, crawling for it, pleading for it, waiting, hoping, hoping.

As things stood, money was the chief cloud over his newly found happiness with Kathleen. Until he got the eighty to a hundred pounds from Bert Flogcrobber, all their arrangements were quite temporary and very unstable. They were living in Bellenger's flat, for instance: but who was paying the rent? The month was up, and there had been no word from Bellenger, and no one had come to turn them out. No doubt Bellenger was too busy with his plans for getting married to bother about what was happening to his flat in Guilford Street. Ha! It would be a joke to dish Bellenger by getting married first! Show old Bellie that two can play at that game! Then there was Julius Kripkin; how long was he going to stay? And could he be relied on to fork out seven and six rent again next week? Julius, who was expecting to be called for the mines any day now, and who was in love with a medical student in the university girls' hostel in Marchmont Street, had been granted the use of Ginsberg's old room, while Ivan and Kathleen occupied the massive double bed. In spite of his mother's tearful opposition, Julius had left home to be near the girl he loved in Marchmont Street and if possible persuade her to come and live with him in Ivan's old room. But Julius was not so blind with love as to ignore that seven and six a week for the use of a room of which the rent was paid by Bellenger, was a piece of pure extortion on Ginsberg's part. He had paid the first week; but would he stay the second week? And if he stayed, would he pay?

Kathleen's job in the illegal divan factory was very insecure, and she was getting tired of it. She did not take well to carpentering, nor to typing, nor to "fiddling", nor to sitting for hours on end in Pedro's International Café Restaurant listening to Penshaw's confidences. Not yet, at any rate; but Penshaw had hopes. That was why he kept her on; that was why he kept most of his employees on — because one day they might be "useful". However, times were not as good as they had been. The Board of

Trade was coming down right and left on the illegal divans. In the cafés of Charlotte Street there was talk of "fascism". Penshaw had sacked half a dozen bums the previous week. He had walked into Pedro's International Café Restaurant, where the bums spent the whole afternoon, and told them that they could go on sitting in there as long as they liked, but he wasn't going to pay them to do so. The axe was descending — who knew where it would fall next? Perhaps on Kathleen?

Any week, Bellenger might come down from Cambridge and say he was giving up the flat, or exchanging it for one in Cambridge. Then they would be out in the street. Finally, the Chinese student would be back in a fortnight, to reclaim his dish-washing sinecure at the Sophisticated Revue Theatre. All in all, money, and the things that depended on money were substantial clouds on these happy last weeks of August and the summer. The most curious thing of all was Bert Flogcrobber's quarter. Ginsberg was to get his twenty-five per cent commission at the end of the quarter. But when did this damnable quarter begin and end? Ginsberg had started doing work for Bert in April; he had finished in August, and there was no mention as yet of any quarterly statement.

But Ginsberg, walking through Mayfair to the mews in which the Sophisticated Revue Theatre was situated, was happier than he had been for many a year. He was happy, not for this reason nor that, but simply because he was alive. And if, on this particular evening, he was more than happy — elated — it was because he and Kathleen had just decided to get married. After all, whatever its longer-term consequences, the actual event of marriage was a great lark. For once in his life, the individual, no matter how insignificant and even despised, took the centre of the stage. Other people were highly interested and congratulatory.

So it was at the Sophisticated Revue Theatre. Ginsberg, the dish-washer, the Soho bum, who had spent a fortnight completely unnoticed at the back of the kitchen watching the fabulous soap substitute dissolve all grease and dirt from the dishes in the sink; Ginsberg, whose name was unknown to anyone but the cook, who called him Greenberg, was singled out by actresses, business-men's wives, musicians, stagehands, and even the manager, for congratulation, drinks, cigarettes, back-slapping, and "for he's a jolly good fellow".

"Good old Goldberg!" they said. "Goldberg's one of the best!"

Only Isaac Kritz, the East End poet, who was working, experimentally, as a waiter in the lounge, and with whom Ginsberg had struck up a friendship of few words, he alone said nothing. But he was a man of silence, lost in some old dream of years ago, a philosopher who thought carefully and conscientiously around and about a subject before touching it. During a quiet interval, Ginsberg came upon Kritz standing in the backyard — which wasn't in the least bit sophisticated — and looking at the sky. Ginsberg thought of Kritz's poem, "East of Aldgate Pump", which had once wrung his heart out in those remote, buried years of childhood and adolescence.

"Wounds of the fog are bleeding.
Along Commercial Road the Jews
Are dark and shiny with brilliantine,
I've got those old Whitechapel blues. . . "

"Hullo, Isaac," said Ivan.

"Oh, hullo, Ivan."

They both stared up into the late evening sky. Up there lay the past, all the dead gazing at them sadly, uncomprehendingly, reproachfully.

"Congratulations," said Isaac Kritz finally. He gave the impression of having come to this conclusion after long, careful deliberation.

"Hey, you two!" called the head-waiter from the kitchen window, "what do you think this is, a rest home?"

Ivan jumped at being thus caught out, and snapped back to the kitchen with smiling alacrity. Kritz, taking his time, refusing to be rushed, moved with severe deliberation to the lounge, there to serve gin conscientiously, grimly, and experimentally.

CHAPTER XXI

GINSBERG WORE HIS VERY BEST TIE, a new check shirt, and his sports jacket, which Kathleen had freshly patched up with discs of leather at the elbows and with neat leather cuffs. His grey flannel trousers were pressed to a knife-edge crease and his chin was the lightest of light blue. A summer dress showed Kathleen at her best, fluttered around her long, sunburnt legs and slim, shapely body. Her arms, face, and neck, too, were becomingly bronzed, for on fine afternoons the illegal divan manufacturers went sunbathing en masse in Regent's Park or at the Bloomsbury open air swimming pool.

They sat with Pam and Julius Kripkin drinking beer in the Museum Tavern before pushing over to Russell Square registry office and getting married. After a couple of drinks, Julius was sent to Charlotte Street to fetch two more witnesses, one male and one female, for the ceremony at three o'clock. Julius made straight for Pedro's International Café Restaurant, where he found a young man named Joe, who had been sitting, in more or less the same position, for three years, pondering whether to go and look for a job and/or a room in which to live. Julius bore down on him, knowing that though Joe was a bum, he had an identity card, was legitimately fixed with the authorities, and could serve as a marriage witness.

Joe greeted him with a brief, friendly smile, waved him into a chair, and thought with relief that now he could postpone for a further couple of hours the unpleasant decision about the job and/or room.

"Look," said Julius, without sitting down, "I wonder if you would —"

"You haven't got a cigarette, I don't suppose?" interrupted Joe. "I'm gasping for one."

Julius gave him a cigarette and explained about Ginsberg's impending marriage and the necessity for a second witness.

"It isn't far, is it?" asked Joe. He hated leaving Pedro's International Café Restaurant.

"Just over in Russell Square," said Julius. "The whole thing won't last ten minutes."

Joe agreed, but insisted on having a cup of tea first.

"I don't suppose you'd care to get the teas, would you?" he added. "I'm a bit hard up at the moment."

Julius bought the teas and waited impatiently while Joe savoured his tea and cigarette at leisure and read half the previous day's evening paper.

"O.K.," said Joe at last. He stood at the doorway of Pedro's, blinking and yawning a little to accustom himself to the fresh air and movement, and followed Julius up Charlotte Street.

Meanwhile, in the Museum Tavern, Pam had momentarily forgotten all about the wedding, because she had recognized among a group of people in the corner Barrel Bramley, editor of the *Super-Highbrow* (A Review of Psychoanalysis and Sculpture). For years Pam had been bombarding Barrel with short stories and articles, had even called at his office in an attempt to meet him personally; but her manuscripts had been unfailingly rejected and her way into Barrel's inner office unfailingly barred by a sardonic blonde secretary. This beastly blonde secretary was not now with Barrel in the corner of the pub; but there were two equally sardonic young women who, Pam gathered from loudly spoken scraps of conversation, were film critics just off to the afternoon show. Oh, if only I could rescue him from such people! thought Pam. For it was not merely out of a desire to get her stories published in the *Super-Highbrow* that she pursued Barrel. She wanted to rescue him from the spiritual torment which he announced in his weekly editorials. She wanted to show him the pleasure to be derived from simple, homely things, from the quiet affection of a trusting friend. . . . Ah, she had not told anybody about her higher love for Barrel; but it was that alone, and not want of offers, which had kept her unmarried all these years. And what a poignant coincidence it was, that on the very day she was organizing the wedding of a friend — almost the last of her unmarried contemporaries — she should be seeing Barrel for the first time!

But there was no chance of getting at him now, not in any way that was at all seemly. Barrel himself gloomily held a glass of gin. The two formidable-looking film critics held conversation across Barrel's sunken head with two men with soprano voices.

"Beastly bore," said one of the film critics.

"Not as bad as book reviewing," said one of the sopranos.

"It's deadly," said the other film critic.

"Art criticism's the worst of the lot," said the other soprano.

"I shall have to say the same as usual," said the film critic. "You know, if this is the sort of film you like, then you will like this film. What are we all drinking?"

Barrel, thought Pam, I could make you happy. We could have a cottage in Surrey. Ours could be the most sensitive of marriages, with books, paintings, music, sculpture, ballet, all tastes in common. And each of us could keep a diary describing our inner feelings, so that posterity could for the first time have a complete picture of the joint lives of two sensitive beings.

"Mine'll be a gin and orange," said Barrel to the film critic.

Julius and Joe were just passing the Fitzroy when Penelope tottered gaily out of the public bar. She was drunk, of course, since the pubs had already been open a couple of hours; but having been drunk twice a day for the previous forty-five years, she was in a quite normal condition and capable of considering rationally Julius's suggestion that she should witness Ginsberg's marriage.

"Bit of a bloody bore," she said. "Still, I like Ivan, he's a nice boy, he once more or less carried me home when I was flat out. Christ! I was stinko that night! Christ! I was stinko! You haven't got a cigarette, have you?"

Julius produced his cigarettes and gave Penelope one; Joe claimed one, too, "for later". Lucky his mother had given him those hundred Players, reflected Julius. The thought of his going into the mines and living away from home was driving her to distraction; and apart from the great hampers prepared for him on his bi-weekly visits to Golders Green, every day a parcel of food and cigarettes and spare clothing arrived at the Guilford Street flat. Julius felt an overwhelming sensation of gratitude and affection towards his mother. She really was a brick. He had a good mind to go back home to-morrow for good.

"Where is it?" said Penelope. "You're a darling for this cigarette. But you are, you know, perfectly sweet. What is your name? I always forget it. Julius? Well, where is it, Julius darling? Where is this bloody wedding? Poor shit! I do feel sorry for anybody getting married. Well, where is it, sweetie pie?"

"Russell Square," said Julius.

"Russell Square! Dear old Russell Square!. . . All right, let's go"

In the Museum Tavern, Penelope waved across to Barrel Bramley, and Barrel waved back to Penelope — they were fellow warriors of Montparnasse in the twenties.

"Ooo-ooh Barrel!"

"Ooo-ooh Penelope!"

Pam felt thoroughly miserable, but she bucked up a little in the hope that perhaps Penelope would on some more suitable occasion introduce her to Barrel.

The ceremony in the Registry Office was business-like and uneventful. Ginsberg paid over the money, received a receipt and marriage certificate, and went off with Kathleen to the Merton Cinema in Tottenham Court Road to see *Amok,* because he fancied something light;

and although the film was a tragedy, having seen it fifteen times before at the dear old Merton, he was certain to go into fits of uncontrollable laughter at every heartrending sequence. Penelope and Joe went back to Pedro's International Café Restaurant to doze till the pubs opened and to ponder whether to look for a job and/or room respectively. Julius decided to pay a surprise visit to his mother in Golders Green, and by eating an enormous meal to warm her dear heart up. Pam went back to Guilford Street to prepare sandwiches for the party, play records on the gramophone, and think of Barrel.

Sandwiches were to be provided at the party, and a certain amount of drink. But in principle every guest was to bring his own drink. On this basis, there was no limit to the number of guests except the capacity of the flat. At first, there was some talk by Pam about the selection of guests; but very soon realizing that this would be hopeless, she agreed that the party would best be thrown open to anybody who should hear of it.

So later in the afternoon, and in the early evening, word got round Charlotte Street that there was to be a party in Bellenger's flat. People spoke vaguely of possibly looking in if they had nothing else to do. Others definitely decided to go; but since it was a bring-your-own-drink-party, they determined to get decently tanked-up before leaving the Corney Arms and the Duchess of Canterbury. In any case, everyone postponed going until later in the evening. The result was, that at eight o'clock, only Ginsberg and Kathleen, returned from the cinema, Julius, returned from Golders Green with another hundred cigarettes, a currant cake and three bottles of wine as a present from his mother, Kroganin, whom Ginsberg had met in the street, and Pam, were sitting in the Guilford Street flat. All except Pam then made as quick a round as possible of the pubs in order to liven up, collect guests and snatch a few drinks. At half-past nine they headed a straggling, noisy procession across

Bloomsbury back to Guilford Street. In addition, more guests promised — or threatened, as the case might be — to come once the pubs had closed. Towards closing time a surprizing number of the most varied people, many of whom Ginsberg had never even seen before, announced their intention of coming to the wedding party. Talk of a party produced a boom in the pubs. There was an unusual amount of drinking and conviviality. Many of those who most frequently and loudly toasted their intention of coming did not reach the flat. They had to stagger down to the tube, out of sheer exhaustion, or hail a taxi home, or collapse on an improvized bed in the nearest illegal divan factory; or they lost their way, or found it more interesting to pair off on benches in the intervening Bloomsbury squares. Nevertheless, a huge crowd of guests finally arrived at the flat. Judged by numbers, noise, and variety, the party was a success.

Ginsberg went through all the stages of drunkenness. First, he was heavily lethargic; then he was noisy and gay. Then everything acquired a wonderful significance. He saw the meaning of life, its tragedy, its beauty, its joy, its pathos. There was not a single one of his guests, or of the entire human race, whom he did not love. Then he fell asleep with his head on Kathleen's lap, while Kathleen, totally exhausted by the excitement and unaccustomed drink, slept even more deeply sitting up, with her back resting against the wall behind the great double bed.

But the third stage of intoxication, the significant stage, lasted long enough for Ginsberg to receive an immense confused impression of all the acquaintances and friends who put in an appearance at the party. Of one or two, he could not be sure whether they actually put in an appearance or whether his intoxicated imagination merely conjured up an hallucinatory glimpse. Bellenger, for instance: he thought he saw — though he could not be sure — Bellenger's head poke round the door, with a girl's head just underneath it. And Kagaranias; he could have sworn Kagaranias shook his hand and muttered: "All de best!" But these events, if they occurred, belonged to the final stages of the party. Earlier, there had been some amusing encounters. Kroganin had been on great form, incomparable, shattering form, and even Pam had insisted on singing an old English madrigal.

For Pam, the party turned out after all to be a success, If there was one cure, she found, for disappointed love, it was to fall in love with someone else. And she had found someone else to rescue from spiritual despair, someone almost as much in need of rescue as Barrel Bramley himself — Angus Sternforth Simms.

Angus Sternforth Simms, reconciled to Panjitawarelam, had decided to look in. He and his friends created a distinguished, literary corner of the party at the back of Ginsberg's room, drinking their own gin and not mixing with the bums who milled around. To begin with, Angus kept his back turned on Isaac Kritz, the only other literary man of consequence in the room, who sat in an armchair smoking his pipe. But eventually Angus, unsure of himself outside the Corney Arms, gave way and called to Kritz above the din:

"I see Faber are bringing out your poems in the autumn!"

Kritz nodded.

"How are they off for paper! It's the deuce, isn't it?"

Kritz shrugged his shoulders.

"I saw Gollancz yesterday. . . "

Pam, having finished singing a madrigal in the other room, offered Angus a sandwich. This was the first time she had been able to catch him unaccompanied by his girl-friend. She noticed how sensitive his face really was, in spite of the coarseness with which he tipped back the gins in a single swallow.

"It was very nice of you to come along," she said. "The backwoods of Bloomsbury," murmured Angus. "I like to keep in touch. Ivan's a very decent sort."

He slung back a gin. With their backs turned disdainfully on the rest of the room, they began an acquaintance which was later to bear fruit in Pam's

second novel —
"A delicate study of a tortured soul"
(The Observer),
"Lives up to the promise of her first novel"
(John O'London's),
"A sensitive and moving tale"
(Sunday Times)
— and Angus Sternforth Simms's witty short story, "The Woman I Loathe". Joe had hit upon a young man, Sam, who was in more or less the same predicament as himself. Sam, too, had been considering for some time whether to look for a job and/or room and had been sleeping in Larry's divan factory, a rival to Penshaw's. What was more, Sam had discovered a part-time job which he was almost tempted to accept. But it was a little too much for one.

"Then why shouldn't we share it?" said Joe.

A brilliant idea, agreed Sam. They could share the part-time job, each working part-time on alternate days, and they could also, perhaps, get a single room between them. Thus, they would be able to sleep on a bed at least one night in two, or even once a day, if they slept in shifts. After such a comfortable rest, they would find no difficulty in sitting the alternate night up at an all-night café or kipping down when necessary in the illegal divan factory.

Kroganin discussed the European food situation with some students newly added to his vast circle of friends.

"Mice," he insisted, was an important factor in some countries. Mice? Yes, mice with which to feed animals. Feed animals with mice?

"But of course! Mice, mice! Verry imporrtant! Mice! Ach!"

"Maize," whispered someone who knew Kroganin well. "Maize, pronounced mice."

"I wars to-day Brritish Council. I wars forr some time assistant editorr magazine. So I said to Mr. Rruperrtson — do you by any chunz gnaw him?"

Gradually Kroganin's voice dominated the party. It

boomed and thundered amiably and incomprehensibly from room to room, until, at about one o'clock, it woke Ginsberg up by roaring in his ear: "You urrr lucky men, sirrr!" He kissed Ginsberg on the cheek and left.

Once Kroganin had gone, the silence brought home to those who remained how few they actually were. Most of the guests had gone to catch the last tube at half-past twelve. There were a few couples asleep in each other's arms on the floor. There was a young man being sick over the sink and a girl who said she was ill on Ginsberg's bed. Ginsberg had a magnificent headache. He felt almost proud of it, because it was surely the most terrific headache ever experienced. What he wanted most in the world now was cold water and fresh air. He gently edged aside the young man who was being sick in the sink and poured himself out several cupfuls of water.

Sobering up, and surveying the wreckage of the flat — the hundreds of cigarette-ends, the smashed glasses, spilt beer, scattered crumbs, trampled sandwiches, burnt tablecloths, lost handkerchiefs, and two circular little heaps of regurgitated food and drink — he regretted not having planned a honeymoon, even if only for a day or two. Money, of course, was the root of the trouble. He had about twelve shillings left, and Kathleen had a couple of pounds. And yet — an intense fury seized him at the thought of it — he had some money. Yes, at least eighty pounds, earned legitimately by his own effort. It was not owed to him, it was *his money!* Why then should he spend his wedding night in this chaos, when he could afford to catch the train to Brighton and do himself well at one of the honeymoon hotels? Or slip away at once to Carmarthenshire and begin the long overdue rest and change which he and Kathleen had been planning?

He came to a sudden decision. What was the time? One-fifteen; admirable, just right. He would catch Bert Flogcrobber alone in his office and he would come out with that cheque if it was the last thing he did. Kathleen wanted him to wait till the morning, but Ginsberg refused to be put off. It was now or never! The money! And the new life!

CHAPTER XXII

IN THE END, reflected Ginsberg, one is alone. He walked on, his head splitting at each step, through the familiar landscape of deserted midnight streets. The traffic lights clicked, green, amber, red, green, amber, red, all the way down Southampton Row, Kingsway, and Fleet Street. He could not think too clearly, with his head rattling and thumping away, but his mind fastened on one thing very firmly: money. That was what he had come out for, and that was what he was going to get. He remembered, too, that he was happy. If his reverie took, out of long habit, a deeply melancholy turn, he thought of Kathleen, and from a central point in his mind happiness radiated outwards.

Passing Kingsway Hall, he was reminded of his walk with Kagaranias in April, just after the idea of *Scamp* had been born. Ah, he had grown old since then; or rather, he corrected himself, he had grown up. He had no more ambition left. Could he say that with absolute sincerity? Yes, with absolute sincerity he could say that he had no more ambition left. It was a case of sour grapes, of course; still, what difference did that make? He wanted to write, but just for the sake of writing, to say his say, unhurriedly, without urgency. Apart from that, he was a nonentity. He had to earn his living right at the bottom, as a labourer, a dish washer, a Soho bum. In any case, not for anything would he work again for Bert Flogcrobber and his crew. He thought with distaste of his forthcoming interview with Bert. But it had to be gone through. Money; that was what he had come out for, and that was what he was going to get.

Ginsberg hurried past the night-porter in the *Daily Post* office. He waved his hand and said: "Just going up to see Mr. Flogcrobber!" The night porter made as if to halt him and ask him to sign a chit, then sank back into his chair and returned to the first edition of the *Daily Post*. He remembered Ginsberg having called several times before at this time of night, so it was no doubt all right.

Bert jumped up from his chair as Ginsberg entered the room. Ginsberg's knock had been peremptory, instead of deferential, and his first words were:

"I've called for my money!"

Bert trembled with anger. He could not control himself. The nerve of this blasted Jew! After having let him down without a day's notice! This miserable reptile speaking to him, Bert Flogcrobber, assistant night-editor of the *Daily Post,* as though he were a Petticoat Lane huckster!

"Get out!" screamed Bert. He could not control his voice either, it went on of its own accord. "Get out! Get out! Get out! Get out!"

Bert too had been drinking, drinking even more heavily than usual for weeks on end. He had been wearing his tight shirt all day, with the collar that squeezed and cut into his neck. Although it had been loosened for five hours, he could still feel its circle of irritation. And his shoes had not yet ceased to give him pangs, after weeks of breaking in. The word Jew rose to his mind; this man was a foreigner, a Jew, one who had no right in the country, one who ought to feel glad if he wasn't kicked out of the way. Bert had continued swiftly along the road begun in the Irish Bar, when he had picked up the leaflet issued by the Association of Freemen and Yeomen of Britain; he was now a member, made allowances for the crudities of the rank and file, and had been elected to the propaganda committee. He refused to argue any longer, or even think, about the word Jew. When he heard it or sensed it, a red-hot needle of rage shot through his temples.

"Get out!" he yelled. "Out! Out! Out!" His voice rose higher and higher till it reached its top note: "Jew!"

"I've called for my money!" roared Ginsberg. "I don't want to argue, I want my money!"

"At the end of the quarter," gasped Bert. His breath was doing what it liked with him, saying what it liked how it liked. Now it sank to a whisper: "Get out. I don't want to see you again. I'll send it to you by post at the end of the quarter —"

"End of the quarter! End of the quarter! I'll give you end of the quarter!"

The infuriated Ginsberg dashed at Bert from the door with fist upraised. Bert dodged round the table which stood in the centre of the room. They dodged and twisted round the table this way and that, pursuing and pursued, until Bert swiftly dashed over to the set of drawers, jerked out the top one, and seized his permanently loaded revolver. Ah, that was better! Now that he had the beautiful thing in his hand, he felt safe. There was a pause, during which Ginsberg and Bert Flogcrobber stood facing each other in a motionless silence broken only by their deep, rapid breathing; while through the nearly soundproof walls came the faint, distant thumping of presses and the muffled roar of vans accelerating in the *Daily Post* garage. Between the two men, the barrel of the revolver wobbled in Bert's trembling hand.

Ginsberg strode forward.

"Put that stupid thing away and give me my cheque," he said.

"If you don't stop I'll fire!" Bert screamed and sobbed. "If you come further I'll fire! If you don't —" "Bang!" went the bullet. "Mung-mung-mung", trailed the echo in that confined space. The bullet missed Ginsberg by about two yards, ricocheted madly from wall to wall, and almost caught Bert in the stomach. Bert stared uncomprehendingly at his hand, at his finger, the finger which had fired the shots of its own accord. Then he flung himself in the chair by his desk, put his head in his hands, and wept. The revolver lay on the table beside him; Ginsberg hastily replaced it in the top drawer from which it had been taken. A boy came in with some papers, put them on the table, looked curiously at Bert, and went out again.

"Why don't you go?" said Bert finally. "I'm not feeling

very well."

"Give me the cheque and I'll go."

"How much?" said Bert wearily. He opened a drawer and drew out his cheque book.

"I estimate that my commission can't be less than eighty and probably isn't more than a hundred."

"I'll write you a cheque for eighty and for God's sake don't let me see your face again."

"Right-o," said Ginsberg with a smile. "Anything to oblige. The only thing is," he added as an afterthought, "I shall have to come for the remainder of my commission, if there is any, at the end of the quarter. Make it a hundred, Bert, there's a pal, and we'll call it a day."

"Pay Mr. Ivan Ginsberg one hundred pounds," wrote Bert savagely. His hand still trembled, however, and there were tears on his cheeks.

"And remember," said Bert, "that's agreed; I shall never again see you or hear from you as long as I live. Now go."

Ginsberg folded the cheque and went. He leapt down the stairs into the vestibule four at a time, half ran past the night-porter into the street. A *Daily Post* van shot down the alleyway at the rear of the building and slowed down for an instant before turning into Fleet Street. Ginsberg flung himself on to the back and fell sprawling among bundles of newspaper. The *Daily Post* van rapidly gathered speed; loaded with its daily quota of truths, half-truths, and downright lies, it shot up Fleet Street towards Holborn. At the traffic lights in Southampton Row, Ginsberg jumped off and walked slowly homewards. He dawdled, he lit a cigarette, stared in shop-windows. There was no hurry now, no hurry at all. The cheque, that bountiful little slip of paper, lay safely in his pocket. He felt again to make sure. Yes, it was still there. In a newsagent's shop, just by a street-lamp, there was a board full of small advertisements. Could they have left it in the window all this time? Ginsberg bent and peered into the bottom corner where it had fallen on its side and been forgotten by the newsagent: it had not yet been taken away. By bending his head sideways and downwards he could still read it:

"Contributions invited to new occasional publication. Lively, controversial, informative. SCAMP, magazine for the younger generation. Payment at the rate of a guinea per thousand words. All communications to SCAMP Publications, Guilford Street, W.C.1."

Available from New London Editions

Available

King Dido by Alexander Baron
(introduction by Ken Worpole)

Rain on the Pavements by Roland Camberton

Rosie Hogarth by Alexander Baron
(introduction by Andrew Whitehead)

Forthcoming

Adrift in Soho by Colin Wilson

The Furnished Room by Laura Del-Rivo

This Bed My Centre by Pamela Hansford Johnson
(introduction by Zoë Fairbairns)

October Day by Frank Griffin
(introduction by Andy Croft)